THE FINAL
BATTLE

HELFORT'S WAR: BOOK V

Betrayed...

"Come on!" Malvern shouted to the unseen guards. "Get this damn screen up."

"Sorry, counselor," a voice said. The screen opened a fraction, and the woman slipped the envelope through the gap. Michael Helfort took it with hands slick with cold sweat.

"Open it," Malvern said, her voice soft.

Michael shook his head. "I can't. I'm sorry, Erica; I just can't."

"You want me to?"

"Not really," Michael replied, misery splashed all across his face. "I don't want to know."

"You need to know. Pass it back."

Michael did as he was told and watched Malvern tear the envelope open, his heart hammering in his chest with painful intensity. She scanned the letter and then looked up at him, the tears in her eyes sparkling in the harsh light. "I'm so sorry," she said, her voice breaking. "The president has turned down your appeal for clemency. Sentence will be carried out one week from today."

"No!" Michael hissed. "She can't have. I trusted her."

He slumped back in his seat, and his head dropped into his hands. "I've been screwed," he said, his voice strengthening as anger pushed fear aside. "They've betrayed me, all of them. Goddamn the bastards all to hell."

Also by Graham Sharp Paul

HELFORT'S WAR*

Book I: *The Battle at the Moons of Hell*
Book II: *The Battle of the Hammer Worlds*
Book III: *The Battle of Devastation Reef*
Book IV: *The Battle for Commitment Planet*

THE GUILD WAR

Book I: *Vendetta*
Book II: *Counterattack (late 2012)*

*Books 1 to 4 of the Helfort's War series are published in the United States by Del Rey Books, an imprint of the Random House Publishing Group, a division of Random House Inc., New York.

THE FINAL BATTLE

HELFORT'S WAR: BOOK V

Graham Sharp Paul

For Vicki. Hang in there.

Acknowledgments

As ever, my thanks to Tara Wynne and Liz Scheier for their support, encouragement and advice.

Hell Bent was in a race it could never win, and Michael Helfort knew it. "How long?" he asked the battered lander's command pilot.

"Provided the battlesats don't get us first," Kat Sedova replied, "the first missile salvo will be inside hard kill radius in two minutes." Her voice was barely audible over the racket of pulsed antiship lasers chewing away at *Hell Bent*'s ceramsteel armor.

Fear churned Michael's guts. It would be five minutes before *Hell Bent* could jump safely into pinchspace. "I guess this is it, then," he said.

"I'll jump us just before the salvo gets that close. We might get lucky."

Michael glanced across *Hell Bent*'s cargo bay. He threw a smile at Shalini Prashad, the best political mind in the New Revolutionary Army's political wing, the Revival; she stared back at him, eyes wide with terror. He turned to the two NRA officers who were sitting alongside him. "We still have a good chance," Michael said, making himself sound confident, "even this deep inside Commitment's gravity well."

"Let's hope so," General Cortez replied, grim-faced. "If we don't make it …" His voice trailed off into silence.

Major Hok said nothing, her face grim.

Nothing more needed to be said. After more than a century of brutal, bloody conflict between the Hammer of Kraa and the Federated Worlds—a conflict fueled by the Hammers' religious fundamentalism—humanspace teetered on the edge of the abyss, and every soul onboard knew it.

The Hammers had been the only polity to weaponize antimatter. None of the other major systems of humanspace had even tried. They had judged it impossible, only to find how wrong they had been when in a single brutal attack the Hammers had used missiles with antimatter warheads to destroy much of the Feds' fleet at the Battle of Comdur.

Now the Hammers were constructing a new antimatter plant—with help from the Pascanicians—to replace the one the Feds had destroyed at Devastation Reef. Once it was on-stream, the Hammers would have the antimatter warheads they needed to defeat not just the Feds but every last system in humanspace. Nothing could stop them. Billions would be plunged into slavery, their only task to serve the all-powerful Empire of the Hammer of Kraa.

Michael closed his eyes. He told his neuronics to bring up his favorite picture of Anna. He sat back and waited for the end.

Monday, March 25, 2402, UD
Offices of the Supreme Council for the
Preservation of the Faith, city of McNair,
Commitment planet

"They'd have had a damn good reason to waste one of their precious landers like that," Jeremiah Polk said. "The NRA and the Revival are gambling and gambling big, and we don't know why."

"Let's be realistic, Chief Councillor," Viktor Solomatin, the Hammer of Kraa's councillor for foreign relations, said. "The only people who can help that heretic scum are the Federated Worlds, but with Caroline Ferrero as moderator, that will never happen."

Polk leaned forward to look Solomatin right in the face. "Care to back that up, Councillor?" he said.

"That's why I wanted to see you, Chief Councillor. The Fed chargé d'affaires has just forwarded me a personal message from Caroline Ferrero. She wants to know whether we would agree to a cease-fire."

"Kraa! The woman hasn't wasted any time," Polk said. He took a deep breath to control a sudden rush of excitement. "She's been moderator for what … a week?" He paused to think. "Two questions," he went on. "Why would the Feds propose a cease-fire, and why would we agree to one?" Again he stopped, a finger tapping his lips. "That said," Polk said, "I think we know the answer to the first question."

"One of my staff members summed it up nicely: Caroline Ferrero is the right appeaser at the right time."

"So it seems, but should we agree to a cease-fire?"

"The Feds always believed they would defeat the Hammer of Kraa. It was an article of faith, but when we dropped antimatter warheads into Fed nearspace—" Solomatin's voice was animated now, his eyes glistening, his excitement unmistakable. "—we destroyed that belief. Ferrero doesn't think the Feds can win, not anymore. That gives us the leverage to accept their offer, but on our terms, not—"

Polk's hand came up. "What terms?" he said.

"The Feds must halt their fleet rebuilding program; they must terminate all research into weaponizing antimatter and agree to verification inspections."

Polk frowned, unconvinced. "The Feds will never agree to that," he said. "Even they aren't that stupid."

"They're frightened. Trust me; they'll agree."

"Morons," Polk said; he shook his head dismissively. "The Fed fleet's still a serious threat; given enough time to rebuild, it could defeat us. So I cannot understand why Ferrero's being so lily-livered. She doesn't have to be."

"It doesn't matter why. We need to negotiate hard to keep the Feds as weak as possible until the Hendrik Island antimatter plant comes online, which it will as long as we keep the Pascanicians happy."

Polk looked hard at Solomatin. "I thought we *were* keeping them happy," he said.

"Oh, we are," Solomatin replied. "We can't afford not to."

"No, we can't," Polk said, his eyes glittering in anticipation, "and if we have to tolerate those bloodsucking assholes to get our new antimatter plant, then that's what we'll do. And when it's operational, the Federated Worlds will never threaten the security of the Hammer of Kraa Worlds again."

Saturday, April 6, 2402, UD
Clevennes, Asthana planet

The young woman put the mug of steaming hot coffee down on the table beside the man's bed and leaned over to look him right in the face. "Feel better?" she asked.

"Yes." The voice was scarcely a whisper.

"You had us worried. Those comatropic drugs are very unpredictable."

"Who are you?"

"Marnie Bakker," she said. "I'm with the Revival. We handle things here on Asthana. It's good to meet you, Michael."

"Ah, yes," Michael mumbled. He looked around. "Where am I?"

"You're now in one of our safe houses. A Revival team smuggled you out of Haaken Military Hospital."

"I don't remember that. Where's Kat Sedova? Is she okay?"

"She's somewhere else. Better that way. This planet is infested with Hammer agents. Everybody knows a Fed lander dropped into Asthana nearspace, so they'll be out looking for you."

Michael's eyes flared wide with alarm. "Looking for me? They don't know I was onboard, do they?"

Bakker shook her head. "Don't worry; they don't. They just like to get their hands on any Feds who end up here."

"What about your people?"

"Cortez and Hok are okay. Prashad didn't make it. The Revival will miss her."

Michael said nothing for a moment; Prashad's death was a serious blow. "We needed her," he went on. "I didn't know her well, but everyone said she had the sharpest political mind of any Hammer. Sorry. You don't like to be called Hammers."

"No, we don't, even though we were all born Hammers. 'Revivalists' will do. Anyway, here's the plan. As soon as the doctor says you're okay to be moved, we'll relocate you to another safe house."

"Cortez and Hok will be there?"

"They will. Sedova, too."

"I hope Admiral Jaruzelska's in a good mood," he said. "We're screwed if she refuses to help us get the Fed government to back the NRA."

"Stop worrying, Michael," Bakker said. "She knows the Hammers have to be beaten, and she knows we can't do that without Fed support, so why wouldn't she?"

6

Because I betrayed the trust she'd always shown in me, Michael thought. *That's why.*

Thursday, April 11, 2402, UD
Graymouth, Asthana planet

Marnie Bakker's eyes betrayed her apprehension as they flicked from side to side in a restless search for anything out of place. Her anxiety was contagious. Michael's nerves were a mess. His mouth was dry, and his heart was racing. For all he knew, there could have been hundreds of Asthanan Community Safety agents in crowds thronging Graymouth's busy town square, waiting for him to break cover, waiting to arrest him, waiting to hand him over to their DocSec masters.

Finally Bakker nodded. She turned to Michael. "Okay," she said. "My people say there's no sign of CommSafe, so I think we're good to go."

"You sure?"

"No, not really. CommSafe has more agents than you've had hot dinners, and even though we do our best to ping them, we can't know them all."

"Great," Michael muttered.

"Let's do it, and don't forget the bailout plan if it all goes to shit."

"I won't," Michael said, sticking close to Bakker as she set off for the Asthana Communications building, the largest and most imposing on the square.

* * *

The months had not been kind to Vice Admiral Jaruzelska. She had aged. Dulled gray by fatigue and stress, her skin was tight across a thin, angular face, her eyes sunk into black-dusted wells.

Jaruzelska was angry: eyes narrowed, cheeks red, lips thinned into a bloodless line, fingers drumming on the desk.

For an eternity after the pinchcomm call stabilized, nothing was said. "Admiral," Michael said at last, "it's good to see—"

"You have one minute, Helfort," Jaruzelska said, "and that is all. If you cannot convince me I should talk longer, the next time you hear me speak will be when I give evidence at your court-martial, and believe me when I say that day will come. You betrayed me, you betrayed the Fleet, you betrayed the Federated Worlds, and for what? A goddamned woman!"

In an instant, fury engulfed Michael. It took an enormous effort to choke back his angry response. He took a deep breath. "What I have done—and why—is irrelevant. This is not the time or the place. I—"

"How dare you!" Jaruzelska barked. "Never in our history has one officer done so much damage, and not just any officer. *You*. The most decorated, the most experienced, the most promising junior officer I have … the fleet has ever seen. And you threw it all away because you loved a woman. It makes no sense, and you must stand trial for what you have done."

"I agree, and if you listen to me, I'll surrender myself to you here on Asthana." The lie threatened to stick in Michael's throat, but he did not much care anymore. If he betrayed Jaruzelska's trust one more time, what did it matter? There was too much at stake.

"That means you'll be court-martialed for what you've done. You do know that?"

"So be it."

Jaruzelska stared at Michael for a good minute without saying a word. Then she nodded, and a fleeting smile flitted across her lips, a smile that came and went in an instant. "You always were a clever little bastard, Helfort."

"Thank you."

"That wasn't a compliment," Jaruzelska said. She paused; her eyes bored into his, her gaze so intense that for a moment Michael was worried that she somehow had uncovered the lie. "Now, stop wasting my time. What is it you want to tell me?"

"Watch this, admiral."

Jaruzelska looked right at Michael for good minute after the holovid clip had ended. "So you want me to come to Asthana to talk with this General Cortez?" she said at last.

"You need to hear it from them, sir. And we need to start moving things forward. We don't have a lot of time."

"You haven't heard the latest news, have you?" she said. "The Fed government has offered the Hammers a cease-fire."

Michael's mouth sagged open. "A cease-fire?"

"Moderator Ferrero and Chief Councillor Polk announced it at a media conference on Scobie's World. Fleet found out only afterward; it seems we weren't important enough to be consulted." The bitterness in Jaruzelska's voice was plain to hear. "She wants to conclude a full peace treaty inside three months."

"Why the rush?" Michael said. "All that does is make the Federated Worlds look weak."

"It does. Problem is that Joe Public thinks a treaty will put an end to the fighting between the Federated Worlds and the Hammers. Let me see ... 'so we can look forward with absolute confidence to a new era of peace and prosperity'; that's what our new moderator said."

"Anyone who thinks the Hammers are interested in peace and prosperity is a moron."

"The average Fed *does* think that. Ferrero's never been more popular."

"So what do we do now?"

"I'll come to Asthana to meet with General Cortez. I'm due some leave, and since everybody thinks the war is over, I don't think that'll be a problem."

"Cortez will be pleased."

"I doubt that, Helfort; not when he understands just how much things have changed back home."

"What are you saying?" Michael protested. "That it's all over? That all we've got to look forward to is life as one of the Hammer Empire's vassal states?"

"I didn't say that, Helfort!" Jaruzelska said with some asperity. "Right now I don't have anything good to tell

Cortez, but if Polk and Ferrero think people like me will just roll over, they are mistaken, so let's not give up just yet. Believe me, we are a very long way from beaten."

It sure as hell doesn't look that way to me, Michael thought. "Understood," was all he said.

"Okay, I'll be in touch as soon as I've made the arrangements. Oh, there's one more thing before I go."

"Sir?"

"I have decided to decline your offer to turn yourself in, Helfort. We have bigger things to worry about right now."

"Thank you," he said.

"Don't thank me. I knew you were lying."

And with that, before Michael could respond, Jaruzelska cut the call and the holovid screen went blank.

Cortez, Hok, and Sedova were sitting around the battered kitchen table waiting for Michael when he and Marnie Bakker walked in.

"Well," Cortez demanded, the strain showing on his face, "what did she say?"

"She'll come to talk with you, General," Michael replied.

"Thank Kraa for that," Cortez said with a broad smile of relief.

"I'm afraid there's some bad news, though. You know that the Federated Worlds has a new moderator?"

"Yes, Caroline Ferrero. What of her?"

11

"We thought she'd tone down the peace rhetoric once she took over the government and became responsible for the security of the Federated Worlds, right?"

"Our political analysts were pretty confident on that score," Cortez said. "Sniping from opposition is one thing; carrying the can for humanspace's wealthiest system is another."

"Well, the analysts were wrong, General. She's offered the Hammers a cease-fire, and they've agreed. The next step is to sit down and negotiate a formal peace treaty."

"We're screwed," Cortez whispered, "absolutely screwed." His head slumped, and his hands massaged his temples as if to make the bad news go away. "I'm not sure how the Revival can survive this," he said, looking up. "Without the Federated Worlds' direct support, the NRA cannot deliver a military victory, and Polk will take full advantage of the, the … what's the phrase?"

"Peace dividend?" Hok said.

"Yes, Polk will use the peace dividend to make sure the Revival cannot win a political victory either."

"Things might look bad right now, General," Michael said, trying to make himself sound upbeat, "but we can have faith in Admiral Jaruzelska. If she says we are a long way from being beaten, then I think we should believe her."

"I wish I could," Cortez said. "Problem is, I can't." He pushed himself to his feet with an obvious effort; he looked like a beaten man. "Come, Major; we have a report to write."

In silence, Michael watched them leave. "Damn, damn, damn," he muttered. "What the hell do we do now?"

"Michael!" Sedova snapped. "Didn't you tell me once it's not over until the Hammers bang the coffin lid down on us?"

"I think they just did."

Sedova thumped the table with both fists "Bullshit!" she snapped. "What is the matter with you?"

Annoyed now, Michael scowled at her. "Piss off. I'm not in the mood for any rah-rah speeches."

"And you won't get one, but you need to lift your game, son."

"And why should I do that? I think it's over; I really do. The Hammers will win; the Feds, the Revival, the NRA will lose; and I'll never see Anna again because Jeremiah fucking Polk will never rest until DocSec gets its hands on me, and when they do ..." Overwhelmed by the extent of the defeat hanging over their heads, Michael could not go on.

"This is not over, Michael. Jaruzelska said so herself. If she says it's all finished, then fine. I'll accept that and go find myself a job somewhere the Hammers won't bother me."

"Have to be a long way away," Michael said. "When it comes to empire building, a megalomaniac like Polk won't stop until he's got his foot on every last system in humanspace."

"I'm sick of your sad face, so I'm off to find a beer. Feel free to join me when you've got your shit back together."

And when will that be? Michael asked himself as Sedova stormed out, slamming the door hard behind her.

Monday, April 22, 2402, UD
Clevennes, Asthana planet

Vice Admiral Jaruzelska had sat silently throughout Cortez's presentation.

Now she leaned forward to look the man in the face. "I have a lot of questions, General, as you would expect, but none I need to ask now. What *is* important is that I'm convinced, and that brings us to the next problem."

"How to get your government to agree." Cortez's face was sour with frustration. "We've been watching the newsvids from the Federated Worlds, and it's … very depressing, I have to say."

"Yes, I'm afraid it is, and things won't get any better. The cease-fire agreement is scheduled to be ratified by our Chamber of Deputies, let me see … yes, in less than twelve hours, and it will be. Ferrero has the numbers on the floor of the chamber, so it's a done deal. The opposition will do what they can, but nobody listens to them, and anyway, there aren't enough of them left to make a difference."

"Not even if we tell everyone what the Pascanicians are doing to restore the Hammers' antimatter capability and what that means not just for the Worlds but for the rest of humanspace?"

"I'm afraid not."

"But why?" Cortez demanded. "Won't the facts speak for themselves?"

Jaruzelska shook her head emphatically. "No. Our intelligence agencies have a different view of what the Pascanicians are up to. Put simply, they've bought the cover story the Hammers have put out that they are helping to modernize your—"

"Not ours," Cortez growled.

Jaruzelska put up a conciliatory hand. "Sorry," she said. "Our intelligence people say the Pascanicians are helping to modernize the Hammers' starship production program, and it will be very hard to change their minds. That means—and please don't take this the wrong way, General Cortez—the Federated Worlds will only have the NRA intelligence you have provided. I'll tell you now; it will be seen as tainted, self-serving, and therefore unreliable."

"So what do we do? We can't just give up."

"No, we can't, though to be honest, I am not at all sure what we do next. I need to get back to the Federated Worlds, meet with some people, see what our options are. Give me a week and we'll talk again."

"I guess that's the best we can ask for," Cortez said, his voice dulled by disappointment.

"I'm afraid it is."

Wednesday, April 24, 2402, UD
Leaving Clevennes, Asthana planet

Michael stared out of the mobibot's window, still depressed by Jaruzelska's less than enthusiastic response to General Cortez. Bakker sat up front in grim silence; all she'd said was that they were heading for a new safe house. Where it was and how long it would take to get there, Michael had no idea. Before long, he drifted into sleep and his head toppled over onto an already unconscious Sedova's shoulder.

Bakker's voice dragged Michael up and out of the darkness. "Wake up!" she shouted, punching his shoulder to get his attention. "Wake up!"

"What's up?" Michael asked, bleary-eyed and confused by the panic in her voice.

"Not sure," Bakker said, "but we were passed by a mobibot five minutes ago, and two more have just turned up behind us. That's not normal, not on this road."

Adrenaline flooded Michael's system. In an instant he was wide awake, and his mind went up a gear as he struggled to work out what to do. "We should abandon this bot, take off on foot."

"Too late. Look out the window."

"Shit," Michael hissed when he spotted the surveillance drones—a cluster of tiny black spots against the morning sky—dropping into position around them.

Then their options ran out. The road ahead was blocked by two mobibots, and four figures, hooded and

16

armed with assault rifles, waited for them. The road behind them was closed off by two more fast-approaching vehicles.

"I'm sorry, guys," she said, her voice thick with defeat. "I think we're about to get screwed."

Fear, malevolent and all-consuming, surged through Michael's body, turning his guts to water and his mind to mush. Every instinct told him he had to get away. He lunged for the door. "Go, Kat, go!" he shouted. He slapped the controls to open and threw himself out. He hit the ground hard, too hard. He rolled and tumbled; gravel ripped his shirt off and tore at his back. He slid to a stop. Ignoring the pain, he started to his feet. He got no farther before he was hit hard in the small of his back, first one blow and then another and another. A microsecond later, every nerve ending in his body exploded into white-hot agony that plunged him into unconsciousness before he'd even reached the ground.

Michael was confused. Why was his face cold and wet? Why was he so tired? He just wanted to sleep, but he was being shaken and the light was getting brighter and brighter. It drove splinters of agony into his brain. His head thrashed from side to side in an attempt to get away. "Too bright," he mumbled. Then a hood was slipped over his head, and the light was gone.

"He's awake," a distant voice said. It was a man's voice: flat, metallic, nasal. The man was using a processor to conceal his accent. With a rush, memory flooded back, and with memory came a raw terror that devoured his self-control, a terror fueled by the awful certainty that somehow the Hammers had found him. "I'll get the medics," the voice said.

Michael put up with the indignity of being stripped naked for a complete medical examination. *It's not like the Hammers to worry too much about the health of their victims*, he thought, *so they must want me in good shape. But why? For a show trial?*

His sprits sank into utter despair.

The examination over, hands grabbed him and lifted him to his feet. "Who are you?" he asked as he was hustled forward.

"Don't waste your time asking questions," the same flat voice said. "You'll get no answers from us. Now, we're going to put you in the shower. You can take your hood off, but do not turn around. If you even think about trying, I'll stunshoot you. Understood?"

"Yeah."

"Good. When you've finished and dried off, tell us. We'll put the hood back on, and you can get dressed. Then we'll take you to a cell. Once you're inside, you can take the hood off, and we'll get you some food. Any time we bang on the door, stand up and put the hood back on. Is that all understood?"

"Yes," Michael said.

"Right, let's do it."

18

Wednesday, May 1, 2402, UD
In pinchspace

The days had dragged by. The daily routine did not change: three good meals, a shower, and a change of clothing. Other than that, he was left alone, no doubt watched by surveillance holocams every second of the day.

He was onboard a starship in pinchspace; Michael had worked that much out. He'd learned nothing else since he'd been kidnapped, and not knowing who his kidnappers were—logic said it had to be the Hammers, since nobody in humanspace wanted to get his hands on him as badly as his nemesis, Chief Councillor Jeremiah Polk—gnawed at him. But no matter how often he asked, he never got an answer.

He lay on his bunk. Boredom and frustration had long since displaced fear; he was beginning to think he would to go insane if the starship didn't get to wherever it was going and soon. He wondered how Anna was; he stifled a stab of anxiety at an unwanted image of her charging forward, assault rifle spitting death as she took on a mob of Hammers single-handed.

A metallic voice interrupted his silent prayer that he would live long enough to hold Anna in his arms again. "We'll be dropping out of pinchspace in five minutes."

"And about time, you asshole!" Michael screamed with sudden fury, erupting to his feet, fists hammering out his fear against the door. But there was no response, and the silence hung heavy. "Jerks," Michael muttered, slumping back onto his bunk.

Hours after they had dropped into normalspace, Michael sensed the subtle changes in the artgrav that told him the starship was decelerating in-system. *Commitment; it has to be Commitment*, he thought. *And that means my day of reckoning is at hand.* He shivered, the memory of the last time the Hammers had gotten their hands on him still red-raw.

A fist hammered on the door. "Stand up, hood on," a voice said.

Michael took a deep breath to steady himself, then did as he'd been told. The door banged back. He was grabbed, plasticuffed, and hustled out of his cell, all without a single word being said, his repeated demands to be told what was going on ignored.

After a long walk, a change of air gave him part of the answer he was looking for: He was in a shuttle.

He was headed dirtside.

A lifetime later, Michael climbed out of the mobibot he had been pushed into after the shuttle had landed. The sun was hot on his back, and even through the hood, the air was thick with the smell of plants running riot.

I'm in the country, he thought, *but which goddamned country?*

"Right, this is what'll happen," a voice said, cutting his plasticuffs off, "so pay attention."

"Yeah," Michael muttered. "Like I give a shit."

He was ignored. "Stay where you are," the voice continued. "In five minutes, take the hood off. You'll see a road. Walk down it. Half a klick on you will come to a small village. You'll be met there. Don't try to run, don't turn back, and don't leave the road. We *will* watch you every step of the way, and I'll stunshoot you if you don't follow my instructions. Understood?"

"Yeah, but what the hell is this all about?"

"Just do what you've been told. You'll find out when you're supposed to."

"Fuck off, you prick," Michael said, by now hopelessly confused. None of it made any sense, but he waited the five minutes anyway. When the time was up, he ripped the hood off and tossed it away. He looked around. It didn't help; he might have been anywhere in humans-pace. He started to walk down the road, too tired and dispirited to do anything else. He reached the village and stopped. It was not much of a place. There was not a soul in sight, but the fact that it was not a Hammer village—for a start, there were none of the propaganda banners the Hammers liked to plaster everywhere—lifted his spirits a fraction.

Why he had been taken off Asthana the way he had, he could not understand, but wherever he had ended up, it was not on a Hammer planet. That was all he cared about right now.

But what the hell was he supposed to do now?

Baffled, he began to think he should go knock on a few doors when a large mobibot came down the road and stopped in front of him. Four men climbed out; they spread out into an arc and walked over to where he stood.

"Michael Helfort?" one of the men asked. "Lieutenant Michael Helfort?"

"Yes," Michael replied, his face twisted into a puzzled frown, "but how'd you know that?"

"I'm Detective Inspector Macauley, Jamuda Planetary Police. I have—"

"Jamuda? What am I doing—"

"Lieutenant!" Macauley barked. "You can ask all the questions you like, but not now, okay?"

"No, it's not okay," Michael snapped back, glaring. "I've been stunshot, kidnapped, dragged halfway across humanspace, and dumped on some shithole of a planet I've never heard of, so if you don't mind, I'll ask all the damn questions I like, and I'll keep on asking until I get some fucking answers, all right?"

Macauley's face hardened. "Listen to me, Helfort. Shut your damn mouth or I'll stunshoot you myself. Is that understood?"

Common sense prevailed. Taking a deep breath, Michael nodded.

"Good. Lieutenant Michael Wallace Helfort, I have here—" Macauley held out a piece of paper. "—a warrant for your arrest pending a formal extradition request from the government of the Federated Worlds. You will be remanded in custody until your extradition hearing. Do you have any questions?"

Hundreds, Michael thought as he took the warrant. He could not speak, stunned into silence by the terrible realization that he must have been betrayed by the one person in humanspace he'd thought he could trust: Vice Admiral Jaruzelska.

"… and then the police turned up," Michael said, "and I was arrested. The rest you know, François."

"Hmm," the fresh-faced man sitting across the table said. "The Federated Worlds was behind your abduction from Asthana; there can be little doubt about that. The problem is that we have no way of proving it."

"Hah!" Michael snorted his derision. "One hell of a coincidence, don't you think?" he said.

"Of course it is, but without hard evidence, that's all it is. I'm sorry, but how you got to Jamuda is irrelevant."

"So what are my options?"

"Limited, to be blunt. The provisional arrest warrant specifies that you will be charged with aggravated grand larceny."

"That doesn't sound so bad," Michael said. He tried to sound flippant. "I did steal three dreadnoughts, after all."

"I know you did, and the Federated Worlds were at war, which is why the charge specifies aggravated grand larceny. The bad news is that's a capital offense …"

"Oh," Michael whispered.

"… and unfortunately for you, Jamudan law permits extradition for capital offenses."

"So what?" Michael said, dismissing the problem with a wave of his hand. "The Federated Worlds haven't executed anyone for centuries."

"That's not a precedent you can rely on," Hammel said. He pulled a piece of paper out of his folder and pushed it across the table. "This is a transcript from one of the Federated Worlds' news networks, and needless to say, your arrest is the headline story."

"Those scum-sucking lowlifes," Michael hissed after he'd read the page. "Bastards," he said, and pushed the page back. "They don't like me … not that they ever did."

"No, they don't, and they're not alone. There's enormous pressure on your government not to waive the death sentence, and that pressure will not go away."

Michael's head dropped into his hands; his mind raced. He looked up again. "You think they'd ask for the death sentence?" he asked.

"I think they will."

"Let them. President Diouf will never allow it."

François Hammel threw his hands up in frustration. "How can you know that?" he snapped. "Things have changed since you were last back home. The Hammers have your people running scared, and even Diouf has her limits."

"I've met the woman, François. I can trust her with my life. I don't think the death sentence will be a problem."

"Your call," Hammel said with a disbelieving shake of his head.

"Any luck tracking down Lieutenant Sedova? Was she kidnapped too?"

"There is no sign of her here on Jamuda. The Feds are only interested in you. Anyway, that's it for now, so I'll see you … let me think … yes, tomorrow afternoon," Hammel said. He pushed his chair back and climbed to his feet. "That'll give me time to talk to the people at Justice. I need to see how they feel about handing a man over to the people who had him kidnapped."

Unable to sleep, Michael lay awake long into the night. If the young lawyer from the public defender's office was right, he was headed for a Fed court. The thought of the fear-fueled storm that would break over his head the minute he stepped onto Fed soil terrified him. He'd had a taste of what lay ahead after the Battle of Devastation Reef. What Giorgio Pantini from World News and his fellow gutterscum from the trashpress had in store for him would make that unhappy time pale into insignificance.

Not that the trashpress was the problem. Staying alive was the problem, and he had trouble seeing how he'd do that.

If he escaped extradition, he would end up dead. Jamuda might be a neutral system, but that would not stop the Hammers from coming after him. By now, it would be no secret where he was being held. He had seen the news reports; the Hammers would have seen it too.

If he was extradited, he'd be tried in a Fed court, found guilty, sentenced to death, and, if his faith in President Diouf was misplaced, executed. And even if he escaped the death penalty, he'd be jailed for the rest of his life.

"Oh, crap," he said under his breath. "I am screwed."

Monday, May 6, 2402, UD
Kovak Remand Center, city of Kovak, planet of Jamuda

"How are you today?"

"Bored shitless," Michael replied. "You guys have the worst holovids."

François Hammel smiled. "True enough," he said. The smile vanished. "I have news, and not good news, I'm afraid."

"Add it to all the rest," Michael muttered. "Come on; tell me."

Hammel pushed a piece of paper across the table at Michael. "This is a warrant for your arrest pending a formal extradition request from the government of the Hammer of Kraa Worlds."

A hand reached into Michael's chest and squeezed his heart hard. "Fuck," he whispered; his head dropped into his hands. "The Hammers never give up." He looked up at his lawyer. "Same old bullshit. The charges, I mean."

"Let me see. On December 17, 2399, Universal Date, in the town of Barkersville, Commitment Planet, Hammer of Kraa Worlds, you murdered Detective

26

Sergeant Kalkov, Commitment Planetary Police Service, and Trooper Askali, Hammer of Kraa Doctrinal Security Service, both in the course of their duties."

"Like I said," Michael muttered, "the same old bullshit."

"Maybe, but this—" Hammel poked the piece of paper. "—means the Feds will have to wait to get their hands on you. I know, I know," he said, putting up a hand to preempt Michael's response. "It's crap, but the court needs to agree that it's crap before it gets thrown out."

"Which it will, right?"

"Jamuda has never extradited anyone to the Hammer of Kraa, because it is a well-established fact that they use torture as a matter of routine …"

"Tell me about it," Michael said.

"… but even the Hammers are entitled to due legal process, and that will add to the time it all takes. We'll go through the Hammer request in detail as soon as I get it from Justice. I'll be back as soon as I've had a chance to look at the Hammer's paperwork."

Back in his cell, Michael lay on his bunk, hands behind his head, and stared up at the ceiling. The Hammers' extradition request was a worry. Not because of the request itself—Hammel's assessment of its chances was probably correct—but because of what it said about the Hammers' determination to get their hands on him.

Michael felt very uncomfortable. Once back on the Federated Worlds, he would be safe. Here on Jamuda, he was not, and that meant the Hammers would be coming for him and soon. He'd never been more certain of anything in his life.

He banged the button on the wall-mounted intercom.

"Yes?" a disembodied man's voice said.

"I need to talk to my lawyer. It's urgent."

The guard closed the door of the booth; Michael flicked on the privacy screen and waited in patient silence until the earnest face of his lawyer appeared on the holovid screen. "Hi, François."

"What can I do for you?"

"I want to see someone from the Fed embassy."

Hammel frowned. "That won't be easy. You're not their favorite person. Can I ask why?"

"The Hammers aren't serious about extraditing me. They—"

"Hold on. I don't think you can say that."

"I can. Like you said, they've never extradited anyone from Jamuda, ever, which means they're wasting their time, and they know it."

"I'm sure they do, but that shouldn't stop them from following legal process."

"Legal process?" Michael rolled his eyes. "Oh, François, give me a break," he said. "This is the fucking Hammers we are talking about. Like they give a damn about due legal process. Come on! They're just trying to slow things down, that's all."

"Eh? Why would they do that?"

"So they can kidnap me and take me back to Commitment for a show trial, that's why. Though why they'd bother, I don't know. They're going to kill me anyway."

"Not sure I'd agree with that." Hammel sounded skeptical.

"Ever been to the Hammer Worlds, François?"

A look of horror crossed the lawyer's face. "Hell, no!"

"Ever met a Hammer?"

"No."

"Heard of Doctrinal Security?"

"Of course. Who hasn't?"

"Well, I've been to the Hammer Worlds." Michael's voice sharpened as anger took over. "I've met lots of Hammers, I've been a prisoner, I've been tortured by DocSec, and I still carry the scars to prove it. So you should believe me when I tell you that those bastards will come after me, and it won't be to read me bedtime stories."

"All right, all right," Hammel said, his hands up, "I believe you. But what can your embassy do?"

"Maybe nothing, but it's worth asking them to lean on the Jamudans to beef up security around here. From what I've seen, a Hammer hit team would have no trouble getting into this place."

"Fine," Hammel said with a sigh. "I'll contact the embassy. You want to talk to them direct?"

"I think that would be best."

"It won't be easy, but leave it to me."

The cell door swung open, and a guard stuck his head in. "Let's go, Helfort. You have a visitor."

"About bloody time," Michael muttered. He got to his feet and followed the man out of the cell and down the corridor to the interview room, a cramped space cut in half by a floor-to-ceiling plasglass divider.

A woman was waiting for him; she looked unhappy. "I'm Colonel K'zekaa," she said once Michael had sat down. "You asked to see me?"

"I did, sir. Thanks for coming."

"Not my decision, Helfort," K'zekaa said, her voice tight, controlled.

"I'm still glad to see you," Michael said. He wondered just who had leaned on K'zekaa; the woman's body language screamed her protest. "Did my lawyer give you the background?"

"He did, and I am not convinced that you are at any risk from the Hammers ... or anyone else, come to that. Jamuda is a neutral system, Helfort, and I am sure the Hammers will respect that. They're not complete animals, you know," K'zekaa added with a condescending curl of the lip.

Michael stared wide-eyed at the woman. "Not complete animals?" he snarled. "You are fucking joking."

"I am not in the habit of saying things I do not mean, Helfort. And watch your language."

You are such a pompous asshole, Michael thought, all his good intentions flying out the window. If the woman wanted a fight, he'd give her a fight. "You're a colonel in planetary defense, am I right?" he asked.

K'zekaa frowned, clearly puzzled by Michael's sudden change of tack. "Yes, I am. But I don't see what that's—"

"I'll tell you what it's got to do with things ... sir," he said, using the pause to make certain K'zekaa did not miss the calculated insult.

K'zekaa didn't; her face flushed with anger.

"So far as I know," Michael continued, "planetary defense has not seen much combat against the Hammers, so I'm guessing that means you haven't either."

"I don't like your tone, Helfort."

"Like I give a shit, Colonel. You are yet another rear-echelon motherfucker, so don't talk to me about the Hammers. I know them, I've fought them, I've been wounded by them, I've been tortured by them, so you can trust me when I tell you that you are wrong. They are animals, and they will come for me. So you can either get off your ass and do something to help keep me alive or piss off and leave me to take my chances. Your call. Which is it to be?"

K'zekaa sat staring at Michael, her mouth working as his angry tirade washed over her. It was a while before she could speak.

"I will ignore all that. You are in enough trouble as it is, so I will put it down to the stress you must be under ..."

"Thank you so much," Michael muttered, his voice all acid.

"... but it does not change my view. The chances of the Hammers coming for you are remote, so you have nothing to worry about. And that's not just my opinion. It's the embassy's opinion as well. But I will do one thing, Helfort: I will pass your concerns on to the people responsible for security around here. Provided they are not insulted by your lack of faith in their ability to protect you—and I wouldn't blame them if they were—maybe they will take steps to address those concerns, however ill considered they might be." K'zekaa stood and pushed her chair back. "And don't talk to me about what I have and have not done, Helfort, because I have always done my duty ... which is more than I can say for you."

With that, K'zekaa turned, banged on the door to be let out, and was gone the instant the door opened.

I do like it when things go well, Michael thought, the anger-pumped adrenaline in his system ebbing fast. Now what would he do? The Hammers would come—of that he was certain—and he did not want to find himself alone and cornered in his cell like a rat when they did.

But just how he could avoid that fate, he had no idea.

Friday, May 24, 2402, UD
Kovak Remand Center

Michael cringed as he stepped into the sunshine to cross to the slab-sided mobibot waiting to take him to court.

He could not help himself. To the north, the remand center was overlooked by a park that rose to a ridge and by commercial buildings to the west and south. A hit team in any of those places would see him. They'd have to be blind not to; the fluorescent orange jumpsuit he was forced to wear as a dangerous, high-flight-risk Category 1 remand prisoner would make sure of that.

And the bad guys would know what time he would be returning after his hearing: the minute the mobibot left Kovak's courts complex. The Hammer hit team would plenty of time to set up.

Michael stepped up into the mobibot's coolness. He allowed the guard to push him into his wire-mesh cage. As usual, the man used more force than he had to. Michael did not complain; not only was it pointless, it provoked the guards. Today he was the last one in, the cages around him full of prisoners headed for their day in court, his arrival greeted as always with a mix of abuse and welcome. Michael ignored it. It was the same old bullshit, and it took a while for him to realize that the prisoner next to him—like Michael, a Cat 1 prisoner in orange—was trying to get his attention, the man's face hard up against the micromesh between their cages.

"Helfort," he whispered. "For fuck's sake, talk to me."

"What do you want? Who are you?"

"I'm Max Hardy. I've got a message for you. I—"

"Who from?"

"Don't know; doesn't matter, so listen up. There's to be an attack on the bot—" Michael's heart began to pound; he wondered how he'd survive handcuffed inside a cage. "—just before we get to the court, as we approach Shanghai Boulevard."

"Thanks for the heads-up, but what am I supposed to do?" Michael demanded. "I'm not going anywhere." He rattled his wrist and ankle chains to reinforce the point.

"Pull your chains apart. Pull hard."

Mystified, Michael did as he was told. To his surprise, the restraints fell away. "What the hell," he hissed. "How did—"

"Don't ask," Hardy said. "Now, one of the guards will unlock the doors before we get to Shanghai. The moment we're hit, wait for my word, then kick your cage door open and follow me out. And stay close."

"What then?"

"I'm going to run. Unless you want the bad guys to blow your brains out, you should do the same."

"See the orange jumpsuit, sport?" Michael hissed. "I won't get 5 meters."

"Better than having your brains blown out. When the bad guys get inside, it'll be a bloodbath, so I know where I'd rather be. Just follow me out and run like hell. You'll be fine."

"Okay," Michael said, "and thanks."

Hardy did not respond, so Michael sat back. His mind reeled. Hope flickered into life, but only for an instant. The whole thing smelled wrong. It was all too pat, too neatly packaged, too convenient. It was a Hammer setup; it had to be. But why would they want him out of the mobibot? If they wanted him dead, why didn't they just blow the bot apart? They wouldn't give a shit about the collateral damage; they never did.

Then it came to him.

The Hammers wanted him alive. That was why they wanted him outside. They couldn't risk trying to extract him. The ever so helpful Max Hardy had been right. It would be absolute pandemonium: smoke, gunfire everywhere, prisoners running around like headless chickens, guards trying to contain the situation until reinforcements arrived. And Michael wasn't the only Cat 1 prisoner onboard. The Hammers would have to pick him out of the eight other Cat 1s, and that would be difficult in all the confusion.

Now it all made sense to Michael.

The Hammers could force their way in to get him, but that would be time-consuming, and the chances of his being killed would be too high. It was all too uncertain, too hard to manage, so the Hammers needed him to get out of the bot under his own steam, and that was the job of Mr. Hardy.

The second Michael appeared, the Hammers would scoop him up and be gone before the Jamudans even had time to think, let alone react.

High risk but high return, and it would have worked if he'd gone along with Hardy's plan.

For a moment he thought he'd found the way out of the trap that had been laid for him: He would stay in the mobibot and keep his head down until it was all over. But it was only for a moment. That would not work. If he failed to show, the Hammers would come in after him. They had to, and they would, guns blazing. That way Michael would die sooner rather than later and a lot less painfully, but that was scant comfort.

He'd rather not die at all.

Much faster than he wanted, the clock ran off the last few seconds. His strategy for survival was little more than a half-baked idea when, with a violent crash, an explosion lifted the front of the mobibot up into the air and dropped it back down with a crunch of torn metal. The impact smashed Michael's head against the side of the cage and tore his scalp open. Blood ran hot down his face and neck.

"Now!" Hardy shouted.

Michael kicked his door open.

"Follow m—" Hardy said.

But Michael was already moving. His arm came up fast from below waist level and drove a fist into Hardy's throat that dropped the man as if he'd been shot. Michael did not waste a second; he plunged into the smoke that was fast filling the prisoner compartment and threw himself at the exit.

The door offered no resistance. Michael tumbled out and hit the road hard. He scrambled to his feet and waved an arm at the door. "Helfort's coming!" he screamed. "Helfort's right behind me."

It was not hard to work out why the Hammers fell for it. Michael was supposed to be the second orange suit out, not the first, and so they waited. Their indecision gave Michael the chance he needed, and he took it. He sprinted to the front of the blazing wreck of the mobibot. Flames scorched his face, smoke eddying and twisting around him as he ran for his life.

Then the Hammers woke up, sending a blizzard of rifle fire in Michael's direction, the air flayed by hypersonic rounds whiplashing past before whanging off into the mobibot's armored skin. But only for a few seconds, and then Michael was around the front of the flaming carcass. He plunged through air thick with acrid fumes that ripped at his throat and lungs. On he ran, keeping the wrecked mobibot between him and the Hammers, praying that his ambushers had been too confident to position anyone to cut him off.

Michael burst clear of the smoke into a scene of complete chaos. The road was choked with bots of every shape and size forced into emergency stops by the city's traffic management system, the spaces between them fast filling with confused and uncertain passengers, most slow to realize that they too were in mortal danger, with barely a handful taking cover as rifle fire filled the air. On Michael ran, barging the standing aside and hurdling the rest.

Just as Michael allowed himself to think he had escaped the Hammer trap, two men, one white-blond and the other with his head shaved so close that the sun glistened off his scalp, stepped from behind a cargobot, assault rifles pointing right at him, rock-steady. "Stop, Helfort!" Baldy screamed. "Stop and drop, right now!"

Michael ignored them, but only until the pair sent a burst of fire shrieking past his head. Sick with defeat, he skidded to a halt. "Okay, okay," he said.

The two men were on him in an instant. Michael screamed as they yanked his arms behind him, brutally indifferent to his pain. Cuffing him, they dragged him to his feet and hustled him away down Shanghai Boulevard.

"Zero, Six. We have him," Michael heard Blondie say.

"Roger that, Zero," the man said a few seconds later. "Egress Bravo, understood. Six, out."

On they went. Michael knew that his chances of survival were fading fast. He had one chance, and he took it. Without warning, he exploded, a single violent movement that drove a shoulder into Baldy even as he rammed his left leg into Blondie's knee, He took both Hammers by surprise, and the three of them fell to the road in a twisted, tangled mess, with Michael kicking out in all directions in an attempt to slow things down.

"You little fucker," Blondie snarled, struggling to get his rifle free.

The fight did not last long. Baldy finished it with a crushing blow from his rifle butt to the side of Michael's head, a blow that drove him to the edge of unconsciousness, the pain blinding in its intensity. But he clawed his way back to the light; to survive, he had to take whatever chances came his way, however slim, however transient.

Cursing, Baldy and Blondie hauled Michael to his feet, and they were on the move again, his body dragged along limp between the two men and into a narrow lane. A few meters down, a small cargobot waited for them.

"Thank Kraa for that," Baldy muttered. "I've had enough of this."

The words snuffed out the last tiny flicker of hope left burning in Michael. It was over; the Hammers had him.

"Me, too," Blondie grunted.

Just short of the ramp, they stopped. "You hold him here," Blondie said, "while I get the ramp down."

"Roger that," Baldy said, dropping Michael to the ground. "You move one millimeter and I'll blow your leg off. Got it?"

"Yeah, yeah … asshole."

Baldy laughed. "Nice try, Helfort. I'll tell you this," he went on as the ramp started on its way down, "I think I'll enjoy—"

A soft, wet slap cut the man off. Baldy stood swaying, his mouth open, a look of surprise on his face. He stayed upright for a few seconds, and then with a soft grunt he crumpled to the ground alongside Michael.

First one and then another and another and another person rushed past, their black jumpsuited figures hung with equipment.

"About time, guys," Michael said.

Saturday, May 25, 2402, UD
Kovak Military Hospital

"I think I owe you an apology, Lieutenant," Colonel K'zekaa said, her head bobbing in embarrassment. "You were quite right about those goddamned Hammers, and I was wrong."

"Thank you, sir," Michael said, his smoke-damaged voice a hoarse croak, "and I'm sorry I was so rude."

K'zekaa waved the apology aside. "Don't worry about it," she said. "I did talk to the Jamudans, though, and they told me they'd take the threat seriously."

"What happens now?"

"Your lawyer hasn't seen you yet?"

"No. You're my first visitor. I told the hospital to tell everyone that I was too tired to talk to them. You must be very persuasive is all I can say."

"Oh, I am. Anyway, to answer your question, nothing happens until a court-appointed doctor says you are fit enough to appear."

"Shit!" Michael said.

"I thought you'd be happy about that. You know what might be waiting for you?"

"I do. My lawyer has been telling me the same thing."

"So why the rush?"

"Two reasons. First, I don't need to worry about the death penalty. The Feds will never execute me. It won't happen. Ever."

"I wouldn't be so sure about that," K'zekaa said with a frown.

"What will be, will be. I can't worry about it. Fact is I cannot go on like this much longer. I didn't want to be here, I never planned to be here, and I wouldn't be if Admiral Ja—if I hadn't been kidnapped. But now that I am, it's tearing me apart. I want closure, and sooner rather than later." Michael paused, taking a deep breath to settle himself down. "I know it won't make any sense to you," he went on, "but you haven't been through what I have."

"No. But I do know this: I've read your file, and I cannot judge you."

The silence that followed was broken when a nurse stuck his head in Michael's room. "Hey!" he said. "What are you doing here? No visitors, so please leave—now."

Saturday, November 9, 2402, UD
Kovak planetary defense base

The door of the holding cell banged open to reveal the substantial figure of Sergeant Habash. "It's time, sir," he said.

"And not soon enough," Michael grumbled. "I've had enough of Jamuda, I can tell you."

"So you keep telling me." Habash chuckled. "We're sorry to see you leave."

"So tell those Fed motherfuckers I'm not coming."

Habash looked right into Michael's eyes. "I wish I could. None of this is right."

"No, Sergeant Habash, it's not. Come on; let's go."

Flanked by two more guards, Michael followed the man out of his cell and down a series of corridors until they reached the prisoner outprocessing center, a bleak room filled with a large contingent of grim-faced fleet police in Fed shipsuits. One of them stepped forward, a dour-looking woman sporting a warrant officer's badges.

"I'm Warrant Officer Yamazaki, Federated Worlds Space Fleet. I have orders to return you to Terranova planet, Lieutenant."

"Show me," Michael demanded.

Yamazaki held out a single sheet of paper. Michael took it and read through the dense legalese. He wasn't left much the wiser. He had no idea whether what he was looking at was valid, but he was determined not to give the Feds any more slack than he had to.

"Looks okay," he conceded, handing the orders back to Yamazaki.

"It is. Now, your hands, sir."

"Is that necessary? There are hundreds of you bastards, you're all bigger than me, and we're inside a planetary defense base. How far do you think I'd get?"

"Just do it, sir," the woman said, her voice flat and cold.

"Why are you such an officious asshole, Warrant Officer Yamazaki?" Michael snapped.

"Now!"

With reluctance, Michael held out his hands. He was cuffed by the largest spacer in the escort. The man ran a thin plasfiber cord from the cuffs to a band on his own wrist. "Oh, come on!" Michael protested. "That's not necessary either."

"Not your call, sir. Let's go."

"No kidding," Michael muttered as he was led out of the cell, with the rest of Yamazaki's team of fleet police falling in around him.

Flanked by his escort, Michael stepped out into a hot Jamuda morning. The sun hammered down. It turned the ceramcrete apron into a blazing sea of heat and light that brought Michael to an abrupt halt, his eyes flooded with sudden tears. "Shit," he hissed, wiping his eyes with the back of a plasticuffed hand.

"Come on, sir," Yamazaki said. "Keep moving."

The warrant officer looked anxious. *As well you should,* Michael thought. The Hammers might deny any responsibility for the abortive attempt to kidnap him, but that had not stopped them from jacking up the rhetoric, with their embassy demanding that he be extradited back to Commitment to face Hammer justice. And Yamazaki would have known every bit as well as Michael did that the Hammers would stop at nothing to get their hands on him.

"Okay, okay," Michael said as they set off again. They had gone a few meters when Michael stopped again. His mouth dropped open. In front of him was the Federated Worlds Space Fleet assault lander waiting to take him back to Terranova.

His heart sank. He was about to come face to face with the very people whom he had betrayed, whose code of honor he had despoiled, whose reputation his actions had so traduced.

The cell door opened to admit a young spacer carrying a tray. "Lunch," the man said.

"Thanks," Michael said, getting to his feet.

The spacer leaned forward. With great care he spit into the food. "Enjoy," he whispered, holding the tray out.

In an instant, rage consumed every part of Michael's being, and he erupted into violence. He smashed the tray aside. His hands lunged for the spacer's throat. He rammed the man back against the bulkhead with a sickening thud that drove the air from his lungs in an explosive *woof*. Michael spun the man around and pulled him back and down to the deck, one fist clubbing his tormentor's face in a brutal, frenzied attack that gave the spacer no chance to protect himself.

Within seconds the cell filled with bodies, and Michael was dragged off. His chest heaved, and his heart pounded. He was still consumed by anger, and his arms and fists lashed out until sheer weight of numbers pinned him down. A soft *pffft* and stinging pain from a gas gun ended his fight. "Tell that little fuck I'll kill him next time I see him," Michael screamed as blackness closed in. "You tell that … little …"

The marine corporal sitting on Michael's unconscious body eased himself off. He stood up, shaking his head. "Now what the hell was that all about?" he asked.

"Who knows?" his buddy said. "But I'd bet it was something—" He reached down to pull the whimpering spacer to his feet. "—this sad sack of shit did."

"Visitor for you," the intercom said.

"Piss off," Michael muttered. He refused to open his eyes even when the cell door opened, furious with himself that he had lost his temper, even more furious that his left wrist had been secured to the bulkhead by a plas-fiber restraint.

"Lieutenant Helfort," a voice said, a woman's voice, authoritative and controlled. "I'm Commander Kadar, captain in command of the FWSS *Pilgrim*."

Discipline, deeply ingrained, forced Michael to his feet. He snapped to attention. "Apologies, sir," he blurted. "I didn't know it was you."

"Don't apologize. Now, first things first." Kadar turned and waved a marine into the cell. "Get that restraint off. That's better," she went on when the man was done. "I'm here to apologize to you. The security holovid showed us what happened. We'll be taking disciplinary action against Spacer Gillespie."

"I'm sorry I lost it," Michael said.

"Pity about all this." Kadar waved a hand at the cell's sterile white bulkheads. "But rules are rules."

"I understand that."

"I know you do." Kadar leaned forward a fraction. "You're not on your own, Helfort—" Her voice had dropped to the faintest of whispers; Michael struggled to hear her. "—so hang in there." Kadar stepped back. "Now," she continued, her voice strong again, "if there is anything you need, just ask. I can't guarantee you'll get it, but anything we can do, we will."

With that she was gone. Michael wondered just what the hell she'd been talking about.

Wednesday, August 20, 2403, UD
Offices of the Supreme Council for the
Preservation of the Faith, McNair City

"Michael Wallace Helfort ..."

If the black-gowned judge was troubled by the gravity of the occasion, her voice did not show it.

"... it is the sentence of this court that you be transferred to a duly authorized place of execution, and there, on the date specified by the minister for planetary security, you be put to death according to law. Take the prisoner down."

"Yes!" Chief Councillor Polk hissed. "It's about time, you piece of Fed garbage." He scowled. "Months and months they took! Can you believe it, Lou?"

"That's the Federated Worlds for you," Lou Nagaro, Polk's chief of staff, said. "Very keen on due process."

Polk snorted derisively. "I'll give the assholes due process," he grunted.

"At least they got there in the end, Chief Councillor. So how about a glass of champagne to celebrate?"

"No, not yet," Polk said with an emphatic shake of the head. "I'll share a bottle of champagne with you, a good bottle from Old Earth, but only when that man is dead and not before. Now go and find out where Councillor Kando and Colonel Hartspring are. I want to see them."

"Sir."

Polk waited in silence until Nagaro returned.

"Kando and Hartspring will be back in McNair tomorrow," Nagaro said.

"Good. I want Kando to make sure that the Feds carry through with this, and I don't care how much we have to spend or who we have to suborn. Helfort must be executed."

"I think Kando can make sure of it."

"He'd better."

"But what about Hartspring? What can a DocSec colonel do?"

"A lot, Lou, a lot. Michael Helfort might be on his way to the gallows, and none too soon, but death's not enough for him. I want him to suffer every minute of every day he has left alive. I want him in so much pain that he'll be begging the Feds to kill him when they strap him into the chair."

Skepticism flitted across Nagaro's face. "Forgive me, Chief Councillor, but how can we do that? The Feds will have Helfort locked away where nobody can reach him. No matter how much we spend, we'll never lay a hand on him."

Polk smiled indulgently at Nagaro. "You never were much of a creative thinker, were you?"

"I don't follow."

"Watch and learn, Lou; watch and learn."

Saturday, September 16, 2403, UD
Federal Supermax Prison, Foundation City,
Terranova planet

Day followed day, each one the same as the last, the routine mind-numbing in its relentless predictability.

It was almost nine in the morning: exercise time. Precisely on the hour, the door would open. He would be called out into the corridor. A pair of guards would escort him out into the yard. He would exercise for an hour and then return to his cell.

The routine never varied.

Except today it did. When the door opened, one of the guards was standing not back as usual but right by the door, a break from routine that struck Michael as odd. It was his least favorite guard, a hard-faced bitch called Loewenthal, always sullen, always as unhelpful as she could be. The woman would have made a perfect DocSec recruit, Michael had decided.

Loewenthal took a half step forward. Her hand brushed Michael's long enough to press a tiny object into his palm.

The guard stepped back as though nothing out of the ordinary had happened. "Just checking," she said. "Let's go."

The lights in Michael's cell burned twenty-four hours a day, but they were dimmed at night. Taking advantage of the gloom, Michael lay on his bunk, his back to the security cameras that watched his every movement. He moistened the inside of his wrist with saliva, then pressed the object—a datastick—hard into his skin. His neuronics took only a second to establish an online connection.

"Upload file?" Michael was asked.

"Go," he responded.

The file took a lifetime to upload. Michael prayed throughout that the prison guards would not break the door down to stop the process and then prayed even harder that somehow Anna had found a way to get a message to him.

"Upload finished," his neuronics said. "Open file?"

"Go."

There was a pause. Michael's anticipation grew, and his elation built. He was convinced the holovid was from Anna. Finally, his neuronics popped a screen into his mind's eye, and he settled down to watch.

"Hello, my love," Michael whispered when Anna appeared. *That's very odd,* he thought. *Why is she in Fleet coveralls? She should be in NRA combat fatigues, surely.*

A few seconds later, the screen faded to black. Disappointment and frustration swamped Michael. "What is going—oh, no," he hissed.

A man had appeared. He had a face no Fed would ever forget. It was more skull than face, with the skin drawn tight over sharp-edged cheekbones. They eyes were deepset and hooded below steel-gray hair that was cropped short. "You murdering dirtbag," Michael whispered as the image steadied.

The man's eyes bored into him as he spoke.

"Hello, Lieutenant Helfort," the man said, his deathskull face stretching into a ghastly smile. "I'm Jeremiah Polk, Chief Councillor of the Hammer of Kraa Worlds. I wanted to tell you how delighted I am that you are to be held to account for your crimes. I am, of course, disappointed that you'll be executed by your Fed countrymen rather than by a DocSec firing squad, but it is a disappointment I can live with.

"And do not think for a second that you will escape. You won't, not this time. To make sure of that, I have authorized my people to spend as much money as they need to ensure that your sentence is not reduced, and you might be surprised just how many Feds are more than happy to help us.

"Even President Diouf will not help you, and spare me all that crap about what a good woman she is. Even she has her price—which we will pay—and …"

"Bullshit," Michael snarled. "Absolute bullshit."

"… as you've noticed we've had no trouble persuading your trashpress to lobby hard for your death sentence to be carried out. But it does strike me that you're getting off too lightly. Because you Feds believe all that human rights garbage, your death will be painless, and you won't suffer as much as you deserve to. I think that is just plain wrong. You should suffer, and I intend to make sure you do.

"'But how?' I hear you say. I'm speaking to you from McNair, hundreds of light-years away, and you're tucked away behind the walls of a Fed maximum-security prison. So what can I do to you? Well, the answer to that …"

Michael's heart lurched. "Oh, no," he whispered. All of a sudden he knew where Polk was going.

"… is to hurt the woman you love, and when I say hurt, I mean in a way no human should ever be made to suffer. And in case you're wondering what those words mean, I am talking about weeks and weeks and weeks of drawn-out agony, torture so exquisite, so relentless that death will be a blessing."

Polk smiled.

"Oh, yes, I'm really looking forward to it, I can tell you," he went on. "Now, let me see." Polk made a show of consulting a piece of paper. "Ah, yes; your Anna has done well. Very well, in fact. I'm told she's a captain in the NRA's 120th Regiment, which is not bad for a woman. We thought you might like to see a picture of her."

Anna reappeared. Michael's breath caught in his throat at the sight. The image was so real, he felt as if he could reach out and touch the woman he loved. Assault rifle in one hand, she was dressed in well-worn NRA combat fatigues. Wayward wisps of fine black hair peeked out from beneath her helmet to hang down over honey-dark skin smeared with dirt. She stood in front of a group of NRA troopers—*She's doing a briefing,* Michael realized—and her deep green eyes blazed as her right hand stabbed out to make a point. It broke Michael's heart to see her, to know how badly he had betrayed her, to know he would never hold her close again, to know she would live while he died.

The picture faded.

"I have to say," Polk went on when he returned, "your Anna is a very beautiful woman. And in case you were interested, one of our agents took that picture last week at a briefing before the 120th attacked one of our planetary defense firebases. One of their more successful operations, I'm sorry to say, and before you ask, she came through without a scratch. As you've worked out by now, my agent in H Company keeps me very well informed. Now it's time for you to meet an old friend. Colonel?"

Michael flinched when Erwin Hartspring appeared. The man terrified him still. The DocSec colonel had been pressed from the same mold as Polk. His face was long and gaunt, his skin wrinkle-cut, stretched tight over prominent cheekbones and windburned to a reddish brown. A long, straight nose dropped to a fine pencil mustache above thin bloodless lips. His hair was cropped to jet-black stubble.

"Hello, Michael," Hartspring said, slapping the palm of his left hand with a riding crop. Michael had never forgotten the short length of cane covered with black leather. "I'm sure you remember me," the man went on. "I mean …"

And you would be right, you psychopath, Michael thought, his hand feeling for where Hartspring's crop had slashed his face open.

"… how could you forget after all we've been through together? Now, the chief councillor has asked me to put together a dedicated unit to hunt down and capture Anna. Team Victor, we've called it—v for 'vengeance,' in case you were wondering—and it will be under my command. Its members will be special forces marines; that gives you some idea of how seriously we are taking this. When Team Victor captures Anna, she will be handed her over to a handpicked team of DocSec …" Hartspring paused to let a smile of unalloyed evil stretch across his skull-like face. "Do I need to say any more?" he continued. "No, I don't think I do. You can use your imagination to fill in the gaps. And don't be in any doubt that we will capture her. Anna is here on Commitment, and you're not, so it's just a matter of time. We'll do our best to get our hands on her before you are executed, but don't worry. Even if we don't, we will get her eventually.

Well, I don't think there's anything more I need to say, so I will sign off now. I'm sure you won't enjoy your last days, but Chief Councillor Polk and I will."

Polk reappeared. "You can believe what Colonel Hartspring says," he said, "if only because I will bring the full might and power of the Hammer Worlds to ensure that he succeeds. Goodbye, Michael."

The holovid stopped; before Michael could do anything to prevent it, the words "File Deleted" appeared on the screen. "Goddammit," he swore, jumping to his feet. "Now what the fuck do I do?"

That was the worst thing. There was nothing, not a damn thing, he could do, and he knew it. What Polk and Hartspring planned to do was the most exquisite torture imaginable. And the torture started now, and it would continue until the day he was taken out and killed.

If I ever get out of here, he vowed, *I will hunt the pair of you down and kill you both.*

There was only problem: He had absolutely no idea how to win his freedom, and until he did, that promise was as empty as the rest of his life.

Friday, December 5, 2403, UD
Federal Supermax Prison, Foundation City,
Terranova planet

Michael stared out of the plasglass window in his cell. It had been—he couldn't be bothered to work it out exactly—months since his appeal had started its laborious journey through the courts, a process never designed to be fast and slowed further by the fact that the Federated Worlds had not executed anyone in living memory. To say those involved were being cautious was a serious understatement.

And every minute of every day, the same question ate away at his sanity: Had Polk and Hartspring succeeded? Time dragged past; not knowing the answer had stripped the life out of him. He was an empty shell, devoid of hope. All he did was exist, a man borne along by forces over which he had no control, forces utterly committed to his destruction.

He swore softly at the prospect of another day the same as the one before and the one before that, each new day dragging past with the same dreary predictability, grinding down what little of his humanity remained.

The anger that had sustained him through the early days, that had fueled his hope that there would be some way out of the trap laid for him by Admiral Jaruzelska's betrayal, had long gone. Even the bitter mix of despair, frustration, and guilt that had followed had not lasted, leached away by the dreary monotony of living a life waiting for death.

Outside his cell, there was nothing new to look at: the same grassy exercise area secured by a double fence of razor wire 3 meters high topped with floodlights and surveillance holocams. Beyond lay more grass and yet more wire, a distant maglev line the only evidence that life went on in the real world.

At the best of times, Michael hated it. Today, it was a dismal sight after days of rain had drained from a leaden sky. It was so depressing that he wouldn't have needed much encouragement to finish it all himself. Not that he could, of course; the never-ending surveillance made sure of that.

"You have a visitor," the squawk box on the wall said. "Stand away from the door."

Michael sighed and did as he'd been told. The door opened, and he was waved forward; surrounded by guards, he followed the familiar path down the corridor to the interview room, too dispirited to ask who had come to see him. "I really am a dead man walking," he muttered under his breath. He managed a fleeting smile. Never was a cliché so true, because he might as well have been dead.

He hoped his parents hadn't come to see him. The stress and uncertainty of the appeal process was tearing them both apart, and Michael knew that nothing he could say or do could help them. Their visits had become so difficult that he had asked them not to come anymore.

But occasionally there was one emotion that troubled him. He tried not to think about the future. Most of the time he succeeded. When he failed, the thought of waited for him was frightening, made worse because he knew what his death would do to those who loved him: his mom and dad and his sister, Sam. And more than any of those, there was Anna, still stuck on Commitment

56

fighting the Hammers, something the people of the Federated Worlds were too gutless to do.

He could only hope that she was still alive, that she had not been taken by Hartspring.

The door to the interview room opened, and his lawyer walked in. He liked Erica Malvern, but her relentless energy was wearing, as was her unshakable confidence that Michael's death sentence would be commuted.

"Morning, Michael," Malvern said, a bright smile on her face as always.

"Erica. What's happening?"

"I've just had word that the president has made her decision on your appeal for clemency, so we should know where we stand any time now."

Gut-wrenching fear tore at Michael's stomach. "No idea what the decision is?" he said, his voice a half-strangled croak.

"Sorry, no. By Federal law, the president's decision must be given to you in writing. But hang in there; I'm sure President Diouf will do the right thing."

"I was sure of that too once, but now …" His voice trailed off into silence. "So all we can do is wait," he went on.

"I'm afraid so. We've done everything that we can."

"What's the trashpress saying?"

"Michael, Michael," Malvern protested. "Don't go there. You know the outcome they want, so why torture yourself?"

"Bastards," Michael muttered. "When the Hammers take over, they'll have a lot to answer for. What's the view in Fleet?"

Malvern frowned. "That's a tough one."

"I know you can't go around conducting opinion polls, Erica, but surely you have some feel."

"Well, as best I can tell, the more senior the person, the more unhappy they are. They don't like the concessions Moderator Ferrero has made to the Hammers. That damn peace treaty's so very one-sided. And it's no secret the Hammers are leaning hard on the government to have your sentence carried out."

"I'm surprised Ferrero hasn't just handed me over," he said. "I know Chief Councillor Polk wants me in front of a DocSec firing squad almost as badly as he wants to be Emperor Jeremiah the First."

The door behind Malvern opened. A guard stuck his head in. "Can I have a word, counselor?" he asked.

"Sure. Back in a second," Malvern said as she slipped out.

"Okay," Michael said. He wondered what was going on. Then it hit him, and hard: the president's decision had arrived. "Please don't let me down," Michael whispered.

Malvern was gone a very long time; Michael's nerves were a mess by the time she reappeared, a slim envelope in her hand. "Is that what I think it is?" he croaked.

"Yes. Come on!" Malvern shouted to the unseen guards. "Get this damn screen up."

"Sorry, counselor," a voice said. The screen opened a fraction, and Malvern slipped the envelope through the gap. Michael took it with hands slick with cold sweat.

"Michael," Malvern said, her voice soft. "Open it."

Michael shook his head. "I can't. I'm sorry, Erica; I just can't."

"You want me to?"

"Not really," Michael replied, misery splashed all across his face. "I don't want to know."

"You need to know. Pass it back."

Michael did as he was told and watched Malvern tear the envelope open, his heart hammering in his chest with painful intensity. She scanned the letter and then looked up at him, the tears in her eyes sparkling in the harsh light. "I'm so sorry," she said, her voice breaking. "The president has turned down your appeal for clemency. Sentence will be carried out one week from today."

"No!" Michael hissed. "She can't have. I trusted her." He slumped back in his seat, and his head dropped into his hands. "I've been screwed.," he said, his voice strengthening as anger pushed fear aside. "Admiral Jaruzelska … that fucking judge … and now Diouf. They've betrayed me, all of them. Goddamn the bastards all to hell."

The silence that followed was a long one. Michael was the first to speak. "That's it. It's over," he said, his voice flat, emotionless. "There's nothing more you can do now, Erica, so you'd better go. But thanks for everything."

"Oh, Michael," Malvern whispered. "I'm so sorry."

"Just go, Erica."

Malvern looked at him for a moment, nodded, and then was gone, leaving Michael alone. "Fuck them all," he muttered. He wondered why he felt so strangely calm. He'd always done his duty as he saw it, and if that wasn't good enough, then so be it. Even looking back, he would not change anything.

The door behind him opened. "Come on," the guard said. "Let's get you back."

Michael nodded. "Sure, Sergeant Valek," he said. Michael liked Valek; the man had always treated him with respect. With the nearly absolute power the guards had over him, he need not have.

"We've heard the news," Valek said when they got to his cell. "I just wanted to say ... how sorry we all are. It's not right, and I know I speak for everyone in the corps."

Michael shook his head, confused. So far as he knew, Sergeant Valek had never been anywhere near the marines. "The corps?" he said. "I don't follow."

"Both of my brothers are marines. We talk a lot. They've told me what you did for the guys at Devastation Reef."

"That was a while ago."

"I know it was, but they tell me that the corps does not forget. Anyway, I need to go. Captain Pillai will be along in an hour to talk to you."

"Okay, and thanks. It helps."

"Not as much as I'd like," Valek said.

"Bad business," Pillai said as he walked into the cell.

60

"You should see it from where I'm sitting."

The man smiled and shook his head. "Before we get started," Pillai went on, "I'd like to say that Sergeant Valek was right. And it's not just the Marine Corps that's pissed. I don't know many people who agree with what's happening. I don't know what anyone else thinks, but I do know the Hammers are behind this."

"Should you be saying that?" Michael said with a worried frown. "Everything's recorded."

"Let me worry about that," Pillai said. "The powers that be have bigger problems on their plate right now."

"They do?"

"Let me see … Yes, at last count, 372 marine officers have resigned their commissions to protest the president's decision. And there are more from Space Fleet, apparently, though the news channels aren't saying how many. But I bet they won't be the last. If this government thinks it can get away with this, then they're stupider than they look."

Michael was shocked into silence; tears pricked at his eyes as emotion washed through him. This he had not expected. "What can I say?" he said. He wiped his eyes.

"You don't need to say a thing. I just hope it helps." Pillai took a deep breath. "Time for business, I'm afraid. You'll leave for Farrisport in two days' time. Once you are there, you will be briefed on what happens … you know …"

Michael did know; he'd thought of nothing else. He took a deep breath to steady himself. "What about visits? I want to see my folks."

"We'll arrange for them to fly to Farrisport. You'll be able to spend as much time with them as you want, right up until the end."

Sunday, December 7, 2403, UD
Foundation City, Terranova planet

Michael sat slumped in his seat, head back and eyes closed, as the suborbital shuttle carrying him and his ten-strong escort of heavily armed guards—talk about over-kill, Michael had thought when they'd fallen in around him—rocketed down the runway and climbed away from Foundation City. The flight to Farrisport promised to be a long one. Michael tried to force himself to sleep, but sleep refused to come, the minutes dragging past second by miserable second.

Michael emerged from the shuttle into a hellish night. The wind drove thick flurries of snow into his face. The cold was intense. It sliced through his prison jumpsuit; his eyes watered with icy tears. Captain Pillai and his team escorted him to where a mobibot waited on the floodlit apron. *So this is where my life ends*, Michael thought as he was led into the welcome warmth of the vehicle.

With a lurch, the mobibot set off. A few minutes later, it stopped, and Michael was fed into the Farrisport machine, the latest in a long line of prisoners that stretched back to the earliest days of the Federation.

An hour later, the machine was satisfied that Michael was who he was supposed to be. Deep scanned for contraband, checked for disease and injury, and dressed in a new jumpsuit, he was spit out by the machine into a cell no different from the one he had left behind. He dropped onto the bunk, tired beyond belief.

"You have a visitor," the intercom announced. "Stand up and wait back from the door."

With a huge effort, Michael got to his feet. The door opened, and a prison service colonel, iron-gray hair cut short above a comfortable round face, stepped in. Her crisp blue uniform was stark against the white sterility of the cell. "I'm Colonel Kallewi," she said. She waved the guards out. "I'm the superintendent of Farrisport Island Prison."

"Wish I could say it was good to meet you, sir," Michael said with a fleeting lopsided smile. Then it hit him hard enough to make his heart pound. "Forgive me," he went on, "but Kallewi? Are you any relation to the commander of my marine detachment in *Redwood*?"

"Yes, I am," Kallewi said, her voice soft. "Janos was my son."

Michael's stomach turned over. This he had not expected. "You've heard ... you know?"

"I received notification that he'd been killed in action, yes."

"I was his captain," Michael said. Kallewi's dignity in her grief made his guilt all the worse. "I was responsible for his being on Commitment. It was … I'm so sorry."

Kallewi said nothing for a moment. "Don't be," she said finally. "I won't say his death has been easy to bear. It hasn't, but Janos was his own man, and he made his own decisions. And he died doing his duty the best way he could, and I won't stand here and tell you or anyone else that he was wrong about that. But I would like to know more of what happened. It would help me and his father."

"Of course."

"Tonight at 20:00 if that's okay."

"I don't think I'm going anywhere," Michael said with a crooked smile.

"Not sure about that."

Michael stared at the woman. *What on earth does she mean by that?* he asked himself.

Kallewi took a deep breath before continuing. "Now, back to business," she said. "There'll be a full briefing for you at 09:00 tomorrow morning on the execution protocol—" Michael flinched; he couldn't help himself. "—and your parents will be arriving at 12:00. You can see them for as long and as often as you wish, though their last visit will have to finish no later than 02:00 on the day."

Six hours, Michael thought. *I will be utterly alone for the last six hours of my life.*

"That's all for now," Kallewi went on. "Any questions?"

"None worth asking."

"Okay. I will see you later."

"Sir."

"Sit," Kallewi said, waving Michael into a seat across a small metal table from her. "Can I call you Michael?" she went on once his escort had left.

"Of course, sir," Michael replied. He was both embarrassed and surprised by the question. In his experience, colonels, even prison service colonels, weren't on first-name terms with junior officers.

"Bear with me a second," Kallewi said. She placed a small silver cube on the table.

Michael stared at the cube to make sure he wasn't hallucinating. He wasn't. He was looking at a near-field jammer; there would be no digital record of anything said or done in this room. Michael did not know much about prison service regulations, but he would have bet what little was left of his life that the device had no business inside Farrisport. "Colonel, forgive me," he said, "but what's going on? I'm pretty sure this thing—" He pointed at the cube. "—is not allowed in here."

"You'd be right."

"So what's happening? Please, I need to know. I can't … I can't …" Michael had to stop to recover his self-control. "This might surprise you," he went on, "but I've had it. I just want this to be over."

"I'm sorry. I can't imagine what you're going through, so let me get to the point."

"Fire away."

Friday, December 12, 2403, UD
Farrisport Island Prison

"It's time."

Michael got to his feet. "I'm ready," he said. It was a complete and utter lie. Only the last dregs of courage and self-control allowed him to keep a body torn by fear under control.

Two guards stepped forward. Hands locked onto his arms. They escorted him down a succession of short corridors. Kallewi and a posse of observers fell in behind, his lawyer too. Erica Malvern's eyes were brimful of tears. Michael was led into a room. Its walls were seamless sheets of blindingly white plasteel, its only furniture a single chair bolted to the floor, its back, arms, and legs fitted with broad plasfiber restraints.

Michael's heart hammered at the walls of his chest. He was eased forward, turned, and pushed gently down into the chair. The guards worked fast to secure the restraints. The awful, unstoppable inevitability of the process threatened to break him apart. With all that remained of his self-control, he made himself stay still.

"Prisoner is secure, sir," one of the guards said, moving back.

Colonel Kallewi stepped forward to stand right in front of Michael, a single sheet of paper in her left hand. She leaned forward. "Hang in there, spacer," she whispered.

Michael said nothing. He was too terrified to speak, even now unable to believe what was about to happen to him.

Kallewi cleared her throat before speaking. "Michael Wallace Helfort. Your final appeal for clemency having been denied by the president of the Federated Worlds in presidential order J-557, a physical copy of which document I have witnessed in person and further confirmed by direct comm with the president herself …"

Michael turned his mind inward. His neuronics cycled through his favorite holopix of Anna, pictures of the best times in his life, pictures rich in hope and happiness. But all of a sudden, it was too much, too painful, and Michael could not take any more. He shut his neuronics down. He opened his eyes and waited for Colonel Kallewi to finish.

"… and now, by the authority vested in me as the superintendent of Farrisport Island Prison, sentence of death will be carried out." Kallewi stepped back. "Proceed," she said.

A guard—she looked very young and very nervous—wheeled a small trolley to where Michael sat. On it rested a plasfiber cylinder from which two corrugated hoses led to a face mask. With well-rehearsed efficiency, the guard placed the face mask over Michael's face, tightening the straps behind his head to form an airtight seal.

"Face mask is secure, sir," the woman said.

"Confirm system is nominal."

The guard's fingers flickered across a small touchpad set below a status screen. "System is nominal."

"Close the vent. Set the system to recirculate."

"Vent closed. System set to recirculate. Carbon dioxide scrubber is active, sir."

"Sentence will now be carried out," Kallewi said.

This is it, Michael thought, knowing with each inhalation that he was one step closer to death as his body burned the oxygen in the system until too little remained to sustain life. It was strange. He felt disconnected from what was going on. As if it were already over. As if he were …

Quietly and with no fuss, the end came, and Michael slipped away into unconsciousness, falling down into the darkness, down to where death awaited.

Why could he not feel anything? Why was did the darkness feel so thick? Why was the silence so absolute?

Was this what it was like to be dead? He was dead, so it had to be.

None of it made any sense, so he lay unmoving until a soft voice reached down to where he drifted. It called him back up from the infinite blackness that cradled his being, urging him to come back to the light. He did not want to go, but the voice was insistent; it nagged at him until he had to leave the warmth and security of the darkness. He drifted up toward a faint point of light. It strengthened as he rose; its brilliance grew and grew until it pushed the darkness aside, and then a blinding white-ness enveloped him, a whiteness so bright that he had to screw his eyes shut against the glare. His head filled with sudden stabbing agony, his heart thrashed at his chest, nausea roiled his stomach.

"Can you hear me?" a voice asked.

He wanted to answer, but his mouth was too dry, his throat too constricted to let the words come. With an ef-fort, he drove air from his lungs and past his lips. "Yes," he croaked.

"Good," the voice said. "You had us worried. That damn drug is dangerous. We're transfusing more nano-bots to mop up the last of the toxins in your system. I'm afraid you'll feel like shit until they're gone, but it won't be long, so hang in there."

"Head hurts," he mumbled. The pain was terrifying in its intensity; it radiated out from behind his forehead in swirling waves of red-hot agony, each more powerful than the last.

"How bad?"

"Bad, real bad."

"Bloody cataleptic drugs," the voice said. "Hold on … okay, I've upped your painkillers."

The pain roared to new heights. He bit down on his lower lip to choke down the scream that built in his throat, his mouth filled with the coppery taste of fresh blood.

"Better?"

He shook his head. A mistake; shards of pain slashed razor-edged through his head. "Stop!" he screamed. "Stop it now! Please!"

"Hang in there."

But he could not. With brutal force, the pain bludgeoned him back to where he had come from.

In an instant, he was awake. He stared up at the ceiling, which was white and featureless except for a single light panel turned down low. He looked around. Judging from the medibot beside his bed, it had to be a hospital, he decided.

But why was he in a hospital? His mind was blank. Panic engulfed him. He could not remember anything, not a damn thing: who he was, where he was, why he was here. All he knew was what his senses were telling him right there and then.

That was it.

Beyond the immediate lay … nothing. Hard as he tried, he could not see past the nothingness. His mind said he existed, but that was the totality of his universe. He had no idea what lay beyond the Spartan confines of his room; that terrified him. But why? He did not know. But he did know one thing for certain: Outside the door lay unimaginable horrors, horrors that would destroy him with casual, uncaring cruelty, horrors that even now might be coming for him. With fear-fueled desperation, he tried to find a way out, to escape, but he could not move.

Without warning, the door opened. A scream of primal terror boiled up from deep inside, a scream that died before it reached his lips. The man who had entered the room was a marine medic, a corporal, there to help him.

He knew all that without thinking. But how did he know? What was a marine? What was a corporal? Why was the man here to help him? None of it made any sense.

"The medibot told me you were conscious," the medic said; he leaned over to look him in the face. "How are you feeling?"

"Confused," he said after a moment's thought.

"Can't remember anything?"

"No. Who am I?"

"You're Michael Helfort."

That did not help. Who the hell was Michael Helfort? "Where am I?"

"A place called Karrigal Creek."

"Never heard—"

With all the shocking impact of a dam bursting, memories exploded inside Michael's head, a torrential, confused kaleidoscope of people, places, and events, a churning mess of sensations that Michal struggled to make sense of. His heart lurched as he remembered with an awful clarity the moment when the prison guard had slipped the mask over his face.

"I'm alive," he whispered. He felt stupid the instant the words came out. Of course he was alive. That had been Colonel Kallewi's promise to him. He'd wanted so badly to believe the woman, but he never had, not even for a second. Throughout those last awful days, he had convinced himself the woman had only wanted to make the inevitable less terrible. But she had been telling him the truth.

"You sure are, spacer," the medic said with a cheerful grin. "Now, let's get you hydrated," he went on, handing Michael a beaker of pale blue fluid. "Get that down you."

All of a sudden aware of how thirsty he was, Michael took the beaker and drained it in one long swallow. "Thanks, Corporal," he said. "Any chance of another one?"

"As many as you like," the man said. "I'll go get a refill."

"Thanks," Michael said. He put his head back and closed his eyes, happy just to luxuriate in the sudden rush of energy surging through his body.

The door opened.

"That was damn quick, Corporal," Michael said. He opened his eyes and looked up, and there she was, a tall, spare figure in Fleet black. "You," he hissed at the sight of Admiral Jaruzelska. "What are you doing here?"

"Hello, Michael," Jaruzelska said, closing the door behind her. "Welcome to Karrigal Creek."

"I am going to kill you," Michael shouted, fists clenching and unclenching as rage surged hot through him, "and that's a fucking promise you can depend on."

"Hold your horses," Jaruzelska said, a trace of iron in her voice. "There's a lot you don't know, so you need to listen before you kick my head in."

"Why the hell should I?" Michael shouted, his voice hoarse. "You lied to me, and then you betrayed me. Do you have any idea—" He tried to sit up, hands reaching out for Jaruzelska. "—what I've been through? Well, do you? No, you don't, you callous bitch! If it's the last thing I ever do, I *will* kill you."

Jaruzelska said nothing. Michael, unable to hold himself upright any longer, collapsed back onto the bed. "Everything that's happened has happened for a good reason," she said.

"So you say," Michael said, his face twisted into a furious mask.

"I do say. Now I'll stand here as long as you like, but in the end you'll have to hear me out," Jaruzelska said, her voice all steel now, "so stop wasting my time. Believe me, I have better things to do."

"Go fuck yourself," he muttered.

"Last chance."

Unwilling to trust her, Michael hesitated. His body trembled as he struggled to regain his composure. "Okay, I will," he said at last, unable to find enough energy to be angry anymore, "though it had better be damn good."

"Oh, it will be. Right, we've a lot to get through, so let's get started," Jaruzelska went on, brisk and business-like. She pulled up a chair and sat down. "First, I would all like to apologize for what you have been put through. It was as unforgivable as it was necessary, and I'm sorry."

"Keep talking," Michael said, grim-faced.

Jaruzelska sighed. "Okay, bear with me as I do this one step at a time," she said. "First, have a look at this holovid clip."

A wall-mounted holovid screen burst into life. It took Michael a few seconds to work out what he was seeing: a flame-shot pillar of smoke that climbed from the blazing wreckage of what looked like a suborbital shuttle. "What's that?" he asked.

"That's all that's left of the shuttle taking your body from Farrisport Island after your execution. As you can see, there could have been no survivors, and your mortal remains are now well and truly incinerated. In fact, my people tell me that the fire was so intense that the recovery team will be lucky to find anything more than a puddle of molten slag."

"But why … Ah, right, I get it," Michael said. "Okay, what's next?"

"Watch this."

The holovid came to life again. It juddered and jumped. Michael struggled to work out what he was watching because the image was so poor, so unsteady. Then it clicked. He was looking at a heavy cargo shuttle, its flame-scorched skin free of any identification markings. The camera moved toward a loaderbot trundling a gray shipping container out of the shuttle's cavernous cargo bay. The letters on the side of the container said: **government of the pascanici league**. The camera continued on to where a man in a coldsuit stood, his face thrown in harsh relief by overhead lights.

There the vid paused to leave the man's mouth frozen half open.

"What the hell was that about?" Michael asked. "That's the worst vid I've ever seen."

"It came from dustcams."

Michael frowned. He'd never heard of dustcams.

"And before you ask, dustcams are low-res speck-size cameras that record three-sixty-degree vid before squirting it back to us via a microsat. We dropped millions of them over a lump of rock on Commitment the Hammers call Hendrik Island. We got plenty of vid, almost all of it useless. But some came through for us, and this is best we have. The analysts think it settled on someone's jacket as he walked past that shuttle."

Michael sat up. "So he tells us something?" he said, studying the man's face with care.

"That piece of slime," Jaruzelska said, pointing a finger at the screen, "is Professor Arnoldsen, and he is the Pascanicians' best magnetic flux engineer. He's probably the best in humanspace as well."

Michael's heart tripped over itself; now he knew why Jaruzelska was showing him the vid clip. "Oh, shit," he whispered. "Antimatter production is all about magnetic flux containment."

"It is."

"Which makes Hendrik Island the Hammer's new antimatter manufacturing plant, and the fact that Arnoldsen is there proves that the Pascanicians are helping them. Looks like the NRA's intelligence reports really were on the money. But how did you know about Hendrik Island?"

"We analyzed Commitment's orbit-to-earth and suborbital traffic for the last ten years."

Michael turned to stare at Jaruzelska, wide-eyed. "You're kidding me. That's petabytes of data."

"Exabytes, actually."

Michael shook his head; he still didn't understand. "But how?"

"After you and your dreadnoughts destroyed the Hammer's antimatter production plant at Devastation Reef in March '01, we all knew the Hammers had to replace the plant. The problem was figuring out where they'd put it. After a lot of debate, our intelligence guys decided that the Hammers would have to locate their new plant as close to home as possible—"

"Of course!" Michael blurted out. "Where the defenses are most concentrated; that way we couldn't take it out again."

"And you can't get much closer to home than dirtside on Commitment."

"So you looked for changes in their traffic patterns," Michael said; over and over, his forefinger stabbed out in his excitement. "You looked for shuttles. Lots of shuttles, all going somewhere they'd never gone before!"

"And that somewhere was Hendrik Island. When we crunched the data, it stuck out like the proverbial dog's balls. Hendrik Island was home to a small research station; it used to have one shuttle a month, if that. Now it's getting hundreds, many of them from the Pascanici League. So now we have hard evidence that proves what the Hammers are up to. That's the good news. The bad news is that none of what you've seen made the slightest impression on the government. Moderator Ferrero and her Worlds First Party always wanted a peace treaty with the Hammers, and nothing was ever going to stop them from getting it."

"I know," Michael said, stony-faced. "I watched the holovid of the signing ceremony. It's a disaster."

"More than you know. One of the terms of the peace treaty was that both parties would halt all antimatter research and production. We, of course, complied. As we now know, the Hammers did not."

"Surely Ferrero insisted that the Hammers prove they weren't in breach of the treaty."

"No, she didn't. She said that would be a betrayal of the bond of trust she'd established with the Hammer of Kraa."

"So the government won't do anything. What happens next?"

"We take direct action. If we sit around and wait, we'll all wake up one day to find Federated Worlds nearspace full of Hammer starships armed with antimatter missiles, and then it's game over. Inside a week, we'll be a vassal state of the Empire of the Hammer of Kraa with Jeremiah Polk our emperor. We don't have a choice. We must stop him."

"But how can you do that? With the greatest respect, I cannot—"

"Can you walk?" Jaruzelska said, cutting him off.

"I guess," Michael said.

"If you can—" Jaruzelska's tone left Michael in no doubt that not being able to walk was not an option. "—I'll get Corporal Wei to find you some clothes and bring you through to the command center."

"Yes, sir," Michael said to her departing figure, a tiny corner of his brain still wondering why he hadn't tried harder to kill the woman.

Light-headed from the effort it took to stay upright, Michael followed Corporal Wei through a security post manned by armed marines. He emerged into a brightly lit space humming with disciplined activity, its walls dominated by holovid screens busy with live video feeds and maps overlaid with thick clusters of tactical icons, along with status boards. The air was buzzing with nervous energy underscored by the buzz of quiet conversations from twenty or so shipsuited spacers and marines.

Admiral Jaruzelska waved him over. "Michael," she said, "it's good to see you up."

"What is this place?" Michael murmured even though he knew. This was a command center, a big one, and it was a command center in the middle of a live operation. But Karrigal Creek? He didn't know where Karrigal Creek was, but he was pretty sure that it formed no part of the Federated Worlds' massive network of command and control centers.

"Ah, good," Jaruzelska said when a man in faded marine greens spotted her and came over. "This is General Adam Nwosu."

"General Nwosu," Michael said, confused. "I'm sorry, but what are you doing here? I thought you'd retired."

"I had," Nwosu said; he was a chunky, well-muscled man, ebony-faced, with soft brown eyes under a wild thatch of arctic-blond hair. "But these are dangerous times, and when Admiral Jaruzelska asked for my assistance—" He shrugged. "—how could I say no?"

They shook hands. Michael was wondering why Jaruzelska would need a superannuated Marine Corps general when a third person—this one in planetary defense uniform—saw them from across the room. "General," Jaruzelska called out. She waved at a tall, cadaverous woman with a bleak and emotionless face illuminated by penetrating blue eyes to come over. "General Fahriye Yilmaz, meet Michael Helfort."

"Good to meet you, sir," Michael, even more puzzled now, said as they shook hands. What was a pair of long-retired generals doing in Karrigal Creek? None of this made any sense, and his confusion was made all the worse by the abrupt change in his fortunes. It was so abrupt that he had to keep reminding himself that it was real, that it was no dream no matter how bizarre and unexpected it seemed.

"And you, Michael," Yilmaz said, her face transformed by the sudden warmth of her smile. "You've done well. We owe you an enormous debt."

"Not really, General," Michael said, bobbing his head, embarrassed.

"We'll catch up later, Fahriye, Adam. Michael, this way," Jaruzelska said. She threaded her way through the controlled confusion and into a small room off to one side. "Sit!" she said, pointing to a chair.

"I get it now," Michael said as Jaruzelska found her seat. "All of that out there—" He waved a hand in the direction of the command center. "—that's the planning team for a military coup. You're going to kick Ferrero out and take over, aren't you?"

"I wish we could," Jaruzelska said, laughing, "but no, sadly, we're not. That was our initial thought, but we realized that a coup would tell the Hammers that something was up. No, we want them to think that nothing has changed right up to the point when it's too late to stop us."

"You're going back to Commitment?"

"We are."

"But there's no way to do that without the government knowing, surely. It's impossible!"

"We don't think so. You should know that. After all, you stole three dreadnoughts from under Fleet's nose. We're planning to do the same, only on a larger scale."

"Hijacking three ships is one thing," Michael protested. "Making off with an entire battle group is quite another, and that's what you'll need. It can't be done. The operation to get the support the NRA needs will be huge. It'll involve tens of thousands of people and fifty, sixty ships, maybe more. There's no way you can maintain operational security. Someone will talk."

"All good points, but stay with me while I go back a bit. I need to give you the full story." Jaruzelska was quiet for a long time. "Did you ever wonder," she continued, "why I threw you to the wolves?"

"A million times a day," Michael said with a flash of resentment, "and don't think for a second that I've forgiven you for that, because I never will."

"We had our reasons."

"Which were?"

"We needed Fleet in particular and the marines and planetary defense as well to see Caroline Ferrero and her government for what they were: lackeys of the Hammers, puppets dancing as Jeremiah Polk pulled the strings. And to do that, I needed to turn you from villain to victim."

"Villain to victim?" Michael shook his head. "That makes no sense."

"Oh, but it does," Jaruzelska assured him, "and here's why. When you stole those three ships, nobody in Fleet agreed with what you'd done. Many felt your arrest was a good thing. They thought it wiped away one of the worst stains on Fleet's record. But a few things changed that. The first was your speech in mitigation at your trial."

"My speech? World News called it ... let me see if I can remember their exact words ... yes, 'a tissue of self-serving lies.'"

"Well, since the Hammers were paying them at the time, what else would they say? But I can tell you this: I have heard a lot of speeches in my time, but yours was a work of genius. Do you know how many times it has been downloaded?"

"No."

"Over a half a billion times, and that's just here on the Federated Worlds. Your speech is famous, Michael, right across humanspace."

"It wasn't me," Michael said, his cheeks reddening with embarrassment. "The credit should go to my dad. I told him what I thought, what the rest of the team thought, why we did it. He was the one who turned all that into something worth hearing."

"He didn't tell you that your speech was put together by the best psycholinguistics team in human history?" Jaruzelska asked with a half smile.

"It was?"

"Oh, yes," Jaruzelska said with a nod. "Their job was to craft the most persuasive speech ever written. You had to convince everyone that even though you were as guilty as hell, you didn't hijack those dreadnoughts be-cause you were a lovelorn fool. You did it because your motives were good, because you could see what the rest of us were too slow, too stubborn, too self-interested to see: that it was only a matter of time before the Hammers smashed us into the dust. And guess what? It worked. Right across the Federated Worlds and especially in the military, your approval rating soared. It's never dropped, and we're making sure it never will. You are a genuine hero, Michael, and you might as well get used to it.

"The death sentence was the second step, and we made sure there was plenty of commentary pointing out that execution is a barbaric institution that has no place in a civilized society. We also made sure that everybody knew that your sentence was imposed because that was what the government wanted."

"Despite the fact that it was handed down by a court? The judge wouldn't have been too happy."

"Let's just say that she is a friend of ours," Jaruzelska said. "We owe her big time."

"You didn't stop there, though, did you?" Michael said. "You spread the idea around that the government pushed for the death penalty only because that was what the Hammers wanted. Am I right?"

"Ferrero the puppet having her strings pulled by Polk the puppet master," Jaruzelska said. "You know what? I think we'll make you a psyops man of you yet," she added with a smile.

"I don't have your sneaky, devious mind, sir. Niccolò Machiavelli would have been proud of you, though. So what came next?"

"The final step was persuading President Diouf to—"

"Whoa, hold on, sir! The president is in on this?"

"No, she's not. All you need to know is that a mutual friend, a man whose advice and guidance Diouf has relied on for most of her adult life, convinced her that the Federated Worlds would be at grave risk if she did not turn down your request for clemency. The president was told only as much as she needed to understand why she was being asked to do something … so extraordinary. In the end she agreed to go along with us, but only when we convinced her that you would not actually be executed."

Relief flooded through Michael; he had not been wrong to trust Diouf.

"And that was when things got very dirty," Jaruzelska went on. "When Diouf turned you down, we had to convince the Worlds that you had been unfairly treated. The Hammers helped us there. We have holovid of the dumb bastards trying to bribe Diouf to let your execution go ahead. Twenty million FedMarks they offered her. She refused it, of course, but we slipped a story to the trash-press saying that she had taken the money. To muddy the waters a bit more, we concocted another story that the Hammers were so pissed by Diouf's refusal that Polk forced Moderator Ferrero to blackmail Diouf into turning down your appeal for clemency."

"Diouf's the closest thing I know to a saint," Michael said; he looked incredulous. "How do you blackmail a saint?"

"Easy. You cook up a story, backed by lots of seemingly credible evidence, that Diouf financed a child slavery racket operating out of the Rogue Planets in the '50s, and then …"

Michael grimaced; that would have hurt Diouf.

"… you give it to the trashpress and tell them that Ferrero was using it to blackmail the president. The story was so juicy, so hot, they just couldn't resist the temptation. They went public with it the day you were executed. The timing could not have been better."

"Then what?"

"The story's already been retracted—needless to say, that's seen by some as part of the government's coverup—and Ferrero and Diouf are going to sue for defamation. But that still leaves people wondering if they'll ever get the truth. Was the president bribed by the Hammers? Did Ferrero blackmail her into abandoning all her principles? And if Diouf wasn't bribed or blackmailed, then why did she go against all her principles and allow your execution to go ahead? Not that it matters, not now. We've got what we need. We've turned you from villain to victim, and the process has seriously undermined Ferrero's credibility, so much so that the average Fed now thinks her appeasement of the Hammers will come back and bite the Federated Worlds in the ass. They don't know how, they don't know when, but they think it will. And that's the environment we need to support what we're trying to do here."

Michael shook his head. "That's really … I was about to say clever, but maybe evil would be a better word."

"I prefer to call it a work of genius," Jaruzelska said with a touch of smugness.

"Maybe it was," Michael snapped. Jaruzelska's conceit angered him, and it showed. "I understand why it had to be done, but from where I'm sitting, it looks much more like a work of bloody-minded torture. I thought I was about to be executed. You could have told me it was all an elaborate hoax. You should have!"

"But we did," Jaruzelska protested. "We made sure Colonel Kallewi told you."

"Hah!" Michael snorted with derision. "That was way too late. By then I wanted to believe what she was saying, but I couldn't. When they strapped me down, I knew for a fact that I was about to die. Didn't matter what anyone had said. I thought they were just trying to make things easier."

"I'm sorry," Jaruzelska said, her voice soft, "really I am."

"You damn well ought to be. You should have told me sooner. And there's one more thing you should know."

"Oh?"

"I got a message from Chief Councillor Polk."

"From Polk?" Jaruzelska's stared at Michael, eyes wide with disbelief. "How could you?"

"One of the guards smuggled it in. I wish I could show it to you, but it was one of those damn one-time messages."

"What did it say?"

"That Polk had authorized my old friend Colonel Hartspring to set up a team to snatch Anna; Team Victor he's called it, and that's a v for 'vengeance' in case you're wondering."

"I remember Hartspring," Jaruzelska said, "but why would they do that?"

"Polk was happy that I was to be executed, but not that happy. If he couldn't have me killed his way, then he wanted to me to die knowing that Hartspring was going after Anna, knowing what would happen to her once Hartspring got his hands on her, and—" Michael broke off, unable to speak anymore.

"Oh, Michael," Jaruzelska whispered; she stretched out her hand to take his. "We had no idea. Why didn't you tell us?"

"What difference would it have made?" Michael said. "I'll tell you: none. After all, what was I? Just another pawn in the game."

"We should have told you earlier," Jaruzelska conceded, "but the group was concerned it would take the edge off what had to be the performance of your life. I'm sorry, but there was a lot at stake, and before you ask, your parents—"

"Shit! I'd forgotten. They think I'm dead! Anna too."

"I'm sorry about Anna. There's no way we can tell her what's really going on, but your folks are both in on the conspiracy, have been for a while now, so don't worry."

Michael's head went down; he was quiet for good minute. "I don't think there's much to be gained in going over this anymore," he said at last, looking up. "What's done is done. All that matters to me now is making sure Anna is alive and stays that way. Well, that and hunting down Polk and Hartspring and killing them when I find them. And I will," he added, his voice raw with anger. "But do me a favor, please. All that Team Victor stuff— can you keep it to yourself? Hartspring is my problem, and I'll deal with him. And I don't want Anna to find out. She has enough to worry about."

"I won't tell anyone. Now, any more questions before we move on?"

"Yes, one. You said there weren't many spacers who agreed with what I did … not to start off with, I mean."

"Yes. Most of Fleet thought you were nothing more than a criminal."

"But what about you? Did you agree with that?"

"Initially, yes, of course I did. Mutiny is mutiny, and we needed those three dreadnoughts you smashed into Commitment planet. But as I read and reread your message telling me what you were doing and why, I began to understand. Then it became obvious that Ferrero would form the next government sooner than anyone thought. When I worked out what that meant, I realized that you and your people had been right and I had been wrong."

"So when you came to Asthana looking like you wanted to tear my head off, that was all an act?"

"Yes."

Michael shook his head. "Well, I'll be damned," he said.

"You will be, almost certainly," Jaruzelska said with a faint smile. "Now, here's how we're going to do this. Juggernaut, we call it, and it starts with …"

Michael sat tucked out of the way, a welcome cup of scalding hot coffee in hand, content to let the fear-induced stress of the past months leach out of his abused psyche. It felt good to know that the controlled chaos around him marked the beginning of the end for the Hammer of Kraa, that soon he would be on his way back to rejoin Anna, that the time when he would stand over Polk and Hartspring and see the terror in their eyes before he killed them both was coming.

Oh, yes, he thought as he took a sip of coffee, *I do feel good … not that I don't have my doubts.*

What Jaruzelska and her fellow conspirators planned to do was mind-boggling in its size and complexity. For all her reassurances, for all her confidence, for all her steely determination not to fail, Michael was struggling to believe they could pull it off. There were a million things that could go wrong, and Michael was in no doubt that his old friend Mister Murphy would be hard at work to make sure they did.

Even if everything did go right, none of it would count if Anna did not make it; he wished he knew how she was. What with her joining the NRA to fight the Hammers and the fact that Hartspring and Team Victor were after her, her life was hanging by a thread. He sighed in frustration. Jaruzelska had promised him a detailed briefing on the situation back on Commitment but wasn't sure when that would happen, so he would have to wait.

Michael put the mug to his lips only to choke on the burning hot coffee, distracted by the arrival of a familiar figure. "I don't believe it," he muttered. He got to his feet and threaded his way across to where a woman in dark gray one-piece shipsuit had followed General Yilmaz into the room.

"Lieutenant Commander Fellsworth!" Michael said, putting out his hand, a broad grin splitting his face.

"Hey, Michael! Admiral Jaruzelska told me I'd find you here," the woman said, taking his hand before folding him into a crushing bear hug. She pushed Michael back and put her hands on his shoulders, then looked right into his face. "It's good to see you," she went on. "I really thought you were a goner this time."

"You and me both."

"I take it you know each other?" Yilmaz said with a good-natured smile.

"Sorry, sir," Fellsworth said. "This man saved my ass back on Commitment. And not just mine. He saved the lives of my people. I ... we owe him."

"I remember," Yilmaz said. "After the *Ishaq* was ambushed, right?"

"Yes," Fellsworth replied; her face twisted with pain for an instant. Michael understood. Pain had nothing to do with it; guilt did.

"I'll catch up with you later, Captain," Yilmaz said. "I need to see Admiral Jaruzelska before she heads back."

"Sir," Fellsworth said.

"Captain?" Michael said when Yilmaz had gone, spotting Fellsworth's rank badges for the first time. "I'm sorry. I didn't notice. Congratulations. Well deserved, I'm sure."

"Thanks, though it has little to do with my talent, such as it is. No, we've lost a lot of good people, too many, so promotion's been fast."

"A bloody war and a sickly season," Michael said.

"An old saying but a good one, and it's certainly been a bloody war. But if those Hammer pigs think we'll let them come out on top after all we've been through, they're damn fools. Right, enough of that. The admiral says I'm to answer any questions you have, but before I do, are you hungry?"

With a start, Michael realized he was, ravenously so. He had lost a good ten kilos since his arrest. Now his body was telling him it was time to put the weight back. "Since you mention it, I am."

"Me too. Come on; the canteen's this way."

"That's better," Fellsworth said, pushing her tray away. "So how's Anna?"

"Anna? Wish I knew," Michael said. "That bloody woman always was a wannabe marine, and now she is one. Last time I heard from her, she was a captain in the NRA's 120th Regiment, so she'll be in the thick of things." Michael sighed. "She always is. Oh, and we're married now. It's Anna Cheung Helfort now."

"I'll be. Well, congratulations and all that. The bride wore white, I hope."

"Combat fatigues, actually. Weddings back on Commitment are low-key affairs." The pain in Michael's voice was obvious.

"It must be hard," Fellsworth said, her voice soft. "Leaving her, I mean."

"It was. It still is. But what's worse is knowing that she'll think me dead, though at least I can see a way through now." His eyes locked onto Fellsworth's. "Will it work?"

"Hmm," Fellsworth replied, "that's the only question that matters, of course, but before I answer, I need to check something. Can you sit tight for a moment?"

"Sure," Michael said, mystified.

Five minutes later Fellsworth was back. "I was right," she said, dropping into her seat. "Jaruzelska's authorized your security clearance, but I can't talk to you until we've uploaded a bomb into your neuronics."

"A neuronics bomb?" Michael's eyes flared wide with alarm. "You've got to be kidding me."

"Nope," Fellsworth said with an emphatic shake of her head.

"But a neuronics bomb? Talk about extreme."

"We can't afford any leaks, so every last member of the conspiracy has one loaded."

"That's as may be, but if anyone puts a neuronics probe into me or I leak any information to anyone not cleared, then *pffft*—" Michael snapped his fingers.

"—my brain implodes and I'm dead." He shivered at the thought. "But you're right," he went on when he saw the sense in it. "There's too much at stake to worry about someone screwing up and dropping dead."

"There is. Jaruzelska's told you what we're planning?"

"She has."

"Well, in that case you already know too much. We need to get that bomb uploaded right away."

"Do I have to? Jaruzelska didn't drop dead. If you can trust her, I think you can trust me."

"She is one of a tiny handful of exceptions. She has to be able to talk to people outside the conspiracy without her head imploding. But you won't be doing that. You're dead, remember?"

"Oh, yes, I am, aren't I?"

"You are, so let's get that bomb into your neuronics."

Michael shivered again; he had been too close to death to want this even though he knew full well he had to do it. "Go on, then," he said with obvious reluctance.

Uploading the bomb was the work of seconds; a few more seconds and a tiny green spot appeared in front of his eyes to confirm that he was talking to someone with the right clearance.

"You good to go?" Fellsworth asked. "See the green spot?"

"Yes," Michael said; he licked lips that were suddenly dry.

"Remember, never give or transmit any operational information to anyone unless that green spot is showing.

If it turns red, the neuronics bomb will arm; any breach of security after that and it will trash your brain, and you'll be dead two seconds later. If it's flashing amber, you are outside a secure facility and must talk neuronics to neuronics, nothing out loud. Got all that?"

Michael nodded; he didn't trust himself to speak.

Fellsworth laughed. "Cheer up. You'll get used to it, I promise."

"I hope so."

"Right, you asked if what we're planning will work. Your question is actually two questions. The first is whether we can keep Juggernaut secure until we are ready to launch."

"And can we?"

"It's a huge ask, but yes, I think we can. As you now know, everyone involved has a neuronics bomb uploaded; all mission information is security-tagged, even the lowest of low-grade stuff; and the overall environment is very good."

Michael shook his head. "The environment?"

"The people we work with, even if they are not part of the conspiracy."

"Ah, you mean Jaruzelska's psyops campaign."

"It's worked, a bit to my surprise. Fleet and the Marine Corps are where they need to be, not every last one of them of course, but enough to put a shell around Juggernaut that Ferrero's people will find almost impossible to penetrate."

"But Ferrero's not alone in this, is she?"

"No, she's not. The police are ... well, they're the police, so they're being kept completely in the dark, and so are the intelligence services."

"What about planetary defense?"

"Well, they've never had to fight the Hammers face to face, so they are much more equivocal. Like most Feds, they now see you as a bit of a hero, and they think Ferrero's gone too far to keep the Hammers happy, but they're also frightened enough not to want to rock Ferrero's boat."

"Which is why General Yilmaz is onboard."

"Yes. Her first job is to convince the planetary defense brass that the Hammers are not to be trusted; her second is to persuade them to stand back and stay out of our way."

"That's it?"

"That's it," Fellsworth said, her voice flat. "They'll stick their heads up their fat butts while Fleet and the Marine Corps take all the risks and do all the dying, but as long as that's all they do, then that's enough."

Michael nodded. "Okay. Next question. Let's assume that we can maintain operational security. What are Juggernaut's chances of success?"

"Not good enough. The last simulation we did says we have a fifty-fifty chance of meeting our mission objectives."

Michael blinked. "Wah!" he said softly. "That's not good. Why?"

"Thanks to the goddamned peace treaty, the Hammers have been able to withdraw most of their fleet to home space. They are many more ships around Commitment than when you dropped dirtside with your three dreadnoughts. But we're working on it."

"Kat Sedova. What's happened to her? And Cortez and Hok."

"Sedova's tucked away safely. We've relocated her to … well, let's just say somewhere the Feds and the Hammers won't find her."

"Good. I was worried. Cortez and Hok. What about them?"

"They are an integral part of the Juggernaut planning team, right here in Karrigal Creek. They're running a sim at the moment, but they'll catch up with you as soon as they can. The admiral's asked them to brief you on the situation back on Commitment. Now, I should get back to work. You have somewhere to get your head down?"

"I do, thanks."

"Good. We're doing another sim of Juggernaut tomorrow morning. Since you're the only person who's actually planned and executed an opposed landing on Commitment, the admiral wants you to sit in."

"Love to."

"08:00, Conference 4."

"I'll be there."

Michael lay on his bunk and stared at the ceiling.

His mind raced as he churned through all that had happened that incredible day. He shook his head. Dead man walking one minute, alive and kicking the next. So why did he feel so disheartened? No, it was worse than that. He felt terrible, his mind blanketed with a sick, flat feeling, a feeling that everything he had done, all he had been through, all he had put Anna and his family through, none of it mattered a damn.

But he knew why. Anna; that was why. While he was out saving humankind—not that the vast majority of them knew it, and even if they did, they probably wouldn't gave a shit—she could well be lying dead in the mud back on Commitment with a bullet in her brain, yet another life wasted in the century-old battle to defeat the Hammer of Kraa.

And for all Jaruzelska's cautious optimism that Juggernaut would succeed, Michael was not so sure. When he had ridden his dreadnoughts down to their fiery deaths on Commitment, the Hammers had been preoccupied fighting the Feds to a standstill. And nobody had ever seen an operation like his Operation Gladiator. Nobody—not the Hammers, not the Feds—would have imagined sacrificing three good ships in a Trojan horse assault the way he had.

Gladiator had succeeded, in part at least, because it had never been done before. So for all Jaruzelska's talk of diversionary operations, surprise, weight of numbers, superior technology, and so on, the Hammers would never allow it to happen again.

Still, he reminded himself, Jaruzelska was the Federated Worlds' most experienced combat commander. All he could do was hope that she would find a way. She had to. If she did not, he would never see Anna again.

Exhaustion washed over him, and he closed his eyes. Sleep was beginning to claim him when there was a knock at his door. "Goddamn it," he muttered, forcing his eyes to open. "Yes, come in," he called out, forcing an unwilling body to its feet.

The door opened. It was Cortez and Hok. For a moment, they all stood staring at one another. Then Cortez stepped forward and folded Michael into a bone-crushing embrace that left him gasping for breath by the time the NRA general released him. "Michael," Cortez said, his voice soft, "we owe you."

Michael flushed, his head bobbing with embarrassment. Then it was Major Hok's turn to take him in her arms, her body soft and welcoming where Cortez's had been solid and unyielding; just the smell of her—the soft scent of flowers—was almost overwhelming. For a moment, there was nowhere Michael would rather be, the hard, tangled knot of fear and uncertainty in his stomach easing for the first time since he had been abducted from Asthana.

Hok let him go and stepped back. "Like the general says, we owe you."

Michael could only shrug his shoulders; he did not trust himself to speak.

"I'll catch you later," Cortez said. "Admiral Jaruzelska wants to talk to me."

"I won't ask how you've been," Hok said once Cortez had left.

"Just look at me," Michael said, finding his voice with an effort. "I feel like I look: a million years old."

Hok broke the awkward silence that followed. "I know it's late," she said, "but I was born a Hammer, so I need coffee and lots of it. I'll fill you in on what's been happening back home while we get our fix."

"That would be good. Lead on."

Michael stared at the holovid screen long after Hok had finished speaking. It was an ugly sight, the cordon of red around the Branxton Ranges speaking more than words ever could of the pressure the Hammers were putting on the NRA's heartland bases. "That doesn't look good," Michael said.

"From a purely military point view, no, it doesn't," Hok said, "but we shouldn't be too pessimistic."

"Hard not to be."

"Look at this way. First of all, the Hammers still have not been able to penetrate our perimeter. Two months ago, the Hammer's MARFOR 3 tried here—" A finger stabbed at the screen. "—with massive support from Fleet assets in low-earth orbits, and the NRA handed them their asses. All the marines had to show for their efforts was rubble and a shitload of casualties."

"Just like the last time," Michael said. "Slow learners, those people."

"Come, come," Hok chided, "be fair. We both know it has a lot more to do with the fact that our bases in the Branxton Ranges are close to invulnerable. We have hundreds of kilometers of caves and tunnels buried deep below tens of thousands of acres of limestone karst. They can drop all the bunker busters they like, but in the end they've got to come in after us. And when they do, we both know they'll never get more than a few klicks inside, 'cause that's when we blow the roof down on them."

"Which is why we are all here," Michael said. "Thanks to its bases, the NRA can survive until hell freezes over, but it cannot defeat the Hammers. Well, not unaided, that is, and that's what Juggernaut is all about."

"Exactly. But there's one more thing working in our favor, and that's the way Chief Councillor Polk and his cronies like to deal with the threats facing them."

"That doesn't make sense," Michael said with a shake of the head. "From where I sit, Polk's tactics have been spectacularly successful. He's screwed the Federated Worlds over every which way, and he'll do the same to the rest of humanspace if we're not careful."

"All true, but he's been able to screw you over only because your government played to his strengths."

"Let me guess: Polk's willingness to use massive force?" Michael said.

"The Feds believe him capable of anything, even destroying an entire system and killing billions," Hok replied after a moment's thought. "Not that he has to go that far. The threat is enough. He fires a couple of antimatter missiles into Terranova nearspace to make the threat real. That scares the crap out of your people, so they elect Caroline Ferrero as moderator, and she promptly folds. In the end, Ferrero gave Polk what he wanted without him actually having to use force."

Michael grimaced. "He would if he had to."

"Don't doubt it. Power is all he cares about. And Polk takes the same approach with his own people: kill thousands to put the fear of Kraa into billions. But he's a fool. Our assessment is that Polk would have won a free and open election in the first few weeks after the peace treaty simply because people believed that things would change for the better with the war over. Well, they were wrong. Things did not get better; they got worse. Four weeks after the treaty was signed, Polk not only ordered the biggest crackdown on dissidents in Hammer history, he told DocSec to purge the marines and planetary defense as well."

"What, again? I'm surprised there's anyone left to purge. Why the hell would he do that?"

"Simple: He doesn't need them anymore. Oldest trick in the dictator's handbook."

"Because if he didn't, they'd go from asset to threat?'

"Exactly. Anyway, it took DocSec a while to get organized, but when they got going, they really got going. We don't have accurate figures, but we think the arrests run into the tens of thousands on Commitment alone, and there are a lot more to come."

Michael shivered. "I suppose that means the DocSec firing squads have been busy?"

"Oh, yes," Hok said. "They arrested fifty officers from the 5th Marine Brigade three weeks ago; two days later, after a mass show trial lasting all of five minutes, they were all taken out and shot."

"Okay, I get it," Michael said. "By cracking down on the minority, Polk thinks he can bluff the majority into falling into line."

"Precisely." Hok shook her head. "Bloody man is a fool. If he'd eased up, the Revival would have lost much of its political legitimacy in the eyes of the average Hammer, and the flow of recruits the NRA depends on would have dried up, along with money and supplies. We'd have withered on the vine, and our Branxton bases would have dropped into Polk's hands without him having to send in the marines. Instead, our support has never been stronger."

Michael looked skeptical. "That doesn't help much, surely," he said.

"It does. Let me tell you; when we launch Juggernaut, we'll be pushing on an open door. Polk won't last a month, and that's because the marines and planetary defense will refuse to fight. Deserters are telling us that the marines are close to mutiny and planetary defense is the same."

"So why isn't Polk worried? He should be."

"Yes, he should. But we think he's decided that they don't matter anymore. The marines and planetary defense have both let him down: the marines by failing to destroy our Branxton bases, planetary defense because they let us escape. Now, thanks to the Pascanicians, he will have his antimatter missiles sooner rather than later, and when he does, nobody in humanspace will be able to stand up against him. To rule humanspace, all he needs is the Hammer Space Fleet, and he's being nice to them … for the moment, at least. So who needs the marines? Who needs planetary defense? Polk doesn't, not anymore."

"The man's insane," Michael said.

"Maybe, but thank Kraa for it. Makes our job easier."

"I hope so," Michael said with obvious feeling.

"Which brings us to the subject of your Anna."

Michael's gut twisted. "Ah, yes," he said, trying not to sound as anxious as he felt, "I was about to ask."

"Relax. Major Anna Cheung Helfort is fine."

Michael's eyebrows shot up. "Major?" he said, incredulous. "I thought she was a captain."

"Oh, she was." Hok chuckled. "But we've just had word she's been promoted."

"What a surprise." Michael sighed. "I always wondered why she didn't join the marines, since being a grunt is obviously what she likes doing."

"She has a gift for it, that's for sure."

"Has she stayed with the 120th?" Michael asked, hoping against hope that she'd been transferred somewhere safer.

"She has. She's been given command of a company."

Michael's gut twisted some more. "Good for her," he forced himself to say. "The 120th is still in the Velmar Mountains?"

"They are, along with the 443rd and the 22nd. They've taken a lot of pressure off the Branxtons and have tied down an entire planetary defense division. The latest intelligence summaries say that those Hammers have been hit so hard that only a handful of their formations are fully combat effective."

Michael knew he should take some comfort in the fact that Anna was up against second-rate troops, but he couldn't. Anna being Anna, she'd be in the thick of it. "Good to hear," he said. "I just wish she knew I was okay."

"Shit! I'm so sorry, Michael; I meant to tell you earlier. I know what Admiral Jaruzelska said, but General Cortez overruled her. He's made sure she knows."

Relief flooded Michael's body. "That was good of him."

"Least we could do."

"Don't let me forget to thank him."

"I won't," Hok said, getting to her feet. "Now, I've got some things I need to do, and if you're half as tired as you look, I think you should turn in."

"You're right, Major," Michael said, all of a sudden conscious of just how exhausted he was. "I'll see you tomorrow?"

"You will."

Friday, January 2, 2404, UD
Hendrik Island antimatter plant, Commitment

"If you'd like to come this way, gentlemen."

Trailed by his chief of staff, Polk followed Doctor Ndegwa past a massive blast door and into a tunnel cut through meters of granite. He tried not to think about the billions of tons of rock that lay between him and fresh air. Past a second blast door, the tunnel opened onto a catwalk overlooking a long cavern. The sight took Polk's breath away. Below a roof studded with massed banks of lights and hung with power cables and air-conditioning ducts, the cavern was packed with a mass of stainless steel pipes and cylinders studded with sensors, valves, and controllers, all hung with thick bundles of cable in a rainbow of colors. It was an enormous three-dimensional puzzle free—to Polk eyes, at least—of logic or structure. How the engineers were able to make sense of it all, he had no idea. His brain ached just looking at it.

"This is Low-Energy Antiproton Facility Number One," Ndegwa said, waving a hand across the chaos. "LEAF-1 we call it, and it's the first of the twenty LEAFs we plan to construct."

"Is it working?" Polk asked, casting a skeptical eye around the cavern. Apart from the rush of the air-conditioning and a myriad of status lights, there was nothing to say that the facility was actually functioning.

"Yes, it is. LEAF-1 came on-stream five weeks ahead of schedule. It's currently operating at 15 percent of its planned capacity, though we plan to be at 100 percent within six months."

"Good. I do not want this project to take one day longer than it absolutely has to. The Hammer of Kraa needs its antimatter capability sooner rather than later. Understood?"

Ndegwa nodded. "Yes, sir. And while we're talking about schedules, there's something I'd like you to see. This way, please."

Polk followed the man along the catwalk and into a small meeting room that was empty except for a table on which sat a plasfiber box.

"This," Ndegwa said, reaching in to pull out an object two-thirds the size of a shoe box, its metallic surface polished to a mirror finish and unbroken except for two ports and a digital readout, "is an antimatter container from our new Mark-50C warhead, and it has been charged with antihydrogen produced by the Hendrik Island plant."

Polk reared back; knowing how close he was to the unimaginable power contained inside the container, he could not help himself. "Kraa's blood," he hissed, "are you fucking mad?"

"It's quite safe, sir," Ndegwa said, dropping the warhead back into its box with a thud that rattled the table and made Polk flinch.

"I know it is," Polk said, cursing himself for letting Ndegwa see his fear. "It was just ... wait. Did you just say it's filled with antihydrogen produced here?"

"I did. And we are well ahead of schedule; we plan to have sixteen operational Mark-50Cs by the end of this year."

"Who else knows about this?" Polk asked, his mind flooded all of a sudden with the strategic possibilities sixteen antimatter-armed missiles opened up.

"Apart from the three of us here, only the people in warhead production."

"What about those Pascanicians scumbags?"

"We do not allow them anywhere near the warheads. They might know all there is to know about magnetic flux engineering, but they have no idea how to weaponize antimatter, and it's my policy to keep it that way."

"Good." Polk turned to Ngaro. "This changes things, Lou," he said. "Find Admiral Kerouac. I want to see him as soon as we get back to McNair."

"Yes, sir."

"Well, Chief Councillor," Admiral Kerouac said, "we'll need to look at this in more detail, but a first strike against the Feds, even with only sixteen Mark-50C warheads in our inventory, would destroy most of their warship construction yards and a good percentage of their fleet as well. There would be considerable collateral damage to the civilian population, though. The majority of their yards are in Clarke orbits around inhabited planets or orbital habitats."

"Like I give a shit about that," Polk said with a snort of derision. "Put together a brief to present to the next

Defense Council meeting. If we're to do this, we need to start planning now."

"Yes, sir."

Saturday, May 22, 2404, UD
Operation Juggernaut headquarters, Karrigal Creek, Terranova

Admiral Jaruzelska looked up as Michael pushed open the door to her office. "Come in; take a seat."

"Sir," Michael replied, mystified by the summons. As Operation Juggernaut's launch approached—not that there was a definite date for J-Day yet—Jaruzelska had become remote and unapproachable. It had been weeks since Michael had done anything more than pass the time of day with her, and even then not often.

And all the time there was the nagging fear that Hartspring might have done to Anna what he had promised to do, a fear feeding an angry frustration that threatened to spiral out of control.

"Right, let's get started," Jaruzelska said. "We've just received an intelligence report from the NRA. It seems the Hammers may have gotten wind that we're up to something. Worse, they know that I am involved. The only good news is that the NRA's source says the Hammers have no firm idea what we're planning, though knowing how their minds work, I'd bet my life their money's on a coup."

"So what does that mean for us?" Michael asked.

"We're bringing Juggernaut forward, probably to the last week of July. It's earlier than we wanted, and we won't have all the auxiliaries we'd like, but that can't be helped. Now that the Hammers suspect something, they'll be pushing hard to find out what we're doing, and I wouldn't discount the possibility of the Hammers running interference as well."

"Interference?"

"They'll pressure Ferrero into taking preemptive action against people like me. They'll try to cut the heads off Juggernaut, and I'm one of the heads. There's a good chance they'll manufacture a crisis to help them do that."

"Like an assassination or something?"

"That would do. It'll be much easier for the Hammers to get Ferrero to move against us if there's a state of emergency in force."

"Will any of this stop Juggernaut?"

"Not if we move fast," Jaruzelska said, "and that's why I need you to go back to Commitment early, through Scobie's."

Michael frowned. "But I'm going back with you, in the *Iron Lance*."

"Pay attention," Jaruzelska snapped, her face marred by a peevish frown. "I said to go back *early*, by way of Scobie's World, before Juggernaut launches."

Michael's stomach knotted. Much as he wanted to go back—if only to see Anna again—doing that meant getting past DocSec border security. "Umm, yes," he said, "I guess." He shrugged. "Can't be any worse than going back in *Iron Lance*." That was a lie; it would be much, much worse. "But can I ask why?"

"You can. The peace treaty allows both sides to maintain their networks of surveillance microsats, but we cannot provide any material support to the Revival and NRA, and that includes comsat networks. Needless to say, Fleet has ignored that prohibition, but thanks to all the ships the Hammers have in Commitment nearspace, our comms have become a very hit or miss business—mostly miss, I'm sorry to say."

"Because we can't afford to get caught?"

"We have to keep the Hammers thinking that we're complying with the treaty. But our bandwidth has been close to zero for most of the last few weeks, and if we're to bring Juggernaut forward, there's a pile of planning material we have to get to the NRA. We can't get dirtside safely without their help."

"And you need a courier to do that?"

"Just in case we don't get our comms back. The NRA and Revival need our latest plans for Operation Juggernaut. We also want to give them a brevity code book."

"Brevity codes?" Michael shook his head in disbelief. "Talk about primitive."

"I know, I know," Jaruzelska replied, "but we need a fallback if we don't have adequate bandwidth to the NRA on J-Day. If we have to make mission-critical changes at the last minute, the NRA has to know."

"Okay, sir," Michael said after a moment's thought. "I can see why you need a courier, but why me?" He paused. "I'm not saying no," he added, "but if I'm going to do this, I need to know."

"Because we have access to only two valid Hammer IDs: yours and Marine Shinoda's—sorry, she's Sergeant Shinoda now. Luckily for us, your IDs were never handed back to the spooks in Department 66 after you both got back from Commitment; it was an administrative error …'

Administrative error, my ass, thought Michael. *Somebody thought they might come in handy one day.*

"… and they've been sitting in Fleet intelligence all this time. We have friends inside 66, but they can't generate brand-new IDs without a lot of very awkward questions being asked. Anyway, will you do it?"

Michael swore under his breath. He shivered at the memory; walking up to the black-uniformed DocSec immigration officers had been one of the hardest things he'd ever had to do. *There's no way I want to do this*, he said to himself, *but how can I say no? Duty has me by the balls, and Jaruzelska knows it.* "There is one problem, admiral," he said eventually. "What about the Hammer's border security records? We left Commitment to go to Scobie's World, and we never went back. Department 66 will need to fix them; otherwise we'll be arrested the minute we arrive."

"They will be," Jaruzelska said with some asperity, impatient now. "We're not stupid. Our friends in 66 can do that without any questions being asked."

Fuck you, Michael thought, glaring back at Jaruzelska. *It's my life you're gambling with.*

Jaruzelska's hands went up when she saw the look on Michael's face. "I'm sorry. You have every right to ask," she said.

"I've been lied to a lot lately," Michael replied. "I don't take much on trust anymore."

"Fair enough." Jaruzelska paused for a few seconds before she went on. "Look. This is not about IDs. I want you to go. You're the best person for the job, and I trust you to get it done."

"Relax, admiral; I'll do it," Michael said. "Has Shinoda agreed?"

"She has. She'll be here next week along with the four marines who'll make up the support team. I've arranged for one of our friends from 66 to be here tomorrow; he'll help with the detailed planning. I'll let you know when he arrives."

"Thank you, sir."

Once outside Jaruzelska's office, Michael stopped. The relationship between him and the admiral had changed. He'd 'yes sir, no sir' the woman until the cows came home.

But trust her? Not a chance.

Tuesday, June 8, 2404, UD
Terranova planetary nearspace

Michael drifted in and out of consciousness. He floated on a sea of drug-induced calm, untroubled by the fact that he had been in a box the size of a coffin inside a container of mining machinery for hours now. What did bother him was an itch somewhere down by his left ankle, an itch he could not reach no matter how hard he wriggled and squirmed. The plasfiber box was simply too small. He did his best to ignore it, but cut off from the outside world except for transient shifts in the ship's artificial gravity field that told him only that he had been moved onboard a shuttle, he had little else to focus on.

He wondered when to start panicking. He should have been released hours ago. Six hours, he had been promised; six hours to clear Fed border security for transfer to the freighter to take him to Lagerfeld.

Right from the start, he'd resigned himself to a long wait. The entire consignment had been lashed with a nearly lethal dose of x-rays during security scanning, sending his neuronics into a near panic, alarms urging him to get the hell out of there. Even now the nano-bots loaded into his system worked furiously to repair the damage to his system the x-rays had inflicted.

In the end, border security must have been satisfied by the scan. Otherwise, they'd have torn the container apart and he'd be in custody. That would have been interesting in light of the fact that he was supposed to be dead. He sighed. So what if things were not running to schedule? As long as his supply of sedatives held out, he didn't care. He tried not to think about how he'd feel if they did run out. Michael suffered, and badly, from claustrophobia, and he had never been in such a tight space.

So he did the only thing he could do: He upped his sedatives and within minutes was asleep.

"Hey, spacer! Wake up!"

Michael opened his eyes. *Where the hell* … Then he remembered. He focused with an effort—he might have overdone the sedatives a bit, he realized—and looked up into Sergeant Shinoda's anxious face.

"Oh, hi," he mumbled.

"You had us worried. Now let's get you out of there."

With an effort, Shinoda and a second marine—one of the four making up the security detail Jaruzelska had insisted on sending along—levered him out of the coffin-like box and stood him on his feet.

Shinoda's nose wrinkled. "I think we left you in there a bit long."

"Now that you mention it," Michael said, flushing with embarrassment, "I think you did. There's only so much those diapers can take, so show me to the shower."

"This way," Shinoda said, standing well clear and pointing to the access door leading from the freighter's cargo bay.

* * *

Michael cradled a welcome cup of coffee as Shinoda popped the silver cube of a near-field jammer onto the table. "So what happened?" Michael asked.

"Those assholes at border security smelled a rat. At first we thought they'd been tipped off, but it turned out they just wanted to know why we were taking mining machinery to Lagerfeld."

"Fair question. The mines there stopped production a century ago. But you showed them our end-user certificates?"

"We did, but of course they had to check. I mean, would you accept an end-user certificate from the Live-in-Hope Mining Company?"

Michael laughed. "I guess not."

"So they checked, and that took a while—" Shinoda turned to glare at the gangly marine sitting alongside her. "—which it need not have done if Marine Clothcock Mitchell here—" She reached out and smacked the back of Mitchell's head. "—hadn't given the border security guys some lip."

"Hey, sarge," the man protested.

"Don't fucking 'hey, sarge' me, Marine Mitchell. I've told you before: Keep your damn mouth shut. If I need you to speak, I'll tell you. Understood?"

Mitchell nodded.

"Anyway," Shinoda continued, "the Live-in-Hope Mining Company duly came back to say that all was aboveboard. Turns out the border security guys thought we might have been planning to sell the consignment to the Rogue Worlds."

"Well, Lagerfeld does trade with them."

"It does."

Michael looked around the battered bulkheads of the tiny compartment that passed for the ship's passenger saloon. "Not the best ship I've ever been in," he said.

"The *Golden Gladiator*?" Shinoda chuckled. "She'll do. The captain's a strange man, the mate's even weirder, but the engineer is solid as rock. We've had a look around. She's an old ship, but they look after her."

"So we'll get to Lagerfeld okay?"

"We will … Let me see; yes, another day and half should see us there."

"Any changes to the plan?"

"None. We transfer to the *President Cruz* as soon as we dock; it breaks orbit four hours later. We should be dirtside on Scobie's on schedule."

"Good," Michael said. The moment of truth was fast approaching; he shivered at the thought of what it would take to get past DocSec security and safely dirtside on Commitment. For all the assurances he had been given by Jaruzelska, by Fellsworth, by the spooks from 66, by the tech guys from intelligence support, the fact was that the Hammers, always obsessed with their border security, were now beyond paranoid.

"You okay?" Shinoda asked.

"Oh, sorry," Michael said. "I was just thinking about DocSec. Can't say I'm looking forward to meeting them again."

"We'll be fine."

"Yeah, we will," Michael said. He tried to ignore the fact that they had a reasonable chance of not making it. "They got anything like a gym onboard this scow?"

"Hey! Don't let the crew hear you calling their beloved *Golden Gladiator* a scow. They'll tear you a new one."

"Oops," Michael said, chuckling. "So no gym?"

"Afraid not. But we have found some mats. We'll be doing unarmed combat drills. Care to join us?"

Michael did not like the way a wolfish grin had appeared on Shinoda's face. He sighed. "I hate marines. All you ever want to do is kick ass."

"Never kicked the ass of a dead man before."

Michael sighed again. "Well, now's your chance. Come on, then. Let's do it."

With frightening speed and power, Shinoda scythed Michael's legs from under him and smashed him into the mat with a sickening thud that drove the air from his lungs. An instant later, Shinoda had somehow gotten her arms around his throat and head, twisting and squeezing until Michael had to slap the mat in surrender.

Gasping, he dragged the air back into tortured lungs sip by agonizing sip. "You fucking bastard," he wheezed.

"Had enough, spacer boy?" Shinoda said. She let him go and rolled away. "Honestly," she said, standing up to pull Michael to his feet, "you Fleet guys are a bunch of pussies. You couldn't fight off a three-legged dog."

"Yeah, right," Michael muttered. He tried to ease the aches out of his back and shoulders. "Anyway, better a pussy than a fucking psycho."

"Not where we're going. Now, you had enough?"

"One more, but show me how you did that throw."

"Sucker! Right, stand like this … yes, okay. Now …"

Michael lay in his bunk in the half darkness. The only sound was the gentle hiss of the air-conditioning. The images of Shinoda and her four marines had stayed with him, stuck in his mind. It had been almost frightening to watch the carefully controlled mix of skill, finesse, speed, and brutality at work. Their drills looked like the real thing. More than once Michael had been sure, absolutely sure, that one of the team members would end up badly injured, even dead.

I might be the man to captain a dreadnought, he thought, *but I want Shinoda and her marines alongside me when the fighting gets up close and personal.*

But all the Shinodas in the world would count for nothing when they came up against DocSec.

DocSec did not need skill, finesse, or speed. They had the only thing they needed: brutality, and plenty of it.

118

Friday, June 11, 2404, UD
City of Foundation, Terranova

"… and we'll have more news as it comes to hand, but for those who have just joined us, we have reports that a shuttle carrying Moderator Ferrero was attacked today as it lifted off from Lenore Island after she addressed a rally of the Federation Peace League. We have been told by sources inside planetary defense that the shuttle was hit by two surface-to-air missiles and was badly damaged but managed to land safely. We also have unconfirmed reports—and I must stress that they are unconfirmed—that Federal Police believe the attack was the work of senior space fleet personnel unhappy about what they believe to be the Ferrero government's appeasement of the Hammers. In response to the incident, a state of emergency is now in force. And now we'll cross to—"

Vice Admiral Jaruzelska cut the neuronics link; reopening her eyes, she looked at the man sitting opposite her for a moment. The café around them was hushed as the midmorning coffee crowd absorbed the shocking news. "I smell the Hammers," she said. "I wonder what took them so long."

"Who knows," Vice Admiral John N'tini replied, pushing his coffee cup away.

"Fleet's been set up, John, and we know why. I'll call the boss to see if she's heard anything. I'll also try Juanita Chou at planetary defense."

"You do that, Angela. I'll see if my FedPol contacts can tell us what's happened."

"Call me if you find out anything."

"Will do."

Jaruzelska and N'tini started to their feet. Two men pushed into the air-conditioned comfort of the café. They bundled aside two patrons trying to leave at the same time.

"Rude bastards," Jaruzelska growled as she watched the men thread their way through the tables. *They're FedPol, and they're coming for us*, she thought.

"I'm Chief Inspector Meir," the older of the two men said, "and this is Sergeant Hardina, Federal Police. You are Admiral Jaruzelska?"

"You already know that," Jaruzelska said.

"And you are Admiral N'tini?" Meir asked.

"Yes," N'tini replied.

"John N'tini and Angela Jaruzelska," Meir said, his voice cold and formal, "I am arresting you both under the provisions of Section 19 of the Emergency Powers Act. In accordance with that act, you will be remanded in custody until a duly authorized Federal Police officer details the charges against you in the Federal Court of Criminal Justice. You are obliged to answer all questions put to you by the Federal Police, and any failure to answer such questions may prejudice your defense. Do you understand?"

Jaruzelska's eyes blazed. "Tell me what the charge is," she spit.

"As I just said, sir, you will be informed of all charges against you when you appear in the Federal Court. Come with me, please."

Jaruzelska turned to N'tini. "What do you think, John? Shall we go?"

"I hate to say it, but I think we'd better do as Mister Plod the Policeman wants."

"Now," Meir said, stone-faced.

Without another word, Jaruzelska and N'tini allowed themselves to be led out of the café. The leaden silence broke into a buzz the moment the door closed behind them.

A young man at a table by the door left his coffee unfinished. He hurried into the street. He walked past where Jaruzelska was refusing to follow N'tini into the waiting police mobibot, her voice strident above the hum of traffic.

"I'm a goddamned admiral, so get your hands off me, Meir. I want to speak to my lawyer before I go anywhere."

"I know who you are, Admiral Jaruzelska," Meir responded, "but I must insist."

Jaruzelska was not looking at Meir. Instead she stared right at the young man. "Insist," she said, her voice loud now, penetrating. "Insist all you like. My mother would not like it."

"Your mother?" Meir said, puzzled by Jaruzelska's sudden change of tack. "Do us all a favor and get in the bot." Meir's body language made it clear that his patience was running out.

"My mother would not like it," Jaruzelska called out again.

"Now! Or I'll cuff you and throw you in the bot myself."

Jaruzelska threw her hands up. "Okay, okay. I'll do it."

The man kept walking, an almost imperceptible nod the only sign that he had heard Jaruzelska.

The door was slammed behind Jaruzelska; she slumped down beside N'tini. "This is a first," John," she said. "Two admirals arrested in one day."

"And there'll be more," N'tini said, twisting his body to be able to look into Jaruzelska's face. "I know a witch hunt when I see one." He lifted an eyebrow in inquiry.

Jaruzelska nodded. "True enough." She sat back as the mobibot accelerated away. Whatever the Hammers were up to, it did not matter now. She had pushed the button to launch Juggernaut. The young man, one of a team that shadowed her every move, had acknowledged receipt of the code phrase. Even now, every unit assigned to the invasion of Commitment would be en route for the deepspace jumping-off point.

Operation Juggernaut had started. There was nothing anyone in the Hammers or Ferrero could do to stop it. True, she'd been forced to initiate the operation early. But she'd spent almost all her adult life fighting the Hammer of Kraa; all her experience told her that Juggernaut's chances of success were almost as good as she could have hoped.

Saturday, June 12, 2404, UD
LMS Golden Gladiator, Lagerfeld system
nearspace

"Captain says we've been given clearance to dock," Shinoda said. "We'll be at the orbital transfer station in a couple of hours."

"And the *President Cruz*?"

"Arrived yesterday. She'll be leaving for Scobie's World on schedule, though we might have a problem."

"A problem?"

"Yup. Seems somebody fired a couple of missiles at our beloved moderator's shuttle. Sadly, the shuttle survived, and so did she."

"An assassination attempt?" Michael said, frowning. His mind raced as he tried to work out what it all meant. "You sure?"

"It's all over the news."

"That doesn't sound good. It's going to destabilize everything, and that's the last thing we need right now."

"It gets worse," Shinoda said. "The shit has really hit the fan. The Feds have arrested most of the officers above the rank of commodore in the fleet. They've been charged with everything from conspiracy to murder to stealing the office teacups."

"What about Admiral Jaruzelska?"

"She wasn't mentioned by name, but yes, almost certainly."

Michael was still stunned by the news. "We'll have to work out how this affects us."

"That'll be hard. Things are pretty chaotic. But there is some good news."

"We could do with some."

"They're saying a large force of Fleet units left Terranovan nearspace without proper authorization only minutes after the arrests. Planetary defense told them to turn back, but they refused. The antiballistic missile batteries were ordered to fire on them, but there was a problem with their fire-control systems. The missiles refused to lock onto ships squawking friendly IFF codes, so they got away."

"I'm shocked," Michael said with a huge grin. "Such incompetence."

"It gets better. Apparently the same thing happened at Comdur."

"They've pushed the button on Juggernaut," Michael said. Then it hit him hard. "The Hammers. They'll know that we're coming after them."

"Will they? How?"

"Why else would an entire task force leave Terranova and Comdur nearspace without authorization from Fleet?"

Shinoda thought about that for a while. "Wouldn't they think," she said, "that it was just ... I don't know ... a precautionary move following the assassination attempt?" She took a deep breath and shook her head.

"No, that makes no sense. Warships don't move without orders."

"They don't, and even if the Hammers aren't sure," Michael said, "they'll assume an attack is on the way. Until the missing units are relocated, they have to, and don't be surprised if they close their nearspace to all civilian traffic."

"Damn," Shinoda muttered, her face bleak, "that wouldn't be good. What do we do now?"

"Push on, find the first dead-letter box on Scobie's. It'll have the latest update on the Juggernaut. There'll be new orders for us."

Shinoda nodded. "I'll go brief the rest of the team."

"Let me guess. On the mats again?"

"Yup."

"Slow learners, you marines."

"Watch it, spacer boy," Shinoda replied with a feral smile as she left.

Michael sat back, wondering where Juggernaut stood now. With Jaruzelska under arrest, Rear Admiral Moussawi was now in command. He was renowned for his mix of surgical skill and ruthless aggression. Michael had heard Jaruzelska describe him as one of the best Fleet commanders the Federated Worlds had ever seen; coming from her, that was high praise. But with the Hammers now expecting an attack, the chances of the operation succeeding had to have worsened no matter how good the commander was.

The butcher's bill for Operation Juggernaut had always promised to be high; it now looked to be much, much worse. Michael could only hope that Moussawi would not be deterred.

Michael dropped his gear onto the deck and rolled into the bunk that occupied most of the cramped economy-class cabin. In the time it had taken to clear arrival formalities—and they had been formalities; Michael had never seen people so disinterested as Lagerfeld's border security officers—the newsvids had reported the closure of Hammer nearspace in anticipation of what Polk himself had said would be a full-scale attack by rogue elements from the Federated Worlds Fleet.

"You got that one right, you Hammer asshole," Michael had muttered.

The mission was screwed. There was no way for him and Shinoda to get to Commitment. It was over. Juggernaut was doomed. And worse than any of that, his chances of seeing Anna again were … he wondered what was less than zero. And he was a nonperson, a dead nonperson. The false identities he had been given would get him dirtside on Scobie's and then onto Commitment, but they weren't good enough to last him the rest of his life.

If he discounted blowing his brains out, his options had dwindled to one: flee to the outer edge of humanspace. There he could find some ratfucked system a thousand light-years from the Hammer of Kraa where nobody gave a damn who you were or what you'd done.

Just the sort of place where a dead nonperson could forget the past and carve out a new life.

Sunday, June 13, 2404, UD
Offices of the Supreme Council, McNair

"… and so, to sum up," said Admiral Kerouac, commander in chief of the Hammer Defense Forces, in a mellow baritone voice that Polk always found faintly patronizing, "in response to a full-scale mutiny of the Federated Worlds space fleet, we are withdrawing every unit we can spare from nonessential operational tasks. Those units are now deployed in Commitment nearspace. And finally, all units are at Operational State 4 and will remain at that level until we have confirmed that the renegade Fed units that left Terranova and Comdur are not planning to attack one of our home planets. Are there …" Kerouac paused as an aide handed him a sheet of paper. "I've just received the latest estimate of the number of ships involved in the mutiny," he went on, "and it seems the Federated Worlds has been unable to account for a total of sixty-six ships."

Polk stared at Kerouac, open-mouthed with disbelief. "Did you say sixty-six ships?"

"I did, sir. Sixty-six ships: one planetary assault vessel, fifty-three warships, and twelve heavy armed auxiliaries. Now, I know that sounds like a lot, but you look at our order of battle, you will see that we have three times that number of warships in Commitment nearspace right now. That will increase by twenty-five when Task Force 41 returns from the Federated Worlds. The Fortitude and Faith systems are equally well defended, and of course we should not forget our orbital battle stations, battle-sats, weapons platforms, and minefields. There can be no doubt that any attack by those renegade Fed units would be suicidal."

"Thank you," Polk said. "Which brings us to the one question I have been asking over and over: What the hell are the Feds up to? Councillor Kando, tell me what your intelligence analysts think."

"We think the renegades will attack Commitment."

"They'll suffer enormous losses if they try, so why would they do that? They're not stupid."

"Hendrik Island, that's why."

Polk shook his head. "We're not even sure the Feds know about Hendrik Island."

"Too many people know about it, Chief Councillor. We must assume they do, just as we have to assume they will do whatever it takes to eliminate our antimatter plant on Hendrik Island. They have to. It's the single greatest ... no, it's the only threat to their survival."

Polk stared at Kando for moment before responding. "That does make sense," he said. "What else is worth risking so many ships?' He turned to Jones. "Your thoughts?"

"It does make sense, sir, even though taking out Hendrik Island cannot be done," Polk's councillor for war responded. "The Feds will not be able to penetrate our orbital defenses. It's simple mathematics, and we've run the simulations—just as the Feds will have—and they all point to the same result: total annihilation. Misguided patriots these renegades might be, but even they won't throw ships away for no reason.

"And even if they did, they'd be wasting their time. Hendrik Island was picked because it is an enormous mass of basalt. The plant is buried so deep inside that even an antimatter weapon dropped right on top would have no effect on its operational capability. An attack would be utterly pointless. We know it, and those renegade Feds will too, but we cannot assume they won't try. Kraa knows, they are an arrogant bunch."

Polk nodded. "So there's no downside in making the assumption that the Feds will try to destroy our antimatter plant?"

"None."

"Won't the Feds just attack elsewhere?"

"There's no point,' Jones said. "The Feds do not have sufficient forces to mount a full-scale ground assault. Anyway, the advice I have been given—" Jones looked at Admiral Kerouac, who nodded his agreement. "—is that sufficient forces would remain to cover any eventuality. And it goes without saying that our forces can be moved as the tactical situation in Commitment nearspace demands."

"Good. Admiral Kerouac, you know what has to be done."

"I do, sir. I will report back to the next Defense Council meeting."

Wednesday, June 16, 2404, UD
New Dublin, Scobie's World

Michael let himself into the small house tucked away out of sight of the road down a tree-lined lane. He dumped his backpack and went through to the kitchen, where Shinoda waited. "Am I clean?" he asked, punching buttons on the foodbot to get himself a mug of coffee.

"Spassky and Akuna have just checked in. No problems, they say. I don't know what the locals do at night, but they don't like to get out and party."

"Where are Mitchell and Prodi?"

"Covering the perimeter. Spassky and Akuna take over from them at midnight."

"Okay." Michael sat down at the table, flicking the ever-present near-field jammer with a finger. "Right, I picked up a datastick from the dead-letter box," he went on. "Admiral Moussawi is going ahead with Operation Juggernaut."

"Yes!" Shinoda hissed. "Good for him. But what about us? What's the plan?"

"There is no plan, not anymore. Our mission has been scrubbed …"

"Shit," Shinoda muttered.

"… and I have orders for you guys to get yourselves to Al-Sufri. Check with the defense attaché there; she'll organize you a ride back home."

"And why would we do that?" Shinoda asked. She shook her head, her face bitter with disappointment. "Fuck the orders," she said. "I refuse to sit around waiting for Jeremiah Polk to tell me I'm now a Hammer citizen. What about you?"

"I'll go to ground. If I can stay out of the locals' hands, I might find a way to get back to Commitment. Money's not a problem. Maybe I can bribe someone to smuggle me in." Michael did not need to look at Shinoda to know what she thought of that proposition. An awkward silence, the silence of defeat, settled over the pair.

"The problem with looking for someone to smuggle you in is time," Shinoda said eventually. "Nobody knows when the Hammers will reopen their shipping routes. It could be months, and you can't survive that long. DocSec will nail you."

"I know, I know," Michael said.

"You got any better ideas?"

"I might," Michael said, a distant look on his face. "To give Juggernaut the best chance of succeeding, the NRA must get those plans and brevity codes before the operation kicks off. So we can't give up on the mission. We have to find a ship to get us to Commitment."

Shinoda frowned, skeptical. "We can probably do that," she said. "There must be plenty sitting around doing nothing right now. But how the hell can we get dirtside? We'd be plasma five seconds after we dropped out of pinchspace."

"I know," Michael conceded. "That is the fatal flaw in my strategy."

"One hell of a flaw," Shinoda muttered. "So what do we do?"

Michael thought about the problem for a few moments. "Let's get everyone together," he said. "Tell them the situation, then give them the options. If they want to head for Al-Sufri, that's fine. If they want to stay, they can."

"And do what, sir?"

"Work out how to do the impossible," he said.

Michael paused to look at each of the marines in turn. He was struck by the intensity on every face. He knew he did not have to ask the question but did anyway.

"So there you have it, guys. There's nothing more I can say, so it's up to you. Go to Al-Sufri or stay and see if we can't drag this mission across the line." He got to his feet. "I'll let you talk it through. Give me a shout when you've decided."

"No need, sir," Mitchell said before Michael even started for the door. "Well, not for me, anyway. The sergeant says I talk too much anyway ... '

"No kidding," Akuna muttered.

"... but I'm in."

"What about the rest of you?" Michael asked. "You in too?"

One after another, heads nodded.

"Well, I guess that's it," Michael continued. "The mission's back on. All we have to do is work out how we can do this."

Shinoda broke the silence that followed. "Let me have first crack at it," she said. "The way I see it, there's one logistics problem—we need a ship and fast—and two tactical problems: We have to survive the Hammer defenses once we drop out of pinchspace, and then we have to get safely dirtside."

"Money will solve the first problem," Michael said.

"Hang on a second, sir," Akuna said. "We're talking merchant ships here, right?"

"Yes."

"We can't just waltz onboard and take over. Merships have lockouts on their controls. If the crewmen don't want to drop into Hammer space, they sure as shit won't let us."

"Goddammit," Michael said, trying not to let a sudden despondency show. In his enthusiasm, he had forgotten. "Of course they do, and I have no idea how we can get the command codes. But that problem can wait. Right now we need to start building a list of issues."

"I'll run the list," Prodi offered.

"Thanks. Once we know what all the problems are, we can start working out how to solve them. Okay, who's next?"

* * *

"So that's it, guys," Michael said. "Get some sleep. I'll keep an eye on things."

"Not so fast, sir," Shinoda said. "Spassky and Akuna, take the perimeter."

"You're a hard woman," Spassky grumbled.

Shinoda ignored her. "Mitchell, Prodi, you take over at … let me see, at six. Now move!"

The marines shuffled out, leaving Michael and Shinoda alone.

"I've found a ship broker, Pinczewski Associates," Michael said. "They have plenty of ships for lease. That's the good news. The bad is the cost. Ship leasing does not come cheap."

"Can we get the money?"

"I've got some ideas," Michael said after a moment's thought, "but let's not get ahead of ourselves. I've set up a meeting for ten this morning with Max Pinczewski. Let me see what he's got to offer, and we'll take it from there, okay?"

"All right, but we'll need a cover story. One of Pinczewski's people is bound to ask what we want the ship for."

"Shit!" Michael swore. "Hadn't thought about that."

"I have," Shinoda said with a smug grin. "Remember the consignment for the Live-in-Hope Mining Company? Fed border security bought that story, so I'm pretty sure our friends at Pinczewski Associates will too. We left the containers in one of the orbital bonded warehouses; it won't be a problem to get them shifted. They are ours, after all."

"And we have the necessary end-user certificates, so problem solved."

"Only ten thousand to go," Shinoda said. They both laughed.

"So, where is the Live-in-Hope Mining Company?"

"The Varakala Cluster."

Michael winced. "Long way. That'll be expensive. Still, we won't worry about that just yet. And let me have a look … yes, that works." He pulled up a chart of the space around the Hammer Worlds on the kitchen holovid screen. "A ship jumping from Scobie's en route to the Varakala Cluster passes within 20 light-years of Commitment. Not as close as I'd like, but a ship suffering a major systems failure, say, here—" Michael's finger stabbed at a point north of Brooks Reef. "—would have to try for Commitment."

Michael paused to study the chart.

"Where," he went on, "the Hammers will do their best to blow us all to hell the moment we dropped into normalspace. But that's a problem for later."

"Which we won't worry about now, sir. You should get some sleep. We'll head into town early. That'll give us plenty of time to check out Mister Pinczewski's place."

"Sounds good," Michael said. "I have to drop off an update for Admiral Moussawi as well. He needs to know what we're planning."

Thursday, June 17, 2404, UD
New Dublin, Scobie's World

"That was easy," Michael said, taking a sip of coffee. "I just hope the *Matrix Starlight* is as good as Max Pinczewski says it is."

"Easy?" Shinoda shook her head. "Thanks to the Hammers, Max Pinczewski has ships sitting on their asses doing fuck all, and we have the money. Of course it was easy."

"Apart from the fact that we don't have the money."

"So what do we do?"

"Only thing I can think of is my father. He can get us the money."

"That'd mean making a pinchcomm call to the Federated Worlds, which I don't like the sound of," Shinoda said. She looked anxious. "Scobie's World is infested with State Security and DocSec agents. It'll be risky."

"No money, no mission, no choice," Michael said, his tone blunt. "We have to, but not here in New Dublin. Somewhere quieter."

"Then the sooner we do it, the better."

"Not perfect," Shinoda said, scanning the plaza at the heart of Charfield, a small town three hours by mobibot from New Dublin. It was a place no Hammer tourists ever came to; in theory, that meant DocSec didn't either.

Michael hoped the theory was right. "It will have to do. Now, any questions?"

Michael shook his head, mouth dry with nerves.

"Off you go, then, and if anything doesn't look right, get out of there fast. You know where we are."

"Got it."

Taking a deep breath, Michael pulled his cap down, adjusted his gloves, and set off through the afternoon throng. Akuna followed 10 meters behind. Michael wondered how many of the locals he passed were security agents.

He found the telecom office without difficulty, a small building off the plaza. It was all but empty. Michael found himself a pinchcomm booth. He punched out the familiar digits and tried not to think about the obscene amount of money he was about to spend.

It took a lifetime to make the connection. The familiar voice of his father came as a shock when he answered.

"Andrew Helfort," he said.

"No questions. Go secure. Use one-time code Blue-65-Kilo."

"Blue-65-Kilo, going secure now."

The voice in Michael's ear turned to mush. Two seconds later his neuronics took over. The mush vanished. Michael put a simple acoustic vocoder to his face. It sealed off his mouth entirely. Then he jammed the vocoder into the mouthpiece on the handset. State Security would crack the encryption Michael was using, but they'd need at least twelve hours to do that, he hoped.

"Can you hear me?" he said.

"I can."

"Good. Now write down these numbers." Michael reeled off a long string of digits. "That's a Kosmos Cash Express branch on Scobie's World. I need you to send all the money in my trust fund to that account, and I mean every last cent, plus as much as you can scrape together. I need clear funds no later than twelve hours from now no matter how much it costs. Got all that?"

"Twelve hours. It'll be done."

"Last thing. Make the transfer payable to Larissa Roberts and the payment password 'romantic' in lowercase."

"Understood. Anything else?"

The catch in his father's voice tore at Michael's soul. He forced himself to finish. "That's it. Got to go. Love you; 'bye."

Michael ripped off the vocoder and smacked the handset back into its cradle. He made his way back to the counter. "I'm done, thanks," he said. "How much do I owe you?"

"Ah," the woman said, "a pinchcomm voice-only call to Federated Worlds. Hold on."

Come on, come on, Michael wanted to scream as she dawdled her way to the answer. "Yes, that'll be 3,500 k-dollars, thank you."

Michael handed over his stored-value card. The woman took another lifetime to process the payment. The tension tore Michael's nerves to shreds. Finally she was done, and Michael took his card back. "Thank you," he said.

He forced himself to walk slowly out into the street. He scanned the passersby and saw nothing out of the ordinary. He let himself relax.

Akuna came up from behind him. "Follow me," she hissed as she walked past. "Mitchell's spotted two State Security mobibots, and they're headed this way."

"Fuck!" Michael said. He was more shaken up than he cared to admit. "That was way too close."

"We were lucky," Shinoda said as the rented mobibot eased itself out into the traffic, with a second vehicle carrying Mitchell and Akuna close behind. "Those State Security bastards were fast."

"They were. I wasn't on the line long, and they got there only minutes after I hung up."

"Preplanned response to all pinchcomm calls to the Federated Worlds, I reckon. As soon as you punched in the numbers, the alarms would have gone off. Paranoid bunch of fucks," Shinoda added dismissively.

"Anyway, it's done." Michael rubbed his face, stress ebbing away to leave him exhausted. "Now all we have to do is collect the money."

"Yup."

"I wonder how Spassky and Prodi did."

Shinoda shook her head. "Haven't heard from them yet, but if anyone can suborn that poor sucker from Matrix Shipping Lines, it's those two."

"I hope so. We are screwed without those control codes."

"They'll get them," Shinoda said. Her voice left no room for doubt. Michael hoped her confidence was well founded. "Money gets you most things in life in my experience," she went on. "Now, let's see. It's eleven hours to Franchette, so I suggest you get some sleep."

"Try and stop me."

Friday, June 18, 2404, UD
Franchette, Scobie's World

"Any problems?" Michael said as the mobibot pulled away.

"Piece of cake, sir," Marine Akuna said, her face still flushed with excitement. "I never knew it was so easy to get someone I've never met to hand over so much money. How good are those Kosmos Cash guys? I give them the name and password, they give me cash. They didn't even ask for any ID."

"You can thank the Hammers and their black economy for that. They love their cash. So how much do we have?"

"A shitload: 950,000 FedMarks, which converts to a bit over 2 million k-dollars."

Michael blinked, taken aback. "Two million k-dollars? You sure?"

"Here's the proof, sir." Akuna handed Michael four cash cards. They were anonymous and untraceable, each a testament to the prodigious rivers of cash that underwrote Scobie's World. Its economy was wholly dependent on the corruption endemic to the Hammer Worlds, to the point where Scobie's World had long since abandoned its own currency in favor of the Kraa-dollar. "There's 500,000 k-dollars on each of those puppies," she said.

Michael sat back, frowning. Thanks to the tireless efforts of his agent, Mitesh—the AI had been spectacularly successful suing the trashpress after the Devastation Reef fiasco—his trust fund had held close to half a million FedMarks, which meant his father had somehow found an extra 450,000. "Right, then; we need to get you off-planet," he said to Akuna after a while.

"Not so fast, sir," Akuna said. "I've been thinking."

Shinoda turned around to look at Akuna. "We've been through this," she said, not unkindly. "Listen up, Nugget."

Michael had to smile. Akuna's given name was Precious; applying the obscure logic that all marines used to generate nicknames, gold was precious, hence Nugget.

"Your cover has been blown. State Security will eventually track down the withdrawal, and when they do, they'll come after you. If we don't get you off-planet fast, you'll never get off, and we can't let DocSec get their hands on you, okay?"

"I understand all that, sarge," Akuna said, "but I've been thinking."

Shinoda rolled her eyes. "Give me strength," she muttered, "a marine who thinks. Go on, then."

"You can get me off-planet the same way we got Lieutenant Helfort off Terranova. It worked for him. Why wouldn't it work for me?"

Michael looked at Shinoda; she shrugged her shoulders. "Why didn't we think of that?" he asked.

"Too much else going on," Shinoda said. She looked at Michael. He nodded. "Okay, then. It worked before, so we can do it again."

"Good," Michael replied. "We need all the marines we can get."

"Thank you, sir," Akuna said.

"Wait until you've been dirtside on Commitment for a few months before you thank anyone," Shinoda muttered, turning back to watch the road ahead.

Saturday, June 19, 2404, UD
New Dublin, Scobie's World

"Five hundred thousand k-dollars?"

Spassky nodded. "That's what Jakob Kalkuz is saying," he said.

Michael swore under his breath. That was a quarter of his fighting fund, and if he'd learned anything during his short stay on Scobie's, it was that there was no such thing as a done deal. Only that morning, Max Pinczewski had been in touch; he had "forgotten" to add the war risk premium to the charter, an omission that had taken another big slice out of his stash. "Does he mean it?" he asked.

Spassky glanced at Prodi, who nodded. "We think so," he said. "Kalkuz is taking a huge risk."

"Can we trust him?"

"No more than any crook on the take, sir."

Michael paused to think the problem through. They had to do a deal with Kalkuz, and time was running out fast. "If he gives us what we need," he said at last, "then I don't have a problem paying him what he wants, but how do we know he hasn't double-crossed us?"

"By giving us the wrong codes, you mean?" Spassky asked.

"Exactly."

Spassky looked at Prodi again. "Stick and I were talking about that, sir. We think it would be best if our Mister Kalkuz came along for the ride. That way—"

"Hold on a sec." Michael turned to Shinoda. "We can do that?" he said. "Kidnap the man and smuggle him aboard the ship?"

"It's an added complication we don't need," Shinoda said, "but I agree with the guys. We won't be here to cut his balls off if he fucks with us, so that means he's got to come along for the ride."

"Fine. So be it." Michael looked at the two marines. "Set up another meeting for tomorrow with Kalkuz," he said. "Tell him he's got a deal but we want him at the spaceport an hour before we leave. He'll get his money when he gives you the codes. Okay?"

"Sir," Spassky and Prodi said as one.

"So now we're smuggling two bodies off-planet." Michael looked at the three marines around the table. "Akuna's not going to be a problem, but Kalkuz is."

"I was just thinking the same thing, sir," Shinoda said. "I don't see how we can kidnap Kalkuz and box him up, not at New Dublin spaceport. It'll be as busy as all hell. There'll be people and security everywhere."

Prodi broke the long silence that followed. "Private shuttle?" she asked.

"That'd work," Shinoda said after a moment's thought. She looked at Michael. "Can we afford one?"

"I can't think of any other way of taking Kalkuz with us," Michael said, "so we'll just have to. I'll talk to Max Pinczewski, see what it will cost us." He took a deep breath. "Right, guys," he said to Spassky and Prodi. "Thanks for all that. Good work."

"Okay then, marines," Shinoda said. "What you waiting for? A medal? Akuna and Mitchell need relieving, so get your asses out there."

"Sarge," the two chorused.

"It's coming together,' Michael said to Shinoda when the pair had gone, "but we still have a serious problem on our hands."

"How to get down to Commitment without getting our butts shot off?"

"Yeah."

"We know the solution to that problem, sir," Shinoda said, breaking the silence that followed.

"I haven't forgotten," Michael said, "but even if we had Fed gear and the time to train, it would still be way too risky. I can't order anyone to do it."

"Look at it this way. Not to be too melodramatic, but Admiral Moussawi has to take his ships right into the jaws of hell. Meanwhile, if we trash *our* mission, we'll be doing what exactly? Sitting on our asses, that's what. So what you're saying is bullshit … with all due respect, sir."

"I hate it when people say 'with all due respect.'"

"So glad you worked out what I really meant, sir," Shinoda said, her voice laced with sarcasm and anger.

"Take it easy, Sergeant Shinoda," Michael said quietly. "I know all about ordering people to risk their lives, and it's not something I've ever done lightly."

"That's as may be, sir, but we have a decision to make and not much time to make it. So decide, sir. Do we scrub the mission, or do we do what we have to do?"

"You've talked to your guys about this?"

"Yes, I have."

"And?"

"They know the risks, and they know the importance of the mission. They'll obey orders, sir, just like I will."

"Like it's that easy," Michael muttered. He sat back. "How do we minimize the risks?" he asked. "No point doing this if we all end up splattered across Commitment."

"The local club has a sim package we can upload into our neuronics. If we spend every hour we can practicing drops, at least we won't all die."

Michael looked into Shinoda's eyes. "Some will, though," he said. "Our special forces guys spend months training before they do their first live drop, and they still lose one or two guys a year."

"It can't be helped, sir. I don't like it any more than you do, but it's the business we're in."

Michael nodded. Shinoda was right. The question wasn't whether they could afford to take the risk. It was whether they could afford not to, the same question already asked of—and answered by—Admiral Moussawi. "Right, then," he said, wondering who among them would not make it. "Unless there are any better suggestions, we'll do it."

"That's a good call, sir."

"Don't patronize me, sergeant," Michael snapped, "and don't confuse debate with indecision. We might be pressed for time, but I won't order you and your marines to do something this dangerous without talking it through first."

Shinoda put her hands up in apology. "I was out of line, sir," she said. "I'm sorry. It won't happen again."

"Forget it. Now, moving on. What's left to do?"

"Let me see. Mitchell and Prodi need to make sure the next safe house is clear. Spassky and Akuna have to meet our man Kalkuz, so that leaves us to go talk to the drop club lunatics."

"Don't knock it," Michael said. "Who knows? It might be fun."

"I doubt that," Shinoda said, grim-faced.

Monday, June 21, 2404, UD
New Dublin, Scobie's World

The cargobot rolled to a stop just short of the tousled-haired man. "Hi, guys," he said as Michael and Shinoda stepped out. "I'm Marco Chang."

You don't look like a crazy to me, Michael thought, looking at the man. If anything, he looked very ordinary. "Alan Fels," he said to Chang. Thanks to the vocalization reprogramming in his neuronics, his voice was thick with the crushed vowels of a native-born Hammer. "This is Suzie."

"Hi, Marco," Shinoda said.

"So," Chang said, "you said you wanted some drop shells?"

"Yeah, we do," Michael replied. "Ours are back on Commitment, and since we're stuck here until the shipping lines reopen—and Kraa knows how long it'll be before that happens—we thought we'd do some drops. Not much else we fancy doing."

"First time I've heard a Hammer say that about this place," Chang said. They set off toward a large shed. A sign over its door declared it to be the headquarters of the New Dublin Drop Club. "Scobie's only claim to fame is that we have everything anyone could ever want … for a price."

You're not kidding, Michael thought.

Chang pushed his hand into a reader to open the door. Michael and Shinoda followed him inside. The room looked like a million other club rooms across humanspace: a small bar, a collection of old chairs and tables, and wall-mounted holovids paging through pix of members doing what members did. Michael frowned when he spotted an old-fashioned wooden board sporting a list of names and dates in gold paint with the words "In Memoriam" across the top. It was a depressingly long list that did nothing to improve Michael's spirits.

If the ghosts of dead members bothered Chang, he did not let it show. "Here we are," the man said. He opened a door off to one side to reveal floor-to-ceiling racks packed with large plasfiber boxes. "You want drop shells, we've got drop shells."

"Aha!" Michael said with forced enthusiasm, peering at the nearest box. "You didn't say you were using G-Series systems … very nice," he added. He wondered how much more bullshit he'd have to come up with, even as he whispered a quiet prayer of thanks for the net's ability to turn people like him into instant experts.

"Oh, yes," Chang said, "we have been for a while now. The F-Series was okay, but nothing beats the G."

Oh really, Michael thought. *Try telling that to the poor bastards on your killed-in-action board.* "No argument there," he said. "Wish we could get them back home.

We've been using Kravax-5531 pods. Our military won't let us use the good stuff."

Chang shook his head. "You guys are nuts," he said. "The 5531 is a killer. You know Boris Chernokov?"

Who the hell was Boris Chernokov? Michael flicked an anxious glance at Shinoda. Despite all the research they had done, there were yawning gaps in their cover story. It would not take much probing by Chang for that to become obvious. "Poor old Boris," he asked.

Chang looked at him with a puzzled frown. "Poor old Boris? Why? Has something happened to him?" he said.

Shit, shit, shit, thought Michael. He had assumed the man had been killed. "Oh, nothing too serious … we hope. Small disagreement with our friends in DocSec." Michael made a show of looking worried. "But we won't talk about it if that's okay."

Chang blinked; living on Scobie's, he'd know all about DocSec. "Sure," he said. "Now, you've got three drops planned, I think you said."

"Yes."

"Fine. These are ten grand each. You do know that?"

"Yeah, yeah; no problem."

"I wish I had half your luck," Chang muttered. "I'm lucky if I can afford to do two drops a year. Anyway, let's get them loaded."

"Not sure that man was convinced we were kosher," Michael said to Shinoda as the cargobot pulled away from a thoughtful-looking Chang.

"I was thinking the same thing. I don't suppose that club of his sees too many bored, cashed-up Hammers."

"I'm damn sure they don't see any. Still, this is Scobie's World, and on Scobie's World cash is king, so I guess he was happy."

"He didn't look too happy as we left."

"You trying to tell me something, Sergeant Shinoda?"

"Hmmm." Shinoda nodded. "Yes ... Right about now, I think he's trying to decide whether he should tell the wrong people about us. State Security might think they run this place, but we both know as well as Chang does that DocSec calls the shots."

"And DocSec likes to shoot people who keep things to themselves. He's covering his ass."

Shinoda thought about that for a moment. "He smelled a rat; that's for sure. He'll tell State Security. I'd bet my life on it."

"Damn," Michael said. "We're way too obvious in this damn cargobot. Chang will have its ID. We need to dump it and fast."

"There!" Shinoda said. She pointed to a narrow lane overhung by thickly canopied trees. "Down there. We'll off-load the boxes and send the cargobot on a wander around town. By the time they pick it up, we'll be long gone."

Michael told the bot to turn down the lane. A kilometer in, they stopped in front of an old building, its security fence long past its use-by date. "This is good enough. If we're fast, nobody will question why we stopped."

"I'll have a look," Shinoda said, getting out. She was back quickly. "I think it's safe to leave the gear here for the time being. Nobody's been near the place in months."

"Let's do it."

Working feverishly, they manhandled the boxes off the cargobot and into the dilapidated building and tucked them away out of sight. It took only minutes, and Michael was more than a bit relieved when the vehicle finally hummed off down the lane.

"I'll get a couple of the guys back with holocams to keep an eye on things," Shinoda said.as they set off.

Shinoda dropped into a chair. "You've got a comm from Spassky, sir," she said.

"Thanks." Michael patched his neuronics into the data feed. He gestured to Shinoda to stay connected. "Go ahead," he said when the man's image appeared.

"We're in position, sir, and the holocams are online."

"Roger that. Any sign of life?"

"None. Quiet as the proverbial."

"Okay. Hang in there. We'll see you in thirty-six hours, and don't lose sight of those damn pods. They cost me a fortune."

Spassky's face cracked into a grin. "Don't worry, sir. They'll still be here."

"I hope so."

Michael cut the link. "Almost there," he said to Shinoda.

"I hope so," Shinoda replied. "I've had enough of Scobie's."

Michael was shocked to see how tired the marine looked. "You and me both," he said. "I think I'll go check the dead-letter box. Hopefully there'll be something from Moussawi."

"I'll come with you, sir," Shinoda said, starting to get to her feet.

"No. You stay put. I'll take Akuna."

Shinoda didn't argue with him.

Akuna walked past where Michael sat waiting on the park bench. "Lovely evening for a walk," she said.

Michael's pulse quickened. Akuna had spotted the telltale; the dead-letter box had something for him. A response from Moussawi? "Yes, it is," he said to Akuna's back.

He waited five minutes, then walked the 300 meters to the box, a cleft in an old tree passed by a meandering path well screened by thick clumps of flowering shrubs. It was the work of only seconds for Michael to reach in and feel around inside. "Yes," he said under his breath as his fingers closed around a datastick. He always wondered how the information in the stick had gotten from wherever Moussawi was holed up waiting for Juggernaut to kick off.

He uploaded the contents. Admiral Moussawi's face appeared; he looked old and tired. What he had to say was short and to the point: J-Day had been put back a week to give Michael and his team more time to make it down to Commitment.

It did not take Michael long to work out the real meaning of the message. Michael had to succeed. Juggernaut depended on it. *Shit*, he thought as he set off to meet up with Akuna. *Talk about pressure of expectations.*

Tuesday, June 22, 2404, UD
New Dublin, Scobie's World

Grabbing a mug of coffee, Shinoda dumped her machine pistol on the table with a clatter and threw herself into a chair across from Michael. "We're all set, sir," she said.

"Good," Michael said. "One last time. We haven't missed anything?"

"No, sir. Spassky and Prodi have confirmed the area's clear, and the cargobot's on its way. They'll meet us at the VIP terminal."

"Anything in the dead-letter box?"

Shinoda shook her head. "Nothing."

"Let's hope that's good news," Michael said. "What about Akuna and Mitchell?"

"In position and ready in case Mister Kalkuz turns up early. You happy about providing backup?"

"Yes," Michael said. "And I've spoken to that bloodsucker Max Pinczewski," he added. "He's confirmed our shuttle's liftoff slot. The *Matrix Starlight*'s organized a cargo shuttle to transfer the mining equipment from the warehouse, so I think we're good to go."

"Provided Kalkuz does what he's supposed to," Shinoda said, sour-faced. "Otherwise we're screwed."

"I don't even want to think about it."

"Nor me. Okay, sir. Gear and weapons check, then we go."

Shinoda broke into Michael's thoughts. "Alfa, this is Bravo," she said.

"Alfa," Michael replied.

"Charlie and Delta"—that was Akuna and Mitchell—"have Tango visual. He's inbound in a red mobibot. Registration begins Yankee Yankee Golf. You have?"

"Wait one ... I have him."

"Roger, stand by."

Michael heaved a sigh of relief. After all the work they'd done, he'd been haunted by the thought that the man might not turn up. But he had. Now all he had to do was give them the codes. Sadly, only time would tell whether what Kalkuz gave them was correct.

Shinoda broke in: "Tango is with Charlie and Delta ... Charlie confirms Tango has handed over the package ... Okay, Tango is down. Alfa, you can move in now."

"On my way," Michael said. He threaded his way through the clutter of parked mobibots. By the time he reached Kalkuz's mobibot, Akuna and Mitchell had bundled the man into their bot, his unconscious form slumped across the backseat. "Any problems?"

"None, sir," Akuna said, handing a slim folder across. "This is what he gave us."

"Thanks. Get him boxed up. I'll see you inside the terminal."

"Roger that."

Michael returned the way he came. His heart hammered at the walls of his chest. He prayed that Kalkuz's greed had done the trick. He slid into his mobibot and closed the door. Taking a deep breath, he opened the folder. Inside was a single piece of paper with the words 'CONFIDENTIAL' and 'MATRIX STARLIGHT—CONTROL CODES' in thick black type below the red and black logo of Matrix Shipping Lines. There were twelve codes; Michael ignored the trivial ones—he did not plan to restore the ship's environmental control system to its baseline settings, nor was he interested in changing the cuisine the foodbots would be serving—until he came to the only code that mattered, the words 'Command Authority' followed by an incomprehensible string of letters and numbers.

"Format and checksum are correct," Michael's neuronics confirmed. *Thank fuck for that*, Michael thought. "Bravo, Alfa. The codes look good. I'm on my way."

"Roger." Shinoda sounded as relieved as Michael felt.

"We okay to go?" Michael asked Shinoda when the rest of the team had arrived.

"We are. Akuna and Kalkuz are fast asleep and safely boxed up, and all our gear is being loaded onto the shuttle now."

"No problems?" No matter how cleverly the boxes had been packed with extraneous foam and metal to disguise their actual contents, smuggling two warm bodies past security, even security as lax as that in force at the VIP terminal, was by no means guaranteed. And they still had to get past a second check before the *Matrix Starlight* could depart, a check that would be conducted to DocSec standards.

"None. All they cared about was explosives. And I've checked with the dispatcher. We can board in five minutes, and the shuttle's cleared for transit to Orbital Warehouse 67-Bravo. We'll have two hours to repack our gear before the *Matrix Starlight* turns up."

Michael grimaced. They would have to hustle. Fitting the boxes holding Akuna and Kalkuz into the containers of mining equipment was going to be a big job.

"I'll be glad when we're off this damn planet," he said. "I never want to see Scobie's World ever again."

"Nor me," Shinoda said, casting a disparaging eye across the handful of people waiting for their shuttles. She shook her head. Michael grinned. The locals did not believe in modesty or discretion; that was obvious. Without exception they were loud, overweight, overdressed, and loaded with enough bling to embarrass even the crassest fashionista. "What a rabble," she added, shaking her head again.

"Welcome aboard, Mister Smuts," the tall, spare man dressed in a faded gray shipsuit said. He looked right into

Michael's face from washed-out blue eyes. "I'm the captain, Ulrik Horda. You'll meet my first mate and chief engineer later. Rajiv and Marty are up to their armpits in a defective cooling pump right now."

"Please, call me Johannes," Michael said, shaking hands. *I must be careful,* he thought. *Underestimating this man would be a mistake.* "Good to meet you. This is my team," he went on, introducing Shinoda and her marines in turn.

"Good to meet you all. Your accommodations are ready; just follow the signs. If you can come with me, Johannes, we can get the formalities out of the way."

"Sure."

Michael followed the captain into the passenger saloon. He took a mug of coffee from the foodbot and sat down.

"Right, let me see," Horda said. "Okay, State Security has cleared you all for departure, so no problems there. I just need a copy of the end-user certificates for your consignment to show to the border security team."

Michael's stomach turned over. "Border security team?" he said. "I didn't think they inspected consignments just transiting through."

"Normally, no," Horda replied, "but these are not normal times. I won't say they are paranoid, but they're pretty close."

Michael did his best to sound relaxed. "Fine," he said, pushing a datastick across to Horda. "The certificates are there. Will we need to open our containers up?"

"Depends on how the bast—how the State Security boys are feeling, but I hope not. We'll miss our departure slot if they do."

"Is that a problem?"

"No, not really. Just means hanging around here for a few more hours. I know you want to keep to schedule, but we'll be able to make up time as we go."

"Good. I'm under orders to get everything installed and working as soon as possible. When's the border security team due?"

"Let me check … They're almost here. We should go meet them."

"Shall I get my team down as well?"

"Hell, no. From past experience, the fewer people hanging around, the better. Spare hands make it easy for them to rip everything apart. If they ask you, most of them are ill and have turned in."

"Ill? As in sick?"

"Swamp fever from the mosquitoes. Big problem on Scobie's. Treatable, of course, but it takes time. Most obvious symptom is a high temperature."

Michael had not wanted to like Captain Horda. It wasn't working. Horda looked to be a good man. Michael hated the thought of what he planned to do to him.

"Okay."

"Come on; we need to go. We've stowed your consignment in the smallest cargo bay we've got; they'll berth on the personnel access airlock. They don't like walking."

Michael trailed along behind Horda along passageways and down ladders. It was a confusing process. He commed Shinoda. "You copy all that?" he asked.

"Yes, sir. Everyone's been told to turn in and get their body temperatures up just in case we have to prove they have this swamp fever thing."

"Just make sure they can get to their personal weapons in a hurry. We'll have to move fast if border security finds something they shouldn't."

"We're all set."

Horda slapped a switch on the bulkhead, and a door opened. "Here we are," he said. "Cargo Bay 6."

They stepped through. It was a small space but big enough to make the consignment of mining gear look embarrassingly insignificant. Michael had already rehearsed his answer to the inevitable question: What's so important about a pile of mining equipment that it requires an entire ship to itself?

The inner airlock door opened. A succession of jumpsuited figures entered the bay carrying search equipment. Horda went over to meet them. "Good to see you again, Lieutenant Hinjo," he said, shaking hands with the first of them, his face lit up by a cheerful smile.

"And you, Ulrik," Hinjo said. "Nice little charter you've got yourself."

"The sort I like, Lieutenant: one client, one consignment, one destination, a simple drop-off and return."

"And this is the client?"

Michael stepped forward. They shook hands. "Johannes Smuts, Lieutenant."

"Mister Smuts." Hinjo waved his team into action. With an ease born of long practice, they spread out, fired up their scanners and probes, and started to check the containers. "And what do you do?" Hinjo went on.

"I'm a technical support manager for BellMineTech; we're from Kelly's Deep. The Live-in-Hope mine is one of the clients I look after.'

Hinjo nodded. "We've been through the cargo manifest, and all seems in order. After all, mining equipment is mining equipment."

Michael's spirits soared, but only for an instant.

"But I must say I am curious to know what is so important, so urgent."

"Live-in-Hope produces iridium-193, and thanks to the current, ah … security situation, demand has gone crazy. The mine has a serious problem with the AI process controllers running its stage 3 production system. They bought cheap AIs from somebody they shouldn't have and are now paying for that mistake. This gear here—" Michael waved a casual hand across the containers. "—is what they should have bought in the first place, and until we get it all installed and set to work, they're not producing so much as gram of iridium. It's costing them a fortune in lost production."

Hinjo nodded again. "If it's all so urgent, why did you waste so much time on Scobie's?"

"Ah, well." Michael fixed a look of worried concern onto his face. "I'm not supposed to talk about it, Lieutenant, but I'm sure I can trust you not to let this go any further."

"Of course."

"We had a contractual disagreement with the client, a serious disagreement."

"A contractual disagreement?" Hinjo said, his face twisting into a supercilious smirk. "They wouldn't pay BellMineTech's exorbitant prices, you mean. You people are all the same."

Michael ignored the insult. "I think that's an accurate summary of the problem, Lieutenant," he said.

"Hmm," Hinjo replied. He walked over to the containers, a finger to his lips tapping out his thoughts. "I think we should have a look inside, don't you?"

"Of course," Michael said, heart pounding. "Which one first?"

"That one," Hinjo said, pointing.

"Can your guys give me a hand?"

"They're busy. Get your men up to help, Mister Smuts."

"Sorry, Lieutenant," Michael said, turning to cut off the customs seals. He pulled open the container doors to reveal a tightly packed mass of metal and plasfiber. "I don't think they'd be much use. Swamp fever, apparently. Must say I don't feel so good myself. Captain, do you have a handlerbot we can use? Some of this equipment is heavy."

"We do," Horda said. "Hold on, I'll go—"

"That won't be necessary," Hinjo said with a dismissive flick of the wrist. "Open the doors on every second container."

"Thank you, Captain Horda," Michael said under his breath as he set to work, trying not to feel even guiltier than he already did.

Wednesday, June 23, 2404, UD
SWMS Matrix Starlight, in pinchspace

"Everyone in position?"

"All sct," Shinoda responded.

"Go!"

Michael and Mitchell walked onto the *Matrix Starlight*'s bridge, a small compartment with two chairs and, an array of holovid screens and consoles with master and backup controls for all the ship's systems.

"Ah, Johannes," Horda said. "I was wondering—"

"Stay where you are, Captain," Michael said, the stunner in his hand pointing right at Horda's chest. "Mitch," he went on, waving the marine forward to plasticuff him.

"Oh, dear." Horda shook his head. He let out a long sigh and held out his wrists. "This is a first. I've never been hijacked. Tell me: Do you have any idea what you're doing?"

"Sadly for you, yes."

"I can't give you the command authority codes. You know that?"

"Don't worry, Captain. I've brought my own."

For the first time, Horda looked worried. "You can't have."

"Tell that to Mister Kalkuz."

"Kalkuz? But he's … oh, crap."

"This way, please, sir," Mitchell said to Horda. Shoulders slumped in defeat, the man allowed himself to be led over to the master console.

Taking a deep breath to steady himself, Michael stood beside the man. In theory, taking control of the ship was easy: Select the right menu, enter the master password, check Horda's DNA and retinas to confirm his identity, then repeat to authorize Michael to take control, and the job was done. Taking another deep breath, he punched in the command authority code. Only when the screen told him to proceed did he allow himself to relax a little. *Poor old Kalkuz*, he thought, waving Horda to step up to be screened, *He could have stayed at home.*

In less than two minutes, the entire process was done. Michael was now the de facto master of the *Matrix Starlight*. "Take the captain to the saloon," he said, putting a comm through to Shinoda.

"The ship is ours," he said when her face appeared.

Shinoda let out a sigh. "That's a relief. We've got the first officer and the chief engineer in the crew mess."

"Any problems?"

"None. Quiet as lambs."

"Okay. Send two of the guys to get Kalkuz and Akuna out of their boxes while I change the navigation plan.

When I'm done, I'll be with the captain. He deserves to know why this is happening to him and his ship."

"Roger that."

"Thanks, Mitchell; I'll take it from here. But leave the door open and stay outside. If he tries anything—" Michael hooked a thumb at Horda. "—shoot him."

"Aye, aye, sir."

Michael reached over the table to cut the plasticuffs off Horda's wrists. "I'm sorry about all this, Captain, but we can't afford to take any chances."

"You're marines," Horda said, sitting back and rubbing his wrists. "Aye, aye, sir, and all that."

"My guys are. I'm a spacer."

"You like to tell me what the fuck is this all about? Forty-six years I've been with Matrix, and this is first time anyone's taken my ship off me."

"I'm sorry about that; I really am."

"Sorry?" Horda snapped. His cheeks flushed red with anger. "That helps."

"I have my reasons."

"I don't give a damn for your reasons," Horda said, his voice a half shout now. "You have no right to hijack my ship, none at all. I'd like to kick your ass."

"I'm sure you would," Michael said; Horda's belligerence irritated him. "But it won't happen. Now you've got a choice. You can sit there mouthing off at me, in which case I'll throw you in one of the storerooms and leave you to rot, or you can shut your mouth, sit back, and let me tell you why we've taken your ship. Your choice."

Horda choked back his response with an obvious effort. "Go on, then; tell me," he said, taking a deep breath. "But I want the truth, okay?"

"You'll get it. First of all, we're not from Kelly's Deep."

"Didn't think you were. The accent wasn't right."

"It's hard to mimic. No, we're Feds."

"Feds?" Horda's eyes widened. "In that case you'd better tell me what this is all about, Johannes." He stopped and stared at Michael for a moment. "Wait," he went on. "Smuts isn't your real name, is it?"

Michael grinned. "No, it's not. I'm Michael Helfort," he said.

"The Michael Helfort? I thought you looked familiar, but I just couldn't work out why. I've seen you on the news. Aren't you supposed to be dead?"

"I am."

"What the hell is going on?"

"Sit back and I'll tell you as much as I can," Michael replied.

"... and like I say, I'm sorry we have to destroy your ship, but given what's at stake, I don't think I can afford to be too sentimental."

"Easy for you to say," Horda muttered; his eyes shimmered with unshed tears. "I've been *Starlight*'s captain for twenty-two years. I hate the thought of what you want to do to her." He paused for a moment, then took a deep breath. "You know the worst of it?"

"No, what?"

"I'm Scobie's born and bred. I loved the place … once. But now?" He shook his head. "I hate it. I've watched the Hammers turn the place into a cesspit with their corruption and sleaze. I never go dirtside anymore. This—" He waved a hand around the saloon's well-worn paneling. "—is our home now."

"You said 'our.' Your first mate and chief engineer; they feel the same way you do?"

"They do. We might not own the *Starlight* …"

Thank goodness for that, Michael thought. *I feel guilty enough as it is.*

"… and I know she's old and might not look much to you, but this is our home, and now you want to destroy it."

"I wish there was—"

Horda put a hand up to stop Michael. "You don't have to say it, son. If it's any comfort, I hate the Hammer too. Doesn't stop the hurt, though."

Michael nodded; he did not trust himself to speak.

"So," Horda went on, "what's the plan and how can we help?"

Michael stared at the man. "Help?" he said. "You want to help?"

Horda shrugged. "Why not? I can't change anything, and to be honest—" He looked around. "—maybe it's time I moved on. Matrix was taken over last year, and the new owners are way too close to the Hammers for my liking."

"How does the rest of the crew feel?"

"Marty hates the management. They think he spends too much on the old girl. It's bullshit, of course. He only spends what he needs to keep her safe, but they don't see it that way. Money's all those bastards care about. They've been making his life a misery."

"What about Rajiv?"

"He'll go with the flow. Always has."

"So what will you do?"

"It's strange, you know," Horda said, looking away at something that existed only in his mind. "We were talking about that only the other day. We'd just done a run to Vatuna-6. Nice place. Lots of jobs for guys like us … and no Hammers within hundreds of light-years. So who knows, we might go there."

"Well, I hope it works out for you."

"It will. Not sure about you guys, though. I've heard a lot of dumb ideas in my time, but what you want to do is just plain crazy."

"Needs must, Captain. Believe me, if there was another way, I wouldn't be here now."

"And what makes you think what you're doing will work for you?" Horda asked.

Why is the bastard looking so smug all of a sudden? Michael wondered with a twinge of concern. "Oh, don't worry; it will," he replied, forcing himself to sound both relaxed and confident.

Horda shook his head. "I'm sure that's what Kalkuz told you, but did the asshole tell you that Matrix ships have a backup protocol to validate all changes of command?"

I don't like the sound of this, Michael thought, concern turning to alarm. "What backup protocol?"

"Oh, dear." Horda shook his head. "Kalkuz is not a man you can trust. I could have told you that."

"Don't screw me around," Michael spit. "If you've got something to tell me, then tell me."

"You have to repeat the entire process within two hours. If you don't, you're locked out and stay locked out. The *Starlight* will only do what we tell it to do."

"Shit!"

"And it gets worse. Next time we drop into normal-space, the ship automatically broadcasts a message telling every man and his dog there's been an attempted hijack. That will bring the cavalry, I would think. Let me see ... yes, our next drop is when we cross Brooks Reef, so it'll be the Hammers who turn up."

Michael's guts had turned to ice. He cursed his stupidity. Not only had Horda just blown his last chance to get back to Commitment clean out of the water, now he knew more about his plans than he should. If Horda opened his mouth ...

"Now, young man," Horda went on. "We have eleven minutes left before you lose control of the *Starlight* forever, so—"

"If you fuck me around," Michael snarled, "I will kill you and the rest of your crew. There's way too much at stake here."

"I'm not sure you're the natural-born killer you're pretending to be, but noted," Horda said; he did not look even slightly concerned.

"Captain!"

"Oh, all right. I'd like to help any way I can. Of course, that means you have to trust me, but since I have you by the balls, I don't think you can afford not to, do you?"

"You're enjoying this."

"Oh, I am, but only because I don't like people taking my ship away from me. No, no." Horda's hand had gone up to forestall Michael's angry response. "I understand why it's necessary, I really do, so don't waste time repeating yourself."

"Fine." Michael tried to keep the desperation out of his voice. "Give me a minute, Captain."

He stepped outside the saloon and put a comm through to Shinoda. "You following this?" he asked her when she came online. The tension on her face was obvious.

"I am."

"Talk to Kalkuz. Ask him if the old buzzard is lying and if there are any more protocols we should know about. Tell him that I'll dump him out the airlock unless he's straight with us."

"Wait one."

Shinoda was gone less than a minute. "He swears Horda's telling the truth, but there is a duress code word as well."

"Which is?"

"It's 'ultimate' in lowercase. You need to key that in as well, and the ship really is ours."

"Got it." Michael stepped back into the saloon. "Let's go," he said.

With ten minutes to go, an icon in the center of the command console's holovid screen was flashing a lurid red. "Now what?" Michael asked Horda.

"I have to enter the command authority code, then do the DNA and retina checks."

"Do it."

When Horda finished, the icon vanished and the screen went blank. *I'll give you another ten seconds to tell me about the duress code*, Michael thought, *and then I will kill—*

"One last thing," Horda said, "is a code word to make sure I'm not being forced to do this—" He chuckled as his fingers flashed over the keypad. "—which of course I'm not. There, done." He stepped back. "The *Matrix Starlight* is all yours."

"It better be," Michael said, grim-faced.

"Relax. I could have screwed you, but I didn't, so let's move on. I suspect you've got a lot to do and not much time to do it in, so let's see what we can do to help."

Thursday, June 24, 2404, UD
Brooks Reef

The man's face loomed large on Captain Horda's holovid screen. The bridge filled with the flattened vowels of a native-born Hammer. "Scobie's World mership *Matrix Starlight*, this is Hammer Warship *Sapphire of Kraa*. Chop vidcomm channel 67. Over."

"*Sapphire of Kraa*, *Matrix Starlight*. Going to 67. Out."

There was a short pause before the Hammer officer's face reappeared. Tucked safely out of view, Michael held his breath. The Hammers had no right to stop and search the *Starlight*, but they might. They had never worried too much about the niceties of international law.

"*Matrix Starlight*, *Sapphire of Kraa*. Transmit ship ID and flight plan on datacomm 441, over."

"*Starlight*, roger, stand by … Okay, *Sapphire of Kraa*; you should have it now."

"Confirmed, stand by … You are cleared for transit, *Starlight*. Be advised that any deviation from your flight plan will result in the use of deadly force without warning."

"*Matrix Starlight*, acknowledged. Out."

Horda cut the link without any of the usual niceties. He sat back and rubbed his face with both hands. "Assholes," he muttered. "Okay, Michael, you can come out now. We'll comm Matrix about the instability in the pinchspace generators once we've cleared the reef. It's in our house code, so the Hammers won't take long to crack it, but we'll be in pinchspace by then."

"Good. There's nothing I can do here, so I'll be down in the cargo bay if you need me."

"I'll be here."

Michael left Horda to ease the *Starlight* into the queue of traffic waiting to cross Brooks Reef, a slash through the fabric of space-time hundreds of light-years across but less than half a million kilometers deep, a gravitational anomaly that no ship could transit in pinchspace and survive.

The cargo bay was a hive of activity. Helped by the first mate and the chief engineer, Shinoda and her marines were cutting the *Starlight* apart, the pieces pushed into towering heaps around the massive cargo bay door. Michael nodded his approval. If the Hammers were to be distracted long enough for him and his marines to survive, the more debris the better. He beckoned Shinoda over.

"This looks good."

Shinoda looked around. She nodded. "You said you wanted 500 cubic meters of junk, so we're got a ways to go yet, but we'll get there."

"I'm still worried about getting a decent spread. All that stuff is no good if it stays in one big clump."

"I know," Shinoda said. "Fifty kilos of plastic explosive would have come in handy."

"Yeah, it would. I think I need to talk to Marty again."

"You do that. I've got a ship to shred."

Michael waited for Marty to finish. With exemplary forbearance, the chief engineer was busy explaining to Marine Prodi why using a laser cutter in close proximity to a high-pressure hydraulic system was a bad thing. Laser cutter ... hydraulics; an idea popped into his head. *That might do it*, he thought.

When Marty had satisfied himself that they weren't all about to be killed, Michael took him to one side.

"What pressure do you keep the ship's atmosphere at, chief?"

"A bit under three-quarters of normal atmospheric pressure."

"What's the hull rated to?"

"Ah, now there's a question." *Starlight's* chief engineer thought for a minute. "Test pressure is two atmospheres," he went on, "but she's designed to cope with three, though I think that's optimistic given her age."

"And can you boost the pressure in just one compartment, say, this one?"

"Sure."

"And the cargo bay door will still open despite that overpressure?"

"All our doors and hatches have to. It's a safety requirement."

"Is your hydraulic fluid flammable?"

"Of course it is," Marty snapped. "You think those penny-pinching management assholes would let me buy the good stuff?"

"How much oxygen do you carry?"

"Oxygen?" By now Marty looked completely baffled. "Um, let me see … We have reserves of 4,000 cubic meters in cryogenic tanks. That's at one atmosphere, of course."

"Sounds like a lot."

"It is, but we're certificated to carry eight crew and forty passengers. We have to be able to keep them alive for three weeks if we have problems with our carbon dioxide scrubbers."

"So if you wanted to fill this cargo bay with oxygen, you could do that?"

"So many questions. I hope you'll tell me what the hell you're talking about, Mister Helfort."

"Sorry, chief, I will. Just bear with me."

Marty sighed and shook his head. "Let me think … not completely, but near enough. The only problem is that you'd have a huge—" The chief engineer stopped as realization dawned. "I see what you're getting at," he said. "Leave it to me. I think I need to do a few calculations."

Shinoda came over to where Michael stood. "We've missed something, sir. Kalkuz. He's no fool. Asking him about the backup protocols would have told him that Horda helped us."

"Damn," Michael said. "I didn't think … and if DocSec get their hands on Kalkuz—and they will—Horda's as good as dead."

"Along with the rest of the crew."

Michael nodded. He felt sick. "No need to ask what I have to do."

"I'm sorry, sir."

"My fault. I should have thought things through before I got you to talk to Kalkuz. Leave it to me. I need to talk to Horda."

Friday, June 25, 2404, UD
Deepspace

Horda sat and stared at the holovid screen. He looked worried; a finger tapped out his concern on the tabletop. "The *Starlight* is not one of your fancy warships," he said after a while. "You do know that?"

"Of course I do," Michael replied; he looked equally troubled. "All I ask is that you get the best you can out of your ship."

"I'll do my best, but will it be enough? I don't believe in committing suicide."

"I don't either, but we have to try. There's too much at stake."

"So you keep telling me," Horda muttered, scowling, "even though you won't tell me exactly why you have to get back to Commitment in such a hurry."

Michael bit his lip in frustration. "Can you drop the *Starlight* where I want it or not?" he asked.

"What if I can't?"

Michael stared at Horda for a long time. "If you can't," he said at last, "then we're screwed and you know it, so do me a favor and answer the fucking question."

"Okay, okay," Horda said, putting his hands out to pacify Michael. "Keep your hair on. Now, let me see. You want me to drop this ship not just into Commitment nearspace but here—" He stabbed a finger out at the screen. "—only 300 or so kilometers above the planet's surface. Right?"

"Right."

"And you want me to do that after a 33-light-year pinchspace jump." Horda shook his head. "The last time you pulled this stunt, you said you dropped your ships 8,000 kilometers out, not 300. And you had the benefit of military-grade AIs. The *Starlight*'s were built before you were even born, and even then they weren't state of the art. Oh, yes, and the Hammers weren't expecting visitors. They are this time."

"Listen," Michael said taking a deep breath to keep a lid on his temper. "I appreciate the positive spin you're putting on things, but can you answer the damn question? Can you put us on the drop datum, yes or no?"

"You're lucky because I've been captain of this ship for twenty-two years, and here—" Horda brought a new screen up on the holovid. "—are the results of every drop I've done in the last five years."

"Holy shit!" Michael hissed after a moment's study. "That's very, very impressive."

Horda nodded. "Yes, it is," he said looking very pleased with himself. "Better than any of your fancy milspec AIs can do, and you know why?"

"Why?"

"You space fleet guys don't spend more than a couple of years in a ship. Me? I've spent years talking to the AIs that run this ship. Oh, I know they're not people, but they might as well be. When I first took command of the *Starlight*, the navigation AI had trouble dropping us into the right system. But we worked on it together, and there are the results."

"I'll be damned."

"From what I've heard, I think you already are."

"Thanks. So you're saying you can do it?"

"As long as you accept that there's no margin for error, none at all, and that we'll all be dead if we miss the drop datum, then yes."

"Thank you."

"You remember I said that I'd miss the *Starlight*, that she was our home?"

"I do."

"It's not the ship I'll miss," Horda said, his voice soft and his eyes glittering with tears. "It's just a whole lot of metal and plasfiber. No, it's those damned AIs …" His voice choked up, and he stopped. "They're like people to me, you know?" he whispered. "No, not people … my friends."

"What can I say?"

"Nothing." Horda took a deep breath. "I'll do what I have to. You said you wanted to talk about Kalkuz?"

"I did. Look, there's no easy way to say this, but the man knows too much. I'm going to have to—"

"Stop!" Horda barked. "I don't want to know. He's your problem. You fix it. Now go."

Michael left, too wracked with guilt to say another word.

"On your feet, Mister Kalkuz," Michael said.

The man looked up. He must have sensed something was wrong. His hands shook. His face was a pasty gray. Sweat beaded on his upper lip. "Why? I've told you everything, I swear."

"Just do it."

"What do you want?" Kalkuz's voice trembled. He got to his feet with obvious reluctance.

"You'll find out."

Mitchell stepped forward and pulled out his stunner. He pointed it at Kalkuz and stunshot him in the chest. Kalkuz dropped to the deck in a twitching, moaning heap. Michael stunshot him again. He stopped moving.

"Let's go," Michael said. He waved Mitchell and Akuna to pick the man up.

Dragging Kalkuz between them, the marines followed Michael. He threaded his way along corridors and down ladders until the group reached one of the midships airlocks. Shinoda was waiting for them; she opened the inner door. "Dump him in there," she said. She looked at Michael. "Let me do this, sir."

Michael turned away and opened an emergency locker to pull out a skinsuit. "We've had that discussion," he replied. "It's my screwup, so I'll fix it."

Shinoda put her mouth to Michael's ear. "Fuck that," she whispered. "I won't let you do this on your own." She leaned past him to pull out a second skinsuit. "And don't argue with me … sir."

Michael was too demoralized to try. "Okay, okay," he muttered. A minute later, he was suited up. "All set?"

Shinoda nodded. "All set," she said.

Michael commed Horda as the two of them stepped into the airlock. The door shut behind them with a soft hiss. "We're ready."

"Roger … External door interlocks released."

Sick to his soul, Michael started the scavenge pump. In seconds the air in the lock had turned to white mist as the pressure dropped. To Michael's horror, Kalkuz's eyes opened; they were wild with fear and stared up at him until anoxia closed them forever. He knew those eyes would come back to haunt him. A lifetime later, the red light over the external door turned to green. Michael froze. He could not finish what his stupidity had started.

"Let me, sir," Shinoda muttered. She pushed Michael aside and punched the controls to open the outer airlock.

Shamed into action, Michael reached down to take hold of Kalkuz. Together he and Shinoda dragged the man's awkward mass to the door.

"On three," Shinoda said. "Stand by … one, two, three!"

Kalkuz's body vanished into the gray mist of pinch-space. Michael threw up.

Saturday, June 26, 2404, UD
New Varanasi nearspace

"All set?" Michael asked.

"All set," Captain Horda replied.

"Let's do it."

Horda nodded. Fingers flew, and he initiated the drop. Michael's world turned itself inside out. A moment later, the navigation plot stabilized.

"Aha," Captain Horda said. He pointed at the string of digits displaying the ship's position. "Read that, spacer boy, and weep. We've jumped a quadrillion kilometers, give or take a few, and we're less than a hundred klicks from the datum."

"Now *that* is very impressive," Michael said. And he meant it. For a beat-up old mership, it was extraordinary.

Horda shrugged. "Thank a great AI. And it helps that we've done the Scobie's-to-Varanasi route more times than I can remember. I swear we know every last ripple and bump in pinchspace. Anyway, that's enough self-congratulation. Let's get the sob story on its way, and then we can piss off."

"Do it," Michael said.

"Varanasi Nearspace Control," Horda said. "This is Scobie's World mership *Matrix Starlight*."

"*Matrix Starlight*, Varanasi," the voice of the duty controller said. "Go channel 42. Out."

"And good morning to you too," Horda muttered as he changed channels. "Varanasi, *Matrix Starlight* on four-two."

"*Matrix Starlight*, we do not hold a valid flight plan for your arrival, and you have dropped outside the designated drop zone."

"Sorry about that, Varanasi. We have major problems with one of our pinchspace nodes."

"Tell that to the inspectors, *Starlight*. You are in breach of Varanasi nearspace navigation regulations. Reverse vector to—"

"Negative, Varanasi."

"What do you mean 'negative', *Starlight*?" The controller sounded angry.

Michael smiled. The woman should sound angry. Ships did not make a habit of refusing to do as they were told. Her instructions had the force of law, and captains who ignored them always paid heavily.

"Regret we are unable to comply with your instructions, Varanasi," Horda said. "Have malfunction on main engines, so cannot maneuver. Am transmitting revised flight plan to you for our transit to Commitment."

"Be advised, *Starlight*. Commitment nearspace is closed."

"I can't help that. It's the only place we can get to. If we try for anywhere else, we're screwed."

"We'll pass on the flight plan, *Starlight*, but I repeat: Commitment nearspace is closed, and any unauthorized incursion risks the use of deadly force."

"Not much choice, Varanasi. Adjusting vector for Commitment now. Wish us luck."

"You'll need it, *Starlight*. And I'm still citing you for breaches of Varanasi navigation regulations. Varanasi Nearspace Control, out."

"Arrogant pricks," Horda muttered. "Right, then," he went on. "We'll jump as soon as we're on vector for Commitment. We'll be there in nineteen hours. Make the most of them. We need to get this right."

"I know," Michael replied, grim-faced. He did not need any reminders. "I'll be down in the cargo bay if you want me."

"Good luck, Michael," Horda said. "Even after what you've done to me, it's been good knowing you. I hope we can meet again someday."

"You and me both," Michael replied with some feeling. "You've got the holovid recordings? Believe me, if those Hammer sons of bitches even think something's not right, they'll make you pay."

"Don't worry," Horda said. He patted a pocket in his shipsuit. "They're safe and sound."

"I'm sorry about Kalkuz."

"Hah!" Horda snorted. "Don't be. That bastard would have screwed us; no doubt about it."

"I think he would have, but I'm still sorry the way it turned out."

"He had other choices. Anyway, you should go. If I'm to drop you where I'm supposed to, then I need to pay attention."

"See you."

Michael made his way to his lifepod. He put his head through the hatch. "Room for one more?" he asked.

"Not really," Akuna said.

"I'm coming in anyway," Michael said. He found his seat and strapped in alongside Spassky, Akuna, and Mitchell. *This is absolute fucking madness*, he thought, looking at the bulky drop shells to which they were about to entrust their lives.

He put his head back to sit out the last few minutes before they dropped. He wanted to go now. He'd had enough of the waiting, of the uncertainty, of not knowing whether Anna was still alive. He glanced at the three marines, who were anonymous behind the closed faceplates of their skinsuits, and prayed that they would all make it through.

Then it was time.

"Stand by," Horda said. "In three … dropping, now!"

In a blaze of ultraviolet radiation, the universe turned itself inside out, and *Starlight* emerged into normalspace. The Hammer response was immediate, a barrage of invective with a simple message: Jump back into pinchspace now or your ship will be blown to plasma. Michael ignored it. He was far more interested to know whether Horda had been able to do what he had promised.

Relief flooded Michael's body. Horda had done it. They were close to the drop datum.

"Downloading updated position and vector data," Horda said. "Stand by to launch pods ... launching."

At that point a great deal happened in a very short span of time.

With a series of *whumps*, explosive charges blasted four of *Starlight*'s lifepods clear of the ship, pushing them out at right angles to the ship's track and away from the planet below, radiating preprogrammed bleats for help across all the international distress frequencies, their presence advertised by blazing double-pulsed orange strobes. There was a heart-stopping pause while *Starlight*'s ponderous bulk rolled into position, then more *whumps* to punch the two lifepods holding Michael and his marines into the ship's wake, back the way she had come.

Seconds later, Shinoda's array of jury-rigged chisels sliced effortlessly through hydraulic lines, venting fluid under enormous pressure. The cargo bay's oxygen-enriched atmosphere filled with a volatile mist that hesitated for a moment, eddying and swirling. Then it detonated. The explosion blasted the cargo door away and drove the carefully assembled piles of scrap out into space. The roiling, tumbling cloud of radar-reflective confusion engulfed the fleeing lifepods. The chaos worsened as Hammer battlesat-mounted lasers seared the *Starlight*'s fabric into rolling clouds of ionized plasfiber and metal. Compartment after compartment was punctured, releasing yet more ice-loaded air and debris into space.

Deep inside the mayhem, the two lifepods trailed the *Starlight* as she drove on to her destruction. As one, engines burst into life and thin pillars of plasma erupted from their sterns to decelerate the pods to a safe speed for reentry.

Michael could do nothing except ride the lifepod out of orbit and down into Commitment's gravity well. He focused his attention on the only number that mattered: the lifepod's speed. If they hit Commitment's upper atmosphere too fast, the stress of reentry would tear their drop shells apart. "Come on, come on," he urged the pod even though the small part of his brain that stayed calm told him that he had nothing to worry about.

So intense was his focus that he missed the Hammer's first attempts to communicate with the lifepods.

"*Matrix Starlight* lifepods, Commitment, over."

When Horda finally deigned to answer, his response was a carefully crafted mélange of bullshit, misinformation, and pathos, all underscored by a torrent of invective against the fucking bastards who had taken his beloved *Starlight* away from him because now the ship he loved was doomed to die. On and on he raved, the Hammer controller's attempts to get a word in edgewise overwhelmed by the endless stream of words.

Horda was so good, Michael did not know whether to laugh or cry. He shut off the audio feed. Enjoyable though it was, what the Hammers had to say was not important. "Okay, guys," he said. "We're close, and provided the Hammers don't shoot at us"—*even the Hammers wouldn't shoot down a lifepod, would they?*—"stand by to abandon ship. Final checks. Skinsuits, drop shells, inertial nav, survival packs."

"All green, sir," came the replies. The voices were thick with apprehension.

The clock ran off the seconds, and the time arrived. Michael armed the emergency jettison mechanism and blew the airlock doors off. Explosive decompression turned the air inside the pod to a thick white mist. His skinsuit stiffened around his body against the hard vacuum. He hoped that Shinoda and her team were okay.

Michael took a deep breath and threw off his safety harness; he forced himself into the airlock, his efforts to squeeze his skinsuited body through made more difficult by the drop shell strapped to his back. "See you on the other side, guys," he said.

He pushed himself out into space and was greeted by the awful sight of the dying *Starlight*. She was finished, her hull slashed and lacerated by antiship lasers. As he watched, the first of the antiballistic missiles punched deep into her carcass; its warhead exploded, blasting a massive cloud of flame and debris outward. A second missile followed, then another, and another.

The end came fast. A missile lanced down to the *Starlight*'s core. An instant later, the ship shivered, then vanished, enveloped by a searing blue-white flash that consumed the entire hull and sent a sphere of incandescent gas into the void.

And when the gas had gone, so too had the *Starlight*.

Clear of the lifepod, Michael tumbled through the vacuum of space. Now all that mattered was survival. Shinoda and her marines either made it or they didn't, and there was not a damn thing he could do to change things.

Thanks to the hours spent in the sims, it was all very straightforward as long as he did not think too long or too often about Commitment's unforgiving surface, which was invisible in the darkness below him. A final check confirmed that the drop shell was good to go. Michael gave the go-ahead. High-pressure gas drove reagents into containers of polymer smartfoam. Foam boiled in the vacuum. Foam expanded to fill the preformed plasfiber shell. Foam wrapped itself around Michael's skinsuited body.

The foam hardened, and Michael was sitting in a crash-resistant cocoon inside a heat-resistant shield. The master AI orchestrating the process fired the solid-fuel boosters to align the shell for reentry. The deceleration kicked Michael hard in the back.

He steeled himself for the ride down and prayed that he would look like just another piece of debris from the ill-fated *Starlight* heading out of orbit for cremation in Commitment's atmosphere, a piece of junk that Hammer planetary defense would not think worth a second glance.

It was a rough ride down, worse than anything the sims had put him through. It was so rough that Michael gave up worrying about the Hammers shooting at him, worrying instead about whether his brain would disintegrate under the pressure of a relentless battering, worrying about being consumed in the ball of fire marking his fall to ground, worrying that the flimsy shell would fall apart in the face of the unbelievable punishment.

When will this ever end? he wondered.

But it did end. So slowly Michael was not even sure it was happening, the pummeling eased and the fiery trail thinned until the shell was no longer needed. The AI blew the shell off and dropped his body into a sickening free fall that ended only when the container on his back popped open. Michael came to a vicious stop as his parachute bit into air thick with cloud and rain, the AI steering him down through the murk toward a rendezvous that only it could see.

"Two hundred meters," the AI told him, "one hundred … fifty … brace … thirty, twenty, ten, brace!"

Michael smashed down through a thin canopy of trees and hit the ground with a thud. His legs absorbed the impact, and he was thrown sideways onto the rain-soaked ground. "Fuuuuck," he whispered. He flicked his visor up to let the rain fall cool and sweet on to his face, "I made it."

Seconds later, a black shape thumped into the ground only meters from where he lay, followed by three more in quick succession. *There should be one more*, Michael thought. He scrambled to his feet to strip off his skin-suit and begin the painful business of gathering in a wet parachute.

Shinoda emerged out of the gloom. "You okay?" she said.

"Sure am," Michael said. "Anyone not make it?"

"Spassky." She paused and spit on the ground. "His shell never deployed; bloody thing was a piece of garbage," she went on. "Next time I'm on Scobie's, I'm going to kill that son of a bitch Chang."

The loss of the lance corporal hit Michael hard. "The poor bastard," Michael muttered. "He must have known he wouldn't make it."

"Yeah." There was a moment's silence. "Anyway," Shinoda said, "now we need to get the hell out of here." She looked around. "First thing, chromaflage capes on and weapons checked … all green? Good. Nugget, Mitch. Start digging. Give me a 2-meter-deep hole in ten minutes or I'll kick your asses. Stick! Find everything we don't need and put it in the hole."

"Yes, sarge," Prodi said.

Shinoda turned to Michael. "You get up that hill and keep an eye out," she said. "I don't think the Hammers were too interested in us, but you never know. They might send drones to have a look."

"Yes, sergeant," Michael said. Machine pistol in hand, he shouldered his pack and set off.

Monday, June 28, 2404, UD
NRA command center, Branxton Ranges,
Commitment

General Vaas looked up when one of his personal aides led Michael in.

"Lieutenant Helfort, sir," Major Davoodi said.

"Thanks, Major," Vaas said. He stood and came around the desk to where Michael waited. "Reentry drop shells!" He shook his head. "Insane, absolutely insane."

"Not the way I planned to come back, General," Michael said as they shook hands. He thought the man looked exhausted, the lines incised over prominent cheekbones deeper than ever. But the eyes had not changed. Even when the man smiled, they stared deep into Michael's soul.

"I can't tell you how good it is to have you back, Michael," Vaas said. He put a hand on Michael's shoulder. "You got my message that Anna's alive and well?"

"I did, thank you, General. I've put in a request to join her. I think my spacer days are over."

"We'll talk about that later. The good news is that Lieutenant Colonel Anna Cheung Helfort has been a right pain in the ass. Not to me, of course. To the Hammers."

Michael blinked. "Did you just say Lieutenant Colonel?"

"A well-deserved promotion," Vaas said with a huge grin. "We've given her command of the 120th's 3rd

Battalion. That's where most of you Feds have ended up." He turned to the wall-mounted holovid screen that dominated one side of the limestone cell he called his office. "Let me show you how the war's going."

Vaas pulled up a tactical display that summarized the NRA's current tactical situation. Michael drew in a sharp breath at the sight.

"No, it's not pretty," Vaas admitted.

It wasn't. Michael didn't bother to count the Hammer units arrayed around the half million square kilometers of limestone karst the NRA called home; there were too many. "Lot of Hammer marines out there, General," he said. "That's new."

"Even the dumbest Hammer general was able to work out that Planetary Ground Defense Force troops are no match for the NRA. I've lost count of how many PGDF units we've torn apart. So Polk managed to convince the Defense Council that they had no choice but to send in the marines."

"Is it as bad as it looks?"

"If you're Jeremiah Polk sitting in your air-conditioned bunker staring at holovid screens, status boards, and tactical displays and you believe the reports you're given, then yes, it looks bad for us."

"I hear a 'but,'" Michael said.

Vass nodded. "You do. Let me see … this is MARFOR 8's area of operations. They sit across our resupply routes down from northern Maranzika, and here—" He pointed to the town of Daleel. "—is where their 8th Brigade is.

Five thousand well-trained, superbly equipped marines. Best unit in the Hammer order of battle."

"Where's the 'but,' General?"

"You remember Operation Medusa?'

Michael grimaced. "How could I forget?" he said. The Hammer's operation to take the NRA Branxton base had given him his first taste of ground combat. He'd hated it: the chaos, the dirt, the smoke, the noise, the sound of hypersonic rounds tearing the air around him, the way death lay waste to those around him, the dead so close that he could smell the metallic, coppery reek of blood hanging in the air.

"Well, as is the Hammer way, Polk had anyone even remotely responsible for Medusa's failure taken out and shot. He started with the commanding general, Baxter, and worked his way down. These guys here—" Again he pointed to the icon that marked the MARFOR 8's position. "—lost every officer above the rank of colonel."

"Shit."

"And Polk did not stop there. He even had a couple of platoon commanders shot."

"Let me guess. Polk thinks the 8th is combat-effective, whereas it's—"

"A fucking mess. The 8th's commanding general and his staff are too frightened to pass any bad news back up the line, so they don't. We have our people on the inside. They tell me that if we attacked them, they'd fold like the proverbial house of cards. And the rest of MARFOR 8 is not much better."

"What about the rest?" Michael asked.

"MARFOR 6 is probably the best of them. Of all the force elements involved in the Medusa fiasco, they performed the best, so they got off lightly. MARFOR 11's somewhere in between. But Polk's kidding himself if he thinks these assholes are a match for us."

"And Anna? What's the 120th up to?"

"They're dug in northeast of McNair, in the Velmar Mountains. They are part of 9 Brigade, and their job is to keep some of the pressure off the Branxtons. And thanks to your Anna and the rest of them, it's working. They've given the Hammers one hell of a beating. A bit too good, actually."

Michael did not like the sound of that. "Too well?"

"Yes. Thanks to that Kraa-damned peace treaty with the Feds, the Hammers were able to transfer three marine forces—MARFORS 21, 33, and 92—in from Faith; 33 and 92 were sent south, and MARFOR 21 has been deployed across the Calderon Gap to make sure our 9th Brigade doesn't pose any threat to McNair City. But what they don't know is that we've managed to get a second brigade up there. It's taken us months to do it, and now we're about to teach the new boys one hell of a lesson."

If it were possible, Michael's heart sank even more; the Hammers outnumbered the NRA three to one. "One hell of a lesson."

"Operation Caradoc," Vaas said, grim-faced. "Part of the deception plan for Juggernaut. And speaking of Juggernaut, thank Kraa you got through with the latest plans and those brevity codes. There are so many damn Hammer ships over this planet, we haven't been able to get messages in or out for the last month."

"You didn't have the latest date?" Michael asked, incredulous.

"No, we did not. We'd have been sitting on our asses twiddling our thumbs when your guys arrived, and that would not have been good."

"No, it wouldn't," he said.

"To take the Hammers' eyes off Juggernaut, we have to make them think the NRA is trying to break out of the Branxtons. We hope ... we think Operation Caradoc will distract them enough to let our people take out the antiballistic missile installations around McNair. We'll also mount attacks on the planetary defense bases at Qian and Kraneveldt, and speaking of Kraneveldt," Vaas said, turning to Michael, "they still haven't finished rebuilding after you trashed the place."

"That seems like a lifetime ago, General," Michael said, his voice soft as he recalled the way his hijacked lander's Henschel HKS-30 cannons had chewed their way through billions of dollars of Hammer hardware, with hypervelocity depleted uranium slugs stitching lines of red dots across ceramcrete aprons, the towering columns of flame-shot black smoke rising skyward, and Corporal Yazdi's adrenaline-fueled triumph as she took out another flier, only to end up in an unmarked grave on a rain-drenched hillside.

"You did well."

"Only if we can finish this. What about the marine bases?"

"We'll mount battalion-strength attacks against Besud, Amokran, and Yamaichi. Beslan Island we can't do much about; it's too hard to get to, but we will run truck bombs into its main gate and perimeter defenses. Won't achieve anything except a lot of smoke and noise, but it'll add to the confusion."

Michael put his hand up. "Hold on, General," he said. "Battalion-strength attacks against marine force bases? I'm sorry, but are you nuts?"

Vaas laughed. "Probably, but have some faith in me. They are only diversionary attacks."

"Still a huge risk."

"Not really. The NRA has a secret weapon: all the marines Polk had shot."

Michael looked skeptical. "I'm sure," he said, "that there are a lot of marines who'd happily cut Polk a new asshole, but that's because they're pissed at what he's done. They won't sit on their asses if the NRA attacks them."

"No, they won't, but we don't need them to. All we need is panic and indecision, and thanks to the ax that Polk hangs over the neck of every planetary defense and marine commander, believe me when I say there'll be plenty of that about."

Michael did not look convinced. "And how can you make sure of that?"

"Let me see … Take Yamaichi. The commanding officer of the marine air wing is one of ours, along with most of his staff. The man's uncle was shot after Medusa, so he didn't need much persuading to lend us a hand. And Besud will find that a large percentage of its ground-attack landers are combat-ineffective as well."

"You can do that?"

"We think so. We own the specialist unit that maintains their fire-control systems."

"What about Amokran?" Michael asked even though something told him that he would not like what Vaas was about to tell him.

"Best we could do is a couple of senior officers in one of their combat logistics battalions. We've given Amokran to Anna's battalion …"

"Oh, no," Michael whispered.

"… and that's because the 3rd is one of the best units we have in the NRA, so I'm afraid they get the hardest targets."

"Can't argue with success, I suppose," Michael said, his voice stiff.

"No, you can't, not in this business. Now, what's next? Oh, yes. What to do with you. Now, I know this will come as a disappointment, but I don't want you joining the 3rd."

Michael blinked; he had assumed the transfer was just a formality. "It doesn't bother me that Anna's the battalion commander, sir."

"I'm sure it doesn't, but it's not that. I have other plans for you. Others may have taken the Juggernaut idea and run with it, but it was your idea, just as what comes next was your idea. Sending you out there," Vaas said, waving an arm, "in the field with an assault rifle in your hand would be a criminal waste of your talents ..."

Maybe so, General, Michael thought, keeping his face wooden, *but that means I'll be spending far too much time away from Anna.*

"... and before you tear my head off, I know what you're thinking. Anna, right?"

"Was I that obvious, sir?"

Vaas chuckled. "I'm psychic, remember?"

"So everyone keeps telling me."

"Look, seeing her won't be a problem, because I want you to be my roving eyes and ears, someone who's not part of the formal command structure, my Devil's advocate, if you like."

"If that's what you want, sir."

"It is. You'll be ... let me see ... yes, let's call you my aide-de-camp."

"Sounds good, sir," Michael said. "For a moment I thought you wanted to bury me somewhere in the bowels of encomm."

"Not a chance, my boy. So trust me, you'll find plenty of opportunities to visit the Velmars."

"Thank you, General."

"Right. The final run-through for Juggernaut is this afternoon. I'd like you to sit in on it, tell me what you think."

"I'll be there, and thanks for giving me so much time. I know how busy you are."

"It's nothing less than you deserve. Anything else?"

"Colonel Hartspring?"

"Now there's a coincidence." Vaas's eyes narrowed. "I haven't forgotten what Hartspring tried to do to you and Anna, and I don't suppose you have either."

"How can I? He hasn't given up."

"What's the scumbag up to now?"

"He runs a unit called Team Victor. It's a personal project of the chief councillor's. When I was in jail waiting to be … you know … a message was smuggled in to tell me Team Victor was planning to kidnap Anna and hand her over to DocSec, and … you can guess the rest."

"That's answered a few questions we had," Vaas said. He shook his head, his face a puzzled frown. "But why would they do that?"

"Polk didn't think I was hurting enough, so he decided to make me really suffer. which I did," Michael whispered.

"Kraa!" Vaas hissed. "They are something, those people. But why are you telling me?"

"I'm going to hunt Hartspring down and kill him, and when I've done that, I'm going after Polk. The time's not yet right, but when it is, I want your word that you'll let me do what I have to do."

"Ah," Vaas said, "that's a tough one. You are one of my best assets, Michael. What if I still need you?"

Michael shrugged his shoulders. "I'll go anyway," he said, "but I'd feel a lot better if you said okay."

"What the hell, fine." Vaas sighed. "When the time's right, come and ask. Unless you are the only thing that stands between us and total defeat, I'll say yes."

Vaas's aide appeared. "General, the staff meeting?" he said.

"Yeah, sorry, Major," Vaas said. "I'll be there in a second. Michael, I have to go."

"Thanks for everything, General. I know how busy you are."

"No problem. Now, I was talking about coincidences, so I think you'll enjoy this." Vaas tossed a small packet to Michael. "One last thing: The next time I see you, I want you in NRA uniform. Is that understood?"

"Yes, sir."

Tucked away in a corner of the staff canteen with a fresh mug of coffee, Michael opened the packet and spilled the contents onto the table: a handwritten note and a gold sunburst on a thin chain.

He picked up the note.

Michael,

One of the NRA's deep penetration units ran into an old friend of yours, a Colonel Hartspring, a few months ago. His unit, a composite DocSec and marine unit; we don't know what they do, blundered into one of our operations. Sadly, the bastards managed to fight their way clear. Hartspring was lucky to get out alive, but he did lose the enclosed in the process. The unit's commander knew about you and Hartspring. He thought the sunburst would look better around your neck, so here it is.

We might have missed him this time, but trust me, his day will come.

Never forget.

Vaas

PS: If that sunburst's not around your neck next time we meet, I will kick your ass.

Michael rolled the sunburst between his fingers. "Oh, yes, Colonel Hartspring," he said under his breath, "your day will come, and that's my promise to you." The pain and suffering the man had promised Anna drove a wave of white-hot anger through his body; fists clenched, he drove his fingers into his palms so hard that the nails drew blood. He took a deep breath to steady himself as he put the sunburst onto the chain and around his neck.

He finished his coffee and set off to find Shinoda to tell her that that he would not be going with her to join the 120th.

The conference room was set with rows of seats arrayed in half circles around a small table and, off to one side, a lectern. As usual, Michael arrived early and slipped unnoticed into a seat at the back.

Slowly the place filled up. Michael checked the face of each new arrival, looking for anyone he knew. But every face was a stranger's except that of Major Davoodi, Vaas's aide, and they'd met that morning for the first time. He'd expected to see Captain Adrissa and the rest of the Fed spacers on her staff, but they were nowhere to be seen.

Strange, he thought. *I wonder where they are.*

Two minutes after the flow of arrivals had slowed to a trickle and then stopped, Davoodi called the gathering to attention as Vaas bustled in, followed by his new chief of staff and two more officers, one of whom he did recognize: Colonel, no, make that Brigadier General Pedersen, Vaas's intelligence chief. As the rest of the brass took their seats at the table, Vaas remained standing, his eyes scanning the room.

Michael's heart sank as he spotted Major Davoodi cutting a path right to him.

"The general would like you down front, Lieutenant," Davoodi whispered.

Oh, damn, Michael thought as he followed the man to where Vaas waited. Davoodi motioned for him to stand alongside the general. "Don't move," Vaas said with a smile.

Michael stood there, baffled.

Vaas turned to look at the assembled officers. "In a moment," he said, "we will start the briefing for what I sincerely hope will be the final battle sim for the NRA's operations in support of Juggernaut. But before we do, I have a presentation to make. All of you here know this man—" To Michael's acute embarrassment, Vaas put his arm around his shoulders. "—if only by reputation. Now, the lieutenant will be pleased to know that I will not prolong his agony much longer, but I do have to say that the Revivalist movement and its military arm, the New Revolutionary Army, owe him an enormous debt of gratitude, a debt we will never be able to repay. But what we can do is make some small recognition of the contribution he has made to our cause, a contribution made in the face of great risk and suffering." Vaas nodded to Davoodi, who stepped forward and handed the general a small box.

Please, no, Michael thought. *I don't want a damn medal; it wouldn't be right.*

"Michael Wallace Helfort," Vaas went on, lifting his voice to fill the room. "By order of the Resistance Council, you are hereby promoted to the rank of colonel in the New Revolutionary Army, effective immediately."

Michael's mouth sagged open as Vaas pinned the eagles to the lapels of his shipsuit and shook his hand. "Congratulations," he said; he leaned forward, and his voice dropped to a whisper. "Call me a misogynistic old Hammer, but we can't have a man outranked by his wife, can we?"

"Er, no," Michael mumbled, more embarrassed than he had ever been, "and thank you, sir."

"Nothing to thank me for," Vaas said. "You earned those eagles." He turned to the crowd. "Colonel Helfort, NRA," he declared, and the room erupted in a storm of applause and cheers that rapidly settled into a rhythmic chant of "N-R-A, N-R-A, N-R-A …"

Vaas let things run for a minute, then lifted his arms to call a halt. "Now, go back to your seat," he said to Michael. "I want you to say nothing and do less. Just listen and watch. I'll hear what you think once the sim is over, okay?"

"Sir."

Vaas turned to address the room. "Time to get down to business," he continued, "but before I do, let me just say one thing. Operation Juggernaut is our last and best chance to take the fight to McNair City, and it is up to each one of you to do whatever it takes to make the operation the success it has to be even if that means sacrificing your life, because we cannot live under the Hammer of Kraa any longer."

A murmur ran through the room; angry or excited, Michael could not say. Whatever it was, he knew Vaas would get what he was asking for.

"Now," Vaas went on, "General Pedersen will run us through the latest intelligence. Once she's done, we'll start."

The disembodied voice of one of the umpires triggered a flood of noise as the ENCOMM staff in command of the NRA forces for the exercise stood down. "End of exercise," he said.

Michael stretched to try to ease the kinks out of his back. He was exhausted. And he had to go talk with Vaas once the hot wash-up was over; that could take hours. He knew Vaas. The man could be up half the night. He sighed. Vaas might be able to get by on four hours of sleep a night, but he couldn't.

"… all of which are relatively minor issues, General, and therefore easily fixed. The only significant weakness I can see is your ability to talk to the task force commander as the operation progresses. As things stand, you will have to rely on the brevity codes I brought in, and even though they are pretty comprehensive, Murphy's Law says one of you will want to say something that's not in the code book."

Vaas nodded. "Anything more we can we do?" he asked.

"No, sir," Michael said. "Not as long as the Hammers dominate nearspace. As fast as you put microsats up, they will hack them down. They're soft targets, and there'll be no shortage of Hammer ships to deal with them."

Vaas sighed. "You're right, of course. We've looked at the problem every which way, and we've end up chasing our tails. We'll have to live with it, I'm afraid."

"I think so, General … though I do have an idea."

"Oh?"

"It'll be chaos out there—"

"That is the general idea," Vaas said with a smile.

"—so can we exploit that to get close to the Hammer brass? We know from experience that they are very top-down, even more so now after all the heads Polk has chopped off. The guys responsible for nearspace defense won't break wind unless some fat-assed flag officer says it's okay."

"That's true."

"So why not add to the chaos by taking out some—hell, make that all—of the key Hammer commanders. Then nobody will know who to ask for orders. They'll be paralyzed. Not forever, of course, but every minute counts."

Vaas shook his head. "Nice idea and we did look at it, but it's a nonstarter, I'm afraid. The minute the shit hits the fan, those bastards will be locked up in their bunkers underneath 10 meters of ceramcrete."

"Not necessarily," Michael said. "Do we know who the commanders are?"

Vaas leaned forward. The fatigue had gone. His eyes sparkled. "You've spotted something, haven't you?"

"Not sure yet, sir."

"We'll see. Now, Hammer commanders. Let me see … yes, we know everyone in the Hammer chain of command, from Polk right down to the commanders of every unit and ship, provided they haven't been shot since we last checked, of course," he added.

"Do you know where they live, where they work, what their routines are?"

"Wait!" Vaas snapped. He jumped to his feet and made for the door. "Major Davoodi!" he shouted. "I want to see General Pedersen. And see if you can find Colonel Tekin. I want him too. Yes, now!"

Vaas dropped back in to his seat. "I think I see what you're driving at, and this is why I promoted you. Ah, good," he said when Pedersen and Tekin appeared. "That was fast."

"Here to serve, General Vaas," Pedersen replied, rubbing a hand across her stubble-cut hair, a faint smile crinkling the skin around her piercing blue eyes.

Vaas chuckled. "Colonel Helfort, this Colonel Tekin," he said, "head of our Hammer personnel intelligence division."

"Michael Helfort. Good to meet you," Michael said, shaking hands with Tekin, a thin, cadaverous man. Like most of the staffers who worked in ENCOMM, the yellowing skin of his face was drawn tight by overwork, stress, and fatigue. Michael wondered when the man had last had a day off.

"So what's up?" Pedersen asked.

"We'll come to that, but first Colonel Helfort has some questions."

"Thank you, sir," Michael said. "How much do we know about the Hammer's senior commanders?"

"What specifically?" Pedersen asked.

"Who they are, what their routines are, where they live, where they work, what watches they stand if they do."

Pedersen turned to Tekin. "I think you'd better take this one, Colonel."

"Wait one … Okay, this org chart," Tekin said when the holovid screen came to life, "shows the entire chain of command: Polk and the Defense Council at the top obviously, the commander in chief, Admiral Kerouac, and then something new, the Commitment Unified Military Command—UNMILCOMM for short; it's the equivalent of our ENCOMM—and on down through the various force elements assigned to the defense of Commitment. And we know pretty much all there is to know about most of them. Not all, of course. We don't have unlimited resources, and given how often Polk purges these people, it can be hard to keep up sometimes."

"So," Michael said, "if I nominated, say, thirty officers in key positions, you would have good up-to-date information on them?"

"Pick one."

"Hmmm, let me see … Let's try Colonel Cerutti, commander of the 455th Antiballistic Missile Regiment."

"Stand by … This is everything we know about the man," Tekin said.

"Wah," Michael whispered. The level of detail impressed him. Even the fact that Cerutti kept a mistress in an apartment ten minutes from his headquarters outside McNair was a matter of record. "So if I said I wanted, say, thirty officers like Cerutti, you could give me that?"

"I could," Tekin said firmly. "More if you wanted."

"This is my suggestion, General," Michael said, turning to Vaas. "Your covert ops people tell you how many two-man hit teams they can put in the field before J-Day. Colonel Tekin selects that many targets; they'd have to be key members of the Hammer chain of command and vulnerable as well. When that's done, the teams are briefed and sent out. Time is short, so they'd have to wing it a bit. That'll make it risky and reduce the chances of success, but hit the right people at the right time and the payback could be huge."

Vaas sat for a moment, then nodded. "General Pedersen?" he said.

"I like it, sir," she said, "and we are good at this sort of operation. Like Colonel Helfort says, hit the right people at the right time and we should be able to turn chaos into catastrophe."

"I agree," Vaas said. He turned to Michael. "Colonel Helfort. I'm putting you in charge of the planning this operation. Colonel Tekin, you'll be part of the team, of course. Major Davoodi!" Vaas bellowed.

The aide stuck his head in. "Sir?"

"Where's Major Gidisu?"

"Wait one, sir … She's on her way back from Yankee-34. She'll be here in two hours."

Michael suppressed a sigh. There would be no sleep for him tonight.

"Get a message to her: 'Expedite return. Need to see you soonest.' Got that?"

"Yes, sir."

"Okay," Vaas said after Davoodi vanished, "are we missing anything? No? Over to you, Colonel Helfort. I'll send Gidisu to join you when I've finished with her."

"We'll get started, sir."

Major Gidisu sat back. She was a small woman, chunkily built, with dark eyes and skin so black that it looked blue in the harsh light of the meeting room. "It's a great idea," she said at last, "and I wish we'd thought of it weeks ago. I'll be pushed to get people out there to do this what with Juggernaut so close now, but let me get back to you."

"How soon?"

"08:00 tomorrow."

"I'll have a list of targets by the same time," Tekin said.

"We'll meet then," Michael said. "Well, I think that's all we can do for now. See you tomorrow."

Tekin nodded. "We'll be here," he said.

All but overwhelmed by exhaustion, Michael set off to find his rack. Getting a few hours' sleep was all he cared about right now. But he hadn't gone more than a few meters when a familiar voice brought him to a halt.

"As I live and breathe, it's Lieutenant Helfort."

Michael swung around. "Well I'll be! Matti Bienefelt!"

"The very same," the woman said. She swept Michael into a bone-crushing embrace he could not resist; Bienefelt outmassed him by a good fifty kilos, not one gram of which was fat. She was huge. "It's good to see you again," she said, pushing him back. "And what the hell are those?" she asked, stabbing a finger at one of the eagles on his lapels.

"You know perfectly well, you insolent dog. I should have you flogged, chief."

Bienefelt laughed, a rumbling belly laugh that shook her enormous frame. "I'd like to see you try, and it's Warrant Officer Bienefelt now, by the way."

"Another undeserved promotion."

"For sure. Speaking of undeserved promotions, I hear your Anna is now a lieutenant colonel."

"Watch it," Michael said with a grin. "But I worry about that woman."

'Well, don't. She's a legend."

"So I'm told. How's the arm?"

Bienefelt held up the stump of her left arm. "This?" she said. "It's fine. Itches like hell sometimes, and I can still feel the fingers, which is weird. They keep promising me a biomech hand, but I think I'll be dead by the time one turns up."

"You still with the 246th?"

"Yup. We don't do much, though a Hammer special forces team had a go at us a week ago. We sent them home wishing they hadn't."

"Where's the rest of the team?"

"Chief Chua and Petty Officer Lim are still running their microfabs; everyone else has joined the 3rd."

"Anna's battalion? What, all of them?"

"Every last one."

"Captain Adrissa too?"

"Yup. She's a grunt. Battalion tried to promote her to lance corporal. She told them to fuck off."

"Captain of a heavy cruiser one day, private soldier the next." Michael shook his head. "Hard to believe."

"You should. Anyway, there are so many Feds in the 3rd, it's unofficially called the Federal Battalion. The Hammers loathe them. Anyway, I've got to get back. Nobody will tell us what's going on, but there's something in the wind; I know it."

"You don't—" Michael said before common sense stopped him.

Bienefelt looked at him, a faint smile on her face. "You know, don't you?" She put up a hand the size of a tray to preempt Michael's response. "Don't say anything. We'll find out what when we're supposed to."

"Thanks, Matti. You look after yourself."

"I will. You too, okay?"

"I promise."

Tuesday, June 29, 2404, UD
NRA command center, Branxton Ranges, Commitment

"That's a damn shame," Major Gidisu said as she frowned at the long list of names Colonel Tekin had put up on the holovid. "I've scraped every barrel and shaken every tree, and the best I can do is sixty-five teams."

"So few," Michael said. "Sorry, Major," he went on, seeing the scowl on Gidisu's face. "I'm not being critical.

211

I know how stretched you are with Juggernaut. It's just a shame we couldn't target everyone on Colonel Tekin's list."

"It is," Gidisu said, "and trust me, I'm sending anyone who can walk and shoot a gun at the same time. I don't have anyone left."

"Your list," Michael said to Tekin, "it's been prioritized?"

Tekin nodded. "Yes. The people the Hammers can least afford to lose are at the top."

"Do you need any more from us?"

"No," Gidisu said. "My ops planners will brief the teams; they'll go out tonight."

Michael frowned. "The Hammers have the Branxtons well and truly sewn up. How will you get everyone out?"

Gidisu smiled. "With the help of our friends inside the Hammer marines, usually in one of their truckbots. And if that's not enough, we'll do what we always do: resort to bribery, corruption, and threats of extreme violence. Works every time. Chief Councillor Polk likes to talk about the ring of steel he has put around the Branxtons, but that's bullshit Hammer propaganda. His ring has more holes in it than a colander. We can always get our people out."

"What about DocSec?"

"After what they've done to the marines, it's a brave DocSec trooper who tries to stop a marine convoy to run identity checks. DocSec won't try unless they're in company strength, and even then they prefer not to."

"It gets better," Tekin said. "Last week we airlifted an entire battalion and all their gear from the Branxtons to the Velmar Mountains, 3,000 kilometers, and all courtesy of a friendly heavy lifter crew from the 662nd Marine Squadron."

"How the hell did you do that?"

"The lifter was returning to Yamaichi for routine maintenance. It made an unscheduled landing to check out a problem, and our guys hopped aboard. Of course, it never went anywhere near Yamaichi. The lifter's now tucked away in a cave in the Velmars. You never know; it might come in handy one day."

Michael shook his head at the brass-balled audacity of it all. "General Vaas said the marines weren't all they seemed to be."

"They're not," Tekin said, "though the general is more positive than we are about the marines' combat ability. Even after all they've been through, they'll still fight if they have to."

"We'll see," Michael said. "Anyway, I think we're done here. Can you keep me posted, Major?"

"Of course."

Michael followed Tekin and Gidisu out and headed for the ENCOMM canteen. He grabbed a bowl of gruel—the only way to describe the green-brown slop produced by the antiquated foodbots—and a mug of coffee and found a quiet corner to eat a belated breakfast. It was a struggle, and not because the food was so indifferent.

No, it was something more basic, and it took him a while to work it out.

When he did, it was simple: Right now, he had nothing to do. Of course, Vaas being Vaas, there'd be another task for him, but only when the general found the time to dig one out.

Until then, he would be just another staff officer hanging around headquarters doing not much while others risked their lives.

Screw that, he thought. Back on Terranova, he had promised to hunt down and kill Polk and Hartspring, and that was what he would do. But Anna came first; more than anything he wanted to be with her again, if only for an hour.

And he knew exactly what he needed to do to get away from ENCOMM and back to her. Dumping the remains of his meal in the recycling, he set off to find General Vaas.

"Sergeant Shinoda. Can you spare a minute?"

"Sure." Shinoda stopped; her eyes narrowed. "Hey, wait! Are those colonel's eagles?"

Michael's face flushed with embarrassment. "Uh, yeah, they are."

"Colonel Helfort … hmmm," Shinoda said. "It does have a certain ring to it."

"Yeah, yeah," Michael muttered; he knew he'd never hear the last of it. "I know you were planning to join the 3rd of the 120th, but I need you for a mission."

"Best I hear what it is, then."

"You will, but before I do, you need to know that it's risky, so you can say no."

"Okay."

Shinoda stood silent for a while when Michael had finished. "Hell of a mission," she said, "not that I'm all that much the wiser."

"Sorry about that," Michael said, "but that's just the way things are. Think of it as taking the long way around to get to the 3rd."

"So why me? There must be hundreds of people here who could do the job."

"Two reasons. First, I'd trust you with my life. Can't say that about anyone else."

"Okay."

"Second, after we've rubbed in a bit of dirt and put on crappy clothes, we look like Hammers. Unlike most of the Feds around here; they're all too big."

Shinoda sighed. "Makes sense," she said, "so I suppose I'll have to say yes. I don't like pissing off colonels."

"Thanks."

"But you'll need to explain to me where we'll get our IDs from. Without them, we won't last an hour out there."

"I don't know how, but Major Gidisu says she can organize them. They'll be good for only forty-eight hours, but that should be enough."

Shinoda nodded. "I'll tell the team I'm not going with them."

Michael put a datastick into Shinoda's hand. "Ask one of the guys to make sure my wife gets this," he said. "I'll be in ENCOMM reading intelligence reports if you need me."

Two hours later, Michael shut down the workstation he'd been allocated by Major Davoodi—an antique holovid atop a battered plasfiber desk tucked away in a laser-cut alcove away from ENCOMM's barely controlled chaos—and sat back. The strength of the NRA's intelligence networks was impressive. Some of the reports he'd read had come from senior sources, some inside the Hammer military and others inside DocSec. *None of them are patriots,* Michael decided, turning to the next report. *They're just rats leaving a sinking ship, and nobody should forget it.*

A voice broke Michael's concentration. It was Davoodi; he put down a welcome mug of coffee. "Thought you might like a brew."

"You're a mind reader, Major," Michael said gratefully. "I've just read the reports on those poor Hammer bastards in the 288th. They must regret the day they decided to mutiny."

"They won't have long to regret anything." Davoodi's face was grim. "We've just got word that DocSec is planning to execute the ringleaders tomorrow."

"They don't waste time, do they?"

Davoodi laughed, a short, bitter laugh without the slightest trace of humor. "They convened an investigating tribunal, mustered what was left of the regiment, found them all guilty, sentenced some to be shot and the rest to the mass driver mines on the Moons of Hell … and that all took less than five minutes."

Michael broke the silence that followed. "But it is significant … that even the Hammer marines have had enough, I mean."

"You're right. People like Polk don't seem to understand that you can't go on beating people forever. In the end, they will fight back."

"And they are, which is good for us, I guess."

"It is. And it's not just the marines. The riots on Faith have flared up again, only this time they've spread to Ksedicja and Cascadia. With a little help from Revivalist agents provocateurs," he added with an evil grin.

"I'd say the Hammers made a big mistake transferring MARFOR 21 back to Commitment. The guy in charge of security on Faith—"

"General Killian."

"Yes, Killian; he must be really pissed."

Davoodi nodded. "That's what we hear, not that complaining is doing him any good. Even though the transfer of MARFOR 21 to Commitment left him dangerously understrength, we don't think he'll get his marines back no matter how stretched planetary defense and DocSec are. All Polk cares about is keeping us bottled up here."

"He's right about that," Michael said. "Once the NRA takes McNair, it's game over, and he knows it."

"Here's hoping," Davoodi said, raising his coffee, "and here's to Juggernaut. The beginning of the end."

Michael raised his mug in response. "To Juggernaut," he echoed. "The beginning of the end."

Wednesday, June 30, 2404, UD
Branxton Base, Commitment

"I'm letting you do this only because we need all the help we can get making Juggernaut a success. You do know that, Colonel Helfort?"

"I understand, General," Michael said with a smile.

Vaas shook his head in mock despair and patted Michael on the back. "Just don't mess it up, that's all. And stay on Tactical Alfa. J-Day might change, and it's critical that you don't go early."

"Yes, sir."

"You must be Shinoda," Vaas said when the sergeant appeared. "Good to meet you," he added. "Now, your job is to keep this man safe and well, and if there's a choice between getting out alive and completing the mission, then getting out alive takes precedence. Is that clearly understood?"

"Understood, sir," Shinoda replied.

"Good luck, Colonel," Vaas said as he turned to leave.

"What was all that about?" she asked as they watched Vaas walk away.

Michael sighed. "He didn't want me to do this, so I had to lean on him a bit. It turns out I have a talent for emotional blackmail."

Shinoda shook her head. "Obviously," she said. "Come on; we should go, col—ah, husband."

"Fall in behind me, woman," Michael said.

"Why are Hammer men such pigs?" Shinoda grumbled sotto voce as they set off.

Shinoda looked around with ill-concealed disapproval as they emerged from the maglev station onto what the maps said was Gwalia's Grand Plaza. "What a total shithole," she said.

Michael had to agree. *Grand Plaza, my ass*, he thought. Dominated by an ornate temple to the Hammer of Kraa, it was a tired and dirty town square much like thousands of others across the Hammer Worlds, he supposed. And there were an awful lot of DocSec personnel around. He swallowed hard. The sooner they were out of the place, the better.

Michael spotted a battered mobibot off to one side of the plaza, its green paint barely visible under what looked like a century's worth of mud, dust, and dents. "There," he said.

"Nothing but the best when you work for you know who," Shinoda whispered.

"I don't care as long as the damn thing works."

And it did, surprisingly well for something that looked like it belonged on the scrap heap, humming softly as it sped out of Gwalia down the main highway northeast to Martinsen.

Ten minutes later, Michael slowed the mobibot. "Bit of history coming up," he said, "on the right in a couple of klicks."

"What history?"

"Gwalia planetary ground defense base ... what's left of it. I crashed the *Red River* into the place," Michael said, his voice matter-of-fact, "More than half a million tons of perfectly good dreadnought moving very, very fast. Needless to say, it was completely trashed. Here we are—holy fuck!"

Michael had seen holovids of the Gwalia base both before and after the *Red River* had come calling, but the sheer scale of the destruction his attack had inflicted still took his breath away. Even now, many months later and with reconstruction work well under way, the place was a wasteland of flame-scarred ceramcrete studded everywhere with the shattered remains of buildings and wrecked aircraft bulldozed into sad heaps.

"You did this?" Shinoda whispered as the devastated remnants of Gwalia rolled past.

"Yup. Taught the Hammers a lesson they won't forget in a hurry, that's for sure."

"I'm not surprised the bastards want to get their hands on you."

Then the base was gone. Nothing was said for a long time.

Eventually a sign appeared. Gwalia County Park, it read. Michael found the turnoff. Another twenty minutes saw them in the park, a sprawling well-forested reserve dissected by creeks feeding into the Jerzic River, which flowed westward to the sea north of McNair. To the east, lay the enormous bulk of the Velmar Mountains. Like the Branxtons, they were a single expanse of limestone lifted into a high plateau that dominated the horizon.

And somewhere in all that vastness were Anna and her battalion. Michael forced himself not to think about her.

The briefing they had been given by Gidisu's people had said the park was busy only at weekends, and so it proved to be. For a good hour they cruised its network of narrow lanes, methodically working their way over to the eastern boundary in the process. They did not see another soul.

"I think that's enough, and that'll do nicely," Shinoda said finally. She pointed to a small picnic area that was set back from the road. "Park up over there."

Michael eased the mobibot off the road. He stopped out of sight of any passersby and under the canopy of a massive fig tree. He climbed out and stretched to ease the stiffness from his back. He looked around. "Doesn't look like anyone's been here for a while," he said.

"It's as good as we'll get." She looked around to get her bearings. "Okay," she went on, pointing to the east. "The Jerzic River's half a klick that way with the missile base another five after that—Down!" she hissed as, without any warning, she hurled herself at Michael and knocked him to the ground. "Make it look real," she whispered.

"What the—"

Whatever Michael was about to say was lost as Shinoda's lips clamped down onto his. He was too surprised by the sheer speed and ferocity of Shinoda's attack to put up anything more than token resistance, resistance that vanished altogether when his senses were overwhelmed by the warmth and scent of her body, his tongue flicking out to meet hers.

Shinoda lifted her head only a fraction but enough to break the kiss. "I know we have history, and I know I said to make it real," she whispered, her breath warm and sweet on his face, "but don't get carried away, spacer boy."

"Like to tell me what you're doing?" Michael whispered back.

"Drone, you idi—sir."

Shinoda didn't have to say it. Michael did feel like an idiot. He could hear the steady, thrumming resonance of engines. A minute later a drone shot overhead and disappeared into the distance.

Pinned to the ground, Michael waited for Shinoda to let him go, something she appeared reluctant to do. Finally she rolled off him and onto her back. She lay there, staring up into the dense mass of greenery that hung over their heads. "Pity about that," she said.

"Pity about what?"

"Lieutenant Colonel Anna Cheung Helfort, that's what."

"Ah," was Michael's only response. He did not trust himself to say any more. He was on very thin ice, and he knew it.

"Come on,' Shinoda said. She scrambled to her feet. "We should move out."

"We should. Think that thing saw us?"

"No. The new Hammer recon drones are a problem, but that version's not," Shinoda replied with a dismissive wave. "That was a KSD-31: no down-facing radar, limited ESM capability, and fitted with infrared and optical sensors only. And one of these—" She pointed at the massive fig tree. "—is as good as cover gets … well, short of a couple of meters of ceramcrete, that is. Right, sir," Shinoda went on, all businesslike, as if the events of a few moments earlier had never happened. "Get geared up and we'll move out. And triple-check your chromaflage. There'll be surveillance drones around, and we can't rely on them all being second-rate KSD-31s."

"Yes, sergeant."

Binoculars to their eyes, Michael and Shinoda lay under their chromaflage capes back from the crest of a ridge that ran parallel to the western boundary of Gwalia Missile Defense Base. The late afternoon sun burned hot on their backs.

The base was huge, laid out in a broad rectangle. It was studded with hexagonal ceramcrete structures that supported armored cupolas. Below each one was a quadruple Goshawk antiballistic missile launcher. The perimeter was secured by three razor-wire fences. They ran in parallel and were studded with posts cluttered with arrays of motion sensors and holocams. A road ran outside the wire, connecting a series of small blockhouses and laser batteries. Beyond the road, the ground had been scraped back to dirt for a good 500 meters. Michael didn't need binoculars to know what the signs set in the ground every 50 meters said. The skull and crossbones symbol that headed each one was enough to tell him that the entire area was thick with mines.

In the center of the base was the command center. It was a brutal building, squat and ugly, built of ceramcrete with massive recessed blastproof doors and topped with an enormous dome that protected the phased array radar installation, its seamless skin blindingly white in the morning sun.

Michael shifted his binoculars onto the only thing that mattered to him and Shinoda: the road connecting the command center to the base's main gate, a substantial installation in its own right, protected from attack by a chicane and flanked by dragon's teeth; the approach was covered by blockhouses.

From the gate ran the one and only road that linked Gwalia Missile Defense Base to the town of Gwalia. It was down that road that Colonel Farrah would drive when Juggernaut happened.

"Seen enough?" Michael murmured. They had been watching for hours now, and he was beginning to get nervous.

"I have," Shinoda said. "Let's get out of here before we get spotted. I'd like to drive the road before it gets dark, and we should make sure the good colonel is still shacked up with his wife in town."

By the time sunset arrived—always a protracted business on Commitment thanks to its forty-nine-hour day—Shinoda had picked a spot along the road linking the missile base to Gwalia. It was a tight curve forced on the engineers by a massive limestone reef that reared up out of flat ground.

Shinoda scuffed the toe of one boot through the dust. "Thanks to all this damn rock, there's not as much vegetation as I'd like," she said, "but this'll do." She looked up and down the road. "I'll put you there—" She pointed to where a small outcrop poked its way clear of a thin fringe of bushes. "—while I go just here, alongside this boulder. Our man will come from that way." She pointed down the road toward Gwalia. "He'll slow right down for the bend, and that's when we'll hit him. We'll put three of the remote holocams down the road. That way we can make absolutely sure we get a positive identification. Be a shame to shoot up the wrong car. And we'll put the fourth camera back toward the base to make sure we don't get blindsided by someone coming from that direction. All make sense?"

"Yup."

"Our primary egress will be 50 meters back from and parallel to the road, back where we'll stash the bot. If that's compromised, we'll follow the reef away from the road up to high ground, drop down to the Jerzic River, turn north, and try to reach the NRA positions in the Velmars on foot."

"Long walk."

"But doable. So what I want you to do is this: First, put the base-side holocam in position. Let me see; yes, you'll need to run fiber back to here. We can't risk a radio datalink, and we can't get direct line of sight, so a laser link is out."

"Roger that."

"And point the bloody thing the right way, toward the base. Got that?"

"Sergeant," Michael protested, "I'm not a complete idiot."

"Maybe not, but you'd be surprised how many times it happens. Now, when you've done that, I'd like you to check our secondary escape route. Try to find a way through that will allow us to move fast; look for good ambush sites and ways to get up onto the reef if we have to. Got all that?"

"Yeah. How far do I go?"

"Let me see ... Five klicks should be enough. But I want you back here no later than four hours from now and watch your chromaflage discipline. There'll be drones for sure. Any questions?"

"Just one. While I'm doing that, where will you be? And I'm not being a smart-ass, sergeant, in case you were wondering. I just want to know where to find you."

"Fair enough. I'll set up the cameras, run the fiber back here, and bring up our supplies in case we have to abandon the bot. And when we've done all that, we'll find somewhere to hole up."

Wednesday, July 7, 2404, UD
Gwalia Road, Commitment

Shinoda commed Michael. "Just received the final go code from ENCOMM," she said. "J-Hour is confirmed for 04:00 Universal. So let me see; yes, that's just on dusk local time."

Finally, Michael thought. *Finally, the beginning of what I really hope will be the end.* He cycled through each of the holocams in turn. "About time," he replied.

"Any sign of life?"

"There's still nothing moving." The road was empty in both directions and had been since the last changeover of the base's watch keepers. *Shit!* Michael thought with a twinge of panic. *We've missed something important, very important.* "I think we might have a snag, sergeant," he said.

"A snag?"

"As soon as the shit hits the fan, the missile base will to go from OPSTAT-4 to OPSTAT-5, and our man will come tearing down the road, right?"

"Which is why we're both here, sir," Shinoda said. She sounded irritated.

"But we haven't seen the base go to OPSTAT-5, have we?"

227

"Not while we've been here, no. Why does that matter?"

"OPSTAT-5 is the same as our general quarters," Michael said, "and that means all the Hammers not on watch have to get back to base to do whatever they do when they're at general quarters. So when Juggernaut kicks off—"

"I get it, I get it!' Shinoda said, cutting him off. "We'll not only see Colonel Farrah, we'll have every man and his fucking dog coming down the road at us. How could I have missed that?"

"Doesn't matter. Question is what we do now."

Shinoda went quiet for a moment. "I know what General Vaas said," she said softly, "but I think we should do what we came to do."

"But the road will be thick with truckloads of PGDF troopers," he said. "I know what Vaas would say."

"So do I, but we're here to take out Farrah, and we can do that no matter how many trucks there are. What happens after that …" Shinoda's voice slid into an uneasy silence.

"It's suicide," Michael said.

"Shit happens. But General Vaas isn't here, so it's your call. If you tell me to abort, we'll abort."

We should abort, Michael thought. *We'll never get away alive.*

He took a deep breath. "No," he said even though he knew he had almost certainly signed their death warrants. "We'll stay. We can't walk away from this, not now."

"I agree," Shinoda said. "Now, let me see ... Yeah, we need to change things to give us a decent chance of getting away. I'm coming to you."

A fleeting ripple shimmered its way toward him. Shinoda eased herself down beside him. "Right," she said. "I'll watch the holovids. When Farrah appears, I'll take him from here. You get back to the base of the reef. See that boulder?"

"The one sticking out of the reef with the trees in front?"

"Yup. Dig in there. You'll flank any PGDF brave enough to try and rush me. These are not frontline troops, so they'll almost certainly fall back to the other side of the road when we hit them. The moment I've dealt with Farrah, we need to pull back along the reef. If we can do that before the Hammers get their shit together, we might just make it."

"Not back to the bot?"

"No. The ground's way too open, and more than likely there'll be more truckbots coming up the road. And remember, when I move, you go too. No heroics; just run like hell. Clear?"

"Yes, sergeant."

"Well, what are you waiting for? Go!"

Michael was dug in beneath the overhang of a massive boulder. He stared out down the road, a thin ribbon of silver-gray in the evening light that lanced down between towering thunderheads, harbingers of yet another storm.

"Stand by." Shinoda's voice came as a shock, so intense was his concentration. "One truck. Let it go."

"Let it go, roger."

The vehicle tore past, tires squealing and scrubbing as it hit the corner so fast that Michael thought it might roll over. Somehow it stayed upright. It left the corner and accelerated hard toward the base, giving Michael a clear view of the PGDF troopers packed into the back. They were all in combat gear and carried assault rifles. *No, not all,* he thought. *One of them has a KAF-08 machine gun upright between his legs.*

His heart sank. What he'd seen wasn't a bunch of seat polishers, people who spent their time tweaking missiles or buried in bunkers staring at tactical displays, punching buttons. No, they were security troops. They might not be marines, but they would know what they were doing.

"Vehicles inbound … stand by … okay," Shinoda said. "I have a red mobibot … Yes, image scan confirms that's our man. Oh, shit. He's got two trucks right behind him. Okay, here's the plan. Open fire when I do. Put a long burst into the target, then shift your fire to the lead truck. Don't let it get too close to us."

"One burst on the target, then shift to the lead truck, roger."

Michael wiped the sweat from his hands, then tightened his grip on the battered assault rifle and peered down the road through the stabilized optical sight.

"Yes," Michael hissed when Colonel Farrah's red mobibot appeared. The man was clearly visible through the plasglass windshield. He was talking animatedly to the three other occupants of the bot. "Bad day to ask for a lift from the boss, boys," he whispered.

The moment the mobibot slowed into the curve, Shinoda opened fire. Michael followed suit an instant later. The windshield disintegrated into a maelstrom of shattered plasglass, but the mobibot kept coming despite the hail of hypersonic rounds tearing it apart. Then its snout bobbed as the emergency brakes bit. It slid to a stop in a screech of tortured tires, a smoking, shredded shambles, the bodies of the men inside thrown forward in bloody ruins.

Michael shifted fire. He settled his optical sight on the cab of the oncoming truckbot. Its sole occupant stared open-mouthed at the carnage ahead. Michael squeezed the trigger and put two rounds into the man's face, dropped his aim to put a long burst into the engine compartment, and emptied the last of his magazine into the camouflaged cover over the truck bed. The truckbot wobbled and swayed before it too shuddered to a halt, but not before its nose had rammed into the bullet-ridden wreck of Colonel Farrah's mobibot and shunted it another 20 meters down the road.

Michael changed magazines and returned to the attack. A blizzard of fire flayed the truck and anyone stupid enough to try to get to his side of the road. But the Hammers were getting their act together. A significant amount of fire was already coming his way, and now the heavy chatter of machine gun fire joined the assault rifles. Rounds smashed at the rocks around him. Razor-sharp fragments of rock spalled off the rocks around him, stinging and burning when they hit his arms and face. The noise and confusion grew. Microgrenades arced across the road and exploded with ear-splitting cracks that filled the air with dust and the acrid smell of high explosive.

The mobibot's microfusion plant blew, followed an instant later by the truck's; the two blue-white balls of light and fire hurled debris in all directions. The concussion was so violent that it picked Michael up and threw him bodily backward; he was left stunned and deafened.

For a moment there was a silence. The respite did not last. The Hammers resumed their attack with full fury.

With an effort, Michael forced his brain back to work. He swore under his breath as he watched the second truck screech to a halt. Troopers spilled out of the back. Michael sent a hail of fire into them, chasing the men off the road into cover. But it was hopeless; there were simply too many of them, and they knew what they were doing. Under cover of heavy suppressing fire, Michael could see one group working its way left past the wreckage of the mobibot; a second was moving to his right. *They're flanking us,* he said to himself. *Come on, Sergeant Shinoda; it's time to move.*

Shinoda had been listening; she stopped firing. Michael put a single sustained burst into the Hammers, then squirmed and rolled away He scrambled to his feet and ran around the base of the reef to where Shinoda waited. He shot past her. "Go!" he shouted over the noise as he led the way along the path he had scouted earlier. The volume of fire thrown at them dropped off as they moved away from the road.

A Hammer drone arrived and settled into orbit overhead. Within seconds, hostile fire flayed the air around them and microgrenades ripped ground and vegetation apart. Michael flinched as a wayward round tore at his hair and a second seared an agonizing path across his left shoulder, the pain short-lived as his neuronics dumped neural blockers and painkillers into his system.

"Bastards saw us," Shinoda yelled.

"No kidding," Michael muttered. He forced his body to run harder. Now he jinked and swerved around rocks and trees. Shredded leaves and branches rained down on his head as the volume of fire intensified.

"Dumb fucks are letting that drone get way too low," Shinoda shouted. "We can take it, but we'll only get one chance, so make it count."

"Got it," Michael said. The drone was impossible to miss; its 4-meter wingspan and chunky body orbited barely 200 meters overhead.

"On three ... one, two, three!"

Michael skidded to a stop. He swung his rifle up, struggling to keep it steady with only one arm. His sight locked onto the drone, and he pulled the trigger the instant the red aiming point settled, his burst joining Shinoda's. Their rounds smashed home even as the controller sent the drone rocketing skyward. "Fuck it," Michael said. "We've miss—"

They hadn't missed. With a sharp crack, the drone's microfusion plant lost containment in an eye-searingly bright ball of blue-white light that bleached all the color and contrast out of the bush around him.

"Nice shooting," Shinoda said. "Now go!"

Michael needed no encouragement. The Hammers would have more drones backed up by ground-attack landers on the way, and they'd almost certainly put a blocking force ahead of them. On he ran; his mouth gaped wide open as he fought to feed air to lungs that screamed in protest. All that mattered was to keep moving. If there were drones overhead, if the Hammers were getting close, if he was being shot at, he neither knew nor cared. Shinoda led the way now; her pace was relentless, and Michael knew he had to keep up with her. She was all that kept him moving. If he fell back, he was finished.

Without warning, the ground only meters ahead of them vanished beneath a hail of destruction that shattered everything in their path. Their headlong rush to safety came to an abrupt halt as they scrambled for cover.

"Lander—" Shinoda shouted before the howling roar of a light attack lander swamped the rest of her words. The blast from its main engines ripped the air apart over their heads. Its huge black bulk banked and climbed away under full power to clear the reef, its starboard wingtip so close that Michael felt he could almost reach out and touch it. "We're trapped," Shinoda went on once the lander had gone. "If we keep moving, they'll spot us."

"So what do we do?"

"Best we can do is go to ground," Shinoda said. She turned to head for the tumbled mass of boulders that fringed the base of the rock reef. "Come on; this way."

"That'll work?" Michael asked with a frown.

"I doubt it, but I can't think of anything better. Here," she said. She squeezed herself into a narrow fissure between two huge rocks. "This will do."

"So what's the plan?" Michael said as he followed her in, wriggling and pushing. The crack was tight. He had to roll onto his side to keep his injured shoulder off the rock wall, praying as he went that none of the Hammers had seen them vanish.

"Hopefully they don't know we're here," Shinoda said, gasping for air, "but if they do, then we'll just have to take as many of them with us as we can."

"That's one hell of a plan," Michael whispered. He lay facedown in the dust to let his legs and lungs recover. With an effort, he lifted his head to look around. Shinoda had picked well. A massive boulder protected them. It lay propped against the rock wall, leaving a clear space a couple of meters wide.

Shinoda had wormed her way over to a second split in the rock and worked her way into it. She pulled back. "Too small to get through," she called over her shoulder, "but a great firing position."

Which means, Michael thought, *our only way out is the way we came in.*

They were trapped. This was the end. There had to be at least forty PGDF troopers in those first two trucks. Even allowing for casualties, he and Shinoda were badly outnumbered, and that was before reinforcements turned up. As they would. And when they did, it was only a matter of time before they were overwhelmed.

Shinoda rolled over and sat up. Her shoulders heaved. "Fuck me dead," she muttered, "I never want to do that again." She turned. "We'll—oh, crap," she whispered when she saw the blood-drenched mess that was Michael's left shoulder. "When did that happen?" she asked.

"A while ago," Michael said, "but it's not as bad as it looks."

"Let me see," Shinoda said. She crouched down, knife in hand, and sliced the arm of his shirt open. "Hmm, you're right; it's nothing too serious. I'll get foam and a field dressing on it," she went on, rummaging through her pack.

"Shiiiit!" Michael hissed through clenched teeth as the woundfoam seared its way into the wound. "Hey, watch it! That stuff hurts."

Shinoda took no notice of Michael's protests. She secured the dressing and patted him on the cheek. "That'll do for now," she said. "Okay, pay attention. You cover left, I'll cover right, and remember: Let your chromaflage and this baby—" She patted the rock. "—do the work. Move as little as possible and let me know if anyone looks like he's going to cause us problems. And do not open fire until I tell you to, understood?"

"Got it."

Michael ignored his shoulder. Thanks to the drugs his neuronics had dumped into his system, it no longer hurt, but it was stiffening fast; his arm was now all but useless. He dragged himself back to the lip of the narrow cleft they had used to get in. He adjusted his chromaflage cape until only a slit for his eyes remained open and raised his head one millimeter at a time to look outside. He scanned the ground for any signs of the Hammers. There were none visible through the scrappy mix of trees and stunted bushes that fell away down the shallow slope in front of their position. He shunted his neuronics vision processor down into the infrared to check the deepening shadows thrown by the last of the evening light. Still nothing.

He eased back a fraction. "All clear here," he whispered.

"And this side. Keep watching."

"Roger,' Michael said, resuming his scan. Shinoda did not need to tell him what it all meant. Either the Hammers had pulled back or they were leaving the lander to—

With no warning, Michael's world exploded. He was galvanized back under cover as cannon shells pulverized the rock. The air turned into a maelstrom of noise and dust. Fragments of rock tore at the arms he had thrown over his head. And then it was quiet. The only sound was the ringing in his ears.

He turned. Shinoda was shouting; he struggled to make sense of her words. "… they'll come for us now," she was saying, "but only open fire when I tell you to. And switch your neuronics on. They know where we are now."

"Yes, sergeant," he croaked, his mouth and throat choked with dust. *This is not good*, he thought when he saw what was headed their way. The men were visible because their chromaflage discipline was so poor. Michael's finger twitched on the trigger of his assault rifle in nervous anticipation. After a while, he stopped counting the number of Hammers working their way forward; all that mattered now was that there were a lot of them. And there'd be many more he couldn't see.

"Stand by," Shinoda said. "You take the group moving across to your left. Stand by—now!"

Michael opened fire. His first rounds hit a trooper in the head as he belly crawled forward; the man slumped facedown onto the ground. Michael shifted aim, dropped another shape, and was moving to his third when retribution arrived, a withering barrage of machine gun fire and microgrenades that forced him back, horribly aware of how bad their tactical situation was. They were pinned down, and it was only a matter of time before one of the Hammers got lucky and dropped a microgrenade down his throat. He tried not to think what that would do to him and Shinoda.

He failed.

But until then, he vowed, he'd take as many of the Hammers as he could. He pushed his rifle over the lip of the entrance and loosed a few rounds at random. That provoked another storm of bullets and microgrenades that forced him back again. "We have to move," he shouted over the steady tap-tap of Shinoda's rifle.

"No kidding, Einstein," Shinoda shouted back. "But where the fuck to?"

"I was hoping you'd tell me," Michael muttered. Since it was only a matter of time before the Hammers got lucky anyway, he decided to not to worry about all the crap they were sending his way. He ignored the incoming fire and pushed himself back up so he could work his rifle along the lines of advancing men. "You scumsuckers!" he shouted. He dropped a Hammer, then another. "We're not dead yet!"

His abuse sparked off another furious response. The air in front of Michael's position filled with bullets and the black shapes of microgrenades. One headed right for him, and time slowed to a crawl. He watched in horrified fascination as the grenade grew bigger, a gray blur against the evening sky.

Exactly what provoked Michael to do what he did, he would never know, but without a moment's thought he burst out of cover. That was what he tried to do, but his left arm refused to play along. He ended up half rolling, half staggering down the short, dusty slope in front of the boulder only a heartbeat before the microgrenade flew over his head. It buried itself in the loose dirt and exploded with a shattering crack.

It was the dirt that saved him. It absorbed the microgrenade's lethal gift of shrapnel. That and the blast; it blasted a ball of dust outward, forcing the Hammers to fire blind. Bullets plucked at Michael's body as he wriggled and squirmed to get away in a frantic, floundering scramble toward a fragmentary image lodged in his memory, the image of an opening between two boulders somewhere in the confusion to his left.

His hand felt the hole before he saw it; without a second's thought, he rammed his body into the opening, chased into safety by wayward bullets. One, its energy almost spent ricocheting off rock, slashed his forehead open. The cut sent blood curtaining down across his face, hot and sticky. He rolled into the back wall of the hole and lay there, wiping the blood out of his eyes.

Shinoda popped into his neuronics. "Where the fuck did you go?" she said, her voice overlaid by the methodical double tap of her rifle.

"Five meters to your right, I think," Michael said. He wormed his way around to peer out of the hole. "Had to move; a Hammer grenade had my name on it."

"I'm not sure what they're up to," Shinoda said. "They seem to have fallen back …"

Now that Shinoda mentioned it, Michael realized that nobody was shooting at him anymore.

"… which means they're regrouping. I think they'll bring the lander in to give us another dose of cannon fire." Michael swore under his breath; for an instant he had allowed himself to think the Hammers might have had enough. "Then they'll move in again."

"Can we move?"

"No point. They'll have us covered."

"Shit."

"Shit is right. Keep your head down until the lander's gone, then just do the best you can."

"Will do." Michael checked Shinoda's biostats. "You okay?" he asked. "Your blood pressure's a bit low."

"Losing a shitload of blood does that to you. Bastards got me in the right arm. But I'll be fine. I've got wound-foam and a dressing on it. Brace yourself. I think I see the lander, and the son of a bitch is coming right for us."

Michael slithered to the back of his hole and curled himself into a ball. He tried not to think what even a single 30-millleter hypersonic cannon shell would do to his body. Then the attack was on them, and Michael's world dissolved into more noise and dust and pain as a rock splinters sliced into him. And when he thought it could get no worse, the air turned a blinding white. An instant later, the ground rammed him bodily upward— he swore the rock he was huddled up against moved as well—and then there was silence, a strange, flat quiet broken only by the skittering of pebbles falling around him. "Sergeant! What—"

Something hard, something unseen, something silent smashed into him and battered his body into unconsciousness.

"Colonel, come on. Wake up, Colonel! Hey! Come on."

Colonel? Michael wondered. *What colonel?*

"Talk to me, you overpromoted asswipe."

Overpromoted asswipe? Michael thought. *That does it.* With an effort, he forced his blood-encrusted eyes open and looked up into Shinoda's face. "I'm going to have you court-martialed for insolence," he rasped.

Shinoda pulled Michael upright and pushed a water tube into his mouth. "Be my guest," she said with a lop-sided grin, "but what makes you think we're going to live long enough?"

"How long was I out?"

"Couple of minutes."

"What the hell just happened?"

"Juggernaut, that's what. I think the good guys just took out Gwalia."

"Gwalia?" Michael frowned. He shook his head to try to clear the mush from his brain. "But the missile base wasn't on the target list. It's too far north to be a priority."

"Maybe Admiral Moussawi changed his mind about that. Anyway, I don't give a rat's ass. Whatever it was, it didn't do the bad guys any favors."

"They're gone?"

"Not gone, dead. I don't think they'll bother us any-more. Anyway, it's time we moved on. Can you stand?"

"Get me free of this damn hole and I will."

Michael's mouth dropped open when he saw the damage the blast had done. In every direction, the sparse vegetation had been stripped. The ground was littered with shattered trunks and shrubs piled in haphazard heaps along the foot of the reef wall. A body lay wrapped around a tree stump. More were scattered across the dirt. "What the hell," he whispered, awestruck by the devastation.

"No time for sightseeing," Shinoda said. She pulled Michael to his feet. He stood, swaying and unsteady. "The Hammers will be mighty pissed by all this, and I don't want to be here when they arrive to see what the hell just happened."

"Wait one," Michael said. He pointed to an object, a white splash in his neuronics-boosted infrared vision, something hot against the cool of the ground. "There; what's that?"

"Does it matter? We do need to go."

"Bear with me, sergeant. I've a got a bad feeling about this."

"Five minutes."

"Two will be plenty." Michael walked over to where the object lay. It was a jagged piece of flame-seared metal. He tried to lift it; it refused to move. "Shit, that is heavy," he said. "Ceramsteel armor, I'd say."

Shinoda frowned. "Ceramsteel armor?" she said. "Where the hell did that come from?"

"A warship, I think." Michael straightened up and scanned the area around the piece of armor. "There," he said. He set off through the debris. He stopped alongside a second piece of metal. "Damn them all to hell," he said softly a moment later.

"What's up?"

"See those?" Michael pointed to a meter-square cluster of holes punched into the metal fragment. "Those are pinchspace vortex generator ports."

"So?"

"Hammer ports are hexagonal; ours are circular.'

"Oh!" Shinoda breathed in sharply. "One of ours?"

"From the size of the array, I'd say a deepspace heavy cruiser. Fucking Hammer bastards. Have a quick look around. It'd be good to identify her if we can."

"Here," Shinoda called out a minute later. She waved Michael over.

"What … Oh, no," Michael said when he spotted the distinctive shape of a skinsuited body. "Who is it?"

Shinoda bent down to turn the body over. Michael was thankful that the helmet visor was so scorched and scarred that he could not see the face. "Chief Petty Officer … N … g … u … Nguyen," she said, reading the name woven into the suit with some difficulty. "Poor bastard. Let me see if I can access the ID. Okay, she was Chief Petty Officer Maddi Nguyen, female, thirty-seven years old, posted to the *Recognizant* two years ago."

Michael's head snapped up in disbelief. "Did you say *Recognizant*?"

"I did."

Michael shook his head in despair. "*Recognizant* was Admiral Moussawi's ship." He took a deep breath to fight back a sudden rush of anger. "Let's go, sergeant. There's nothing more we can do for any of them."

They set off without another word, a pair of smoke-blackened, blood-soaked wrecks. *What a sight we must be*, Michael thought. *And how will we stay out of the Hammer's hands? We'll be lucky to get ten klicks …*

He stopped. "Sergeant, hold on."

Shinoda looked around. "What's up?" she asked.

"Look at the blast pattern," Michael said. "The way the trees are lying, I'd say the *Recognizant* blew up somewhere to the northwest and was close to the ground when she did. That means the reef will have deflected some of the blast wave. Our mobibot was in a gully. It might still be there."

"There's only one way to find out," Shinoda said. "Let's go see."

The approaches to Gwalia were a sprawling master class in mindless devastation; the town itself was not much better.

"This'll teach the bastards to fuck with us," was all Shinoda said as they were waved through a DocSec security point without so much as a cursory ID check. They rolled on through the Grand Plaza. It was a rubble- and rubbish-strewn wasteland lit with clusters of arc lights. The temple to the might and power of the Hammer of Kraa had been reduced to a mound of debris, and everywhere emergency services teams were crawling over the ruins looking for survivors. Michael felt like cheering at the sight.

Just past the edge of the town, the mobibot came to a stop behind a line of mobibots drawn up at another DocSec checkpoint. The troopers were visible only as black cutouts against their mobibots' headlights.

"Looking for looters?" Michael said.

"I reckon," Shinoda said. "Some people can't help themselves. Hey, what's happening?"

"I don't believe it," Michael said.

Three DocSec troopers were laying into the occupants of the first bot with boots and truncheons. It was a merciless attack. Deep inside Michael something snapped. "Screw this," he snarled. He reached for his rifle with his good arm and climbed out of the bot. He tucked the butt of the rifle under his armpit. *I hope those DocSec pigs don't fight back*, he thought. *We'd have trouble dealing with a bunch of schoolkids.* "You coming?" he asked Shinoda.

"Just try to stop me," the sergeant replied.

Faces stared open-mouthed at the two blood-soaked apparitions. Michael and Shinoda walked down the line of bots to where the DocSec troopers were kicking the life out of the three people on the ground.

"Hey, assholes!" Michael shouted. He lifted the barrel of his rifle to cover the men.

The troopers stopped and looked around. "Who the fuck are you?" one of them snarled.

"We're NRA," Michael said, his voice flat, "and you're dead."

The troopers reached for their pistols. They were three seconds too slow. With clinical efficiency, Michael and Shinoda shot the men. The impact toppled the troopers away and onto their backs. Shinoda walked over. She took a pistol from a dead fist. She checked each man in turn and dispatched the two who were still alive with single shots to the head.

She stood back and spit on the ground. "DocSec scum," she said flatly.

Michael turned. "Go," he shouted at the line of bots. "You weren't here, but never forget that the NRA is your best and only hope of destroying Doctrinal Security. Now go!"

For a moment nobody moved. Then, one after another, the bots accelerated away. Their occupants, wide-eyed with fear, stared back at the specters standing over the dead troopers.

Michael looked around once the last bot had disappeared. "Maybe this wasn't the smartest thing we could have done," he said. "What the hell do we do with this lot?"

"We'll dump the bodies into their bot, then put it on auto and send it to McNair," Shinoda said. "We'll be long gone by the time anybody pulls it over."

Ten backbreaking minutes later, the DocSec vehicle had been dispatched with its grisly load, though not before Michael had stripped the sunburst insignia from their collars, and they were on their way north to Martinsen.

Shinoda's plan was simple. They would head for the hills, and if DocSec tried to arrest them, they'd blow them aside and keep going. That was one hell of a plan, Michael had said: short, sharp, and simple enough for even the dumbest marine. "That'd be you, sergeant," he'd added, dodging a halfhearted kick from Shinoda.

The mobibot hummed on into the night. "You look like you've had it," Shinoda said. "I'll keep an eye on things."

Michael wanted to argue but could not. He was utterly exhausted. "I'll take over in two hours, sergeant," he said.

"Roger that."

Ten seconds later, Michael was asleep.

Thursday, July 15, 2404, UD
Sector Kilo, Velmar Mountains base,
Commitment

It would be a long time before Michael forgot the weeklong trek to safety: uphill and across rough country, with hours wasted dodging around Hammer positions or hiding from resupply convoys, foot patrols, and drones. To add to their misery, the rain set in early and heavy, and all the time his shoulder protested the abuse it was being given.

But they had made it, though Michael had no idea how. All he could remember of the last few days was a blur of pain, hunger, and exhaustion. Now he was content to sit back and nurse his shoulder—it had been cleaned, stitched, and bandaged, and the pain had subsided to a grumbling ache—as a battered buggy carried them through the tangled network of caves and tunnels that made up the NRA's Velmar base.

"Kilo-5," he said to Shinoda as the buggy slowed to a halt, its aged brakes screeching in protest. "This is us."

What a pair of old crocks, Michael thought as he looked around. He tried but failed to massage the ache out of his legs. He pointed at a doorway cut out of the rock wall under a sign that read "3/120 Bn HQ." "That's it," he said.

"No doubt about it," Shinoda said as they walked over. "I'd know that ugly scumsucker anywhere. Hey! Lance Corporal T'zavara, you useless maggot!" she shouted at the marine manning the security post.

The woman's heavily bandaged head snapped around. Her mouth sagged open when she saw who was calling her. "Sergeant Shinoda!" she said. "We weren't expecting you."

"I'm sure you weren't. Don't you NRA types stand up in front of a senior officer?"

"Senior off—"

"This is Colonel Helfort," Shinoda said.

"No, it's not. Oh, *that* Helfort. Sorry, sir," T'zavara gabbled, shooting to her feet. "I wasn't paying attention. I thought you … but now you're a … I had—"

Michael put up his hand to stop the flow of words. "Shut up, Corporal." He had to force himself to keep a straight face as T'zavara struggled to work out what was happening. "Now go tell your commanding officer that Colonel Helfort is here to see her," he said.

"Hancock!" T'zavara said, turning to the marine beside her, "what are you waiting for? Go!"

"Yes, Corporal," the man said before bolting down the passageway.

"What happened to your head?" Michael asked T'zavara while they waited.

"Shrapnel from a Hammer air burst, sir," she replied. "Nothing serious."

"The Amokran operation?"

"Yes, sir. It was a bitch."

"Lot of casualties?"

"Too many, sir. But we gave those Hammer bastards one hell of a kicking. There were a lot of them, but … I don't know, they didn't fight hard." She shook her head. "Not as hard as they used to."

Shinoda put her mouth to Michael's ear. "If you don't ask her, I will, sir," she whispered, "so get on with it."

"Ah, right," Michael mumbled, mortified that he had been so obvious. "Colonel Helfort," he said. "Did she come through okay?"

"She did, sir. The Hammers sent a special forces unit to attack battalion headquarters. It was touch and go for a while, but we kicked them back to where they came from. Don't think they'll try that stunt again in a hurry."

Sheer euphoria kicked Michael's heart into overdrive. "Good to hear," he said. "When—"

"Michael."

His head snapped around. "Anna," he said.

"You big lump," Anna sighed. "What have you done to yourself? Come with me. And you can close your mouth now, Lance Corporal T'zavara."

Michael lay back beside Anna, exhausted by the animal ferocity of their reunion. "I don't suppose I need to say how glad I am to be back," he whispered.

"I can't say I'm totally convinced, spacer boy."

Michael rolled his eyes. "Give me strength," he muttered.

"You'll need it," Anna said, "so shut up and come here."

"… and so here I am," Michael said.

Tucked away in a quiet corner of the canteen, it had taken him a good hour to finish his account of all that had happened. Leave nothing out, he had been instructed, not even the smallest detail, and he hadn't.

Anna looked at him for a long time before she pushed her bowl away and sat back. "I should hate you, you know," she said breaking the long silence that followed. "I really thought you were dead."

"I know, but … things just happened. Truth is, once Jaruzelska turned me in, I wasn't in control of things anymore.'

"It was bad enough for me." Anna's voice was soft. "I can't imagine what it was like for you."

"It wasn't the best time of my life, I'd have to say, but I'm here now, and that's all that matters."

"It is," Anna whispered; she took his hand in hers.

The silence that followed was a long one. "Hey, drink your coffee," Anna said much later, "or it'll get cold."

Michael took a sip and screwed up his face. "Ugh!" he said. "It already is."

"That's good, because my mug's empty, so you can get us both a refill."

Michael shook his head in despair. "You are so manipulative," he muttered. "I'm a wounded trooper with only one working arm. It's *you* who should get *me* a fresh brew."

Anna squeezed his hand. "You know I love you, right?" she whispered. "With all my heart and all my soul."

"Yes," Michael said with a frown, thrown by her abrupt change of tack, "I do."

"So get off your ass and get my coffee."

Michael did as he was told.

"Here you go," he said when he got back. It had been a struggle to keep the scalding hot coffee in the mugs one-handed. He sat back down and pushed Anna's across the table. "You know something?"

"What?'

"It's one of life's great mysteries," he said, taking a cautious sip from his mug, "how the locals can brew such good coffee without being able to produce decent food." He poked his bowl of gruel with a dismissive finger.

Anna laughed. "You should hear the moaning I have to put up with. It's the battalion's number one complaint."

"I'm not surprised. Listen, there's something I need to tell you."

"Sound ominous."

"Ah, yes ... well, it is, actually."

The smile slid off Anna's face. "Go on, then."

"Lance Corporal T'zavara told me a Hammer special forces unit attacked your headquarters during the Amokran operation."

"Yes, one did. But Branxton warned us that something was in the wind, so when they turned up, we were ready for them."

"T'zavara said you kicked their asses."

"Oh, we did. But it was strange."

"How strange?"

"It was out of character. It's not what the Hammers do ... Well, they might try to take out a brigade or divisional headquarters, but never a battalion."

"Anything else strike you as strange?"

Anna thought for a moment before responding. "Yes," she said, "now that you mention it, there was. Some of my guys swore there was a DocSec officer in charge, which is crap, of course. No marine unit would let one of those DocSec rats take command."

"They weren't wrong," Michael said, "but—"

Anna's face hardened. "Stop screwing me around and tell me the whole story."

"I will. I just wanted to be sure we were talking about the same unit."

"Michael!"

"The unit is called Team Victor. It's commanded by Colonel Hartspring—" Anna flinched. "—and its mission is to capture you alive, hand you over to DocSec, and then ... well, I don't need to say any more."

"But why would they do that?" Anna shook her head. "Surely they've got bigger fish to fry."

"Not in Chief Councillor Polk's mind. If the man's not insane, he's awfully close to it. He wanted me to go to my death knowing what he planned to do to you, knowing that there was not a damn thing I could do about it."

"The son of a bitch. Well, fuck Polk. Didn't work, did it? I'm here with you." Anna sat back. She looked at Michael for a moment; her eyes narrowed. "I know you, Michael Helfort, and well enough to know that there's something else you're not telling me."

Michael threw his hands up. "Okay, okay," he said. "ENCOMM told you that I'm one of Vaas's aides?"

"They did. Aide-de-camp or some such bullshit title. Too good to join us grunts down in the mud, eh?"

"No!" Michael protested. He paused. "I *am* his ADC," he went on, "but when the time's right, I'm going after Hartspring, and once I've dealt with him, Polk's next. I just wanted you to understand why."

"Dealt with him. You mean kill him, don't you?"

Michael nodded.

Anna stared at him; her eyes filled with tears. "Oh, Michael,' she said, a catch in her voice, "let it go. Forget Hartspring, forget Polk … please. The Revival and the NRA will deal with them. Do your best for Vaas and help us finish this damn war. Then we can all go home and get on with our lives."

"I can't do that," he said. "Not after what those two have done."

"You can't do that? That's it?"

"I'm sorry, but yes, it is. I love you more than I can ever say, but I have to do this. Tell me it's okay."

Anna stared at him.

The silence dragged on until Michael could not stand it anymore. "Anna," he said, "Anna, please—"

"I can't say it's okay," Anna said, "because it's not. It's crazy, it's stupid, it's dangerous—"

"But Anna!"

"—and it frightens me to death just thinking about it. After all you've been through, don't you think you've done enough, taken enough risks?" Anna rolled her eyes and sighed. "Why am I saying that? Of course you don't. Look, if going after Polk and Hartspring is what you have to do, then go ahead. Nothing I can say will stop you. Just promise—" The words caught in her throat and forced her to stop for a moment. "—that we will leave this pissant planet together when all this is over."

"I promise … and no more of that crazy marine shit from you," he added.

Anna smiled through tears. "I promise. Oh, crap! Look at the time. I have to go." She got to her feet. "My leave pass expires in … let me see, yes, in ten minutes."

"Leave pass?"

"Colonel Balaghi said he would kick my ass all the way to McNair if he saw me back in battalion headquarters before 22:00. But I do need to go. I've got a lot to do. I'll see you back at my billet, though who knows when."

"Go," Michael said. He climbed to his feet and folded Anna into a clumsy one-armed embrace. "I'll be waiting."

She kissed him, then pushed him away. "You'd better be," she murmured.

Saturday, July 17, 2404, UD
Sector Kilo, Velmar Mountains base,
Commitment

"Come on, lard ass. Colonel Balaghi and the 120th Regiment await the arrival of General Vaas's illustrious aide-de-camp."

"Piss off, you heartless woman," Michael muttered.

"I'll see you later," Anna said, pushing his head back to kiss him full on the mouth.

"Okay."

Forcing his unwilling body upright and out of the bunk, Michael groaned as the weight came onto his left arm. The medics had said his shoulder was healing well, but that didn't stop it from hurting like hell. He was soon dressed and on his way, the battered buggy rattling and banging along the tunnel to where the 120th had its headquarters.

Colonel Balaghi turned out to be a man of Michael's height and, unusually for an NRA trooper, well padded to the point of being rotund. His face was open and welcoming, with deep laughter lines etched around warm brown eyes and a mouth that smiled a lot, his teeth brilliant against mahogany skin.

Michael liked the man the instant they met.

"Welcome, Colonel Helfort," Balaghi said, crushing Michael's hand in his. "Call me Joe.'

"Michael Helfort," Michael said, doing his best to crush Balaghi's hand back and failing.

"This way. Coffee?"

"Yes, please."

Michael followed the man through the regimental command center and into a small cell-like office. He felt awkward. He had checked Balaghi's bio. The man was many years his senior and had picked up a gun to fight the Hammer before Michael was born, yet they were equals as far as the NRA was concerned.

Awkward? he thought as he took a seat. *This is downright embarrassing. I feel like a fraud.*

If any of that bothered Balaghi, it did not show.

"General Vaas said to expect you," Balaghi said once the coffee had arrived, "though I'm assuming your visit had more to do with seeing the other Colonel Helfort."

"I cannot tell a lie, Joe, so yes, it was."

Balaghi laughed, a rich, infectious laugh that had Michael laughing too. "Vaas tells me you're his new aide-de-camp."

"I am."

Balaghi leaned forward, the smile gone. "I think that's good," he said. "The NRA is getting so big, it's hard for the brass to know what's really going on sometimes. But …"

Oh, shit, Michael thought. *He thinks I'm Vaas's spy.*

"… you should understand one thing," Balaghi said, the sudden steel in his voice taking Michael by surprise. "You can go anywhere, talk to anyone about anything you like, but if there's something I should know, you must tell me. Okay?"

"I wouldn't do it any other way," Michael said, reminded again that he would have to tread carefully.

"That's good," Balaghi said, sitting back with a huge smile. "Now that the end is in sight, there are far too many politicians crawling out of the NRA's woodwork for my liking."

"You think the end is in sight?"

"I do, though it's not a done deal. We still haven't worked out how to deal with John Calverson."

"Calverson? The Teacher of Worlds?"

"Yes, him. He's the man Jeremiah Polk fears more than anyone else. Calverson snaps his fingers and his priests can have 50 million Hammers on the streets, and they wouldn't be rooting for us, I can tell you."

"And will he snap his fingers?"

"Of course. We might win this war—we will win this war—but winning the peace is another matter. Calverson knows the threat we pose to all that fundamentalist bullshit the Brethren depend on. The Word of Kraa is the single largest organization in the Worlds, and it is the most corrupt. He will fight us to a standstill to make sure it survives. He has to."

"So what are we doing about it?"

"Nothing, which is why I'm dropping the problem onto your shoulders."

"Ah, okay. I think I've just found my first assignment."

"You have. Look, the problem is this: ENCOMM is a military beast; its solutions are military solutions. The Resistance Council is a political beast, so its solutions are political."

"Why isn't the Resistance Council concerned about Calverson?"

"It's ironic. They're not concerned because of the success of Juggernaut. It delivered everything ENCOMM wanted and more. It even delivered a solution to those Kraa-damned orbital kinetics the Hammers love to drop on us."

"The mobile laser batteries, you mean?"

"Yup. We're very happy to see them, I have to tell you. We can cope with almost everything the Hammers throw at us, but not tungsten-carbide slugs spearing down out of space."

"So what's the problem?"

"ENCOMM says it can finish off Polk and his apparat-chiks quickly and effectively."

"A military solution to a military problem?"

"Exactly. And they're wrong. Calverson has to be neutralized. If he isn't, we'll still be fighting this damn war in ten years' time."

"How do we do that?"

Balaghi threw up his hands. "That's the problem," he said. "I have no idea. That's why I can't convince the brass they've got it wrong. And there's no way I can talk to anyone outside the NRA. Vaas would kick my ass if I tried."

Michael smiled; Anna had said Balaghi was sharp. She was right. "But I can?" he said.

"That's between you and Vaas."

"Leave it to me."

"Thanks. Want to hear what the 3rd's been up to?"

"Please."

"Well, they're unofficially known as the Federal Battalion since there are so many of you off-world heretic scum on its books."

"Gee, thanks," Michael said.

"You're welcome," Balaghi said with a big grin. "I prefer to call them my Shock Battalion …"

Michael winced at the images that conjured.

"… because they never, ever falter. They hit the Hammers like a bomb and keep on hitting."

"They have reason. Feds don't like the Hammers any more than the NRA does."

"That's part of it, for sure. But that woman." Balaghi shook his head. "I've never met anyone like her. She's a natural-born soldier—Kraa knows why she ever became a spacer—and she has a gift for bringing order out of chaos. Her people would follow her anywhere."

"She's a remarkable woman," Michael said, proud and appalled at one and the same time.

"That she is. She tell you about the Amokran operation?"

"No."

"Ah, well, I'm not surprised. It was a bloodbath, and that Hammer special forces unit did not help, I can tell you."

"I heard about that."

"I bet Anna didn't tell you that she killed three of the bastards with her bare hands ... well, not quite. She killed two with her pistol and one with a knife."

Michael looked at Balaghi in horror. "She didn't say anything about that," he muttered.

"Somehow I don't think the Hammers will mess with the boss of my Shock Battalion again."

I wish that were true, thought Michael.

"Now, you'll have to forgive me," Balaghi said, "but I have to go see Brigade."

"I have to get back too," Michael said, standing up, "and I need to catch up with some of the Feds before I go." They shook hands. "Good to meet you, Joe."

"Likewise. And let me know how you do with the Calverson problem."

"I will."

"Bye, Anna," Michael said, kissing her long and hard.

"Look after yourself, Michael," Anna said, holding him tight. "And no heroics, okay?'

"You're one to talk," he said, breaking the embrace with reluctance, "but no heroics. I'd better go."

"Yeah."

"You ready, sergeant?" Michael said to Shinoda, who was standing a discreet distance away.

Shinoda nodded. "Always, sir," she said, shouldering her rifle and pack.

They climbed into the buggy; with a jerk, it moved off. Michael's eyes stayed locked on the solitary figure of Anna until she was lost to view.

Michael slumped back, drained of all emotion. It wasn't just the intensity of Anna's farewell. No, even a good two hours later, it was the impact the 3rd Battalion had made on him that still resonated through every fiber of his being.

Nothing had prepared him for the brutal power of the Federal Battalion's battle cry, the air filling with the thunderous roars of 'Remember Comdur, remember Comdur, remember Comdur,' on and on until Michael's ears rang.

When the parade was over, the men and woman of the battalion were no less impressive in person. Even though he'd spent barely more than a few seconds with each one, he had been left in no doubt that their commitment to finishing the job at hand was real.

Then there was Anna. She might have been over-topped and outmassed by all but a handful of her troopers, but there was no doubting who was in command, a remarkable thing considering how many in her battalion had once been senior to her. Michael had been forced to suppress a smile at the incongruous sight of Fleet Captain, now NRA Trooper, Adrissa standing motionless in the ranks as Anna's second in command—a marine major—had reported the battalion all present and correct to her.

And Adrissa was only one of more than twenty former warship captains in the battalion.

It had been an astonishing display, one that had frightened Michael almost as much as it had impressed him. Trying not to think about how much time Anna and the Federal Battalion would spend in harm's way over the coming months, he slipped off to sleep.

Sunday, July 18, 2404, UD
ENCOMM, Branxton base

Much of the journey back to the Branxtons had been courtesy of an obliging Hammer marine warrant officer commanding a resupply convoy. Michael still found it hard to believe. He made his way to the security post outside ENCOMM.

"General Vaas wants to see you, Colonel. His office, 15:00," the trooper said once he'd checked Michael's identity.

"Thanks. I'll be there."

Michael walked down the rock-cut tunnel to the en-comm canteen, not that he wanted a bowl of its piss-poor gruel, but a coffee would be nice. Mug in hand, he searched for somewhere to sit and came to an abrupt stop, halted by the familiar sight of Admiral Jaruzelska.

"I don't believe it, sir," he said making his way over. "What on earth are you doing here?"

"Well you may ask, Take a seat, and to answer your question, I had the poor old *Iron Fist* shot out from under me. We were lucky; the crew had time to get to the landers, so here we all are."

"This is the last place I expected to see you. The last I heard, you'd been arrested."

"I was," Jaruzelska said, "but it was all bullshit. They had to drop the charges, and since Juggernaut was my baby, there was only one place I could be."

"Speaking of Juggernaut, have you heard about *Recognizant*? I was outside of Gwalia; we found some of the wreckage and a body."

"I did hear. Hell of a shame. Admiral Moussawi was one of our best. I'll miss him."

"I'm a bit out of touch, sir," Michael said after a pause. "How did Juggernaut go?"

"Better than we expected, though I hate thinking about the ships and spacers we lost. We got almost all of the landers dirtside, and although they took a bit of punishment early on, we were able to keep those bloody orbital kinetics at bay once we got our laser batteries deployed." Jaruzelska frowned. "Those orbital kinetics are nasty, and don't the Hammers just love them."

"Tell me about it, sir."

"The Hammers don't seem to care what they do to this planet of theirs. One of the ENCOMM guys told me they use tacnuke bunker busters."

"Not often. They're not very effective; the Branxtons are so huge and the limestone is hundreds of meters thick. The locals hate them, of course, and it's one thing they aren't afraid to object to. Even Polk and his thugs can't ignore such an emotional issue."

"Using nuclear weapons on your own home planet." Jaruzelska shook her head. "That is unbelievable."

"Does anyone have a feel for how the Hammers see things now?" Michael asked.

"Now, that is an interesting question," Jaruzelska replied, "and yes, the NRA does. You've got to give it to them. Their intelligence networks are superb." She paused. "There's a report you should see. What's your security clearance?" she said.

"Top Secret Gold," Michael said, pushing his NRA identity card over for Jaruzelska to check.

"That will do," the admiral said. "Come with me."

Michael sat back from the holovid screen. "That's impressive, admiral," he said, "and this man Ngaro is right when he says UNMILCOMM's assessment of Operation Juggernaut was, let me see ... yes, 'overly optimistic.'"

"He's not Chief Councillor Polk's chief of staff because he's an idiot; that's for sure."

"Look here," Michael said, his finger stabbing out at the screen, "where he says 'Operation Juggernaut has given the NRA a mobile missile and laser defense capability, a capability that will allow them to sustain offensive operations outside their Branxton and Velmar bases for the first time.' That must mean they know the NRA will attack McNair."

"Of course they do, and that's the problem with the NRA's strategy. It's all so obvious."

"What choice do they have, sir? The NRA has to take McNair if they want to get rid of Polk and his crew."

"This is now a war of attrition, Michael. The next time the NRA breaks out, all the Hammers have to do is throw everything at them, then grind them down and go on doing that until there is nothing left of the NRA but blood and dust."

Doubt clouded Michael's face. *I've never looked past Juggernaut*, he realized. *I've always assumed that taking McNair was just a matter of time.*

"And all the Hammers have to do is keep it together," Jaruzelska went on. "Don't forget that they have the resources of three industrialized worlds to draw on. That gives them more men, more armor, more missiles, more ordnance, more of everything. If they can outlast the NRA, then they win. Simple as that."

Michael shook his head. "Ngaro's not at all confident they can do that,' he said. "He says morale in the military is at an all-time low and civil unrest is becoming a serious problem."

"He can thank the Revival for that. Their agents are doing a good job of destabilizing things. Mindless vandalism, flash mobs hurling bricks and Molotov cocktails, sabotage shutting down factories, crippling transport, and disrupting power supplies, and no matter how brutally DocSec cracks down, it's not showing any signs of stopping. If the Hammers are to lose this war, then that's why."

"So we've got a chance?" Michael asked.

"Oh, yes; just not as good a chance as I would have liked."

Michael tried not to think what failure meant. "So what are your plans now, sir?"

"I'm joining your Anna's battalion along with all the other Feds ENCOMM doesn't have jobs for. We leave tomorrow."

"You're … You are kidding me, sir!" Michael said, eyes wide with surprise.

"Think I'm too old?"

"No, no, no," Michael protested. "Just seems a waste of … you know … a waste of an admiral."

"The NRA doesn't need any admirals, Michael. It needs soldiers. Besides, what else would I do? I can use a gun, I can take orders, I'm a bit old but I'm fit, and it'll be nice for someone else to do the worrying for a change."

"Fair enough, sir," Michael said, still trying to get his head around the idea of an NRA battalion stuffed with top brass playing at soldiers and commanded by an ex-lieutenant; he wondered how much more bizarre it could get. "Well, good luck with that, sir," he continued, getting to his feet. "I'm here to see General Vaas, and I've got a few things to do first, so I'd best get going."

"Off you go, but take care. We're almost there."

"I will, sir."

Vaas looked up as Michael walked in. *Oh, crap,* Michael thought when he saw the thunderous look on the man's face. *I'm about to get my ass kicked.* "You wanted to see me, sir?" he asked.

Vaas said nothing for a moment, then nodded. "Yes," he said, his voice soft. He looked at Michael for a minute; his eyes were hard and unforgiving. "Now," he went on, "did you or did you not understand my orders before you left for Gwalia?"

"Yes, sir, I did."

"But you chose not to obey them. Is that it?"

"I'm not sure I follow you, sir."

"Don't mess with me, Colonel Helfort. I ordered you not to take any unnecessary risks, but you went ahead and did anyway."

"Yes, sir," Michael said. "Sorry, sir."

Vaas threw his hands up. "Oh, for fuck's sake, sit down. I was briefed on what happened at Gwalia this morning. What the hell were you thinking?"

"Of the mission, sir."

"No, you weren't," Vaas snapped. "The only mission that matters is defeating the Hammers, not blowing the head off the Gwalia base commander. Kraa damn it! I don't need you to do low-level shit like that. You're no good to me dead, and if I cannot trust you to obey orders, you are useless. I have to be able to trust you; you must see that."

"I'm sorry, General," Michael said, and he was. Deep down he'd always known what the right decision had been; the problem was that he had been too caught up in the moment to walk away as he should have. "It won't happen again."

Vaas looked at him; after a while, he nodded. "Nobody doubts your bravery or your dedication," he said, his voice all the more damning for its absolute lack of emotion, "but I do doubt your self-discipline. I'm not giving you any more chances, Michael. Disobey an order again, no matter how dumb you think it is, and I'll bust you down to trooper. And if I do, you won't be joining the Federal Battalion. You'll be spending the rest of this Kraa-damned war on sector security. Do you understand me?"

"Yes, sir."

"When we're done here, I expect you to kick the ass of that sergeant of yours. She had her orders too, and I don't give a damn whether you overruled her or not. She knew what she had to do."

"I'll do that, sir."

"Speaking of security, you'll be getting your own close protection detail. Call me a slow learner, but Sergeant Shinoda will be in charge, and ENCOMM is giving you four troopers with the right training and experience. You are to make it quite clear to Shinoda and the rest of the team that they are to take you by the scruff of your miserable neck and drag you to safety anytime they think your life is in danger whether you want to be dragged or not, and that's not a suggestion, Colonel Helfort. That's an order, and I expect it to be obeyed to the letter. Is that understood?"

"Understood, sir," Michael said through gritted teeth.

"Good. We won't mention this lapse of yours again. Now, how is Colonel Balaghi?"

"In a word, optimistic, sir."

"That's good to know. He's a thinker, that man. Any issues I should know about?"

"One, but I'd like another couple of days to talk it through with the political affairs people over at the Resistance Council."

That got Vaas's attention. "The Resistance Council?" he said, eyebrows raised. "A bit out of our area of operations, isn't it?"

"Yes, it is, General. But as I see things, working across the boundaries is precisely what I'm supposed to do."

"Can't argue with that, but the Resistance Council can be prickly if they think the NRA is interfering in their business, so be careful."

"I will be, sir."

"Good. Let me know when you're ready to brief me."

"So is that clear?"

"As crystal, sir," Shinoda said.

"I hope so," Michael said. "I do not want another kicking like that again."

"It won't be a problem, sir. And I'll make sure the rest of the detail understands things as well."

"Who have we got?"

"Corporal Bavalek, and troopers Kleber, Mallory, and Delabi. They were all Hammer marines once, so they're competent, well trained, and experienced."

"I'll catch up with them when we move out in thirty minutes."

"Where are we off to now?"

"The Resistance Council."

Shinoda's eyebrows lifted a fraction. "Thirty minutes, Resistance Council, got it," she said. "We'll be ready."

Michael looked at Martin Ruark for a moment. The more the Resistance Council's authority on the Hammer's bizarre state-sponsored religion told him about the Word of Kraa, the more he realized how little he knew. "So," he said, choosing his words carefully, "the Teacher of Worlds has the power of life or death over everyone below him: every high prelate, every priest, every deacon, every acolyte?"

"Every last member of the Brethren," Ruark said. "They take what is called the Vow of Absolute Submission. That means there is no appeal against any decision made by Calverson. It's very simple: The Brethren obey or they die."

"What about Calverson? Who controls him?"

"In theory, his imaginary friend in the sky." Ruark pointed to the ceiling with a grimace. "But in practice, he is constrained only by the networks of mutual obligation that govern all Hammer politics. Just like any senior Hammer, Calverson has to negotiate to get what he wants, though nobody should be in any doubt that he is an immensely powerful man."

"But if he says 'jump' to the Brethren, they jump?"

"They do. And Calverson is not afraid to take Polk on, especially if he believes the Doctrine of Kraa is under threat. Remember the Salvation operation?"

"How can I forget?" Michael said. "We lost eleven ships that day."

"That was all Calverson's doing. He leaned on Polk to send a task force to clean out a breakaway Hammer sect on a pissant planet nobody cared about. And yes, it did cost you Feds eleven ships, but the Hammer fleet lost even more."

"And he can do that because it is the Word of Kraa that gives the entire apparatus of government, Polk included, its legitimacy?"

"Exactly."

"So Calverson will interpret any attack on Polk as an attack on the Word?"

"He has no choice, really," Ruark said. "The two systems, secular government and religious practice, are intertwined. One protects and nurtures the other."

"Why hasn't this problem been addressed in the planning for the attack on McNair?" he asked.

"I've tried," Ruark said with a tired frown, "and the Council has tried, but ENCOMM says it isn't necessary. Their plan is to take McNair, destroy Polk along with DocSec and the entire apparatus of government, and then move on to deal with Calverson."

"Will that work?"

"I don't think so. Calverson will see any change to the status quo as an attack on him, and he will react with all the power he can command. And it doesn't take him long to mobilize his forces. He can have the Brethren in their pulpits and on the streets telling the faithful what to do inside a day. I think … I'm absolutely convinced that Calverson's strategy will be to make the Worlds ungovernable until the status quo is restored."

"Which means putting DocSec back in charge?"

"Yes. That will never happen, of course, so we'll be facing decades of civil war until things shake themselves out. Regime change is like that."

"So how do you neutralize the man?"

Ruark took his time answering the question. "First, you suborn his deputy," he said finally, "a man called Rakesh Malfroy. He's a nasty piece of work: very ambitious and utterly ruthless. And then you kill Calverson. Malfroy takes over, and he keeps the Brethren under control until the new teacher is elected, one who is prepared to work with us."

"Can Malfroy be bought?"

"Hah!" Ruark snorted in derision. "Of course," he said. "The man's a Hammer, isn't he? He was born to sell himself to the highest bidder."

"Money or power?"

"He's almost as rich as Calverson, so money's not a big motivator. No, he wants what he hasn't got: power."

Michael frowned. "But if the NRA topples Polk and DocSec," he said, "the power Malfroy would have as Teacher of Worlds disappears. So why would he go along? He won't."

"We don't live in an ideal world."

There was a long silence while Michael digested the uncomfortable fact that solving the Calverson problem wouldn't be easy.

"So suborning Malfroy is most likely impossible," Michael said eventually.

Ruark nodded. "I'm afraid so."

"Why not kill both Calverson and Malfroy?"

"Same problem, different person. Henry Ndegwa is third in line, and he understands the game every bit as well as Calverson and Malfroy."

"Bloody hell. Help me here, Martin. How can we fix this? We need to."

"I know we do. The only solution I can think of is deceit."

"Deceit?"

"Yes. We take Calverson and Malfroy out of circulation while making it look as if they are safe and well. That neutralizes Henry Ndegwa; he won't even break wind without Calverson's say-so. Calverson and Malfroy issue a string of communiqués telling the brethren to stay firmly on the fence until the new government is in place. That gives the NRA the breathing space they need to deal with Polk and the Hammer military. Then Calverson and Malfroy, along with Ndegwa and every other senior member of the Brethren while we're at it, are made an offer they cannot refuse."

"Let me guess: cooperate or die."

"You got it."

"Shit," Michael hissed. "You don't want much."

"It's the only way."

"No wonder ENCOMM hasn't wanted to get involved," Michael said. "I don't blame them."

"Maybe not, but it needs to be done. If it isn't, then like I said, we can win the war only to lose the peace."

"I agree. So can we work up a detailed proposal? I'll only get one chance to convince Vaas, and I need to get it right."

"We can."

"Now?"

"If I must," Ruark sighed. "I hate all-nighters, but if that's what it takes. Let me go tell my boss what we're planning—he'll need to sign off when we're done—and then we'll get started."

Monday, July 19, 2404, UD
ENCOMM, Branxton base

"I've read your report," Vaas said, grim-faced, "and it was something I did not enjoy."

"It's a much bigger problem than we thought, sir."

"And even harder to resolve."

"Yes."

"Kraa damn it," Vaas muttered; Michael thought he looked exhausted. "You're sure about this?"

"Yes, sir. Calverson and Malfroy can never stop the NRA from winning the war. The peace is another matter."

"I hate to say it, but I think that's right. Leave it with me. I'll present it for discussion at the next staff meeting, and thanks, Michael. You've done a good job. This is exactly why I don't want you swanning around being shot at."

"Happy to help, General."

"Good, because I want you to ride shotgun on a trial we're doing tomorrow. Go see Major Marcovitz. She'll brief you; she knows what I want."

"Sir."

* * *

"What's the scoop, sir?" Shinoda asked as she and the rest of the security detail followed Michael into the mag-lev carriage for the long journey across the Branxtons.

"The 656th is doing trials of the first NRA-built mobile laser batteries, and General Vaas thinks the engineers are being a bit overoptimistic about how well they'll work. He wants us to make sure there's no cheating."

"Sounds good to me, sir," Shinoda said.

"Make sure you bring your helmets. There'll be a lot of orbital kinetics coming our way."

"Oh, great," Shinoda muttered.

Tuesday, September 2, 2404, UD
Federal Battalion headquarters, Velmar base

"Every one?"

"I'm afraid so, admiral," General Vaas said. "All the Juggernaut prisoners were shot yesterday by two DocSec battalions: the 154th and 352nd."

"What animal would do such a thing?" Jaruzelska whispered, her face twisted into a mask of pain. Vaas thought the woman had aged ten years in as many seconds.

"Jeremiah Polk."

"Why didn't we know?"

"I can't answer that, but I will find out. And we will find out the names of the DocSec troopers involved, and when we do, we will hunt them down, every last one."

"I hope so. And thanks for telling me."

"As the ranking Fed officer on Commitment, I thought you should know first."

"Me, the ranking Fed officer on Commitment?" Jaruzelska said with a twisted smile of pain and loss. "Not anymore, General. I'm just a trooper now."

"Ah, yes, you're right." Vaas thought for a moment. "Perhaps I should put a comm through to Colonel Helfort."

"No, let me talk to her. She should brief the battalion. If you could sit on this until then, that'd be good."

"We will."

Friday, September 17, 2404, UD
ENCOMM billets, Branxton base

Michael was beyond exhausted.

As week followed week, Vaas had thrown task after task at Michael, the pace relentless as the launch of Operation Tortoise approached. The name still made Michael smile, and it was very apt. The NRA would make its push for McNair under a missile screen exactly as the Roman Army had moved forward under its testudo of shields. And every bit as unstoppable, Michael hoped.

But Tortoise could wait. If he didn't get some sleep, he would collapse. Michael eased his aching body down onto his bunk and kicked off his boots, collapsing back with a grateful sigh. *It won't be long now*, he reassured himself as sleep claimed him.

Sleep did not have him for long. A hand reached down to drag him awake.

"What?" he mumbled.

"General Vaas wants you, sir."

Michael groaned. "You're fu—"

"Now, sir."

"Okay, okay. I'll be there in two," Michael said, cursing under his breath when he realized that he had been asleep for all of an hour. With an effort, he sat up. Forcing feet into boots, he set off for Vaas's office, pausing only to liberate a mug of coffee from the drinkbot. He wouldn't have made it otherwise.

Vaas waved him into his office. "Sit!" he said. "I'll be with you in a minute."

Michael did as he was ordered, wondering if the man ever slept. And what the hell did he want now? Michael hadn't been back in ENCOMM long enough for the bloody man to dream up a new mission, surely.

"Right," Vaas said, turning his attention back to Michael at last. "The Revival Council has finally given the go-ahead for Tortoise."

"Taken a while," Michael said. He wondered why Vaas had dragged him out of his rack to tell him the news.

"Some of our Hammer friends took longer than the Council expected to see the merits of the Revivalist cause."

"So Polk's on his own, General?"

"He will be when it becomes obvious that the Hammers might lose this war. He'll find key members of his Supreme Council have gone AWOL, along with the planetary councillors from Faith and Fortitude, and that means it's time."

Michael frowned; then it clicked. "Ah, you mean Hartspring and Polk?"

"I do. I thought I'd spare you the humiliation of going down on bended knee to beg me to let you go kill the slimeballs."

"I'm touched by your consideration, General."

Vaas grinned. "You remember the Calverson and Malfroy operation?" he asked.

"Operation Tanglevine? Of course. You asked me to keep an eye on their training."

"Which you did, I know. Anyway, I was thinking that it's as good a way as any to get you right into McNair without having your ass shot off. And that way, you'll be there before Polk sees the writing on the wall and tries to run for it."

"That sounds good, General."

"One condition. I want you to take any of your security team dumb enough to volunteer to go along. I accept that you'll always do your best to get yourself killed, but let's lower the odds a bit, shall we?"

"Yes, sir."

"So what are you waiting for? Tanglevine kicks off in forty-eight hours, so get your ass in gear!"

"Where are we off to now, sir?" Shinoda asked as the maglev accelerated away.

"Portal Zulu-36."

"Again? You like that place. Do you know what happens after that?"

"Well, that depends on you and the guys. I'm not the general's aide-de-camp anymore."

That got Shinoda's attention. "You're not?" she said. "Have you been … you know?"

"What, sacked?" Michael laughed and shook his head. "No. The general's approved my request to go take care of some private business."

"Private business? I think you'd better tell me what you're talking about, sir."

"Let me tell you about a man called Hartspring, a DocSec colonel."

Shinoda looked at Michael wide-eyed when he'd finished. "That's one hell of a story, sir," she said. "I never knew."

"No reason why you should."

"I suppose." Shinoda paused. "But I can see why you're going after him," she went on. "I'd do the same in your shoes. But what about us?"

"That's a good question. If you want to come along, then I'd be very happy about that. If not, then that's fine also. It's entirely up to you; I wouldn't blame you if you didn't, and I'm not just saying that. It really is up to you."

Shinoda thought for a moment before responding. "I need to know a bit more. This Hartspring; where is he?"

"Last report put him in McNair. General Vaas has organized me a ride in with Major Moore's 385th

Independent Company. Tell you what; why don't I comm you the order for Operation Tanglevine. That'll explain everything. Wake me up when you've finished."

Twenty minutes later, Shinoda had finished. She shook Michael awake.

"You done?" Michael said, rubbing eyes gritty and red with fatigue. "What do you reckon?"

"I'd like to think that whoever wrote that op order did it as a joke, but something tells me I'd be wrong."

"It's for real, I'm afraid."

"The unit assigned to Tanglevine, this 385th Independent Company; what do we know about them?"

"It's been handpicked. All men, of course, since the Hammers don't have women in combat roles. All ex-marines, most with special forces training. Two rifle platoons, one support and heavy weapons, a headquarters platoon, and a platoon to provide specialized communications, linguistic, and psyops support. About 120 pairs of boots all told."

"Not a hell of a lot considering what they have to do."

"General Vaas thinks the keys to success are speed and finesse, not force. He was worried that making the unit larger would just make things too unwieldy."

"How well do you know the 385th?"

"Very well. I was one of the team who picked them, and I sat in on as many of their exercises as I could. Thanks to a full-size mock-up of the High Temple complex, their training was very realistic. All in all, they're good, very good."

"Ah, now I get it," Shinoda said. "That was why we went there so often."

"It was. Sorry I was so secretive. Remember when we went over to the Resistance Council? That was where Tanglevine started, and Vaas never let me step away from it."

"And they're happy for you go along?"

"I spoke to Major Moore before we left, and yes, he's happy."

"And he'd be okay with us too?"

"Yes, but like I said, it's up to you."

"Tell you what, sir. It's a long run to Zulu-36, so let me think about it. We can talk again when we get there. If I'm in, I'll brief the guys and let you know what they decide."

"Makes sense. Now, if you don't mind, I want to catch up on my sleep."

Tuesday, September 28, 2404, UD
Portal Zulu-36, Branxton base

The approaches to Portal Zulu-36, one of the hundreds that accessed the maze of tunnels, caves, and caverns making up the NRA's Branxton base, were seething with activity. The air was heavy with tension and filled with the nervous murmur of troopers waiting to jump off, the crush made worse by the landers and missile batteries lined up nose to tail.

Michael pushed his way through to where the 385th Independent Company waited for him. "All set?" he asked the 385th's commander, Major Moore. Michael liked the man. Behind the stern, unforgiving face of the hard-bitten NRA veteran—which he was—lay a warm heart and generous spirit, a remarkable thing given the inhuman cruelty DocSec had inflicted on his family.

Moore nodded. "We are," he said, running his eye across the 385th. "ENCOMM's made a couple of minor tweaks to Tortoise, but they don't affect us."

"Pleased to hear it," Michael said, trying to ignore a sudden attack of nerves that filled his stomach with slowly churning acid, "I just want to get going."

"Me too," Moore said. "Now, I'm happy for your guys to give us a hand when we get to McNair, but you don't have to, you know."

"Here to help, Major," Michael said. "It's the least we can do."

"Thanks." Moore looked at Michael's security detail, whose members were dressed like everyone else, Michael included, in the combat fatigues of Hammer marines. "Even with their visors up you'd never know that two of them were women," he said with a grin.

"Don't tell them that." Michael chuckled. "But I still worry about them compromising the operation, you know, if we're stopped. Their IDs might say they're men, but it won't take long to disprove that."

"Shit!" Moore said. "I knew there was something I had to tell you. I got word an hour ago. DocSec has just made changes to the way their ID knowledge base works. None of our civilian IDs are any good anymore."

"They're not? But what about checkpoints? How will you get through?"

"The old-fashioned way," Moore said. He lifted his assault rifle with an evil grin. "And it's not such a problem. Our orders look genuine. Hell, they are genuine, authorized by the 273rd Transport Regiment's commanding officer himself, not that he knows that. So the marines won't be checking IDs, and those DocSec pigs aren't too keen to pull marine convoys over these days, so they won't be either. They know what happens when they try. Don't worry; we'll have no problems getting to McNair."

"I hope so," Michael said, looking around for a comm box, "but I need to check if ours are okay."

"I already have. Your IDs are screwed too. Once you're in McNair and on your own, they won't help you if DocSec pulls you over."

"Damn!" Michael grumbled.

"You'll be fine. Keep those visors down, look aggressive, and maybe DocSec will leave you alone."

Then it was time. "Move out," Moore ordered, and the 385th headed out into a rain-swept night. Michael, Shinoda, and the four members of his security detail fell in behind, the darkness flaring as NRA air-defense batteries engaged the flood of incoming Hammer kinetics.

Friday, October 1, 2404, UD
War room, offices of the Supreme Council, McNair

Admiral Kerouac cleared his throat before proceeding. "And so to sum up: Although it is still very early days, the heretics' strategy is clear: a two-pronged operation mounted from their Branxton and Velmar bases. It's an operation that relies on two things: speed and the Feds' air and missile defense assets. Its objective is McNair. Our response …"

The man looked nervous, Polk thought, as well he should. The NRA's assault was the greatest threat the Hammer of Kraa had ever faced.

"… depends on our ability to mobilize overwhelming forces to defend McNair. In the end, it is weight of numbers that will determine the outcome of this battle, and we have the numbers; the heretics do not. They have no reinforcements, no new supplies; they cannot draw on the resources of three systems as we can. They have to finish the job with the assets they started with. That's their weakness, and it will prove to be fatal. Are there any questions?"

"What makes you think we can mobilize outstanding force, admiral?" Councillor Kando asked.

"I don't understand your point," Kerouac replied. "The orders transferring … Let me see …" Kerouac said as he consulted his notes. "Yes, the orders transferring MARFORS 35, 66, 87, 66, and 46 to the McNair theater of operations went out last night as soon as the scale of the threat became apparent."

"Well, then. Let's start with MARFOR 87. It's currently tasked in support of DocSec counterinsurgency operations across South Barassia, so what in Kraa's name makes you think you can just pull them out? Did you even talk to the planetary councillor before the orders were issued?"

"No, Councillor, I did not."

"You damn well should have," Kando barked, his forefinger stabbing out at Kerouac. "The marines of MARFOR 87 are staying until the heretics are under control. And that's why I'm questioning your assumption that you can mobilize overwhelming forces."

Polk sat back as voices fueled by fear and anger engulfed the war room. Even if the marines being used to maintain order across the three Hammer worlds stayed put, he still thought the NRA could be beaten, but all of a sudden the chances were not looking as good.

It is time, Polk decided, *to bring my plans for a long and comfortable retirement forward.*

Monday, October 3, 2404, UD
Cordus-Perdan Highway, Commitment

"Shiiiiiit!" Michael hissed, burying his head as a Hammer ground-attack lander flashed overhead, trailing fire and smoke. Seconds later, it slammed into the ground barely 500 meters ahead of where the 385th waited, its enormous mass blasting debris in all directions. "That was a bit close."

"Very," Shinoda said. "Looks like our missile batter—"

Without any warning, the lander's fusion plants blew, unleashing a ball of blue-white light that seared all the darkness out of the night sky. An instant later, the shock wave hit, hammering Michael's body down into the dirt, the air filled with the awful screeching of torn metal howling past the lander.

"I don't think we have to worry about survivors," Shinoda said, looking at the pillar of smoke and flame climbing away from the shattered wreck.

"Reckon not, though—hold on, sergeant," he said as his earpiece crackled into life, "ENCOMM's on the line."

Major Moore's voice was instantly recognizable. "Corndog, this is Gridlock-One, over," he said.

"Route Alfa to your RV point is now clear. Confirm ready to move out."

"Confirmed. Gridlock-One is ready to move."

"Roger, stand by, Gridlock-One. We are still waiting for Starburst to confirm your right flank is secure."

"Request you expedite Starburst. We are behind schedule."

"Understood, Gridlock-One. Corndog, out."

Michael swore under his breath not for his own sake but for Moore's. The 385th had been held up for two hours waiting for NRA ground-attack landers to clear the way through to McNair and for Starburst—10 Brigade—to secure the high ground to the right of their line of advance. And time was the one thing Moore had very little of. For Tanglevine to succeed, he had to have Calverson and Malfroy in custody before Polk realized that the breakout from the Branxtons could not be stopped until it reached McNair.

The moment Polk did, he would pull every lever he could to stave off defeat, and that would include mobilizing Calverson and the Brethren.

It was twenty long minutes later before the 385th moved off again. The company moved fast down the long wooded foothills of the Branxtons, the path ahead cleared for them all the way down to the Oxus River by units from 10 Brigade. The sky to Michael's left was filled with a flickering light show that marked the NRA's relentless push toward McNair. The air shook with the thunder of landers wheeling overhead, the slashing screech of missiles streaking to intercept incoming Hammer attacks, and the popping bangs as laser batteries intercepted the never-ending rain of kinetics the Hammers were dropping on the advancing NRA.

Moore stopped the 385th just short of the Oxus River. A trooper ran back to where Michael and his team waited. "The major says the transport's waiting across the bridge, but we're behind schedule," the man said. "You'll need to get a move on as soon as we've cleared the road. Those truckbots are leaving in ten whether we're there or not, so don't let your people lag."

"They won't," Michael said.

The order came. The 385th stampeded for the bridge. Any pretense at concealment was abandoned in the frantic rush. Pounding along with his team, Michael prayed that the hard-pressed Hammers would be too busy to wonder why a company-size unit dressed in regulation Hammer marine combat gear and sporting the Hammers' IFF codes of the day was running away from the front line toward a line of truckbots.

Michael looked around the rain-slicked square fronting the High Temple complex. It was deserted and looked like it would stay that way. Moore's men had not wasted any time, attacking the small access door beside the massive bronze gates, the only access to the complex that opened into the Plaza of Redemption.

The door gave way, and the 385th poured through, leaving Michael at the gate. He and his troopers got busy: unboxing and launching a cluster of microdrones, then fast-fixing claymores to the complex's towering outer wall, their chromaflage shapes invisible against the lichen-splashed blocks of stone. More claymores went in an arc to protect the main gate inside and out before heavy weapons and shoulder-launched missiles were positioned ready for use.

Finally, they had done all they could.

It was not enough, of course. The temple complex was indefensible, but only if the Hammers broke the absolute taboos that prohibited vehicles from entering; even the airspace was sacred, which ruled out an air assault.

Only one unit was allowed into the complex—DocSec's 1155th Special Company—and it had to be invited in by the Teacher of Worlds. Everyone else was deemed profane and denied entry, which ruled out an old-fashioned ground assault.

If the taboos held, it was a stalemate: Hammers outside, Moore and his hostages inside. But Michael had to wonder how long all that superstitious claptrap would restrain the Polk. The man needed Calverson and the Brethren; surely he'd send in DocSec, boots, guns, and all. But until he did, Calverson would only say—appear to say, to be more accurate—what the NRA wanted him to say, which he would thanks to a Fed-supplied avatar AI, one of the best in all humanspace.

Shinoda dropped down beside him. "That's everything," she said.

Michael nodded, cycling his neuronics through the holovid feeds coming back from the microdrones. "Still quiet out there," he said. "I've checked the entire perimeter. There's nothing moving."

"I've checked the net, sir," Shinoda said. "DocSec has locked the city down. Anyone breaching the curfew will be shot."

"Why am I not surprised?"

Michael patched his neuronics into the holovid feed coming from Moore's helmet-mounted holocam. The 385th had moved fast along the colonnades that flanked the plaza, men peeling off to secure the flanks and cut the fiber-optic cables connecting the temple complex's comm hub to the outside world and others seeding the area with short-range jammers.

Inside the complex, there was no sign of life. Martin Ruark had told him that the place housed around 500 Brethren along with the same number of support staff. The latter were at home. They were forbidden to be in the complex between six at night and six in the morning.

But where was the Brethren?

Moore's men pushed through the second wall. Ahead lay the temple sanctuary. Protected by yet another wall, it hosted the massive bulk of the High Temple and the modest buildings that were home to Calverson, Malfroy, and the rest of the senior Brethren.

Something was wrong: The door beside the gate into the sanctuary was open. It should have been shut. "Cover," Moore's voice snapped in Michael's earpiece.

Michael had to stifle a laugh. A pair of Brethren, their plain brown cowls marking them out as junior acolytes, emerged from the door. Formless shapes broke away from the shadows and bundled them away.

"One, Bravo," a voice said. *Lieutenant Horta, 2 Platoon*, Michael said to himself. "I have two acolytes. They confirm Tango-One and Tango-Two are in the High Temple with the Brethren."

Michael felt for Moore. The High Temple was huge. It had more entrances than the 385th could cover, and if that wasn't bad enough, they'd have to pick their targets out of a large crowd of Brethren.

"Niner-Niner, this is One. Fallback Kilo, Fallback Kilo now!" Moore said. Directed at the entire unit, the order sent the 385th pouring through the gate into the sanctuary. Moore's men ran hard for the temple. They split into six units: four groups to cover the building's perimeter, one to secure their egress, and a snatch squad to locate and extract Calverson and Malfroy.

Tanglevine hung in the balance. Moore did not have the reserves to deal with any more complications.

"Squatter, this is One," Moore said to the snatch team. "Building secured. Go!"

The snatch team sprinted through the High Temple's imposing bronze doors, each a good 10 meters high. They stood open, spilling golden light into the night. The image from the team leader's holocam flared. Michael blinked in the light scintillating off the gold- and jewel-encrusted walls. Hundreds of voices filled the air with their chanting. The team ran down a passageway parallel to the main chamber. Arched openings every 10 meters opened onto the assembled mass of Brethren. Brethren packed the brilliantly lit space.

"One, Squatter," the leader of the snatch team said. "In position. We have eyes on Tango-One and Tango-Two. We're ready."

"One, roger ... Stand by ... go!" Moore barked a microsecond after a small explosive charge blew the building's switchboard apart. Darkness engulfed the proceedings. A brace of grenades skittered across the marble floor and popped into life, spewing gas and smoke in all directions. A volley of flashbangs followed as the snatch squad exploded into the main temple chamber.

Michael would never forget the confusion and fear on the two targets' faces, which he could see for a split second in the searing flare of the flashbangs. The men stared, open-mouthed. Then the snatch squad was on them, three to each target. They half lifted, half dragged Calverson and Malfroy off the altar steps, out the door, and into the courtyard.

"Niner-niner," Moore's voice said in Michael's ear, "Whiskey, Whiskey, Whiskey, now!"

The 385th needed no encouragement to withdraw. They ran hard. The team tasked with securing their flanks pulled back with them. *It's all going too well,* Michael thought as Moore's men passed through the gate in the second wall. Where were the Hammers? There had to be someone with enough presence of mind to find a way to get a message to the police or DocSec that the Hammer's most sacred building had just been attacked.

There was. A police drone dropped into orbit outside the walls of the temple complex. It didn't last long as a missile slashed it out of the sky. The shattered wreck tumbled out of the air, hit the ground, and exploded. The blast stripped the elaborate tiles off every roof and tossed them away in a confetti of shattered terra-cotta.

Breathing hard, Major Moore arrived back at the main gate. Boots sliding across wet pavement, he skidded to a stop where Michael and Shinoda waited.

"Great job, Major," Michael said, and he meant it. Moore and all the troopers with him stripped off, replacing their marine combat fatigues with DocSec black. Despite himself, Michael shivered at the sight.

"Long way to go yet," Moore said. "How do I look?"

"I feel like blowing your head off," Michael said.

Moore chuckled. "We can take it from here. Thanks and good luck."

"It's been an honor, Major Moore. Let's go, Sergeant Shinoda."

Monday, October 4, 2404, UD
Ludovici commercial district, McNair

They moved slowly, ducking out of sight whenever the microdrones screening their advance warned of a DocSec patrol or a passing surveillance drone. Five kilometers from the temple complex through nearly deserted streets, they reached the safe house. The office on the fringe of McNair's commercial district was a tired, decaying monument to the economic cost of the Hammer's commitment to decades of war.

Tucked away behind an abandoned cluster of reeking dumpsters, Michael scanned the area around the building. He spotted a broken crate tossed into the weed-infested remnants of a flower bed "There's the telltale," he whispered to Shinoda. The crate was red: The building had been checked by an NRA countersurveillance team some time in the last two hours and was clean.

"Looks good," Shinoda murmured. "Bavalek, Mallory, Go make sure."

The two troopers eased themselves out of cover and slid down the road to the building, shapeless blurs oozing and rippling across the cracked ceramcrete. They disappeared, one through the front doors and the other around the back.

Ten minutes later, the doorway shimmered, its frame softening for an instant. Michael waited. Precisely thirty seconds later, the same thing happened.

"We're in," Shinoda said. "Let's go."

An hour later, Michael gave a nod of satisfaction "That's it," he said. "We're online to ENCOMM. Okay, let's see what's been happening. Here we go."

The sheet of holopaper Shinoda had tacked to the wall came to life as ENCOMM's latest summary of operations appeared. The OPSUM was a complex display of icons splashed across the approaches to McNair. "Not going so well," Shinoda said, pointing to icons marking the NRA's front line. "Army Group South should have taken Perkins by now."

Michael nodded. Shinoda was right. Perkins was one of the largest planetary ground defense bases in the McNair basin. It anchored the western end of the Hammer's front line. The NRA had to take it before any full-scale assault on McNair.

"But look at this," Michael said. He pointed to the front line between McNair and the Velmars. "Army Group East is way ahead of schedule."

"Wah!" Shinoda hissed. "They've torn the Hammers apart. They've already taken Yallan."

"They have, and I can see why." Michael tapped the icons showing the positions of the Hammer units defending McNair. "The Hammers have screwed up. They've pulled forces away from the Valmars to reinforce the Branxton front. No wonder the NRA's having trouble taking Perkins."

"Which changes things."

"It does. We don't have as much time as we thought. The way things are going, Army Group East could be in McNair before the end of the month."

"Maybe, sir, but they'll have one hell of a job getting across the Oxus River. What's ENCOMM saying about Team Victor?"

"Wait one," Michael said. He drilled down though the datafeeds that summarized everything ENCOMM thought it knew about the Hammer's order of battle. "Last report I got from ENCOMM put them here in McNair, which is why we're sitting in this dump. Right; here we are … shit! Hartspring's not in McNair anymore."

"So where is the scumsucker?"

"Hold on … Okay, a data intercept put Team Victor at Cooperbridge six hours ago."

"Cooperbridge," Shinoda said, looking thoughtful. "So where's the 120th?"

Michael's finger stabbed at the display. "Here, at Yallan." He shook his head. "I'd bet my ass that Colonel Balaghi used the 3rd Battalion to take the Yallan planetary defense base. Do you believe in coincidences, sergeant?"

"No, I don't."

"Nor do I. Team Victor and Hartspring aren't sitting in Cooperbridge to do some fishing. They're there because Cooperbridge is the closest river crossing to Yallan."

"I agree." Shinoda paused to study the display. "I think we've got two choices, sir," she went on. "We can go to Hartspring in Cooperbridge, or we can stick to plan A and wait for him to come to us."

"What do you think?"

"I think we should go to him, sir. We know where he is, and we know why he's there. In a week's time?" Shinoda shrugged. "Hartspring could be anywhere."

"Rats and sinking ships?"

"You got that right," Shinoda said. "Hartspring will cut and run. It's only a matter of time."

"MARFOR 21's dug in around Cooperbridge," Michael said. "We'd have to get through them."

"If we could make it as far as Kumasi," Shinoda said, pointing to a small town 15 or so kilometers short of Cooperbridge and the Oxus River, "that'd be a start."

Michael thought the options through. Cooperbridge or McNair. Cooperbridge, he decided finally. That was where Hartspring was, Anna was across the river, and Shinoda was right. Hartspring's time was running out, and he'd know it. If the man had any sense, he'd head for the hills before the mob ripped him apart.

This is not a good time to be one of DocSec's finest, Michael thought. "Cooperbridge," he said. "I think that's our best chance."

"I agree, but first we've got to get to Kumasi."

There was an awkward silence as Michael and Shinoda digested the awkward fact that they had a serious problem on their hands. "Bloody hell," the sergeant muttered. "Why don't we just catch a fucking taxi?"

Michael stiffened. "Now there's a thought," he said, a thoughtful look on his face.

"I was joking, sir," Shinoda said with a scowl.

"Hold on … Where the hell did I put it?"

"Put what?"

"This!" Michael said, pulling a card out of his pack with a huge grin. "It's one of the cards I used on Scobie's, and it's still got over forty-five grand on it. Think that'll get us a lift to Kumasi?"

Shinoda grinned back. "I reckon."

"Let's find ourselves a truckbot and a greedy dispatcher."

"The McNair Logistics Center is the place to start. I'll get a couple of our drones over there."

Ten minutes later, the holovid feeds from the micro-drones stabilized. "Shiiiiit! It's huge," Michael said.

"It has to be. It supplies the entire Branxton front."

Michael stared at the screen. "I don't think this is an option," he said. "It's too busy, too complicated. Where would we start? And we'd have to get across town without being stopped, which won't be easy. I'm not so worried about DocSec—we know they tend to leave marines alone—but without military IDs and proper orders, we won't fool the military police."

"All of which was we why decided to wait for Hartspring in McNair," Shinoda said, glum-faced.

"Let's stew on it," Michael said. "I'd like to see if Major Moore has convinced Calverson to cooperate."

It was the work of seconds to tune into the holovid broadcast net and a few more to find what passed for a news channel. The news anchor—as always with Hammer newsvids, a blond woman groomed to within an inch of her life—filled the screen.

"… a spokesman for General Barrani said. UNMILCOMM has since confirmed that our forces are making a strategic withdrawal across the Oxus River east of the city after heavy fighting around Yallan and Cooperbridge, though they still hold Paarl and the strategically important town of Ahenkro Junction. South of the city, the heretic advance has been stopped on a line from Perkins through Lukhet Junction to Jarrenburg, again after extremely heavy fighting that inflicted what the spokesman said were unsustainable losses of men and equipment on the heretics.

"The UNMILCOMM spokesman went on to say that a counteroffensive would be launched within days but refused to confirm where the thrust of that operation would be. Our military analysts, however, remain certain that the NRA ... ah, I'm sorry, I should have said the heretic offensive north from the Branxton Ranges still remains the principal threat to the security of McNair even though there can be no doubt that the heretics are so seriously overextended that their defeat is only a matter of time."

Michael smiled; he might have imagined it of course, but he was sure a narrowing of the anchor's eyes had betrayed what she thought of that piece of Hammer self-delusion.

"Meanwhile," the woman continued, "in other news, Doctrinal Security has reported the arrest of nine citizens; they have been convicted of spreading malicious rumors that our beloved Teacher of Worlds had been kidnapped by a Revivalist suicide squad. Doctrinal Security has told us that they will be sentenced tomorrow. According to our analysts, that crime carries the death penalty. In a holovid broadcast from his residence inside the High Temple complex, our beloved Teacher of Worlds confirmed that he is quite safe and well. He went on to say that all peoples of the Worlds should remain calm and follow the instructions of the temple Brethren. Now was not the time, Teacher Calverson stressed, for Kraa-fearing citizens to rise up against the heretics. The sacred task of defeating those who dared to attack the great city of McNair should be left to our heroic soldiers, marines, and spacers, men who will gladly give their lives to secure final victory. Teacher Calverson ..."

Michael chuckled as Shinoda put her finger into her mouth and made a retching sound.

"… also expressed his absolute confidence in the leadership of Chief Councillor Polk and said that it was only a matter of time before the heretics would be destroyed and their souls condemned by the Word of Kraa to eternal damnation.

"However, a spokesman from the Office of the Chief Councillor told us that the situation at the High Temple complex was, and I quote, 'unsatisfactory.' Even when asked repeatedly what he meant by that, the spokesman refused to say. He said only that the authorities had asked that a Doctrinal Security team be allowed access to the complex to ensure the ongoing safety of the Teacher of Worlds but that Teacher Calverson had yet to respond to the request.

"In other developments, sources close to the councillor for internal security have confirmed that outbreaks of civil unrest have been reported right across the Hammer Worlds. We go now to our reporter on Faith."

"Looks like Moore has pulled it off," Michael said, switching the screen back to the tactical display.

"I'd say so, though Polk clearly smells a rat."

"He does, but until he gets his hands on Calverson, there's not a damn thing he can do about it." He paused. "So," he went on, "Kumasi. How do we get there?"

"Put the microdrone feed back up … Look at that," Shinoda said. She pointed at the frenetic activity visible all across the logistics center. "We haven't got a chance, and look outside the place. The Hammers know how important the place is, and it has the security to match. We wouldn't even get close."

"You're right," Michael said. "And they'll be clearing the roads of all nonmilitary traffic, so we can't make our own way there. I think we're screwed, sergeant. If we hijacked a flier, we'd be shot down. It's too far too walk, and I don't fancy swimming upriver."

The silence that followed was a long one, interrupted only by the arrival of Trooper Kleber, his always amiable visage split by a huge grin. "Corporal Bavalek's found an old coffeebot that works, sir," he said. "He's cleaned it up, so we'll have a brew for you any minute."

"That man's a hero," Shinoda said.

"So what's next, sir?" Kleber asked.

"No change," Michael replied. "Remain here until the Hammers have been pushed back into the city, then go find our man."

"Where is he now, sir?"

"Cooperbridge."

"Be better to hit the bastard there, sir."

Michael sighed. "That's what we think, but we're having trouble seeing how to get there."

"Easy. Use the river."

"Use the river?" Michael said, incredulous.

"Yes. UNMILCOMM uses it to ship anything that's too big to go by road. Heavy equipment, tanks, missile batteries, replacement power plants, and so on."

"But that'd be too slow, surely. Must take them days."

"No, no. The barges are just big catamarans, but they do ten, maybe fifteen klicks an hour. Doesn't sound like much, but that'll get you to Paarl and Ahenkro Junction in under a day."

"I'll be damned," Michael said, filled with sudden elation. "That still leaves us with the small problem of how we hitch a lift."

"Well, there's nothing I can do to help you there, sir …"

Crap, thought Michael. *Why is everything always so damn hard?*

"… but Delabi might. Isn't she from Nawadji?"

"Nawadji?'

"Suburb down by the docks. She—"

The concussion was savage, an ear-shattering blast that took the building and threw it side to side, knocking the three of them to the floor, ceiling tiles raining down on them, the air thick with the dirt and dust of decades. The impact was so powerful that Michael thought for a moment that the place might collapse. Coughing and sputtering, he staggered to his feet, wiping the muck out of his eyes and mouth. "What the hell was that?" he croaked.

Shinoda just shook her head. She could not speak. She stood there hacking and spitting as she tried to clear her throat and lungs.

Kleber dragged himself upright. Like Shinoda, he was doing his best to cough his lungs up. "Kraa!" he said. "That would have spoiled someone's day."

"Any idea what it was?" Michael croaked. He tried to get the microdrones back online. The datafeed was dead.

"I'll go check," Kleber said.

"I'll go make sure the rest of the team is okay," Shinoda said.

Kleber was back barely a minute later. "Looks like our guys took out the ordnance depot out at Sanz. It's the only thing out there big enough to cause an explosion like that."

Michael's mind was racing. The blast would have caused chaos right across the city; DocSec and everyone else would have their hands full. They'd be too busy to worry about a bunch of marines. He took the risk and commed Shinoda.

"Now's our chance to get down to Nawadji, sergeant."

"I agree, but best you come to the ground level."

"Why? What's up?"

"You'll see."

Michael raced down the stairs two at a time. He burst out of the stairwell, skidding to a halt. He didn't need Shinoda to tell him what had happened. One sniff did that. The air was thick with the metallic smell of fresh blood, the floor and walls drenched. "Oh, no," he said at the awful sight.

Shinoda was crouched beside a body; it lay on its back with arms outstretched. It did not look right to Michael. An instant later he had worked out why. The head had vanished, and Michael reeled back before turning to spew up the contents of his stomach, heaving and retching until there was nothing left to bring up.

"Who was it?" he asked, wiping the bile from his lips.

"Corporal Bavalek. He was bringing us coffee." Shinoda waved a hand at the shattered remnants of mugs, the brown of coffee splashed across the crimson horror spreading slowly across the floor. "I think a sheet of plasglass took him out. He never had a chance, poor bastard."

"Go get the team ready to move. And see if Delabi can think of somebody who can get us on one of those barges."

"I'll get one of the guys to take care—"

"I'll take care of it!" Michael's voice slashed through the air. "Just do it, Sergeant Shinoda."

Shinoda looked at him for a moment, then nodded. "We'll be by the front door," she said.

"I'll be as fast as I can," he said, already stripping off his combat fatigues down to his shorts. After a brief search, the best Michael could find was an old plasfiber box. "I'm sorry I couldn't find something better, Corporal Bavalek," he said as he struggled to maneuver the corpse into the box, its mass awkward and slippery.

Finally the body was in the box. Michael went to find Bavalek's head. When he did, he wished he hadn't. It lay against a toppled desk. Eyes wide open stared accusingly up at him, and the mouth was slightly open in surprise. Struggling to keep his stomach under control, Michael picked up the grisly object with bloodied hands and placed it with the body. He closed the lid. The relief was overwhelming.

"We'll come back for you and do this properly, I promise," Michael whispered before losing control of his stomach again, his body convulsing as spasm after spasm wracked his body.

Michael went to clean up.

Twenty minutes later, they were on their way to Nawadji, the air full of the sound of sirens overlaid with the thunderous roar of lifters shuttling emergency crews to the disaster site, with police and DocSec bots racing past. Not one paid the slightest attention to the dust-caked group of marines running hard through the debris-littered street. On they ran. Michael forced the pace. He wanted the pain from burning muscles to flush the guilt of Bavalek's death out of his mind.

Not that it did.

Delabi trotted back to where Michael and the rest waited tucked out of sight down a narrow alley.

"One of my cousins is waiting down by the wharf," she said. "He's not happy but says he'll put us in touch with someone who can help us out."

"Can we trust him? Michael asked.

"Not really," Delabi said. "But he likes money, and the slimy bastard's always been a greedy little crapstick. Besides, I said we'd come tear his balls off and stuff them down his throat if he messed with us." She smiled, a smile of feral savagery. "I think he believed me."

"I would," Shinoda whispered.

"Any DocSec around?" Michael asked.

"None. We should go, sir. Before he loses his nerve."

"Lead on."

Michael followed Delabi. The street ran down to a wall of razor wire that secured the wharf. Inside, cranes maneuvered massive loads off low-loaders and onto waiting barges. The few men around paid them no attention. Delabi turned right at the wire. A hundred meters on, a solitary figure waited outside a gate. His head swung from side to side.

"He looks nervous," Michael said.

"He should be," Delabi said. "He told me DocSec took five men away last week for smuggling booze and weed to the marines at Paarl."

"So why's he doing this?" Michael asked, pointing to the security holocams perched atop the wire. "The holovid records will show him waiting for us."

"Easy. We pay him, he pays off wharf security, and everybody's happy. This is nothing new. It's been going on forever."

Delabi's cousin did not wait for them. He waved at them to follow, then went in through the gate. He stopped only when screened by a wall of cargo containers.

"This is—" Delabi started to say.

"No names," the cousin snapped, cutting Delabi off, still doing his head-on-a-stick routine. "Just call me ... Max will do."

"Fine, Max," Michael said. "Which barge?"

"The *Merrioneth Star*. Barry Ho is the captain. They're just finishing loading and will be sailing inside an hour."

"How much?"

"Forty grand."

Michael glanced at Delabi and Shinoda. They both nodded.

"Okay," he said.

"Pay me now," Max said, "then wait here while I go make sure Captain Ho's ready for you."

"You little fuck," Michael hissed. His hand shot out and took Max by the throat. He squeezed so hard that Max could not break the death grip on his windpipe. Michael pushed Max away, sending him backward, tripping over his own feet and falling to the ground.

"Hey," Max protested, massaging his throat. "What are you doing? You can piss off. There's no way I'm doing business with you assholes," he added, starting to his feet.

Michael kicked him in the crotch, and again Max fell back with a soft scream. He folded his body into a ball, hands between his legs, whimpering. "Get him up," Michael ordered.

Kleber and Mallory obliged, dragging Max, wild-eyed with fear, to his feet. "I don't have time to play games, Max, so here's the deal. Take us to this Captain Ho, and then—"

Max must have been dredging down deep to find the last dregs of defiance. "Fuck you!" he snarled. "Why would I do that?"

This time Kleber did the honors, planting a fist in Max's gut. The blow doubled Max over and drove the air out of his lungs with an explosive *whoof.*

"Now, Max," Michael said when the man had recovered, "you're wasting my time. Just do what I say or I'll cut your weaselly throat and drop you in the river. You know what? I think that's what we'll do anyway. I'm sure Captain Ho will talk to us anyway, so thanks for that."

Terror flared in Max's eyes. "No, no, no," he gabbled. "You've got to believe me. He won't talk to you. We've had way too much trouble with DocSec."

Michael nodded. "I can understand that," he said, "so I'll trust you. But if you mess with me, I *will* kill you. Do you understand?"

Max nodded in furious agreement.

"Good. Well, what the fuck are you waiting for? Let's go!"

Captain Ho was a small, dumpy man dressed in faded blue overalls and a battered cap. His nut-brown face was deeply lined and sported a precisely trimmed goatee. He stared at Michael from blue eyes as hard as pebbles. "You don't want much," he said at last. He looked unimpressed by the motley crew arranged in front of him.

"Yes or no?" Michael said.

"Thirty grand, you said?"

"Ten now, twenty when we get to Ahenkro Junction."

"Fifteen and fifteen."

"Deal. When do we leave?"

310

"Hey, what about me?" Max said, his voice thick with complaint. "I should be paid something. It's only fair."

"Mind if we bring this piece of crap along with us?" Michael asked.

"As long as I don't have to listen to him," Ho replied, a look of utter contempt on his face.

"Oh, come on, Barry," Max said; his voice was now an aggrieved whine. "How long have we been friends?"

Ho stared at Max like he was something he'd just scraped off his shoe. "You've never been any friend of mine," he said. He turned back to Michael. "I'll get you some duct tape and cable ties. You can leave the little fuck here when you're done. I'll stash him in the power room."

"Where will you put us?" Michael asked.

Ho thought about that for a moment. "I've got just the place," he said.

"Sergeant, can you take care of this," Michael said, hooking a thumb at Max, "while I go with the captain?"

"My pleasure, sir."

Michael followed Ho aft, out of the barge's bridge and down a ladder to the cargo deck, a flat metal deck covered in massive shapes under chromaflaged netting.

Ho lifted the netting. "Here you go," he said. "No better place for you to stay out of sight."

Michael shook his head. He was stunned by the awesome mass of armored ceramsteel in front of him. He looked closer. "I'd say that this is an Aqaba main battle tank."

"You'd be right," Ho said, "and I've got five more of them onboard. Anyway, get your lot inside this one; we'll be getting under way shortly. And don't come out unless I tell you to. We'll have an escort, and they're a nosy bunch."

"An escort?"

"The NRA occasionally has a go at the barges. Sank two a few days ago, so now we have a couple of patrol boats to keep an eye on things."

"Got it."

"There's just one more thing," Ho said. "Where's my money?"

Michael stared around the inside of the tank, which was dimly lit by the soft glow of emergency lights. This one was the manned version, designed to control a squadron of unmanned Aqabas. By Fed standards, it was crude, and because it did not use AIs, it carried a crew of five where the Feds would have managed with one.

Crude or not, it was an impressive machine. Michael would never forget how they had looked advancing toward his position during the Hammers' abortive attempt to take the NRA's Branxton base. The Aqabas had been a terrifying sight. An autoloaded 95-millimeter hypervelocity gun backed up by missile pods and defensive lasers made sure of that. At that point an idea popped into his mind, fully formed and ready to go.

But was it feasible? he wondered.

"Hey," he said to Sergeant Shinoda, "you ever operate one of these things?"

"Me? Hell, no. First time I've ever seen one up close."

"I have, sir," Mallory called out from one of the drone tank controller's positions. "I was in a logistics battalion attached to a marine armored division."

"Easy to drive?"

"Far as I remember. I think there's a simulator which shows you how everything works."

"And how do you start it up?"

"Let me see. The panel to your left ... yes, that one. Lift the safety flap, put the switch to the first position, and that fires up the fuel cells. One more click brings the auxiliary fusion plant online. Flicking the switch all the way brings up the main propulsion plant."

"What?" Michael said, unconvinced. "It's that easy?"

"It is ... well, once you've inputted the right authorization code, of course."

"I knew there had to be a catch," Michael said, the disappointment bitter.

Mallory stared at him. "Are you thinking of using this thing, sir?"

Michael nodded. "I was," he said, "but without the authorization code, it's just a big useless lump of ceramsteel."

"It is, but in my day, tanks straight out of the factory," Mallory said, looking around, "which this one almost certainly is, all had the same factory code."

"Which was?"

"Ah, now let me see …" Michael felt as if he were about to explode. "I think it was 'system' … Yeah, it was."

"'System'?" Michael hissed. "The code is s-y-s-t-e-m? You got to be shitting me."

"I am not, sir," Mallory said a touch defensively.

"Well, there's only one way to find out."

"Let's do it, sir."

So they did, and Michael found out that no, Trooper Mallory was not shitting him. "Well I'll be damned," he whispered as the cramped crew compartment came alive in a coruscating display of colored status lights and ho-lovid panels. "Is this thing armed?"

"Wait one," Mallory said. Her fingers flew over one of the panels. "It is. It has full loads: 95-millimeter projectiles, machine gun rounds, missiles, decoys, smoke grenades, chaff dispensers, everything."

"That's standard operating procedure for heavy weapons systems being shipped into a combat zone," Shinoda said. "It means they can go straight into action if needed."

An evil smile crossed Michael's face. "Well, things are looking up," he said. He looked around. "Anyone fancy being a Hammer tank commander?"

Mallory had been dead right, Michael realized. Driving the Aqaba was simplicity itself. Once set to auto, the weapons systems pretty much took care of themselves once the target priorities had been set. "Let's take five," he said. "Somebody open a hatch; this place smells like a brothel."

"You would know," a voice said in a stage whisper, provoking an outbreak of laughter.

"Yeah, yeah," Michael said.

Kleber pushed open the hatch; he peered out.

"Anything worth looking at?" Michael asked.

"Nothing."

"Back to work then, folks. We'll keep at it for another hour, then decide what to do with our newfound skills."

"There's too much we don't know, sir," Shinoda said. "You'll have to go talk with the captain."

Michael grimaced. "I was hoping I wouldn't have to."

"I know. He won't be happy; that's for sure."

"Maybe he will be if I give him what's left on my card."

"DocSec will come after him. You do know that?"

"I do." Michael sighed. "Let me see what he says." He slipped through Aqaba's hatch and wriggled his way out from under the netting. He paused to make sure there were no patrol boats in sight, then adjusted his chromaflage cape and made his way to the bridge.

Captain Ho spun around in his chair when Michael appeared. The man did not look happy to see him. "Kraa damn it," he snapped, "I thought I told you to stay put. The Hammers are like flies on shit out there. They have surveillance all over this river."

"I know, and I'm sorry, but we need to talk. Besides, this cape is too good for any Hammer holovid."

Ho's eyes narrowed. "I thought there was something odd about you," he said. "You're not a Hammer, are you?"

For a moment Michael toyed with the idea of lying, then decided the truth might pay better dividends. In any case, Ho had them by the balls; for all Michael knew, he already had DocSec waiting for them on the wharf at Ahenkro Junction. "No," Michael said. "I'm a Fed."

"I knew it." Ho paused. "See this?" he went on, pointing to a red button on the arm of his chair only a few centimeters from the tips of his fingers.

Michael nodded.

"That's the hijack alarm. If I push it, it locks down. Unless I release it inside five seconds, the sky falls in on your head. You might kill me, but you won't get to the button in time, I can guarantee that."

Michael sighed. "Nobody's going to kill anybody," he said, "so spare me the threats. I'm here to talk to you, that's all. If you can't give me what I ask, we'll go over the side where and when you tell us to, and you'll never see us again."

The tension was palpable, Captain Ho's body radiating mistrust. "I can listen," he said eventually, his finger not moving one millimeter. "What do you want?"

"One of my guys was a Hammer tanker, so this is what we thought we'd do ..."

"Kraa!" Ho hissed through pursed lips when Michael had finished. "That's a big ask."

"It's important. You must know that."

"I was a planetary defense officer once." Ho looked away. "I spent most of my time on oceangoing missile defense platforms, so I never saw combat against the NRA,

316

though I knew plenty of people who did. Some were friends of mine. Quite a few of them are dead now ..."

Michael's spirits sank.

"... killed in action, so there's no way I'd do anything to help the NRA ..."

Michael's spirits fell through the floor and kept on going.

"... but on the other hand, a lot more have been killed over the years by DocSec, so I don't owe them any loyalty either, and I hate all that Word of Kraa bullshit. No, I owe all my loyalty to myself, not to anything or anybody else. Just me. This might be my home," he said, waving a hand around the bridge, "but I don't own the *Merrioneth Star*, and I don't have any family here. Ten years ago my whore of a wife buggered off with a DocSec major, and my kids had the gumption to get the hell out of the Hammer Worlds the first chance they could."

Michael had been biting his lip to keep from interrupting. Would the damn man cooperate or not? Ho seemed to have stopped, so Michael took his chance. "Does that mean you'll help us?" he asked.

"Depends on how much you've got left on that card of yours."

"A bit over fifteen grand. If you want it, it's all yours."

Another wave of the hand. "It'll be the end of this, you know," Ho said.

"Your call. But you need to make a decision soon. It won't be long before we reach the Ahenkro Junction wharf."

Ho nodded. "I know," he said. The seconds dragged past before Ho spoke again. "One condition."

"Name it."

"I need to be on my way downriver before you make any move. If I'm alongside when the shit hits the fan, I'm dead meat."

"How much lead time do you need?"

"An hour."

"Okay, but it all depends on how the unloading works. Tell me how the Hammers do that."

"Well, first ..."

Wednesday, October 6, 2404, UD
Ahenkro Junction, Commitment

A series of gentle bumps told Michael that the *Merrioneth Star* finally had berthed. He had been going quietly mad waiting. They had fallen badly behind schedule, and Ho had not seen fit to tell them why.

Ho's voice was crackled and tinny in the earpiece of Michael's headset. "Sorry about the delay," he said. "The convoy before us was attacked by the NRA."

"We wondered what was happening. Did they have any luck?" Even as he spoke, Michael cursed his stupidity. Ho would know the captains in the convoy.

"Not if you were the poor buggers on the three barges they sank," Ho said. If Michael's insensitivity had bothered the man, he wasn't letting it show. "You ready?"

"We are. Just let us know when the driver comes aboard."

"Will do."

Time crawled. Michael wondered why the Hammers were taking so long. A barge load of Aqabas was a sitting duck. He tried not to think what would happen if the Fed ground-attack landers came back.

"They've got the tarps off," Ho said twenty long minutes later, "and now they're putting the ramps in place, so stand by."

"Roger. Okay, folks. Any minute now."

"I've been ready for the last four hours," Shinoda muttered from where she and Kleber waited by the hatch, looks of anticipation on their faces.

"Here he comes," Ho said. A few minutes later, the hatch eased back out of its frame. A pair of legs swung in, followed by the body and then the head of one very shocked Hammer. Shinoda and Kleber dragged him in, one of Kleber's meaty hands clamped down across the man's mouth. It was only work of seconds before the Hammer had been cable tied into the commander's seat. His eyes bulged in terror.

"Now, sonny boy," Shinoda said, putting the tip of an enormous knife to the end of the man's nose, "I'm going to tell my friend here to take his hand away. When he does, you keep your mouth shut and you listen carefully to what we have to say because—" She pushed the knife in a fraction; a tiny jewel of blood oozed out from the tip. "—we don't want you to make any mistakes. Understood?"

Shinoda pulled the knife back. The man nodded, his face white with terror. He looked young and afraid.

Kleber pulled his hand away. Michael leaned forward. "Okay," he said, "do what we want and you'll be fine. That's my promise. Now, take a deep breath and tell me your name."

"Jo-jo-jonah Patel," the man stammered. "Marine Jonah Patel."

"That's good, Jonah; that's really good," Michael said, keeping his voice calm, soothing. He was relieved to see the man relax a fraction. "Now, what's the first thing you have to do?"

"Power up all six tanks." Patel's voice shook.

"Okay, then that's what we want you to do, but remember, we do know how Aqabas work, so no mistakes, okay?"

Patel nodded his head hard. "Go on, then," Michael prompted.

Patel's fingers flashed across the tank commander's master control panel. The Aqaba's massive bulk trembled as the main fusion plant powered up. Michael left him to it. He wanted to check what was happening outside. Nothing to worry them, he was happy to see. He flicked the holocam down into the infrared. The heat signatures of two men appeared, stark patches of white in the cool of early morning.

"All six tanks are online and nominal," Patel said. "I need to call that in."

"Go on."

"Okay. Wharf, this is Tank 1; we are ready to move."

"Patel, you worm," an angry voice barked. "Where the hell have you been? You think I've got all day?"

"Sorry, sarge. Tank 3 had a transient on her auxiliary power control module."

Michael held his breath. Did an Aqaba even have such a thing? He glanced at Mallory, not at all happy when she shrugged her shoulders.

"Is it stable now?" the supervisor said a lifetime later.

"Affirmative.'

"Then what are you waiting for?" the man roared. "Get those fucking tanks off that fucking barge now! Take them to Golf-8."

"Golf-8, roger that, sarge."

"Do it," Michael whispered. He watched as the young marine fed power to the drive train. He spun the tank on the spot, then eased its huge bulk down the ceramsteel ramp onto the wharf. His hand was soft on the sidestick controller. *You've done this before*, Michael thought. He admired the man's effortless precision.

Patel soon had the Aqaba off the barge. It moved steadily up a muddy track. Michael watched the ho-lovid screens with interest. *The Hammers are not messing around*, he thought. *I've never seen so much ordnance in one place.*

"This is where I park it," Patel said. He spun the tank around and reversed into a wide gap between yet more Aqabas.

Michael wondered many of the damn things they had. "Now what?" he asked Patel.

"I bring the rest ashore and park them."

"Okay. Do it."

Patel did just that. "Wharf, this is Tank 1," he said when he'd parked the last Aqaba. "All done, sarge."

"Roger," the supervisor said.

"What will he want you to do next?"

Patel shook his head. "I don't know who you are," he said, the tremble back in his voice, "but I've done what you want, so let me go and I won't say anything to anybody."

"I don't think so," Michael said. "Answer my question. What will the supervisor want you to do next?"

Patel just stared at him, mouth clamped shut, face set in an obstinate scowl. Michael sighed. "You're not being smart. You help me, I'll let you go. How about it?"

The Hammer marine shook his head. "No," he whispered.

"Jonah, my man," Michael sighed, his hand reaching out to take him by the throat. "Screw me around anymore and I will kill you." His grip tightened, crushing Patel's windpipe until he had to struggle to breathe. "Now, which is it to be?" Michael went on, letting go. "And make up your mind quickly. I've got better things to do."

Patel's face crumpled in defeat as he dragged air back into his lungs. "Okay, okay," he croaked, his newfound courage gone. "I've got to run systems tests on all six tanks. We have to make sure the depot hasn't sent us any duds. Once that's done, I shut them down and go back to the wharf for the next load."

"How long?"

"The testing's automated, so a couple of minutes each."

Michael swore. He'd promised Ho he would give him an hour; he still had a good thirty minutes left.

"Do the tests but call in a defect. Make it one that'll take at least half an hour to fix. Understood?"

"Sergeant Miyashita won't be happy."

"A defect's a defect. It's not your fault."

"Maybe not, but he'll still kick my ass."

"That can't be helped."

Patel sighed a sigh of resignation. "I don't think I've got much choice," he said.

"Not if you want to stay alive, no, you don't."

"Okay … Wharf, Tank One."

"Where the fuck are you, Patel? I need you down here now!"

"Sorry, sarge. Tank Three's still showing problems on its auxiliary power control module. I'll have to replace it."

"You useless dipstick," Miyashita shouted. There was a moment's silence, and Michael held his breath, praying that Patel wasn't told to leave it for later. "Fix it," the man said finally, "but fast, understood?"

"Yes, sarge."

"Why do you put up with it?" Michael asked when the circuit went dead.

Patel shrugged. "It's the way things are."

"They don't have to be. Come with us."

Patel stared at Michael. "You're NRA, right?"

"We are."

"My corporal says the NRA is winning this war."

Michael's eyes opened in astonishment. "He said that?"

"He did. Haven't seen him since. He did a runner. He was the tenth this week. So is it true … that we're losing, I mean?"

"You want an honest answer to that?"

"Hah!" the man snorted. "That'd be a change."

"I think we'll win, but it's still too early to be sure."

"That's what I think."

"So come with us."

"No," Patel said, shaking his head. "I can't do that. My two brothers are in the marines. DocSec would shoot them."

Michael didn't doubt it. DocSec was big on guilt by association. "We'll have to tie you up and dump you, then," he said.

Patel managed a lopsided grin. "Just don't hit me too hard."

Michael grinned back. "No more than we have to, Marine Jonah Patel. And you can tell them that we belted you the moment you got into this thing."

"Oh, don't worry. I will. Just let me wipe the holovid records before you do."

Kleber and Delabi climbed back into the Aqaba. "The poor bastard's sleeping like a baby," Delabi said. "His head will hurt like hell when he wakes up."

"Better that way than having it kicked in by DocSec," Michael said. "Positions everyone. Last questions ... no? Right, report when ready to roll."

One by one, Michael's team brought their tanks on-line and reported in. "Right, folks," Michael said. "We need mayhem and lots of it. Wait until I give the word, then shoot at anything that crosses your path, but air-defense assets are a priority, so go for them if you can. Let's go."

Michael took a deep breath to quell an attack of nerves. He had a right to be nervous; they were surrounded by thousands of Hammers. He gripped the sidestick controller in his left hand and eased it forward. The Aqaba lurched ahead, forcing him to push the stick left. The tank swung around, narrowly missing a startled marine who appeared from nowhere. It was harder in real life than on the simulator, Michael realized. He sent the tank zigzagging through the packed ranks of Hammer heavy ordnance. His erratic steering produced a great deal of shouting and fist waving. He ignored it and brushed the Hammers aside. The rest of the tanks followed behind, a crazy conga line of heavy armor.

"Sorry about that," Shinoda said. She'd overcontrolled and driven her tank over the back end of a mobile missile battery. The maneuver sent a passing officer into paroxysms of rage. Assault rifle in hand, he ran alongside the tank, shouting at it to stop. External hull-mounted microphones picked up his voice. The torrent of abuse racketed around the inside of the tank.

"Tank Three," Michael said to Kleber. Even if the Hammers hadn't woken up to the fact that five of their Aqabas were being stolen, they soon would. "Shoot that mouthy asshole."

"Three, roger."

Michael watched as Kleber fired a short burst from one of his tank's machine guns. The rounds picked the man up and tossed him away to one side.

"Nice shooting, Kleber," Michael said. "All tanks, fire at will."

There was only the briefest of pauses before the 95-millimeter autoloading gun on Michael's tank crashed into life. It sent a hypervelocity round ripping effortlessly through a cluster of thin-skinned mobile air-defense batteries, then another and another before one got lucky and smashed into a missile warhead. The explosion that followed was close, violent. The Aqaba was punched bodily to one side. Not even bothering to select a target, Michael traversed the gun, firing as he went. Its rhythmic metallic crash was joined now by machine guns flaying the air around any Hammer stupid enough to stick his head up while grenade launchers dropped infrared absorbing smoke to protect their flanks. The column roared through the ordnance park and smashed through the perimeter wire. They turned hard right and accelerated in a headlong rush for the bridge across the Oxus River. Behind them, tumbling columns of smoke climbed away from the blazing wreckage of MARFOR 21's heavy ordnance reserves.

Still the Hammers seemed paralyzed by events. Nobody tried to stop the tanks. They kept moving and smashed aside anything that got in their way. They let 95-millimeter guns loose at anything even remotely like a worthwhile target, right down to a small all-terrain vehicle full of what Michael hoped was Hammer brass. The furious barrage of fire scattered marines in all directions; only a handful had the presence of mind to fire back, an exercise in futility.

The marine in charge of the checkpoint at the massive bridge spanning the Oxus River was as brave as he was foolish. Flanked by a pair of Sampan antitank missile batteries that would have done the job for him if he had be bothered to take the time to think—until rounds from Kleber's and Mallory's tanks tore their guts out—he stood in the middle of the road, hand raised. His marines, smarter and much less brave, did not wait to see what would happen, hurling themselves out of the oncoming tanks' path. At the last moment, the man woke up to the fact that no amount of arm waving would stop an Aqaba. In a convulsive, panic-stricken leap, he hurled himself to one side, only to be caught by the tank's leading edge, his body tossed clean over the parapet and into the water far below, the tank's microphones picking up his despairing scream as he fell to his death.

They were almost halfway across the bridge by the time the Hammers decided to take the problem seriously. Hostile fire alarms shrieked inside the Aqaba. The holovid screen looking down the bridge flared white as the tank's fire-control system responded to a cluster of incoming Sampan missiles. The attack was over in seconds. Defensive lasers slashed the missiles out of the air; their warheads exploded to send missile debris ricocheting off the hull in a cacophony of metallic whanging that made Michael's ears ring. The noise did not let up. The tank's 95-millimeter gun tracked the missiles back to their launch point. It poured rounds into the missile battery. Again the screens whited out as a power plant lost containment, the blast smashing men and ordnance aside as the five tanks roared past and into the night.

Across the bridge, Michael swung the Aqaba left onto the road to Kumasi, the hull now reverberating as they took fire. *Light cannon*, Michael reckoned, *and there'll be worse to come and soon.*

"Engage autofollow," he shouted. He punched instructions into the master panel to tell the tank to take the road to Kumasi. Now the rest would follow wherever the lead tank went. "Kleber, get the hatch open; everyone stand by to bail out."

The hatch opened with a crash. It was bedlam outside. The noise of tracks on the road and the pounding of incoming cannon fire were overwhelming. "Hold on," Michael shouted. He slammed on the brakes. The tracks screamed in protest as the tank slid to walking pace. "Go, go, go!"

None of them hesitated, diving through the hatch after their packs and personal weapons. Delabi was the last to go. The instant she vanished, Michael mashed the throttle onto the stops, locked the controls, and followed, rolling and tumbling to a pain-filled halt that left him staring up into the sky, stunned and unable to move.

"Come on, sir," Shinoda said, dragging him to his feet. "We need to get out of here."

Groggy, Michael forced himself to follow Shinoda. They ran hard for the cover of the trees. In the distance, the rumble of ground-attack landers was clearly audible. The night sky to the northeast flickered red and white as the NRA and the Hammers traded artillery fire.

Tuesday, October 12, 2404, UD
Outside Cooperbridge, Commitment

"I think we're hooked in," Shinoda said, "so stand by … Okay, the link's up. We're into ENCOMM … and we have the latest OPSUM."

Michael skimmed the high-level summaries, pleased to see that the battle for McNair was going well for the NRA, and no wonder. The Hammers' planetary councillors were still refusing to release the marine divisions they needed to keep a lid on civil unrest; UNMILCOMM was not getting the reserves it needed to contain a rampaging NRA.

If I were Chief Councillor Polk, Michael said to himself, *I think I'd be making plans to get as far away from Commitment as I could.*

He turned his attention to the mass of data summarizing the disposition of NRA and Hammer units along what ENCOMM was now calling the Yallan Salient, both happy and concerned to see that the 120th had been pulled out of the line and into reserve. *There's only one reason for that,* he thought. *Anna's battalion has been taking heavy punishment.*

Michael burrowed down into the OPSUM. He located Team Victor; Hartspring was still in Cooperbridge. He closed the OPSUM. But one thing bothered him; it had been bothering him for a while.

The Hammer of Kraa's survival, the fate of billions, the future of humanspace—they all hung in the balance. Compared with that, Team Victor was an irrelevance. So why did ENCOMM always know exactly where it was? Michael was no expert, but he knew how fast changing, how chaotic combat was, and good as the NRA's intelligence system was, surely it wasn't that good. He was missing something; he was sure of it.

Shinoda broke his train of thought. "I see Team Victor hasn't moved," she said. "I'll get the team ready to move out."

"Hold on for a second," Michael said. "I've been thinking about things."

"And?"

"It's up to me now. I can't ask you to go with me into Cooperbr—"

"Whoa!" Shinoda said. "Hold it there just one fucking second, sir. I don't know about the rest of the team, but I haven't come all this way to stop now. I want Hartspring almost as much as you do."

"Look, sergeant. I appreciate the sentiment, but you'll have to tell me how we'd get past the military police. We're talking about going into a combat zone without valid orders. We belong to a unit that does not appear in the Hammer order of battle, and we have IDs we know are useless. They'll nail us in a heartbeat."

"And you *do* have valid orders to show the MPs?" Shinoda said. She looked exasperated. "And which unit *do* you belong to? Show us your ID; who *are* you, exactly?"

Michael put his hands up in defeat. "I know, I know, but one man on his own has a chance of getting through. Five don't."

"That is a complete crock, sir, and you know it. If we go as marines, then you're right. We will get nailed. But a bunch of civilians has a chance. The marines are not DocSec. They won't give a shit who we are. Even if they look at our IDs—which they won't—they won't check them out. They have better things to do."

Michael knew all that. He'd just been hoping that Shinoda wouldn't pick up on the flaws in his argument. "Doesn't matter," he said. "Decision's made. I'm going in on my own while you guys go to ground until the NRA gets here."

"What? You want me to sit around on my ass waiting?" Shinoda shook her head dismissively. "Forgive my language, sir, but fuck that."

"This is my fight, Sergeant Shinoda, not yours. So butt out and let me fight it, okay?"

"My fight's killing Hammers, sir, and I'm not too fussy about which ones, so this is what we're going to do: We'll go to Cooperbridge, find Hartspring, and when we do, you can kill him. Okay?"

Michael's head dropped; he could see the determination on Shinoda's face and knew when he was defeated. "Why can't you just do as you are ordered?"

Shinoda grinned at him. "I'll take that as a yes, shall I?"

"Suppose you'd better. Go talk to the guys, make sure they're okay with it, then we'll move out. We need—" His fingers plucked at his combat fatigues. "—to find something to replace these."

Michael checked to make sure his assault rifle was safely tucked away under his coat. It was. He turned to look at Shinoda. He threw an admiring glance at the heavy skirt and embroidered blouse favored by older Hammer women. "I must say, you do look very fetching, Sergeant Shinoda," he said. "All those rough, tough Hammer marines will not be able to keep their hands off you."

"You may be a colonel now, sir," Shinoda growled, "but that won't stop me from belting you. Besides, you look like a pig farmer fallen on hard times."

Michael laughed. Shinoda was right; he did. "We all set?"

"We are."

"Let's go, then."

Michael followed Shinoda and the rest of the team down the road out of the village to the junction with the Cooperbridge-Kumasi highway, the ceramcrete road already hot in the midmorning sun. He didn't know whether to laugh or cry. Dressed in clothes dragged from the shattered ruins of a small village mall, they were a sorry-looking lot. But so were all the other civilians they had seen, and Michael knew they'd be all but invisible to the Hammer marines.

Because they were lost amid the flow of Hammer truckbots forcing their way down a road clogged with civilians, the walk into town was uneventful. The Hammer military police showed not the slightest interest in their small group. Since they were the only people heading into Cooperbridge while every other civilian was getting the hell out, Michael had thought they would. But they hadn't. The marines were content to wave them through without even the most cursory check of their IDs.

Michael called a halt just short of Cooperbridge's plaza. Like all Hammer towns, it was a massive space dominated by the inevitable temple. It was still intact, but its facade was badly scarred by shrapnel. The buildings on either side lay in ruins, now just piles of smoking rubble.

Michael waved the team to close in. "Right," he said, "you've all got your search areas. We meet at the corner of Herriot and Chang in eight hours. Keep an ear on channel 643; any problems, let everyone know. And remember, if you locate the target, call it in, get as many holocams set up as you can, then bug out. I do not want Hartspring getting spooked. Any last questions? ... No? Okay, let's move out, and remember, keep your heads down and try to stay clear of the surveillance cameras. There's a lot of them, but they're very easy to spot."

The team split up, and Michael set off. He tried not to be daunted by the size of the task that lay ahead. Cooperbridge was a big place. Finding Colonel Hartspring's unit would have been difficult at the best of times, let alone amid the chaos of the last major town before the front line. And it was chaos. Hammer units— some in good order and going up the line, others tattered, some badly mauled, coming back down—clogged the streets. Truckbots hauling supplies made the confusion worse. They forced their way through the mayhem, weaving around the debris from destroyed buildings and between armored, air-defense, and antitank units parked and waiting to move.

Something tells me, Michael thought, *that the Hammers are not planning to give Cooperbridge up without one hell of a fight.*

Michael walked down the shattered remnants of what must once have been an attractive tree-lined boulevard. His eyes never stopped moving in the search for surveillance cameras. He was relieved to see that he was not the only one with a death wish. There weren't many civilians around, but enough for him not to stand out. They were a sad-looking bunch, poorly dressed and dirty. They all had looks of shocked disbelief on their faces.

Michael rounded a corner and was confronted by the sight of a Goombah air-defense battery. Its tracked launch vehicle, power plant, and command trailer all but filled the road. He started to make his way toward the battery. The screeching of a siren brought him to a stop; he wondered what it meant. And then he realized. Frantic now, he turned and threw himself over a small wall in a desperate attempt to reach the safety of a small concrete enclosure. He crashed into the ground and slid to a stop. He clamped his hands over his ears even as the world around him was torn apart by the savage back blast from missiles screaming skyward. Rocket motor efflux hit the ground and exploded outward. Fingers of hot gas lashed his body, scorching his hands and neck.

The silence that followed was shocking in its intensity. Michael lay there for a minute, breathing air bitter with the acrid smell of burned propellant. He stumbled to his feet. He shook his head to clear the ringing from his ears and tried to ignore the pain from his burned hands, his body racked by coughs as it fought to expel the crud from his lungs.

It wasn't until a hand fell on his shoulder that Michael realized somebody was talking to him. It was a while before he could make sense of what the hulking Hammer marine was saying.

"Can't you read, you idiot?" the man was saying, pointing to a small dust-coated sign sitting a good 50 meters away.

"Sorry," Michael mumbled, "didn't see it."

The marine shook his head. "Fucking civilians," he said. "You are damn lucky you weren't killed … Kraa! Look at your hands!"

Michael did, then wished he hadn't. *No wonder my hands hurt*, he thought as he looked at the blistered red skin.

"Go down there," the marine went on, pointing along the street, "about 300 meters. You'll find an aid post. They'll fix you up. What are you waiting for?" he said when Michael hesitated. "Go on. It'll be okay. Tell them Sergeant Jalevi from the 654th Air Defense sent you."

A marine aid post was the last place Michael wanted to go, but with the man so insistent, he didn't have much choice.

"Thanks," he muttered, setting off.

"And stay away from our batteries, you hear?" the man called out. "By the way, just what the hell are you doing around here?"

Michael just waved a hand and kept walking. With an effort, he resisted the urge to break into a run; a quick glance confirmed that the marine was still watching him, the man's face set in a suspicious frown. Michael found the aid post; it was hard to miss the olive drab tent marked with massive red crosses. "Bastard Hammers," Michael muttered under his breath when he saw a battalion command and control half-track parked so close that no NRA landers would attack it for fear of hitting the aid post.

Resisting the temptation to toss a microgrenade at the half-track, Michael went inside the tent. "What the fuck do you want?" one of the medics said, looking up. "We don't treat civilians."

"Sergeant Jalevi of the 654th Air Defense sent me," Michael said. He waved hands now scarlet and spotted with suppurating blisters.

"Oh, did he?"

"Yes," Michael said, reining in the urge to kick the man in the crotch. "I got a bit close to one of his missile launches."

"What a fucking idiot." The man got to his feet with a sigh. "Come on, then."

With the use of his hands restored thanks to thin sheets of burnskin, Michael stepped out of the aid center and looked around. The medic had turned out to be anything but an asshole. Mostly the man was pissed. Without ever actually saying so, he seemed convinced that things were going badly for the Hammers.

That was all Michael managed to get out of the man. Even after a lot of bullshit about finding his uncle—a mythical civilian liaison officer with a joint DocSec-marine unit—he had learned nothing that might help him track down Hartspring.

"Shit!" he hissed when he spotted Sergeant Jalevi. He was coming his way flanked by four marines, a determined look on his face. Michael didn't wait. Turning away, he sprinted down the street, head down and arms pumping.

"Hey!" Jalevi shouted. "Stop or I'll blow your damn head off!"

Michael kept moving, weaving from side to side. With a good 20 meters still to go before he reached the safety of the next cross street, a burst of rifle fire shredded the air around his ears.

"Last chance, asshole," Jalevi called, sending another burst Michael's way.

"Okay, okay," Michael shouted back. He raised his hands in the air and slowed to a trot. He risked a glance over his shoulder. Jalevi and his marines had slowed too; their guns no longer pointed his way.

With 10 meters to go to the corner, Michael took a deep breath and exploded into a sprint and ran for his life. He'd barely made the corner before Jalevi's men sent a furious volley of rifle fire down the street. A well-aimed round plucked at the sleeve of his jacket as Michael skidded around the store on the corner.

"Oh, shit!" he muttered. Up ahead, a platoon of marines was scattered across the road in untidy confusion. "Help me! Heretics!" he shouted, pointing back to the corner store, which was being chewed apart by sustained bursts of rifle fire. "Heretics, coming this way! Get up, get up!"

The marines needed no encouragement. They leaped to their feet, unslung their weapons, and stampeded past. Michael slipped a microgrenade out of his pocket; he turned and tossed it high in the air. The small black shape dropped right into the mass of men and exploded with a flat crack that dropped marines to the ground screaming in pain, with the rest of the platoon skittering outward. The men nearest the corner needed no prompting to return fire at the oncoming Jalevi and his men, the noise rising to a crescendo as both sides hosed fire up and down the street.

By the time common sense prevailed and the shooting died away, Michael was five blocks away, holed up in the ruins of a small office building. He lay back, chest heaving as oxygen-starved lungs fought for air, and cursed his luck. It would take the Hammers a while to sort out the shambles he had left behind, but sort it out they would. And when they did, they would come looking for a scruffy man in civilian clothes, of medium height, with a stocky build and unruly brown hair.

There wouldn't be many of those in Cooperbridge.

At best he had a day. Almost certainly, the marines would assume the man they were looking for was a deserter, which meant DocSec would get involved. And if they did, it was only a matter of time before Colonel

Hartspring knew that the man Chief Councillor Polk wanted so badly to get his hands on was in Cooperbridge.

At that point the shit would really hit the fan. He groaned out loud. He was screwed. So much for his plan to slip into the town unseen, find Hartspring, and send him to join the rest of his Kraa-loving buddies kissing ass in Kraa heaven. Much as he wanted to have his revenge, a small shred of common sense told him that this was neither the time nor the place. It was time to abort and get the hell out while they still had a chance.

Hartspring would have to wait for another time.

He was fumbling for the transmit switch on his radio when his earpiece burst into life. It was Kleber. "Banjo, this is Two. Tango located in building southeast corner Harkness and N'debele. Putting surveillance cams in place. Will withdraw to Papa-Six. Acknowledge."

"Two, Banjo, Tango at Harkness and N'debele, acknowledged," Michael said, exultant, any thought of aborting the mission gone. "Niner Niner, this is Banjo," he went on. "Implement chromaflage discipline now. Move to Papa-Six when ready. Acknowledge."

One by one Shinoda and the rest of the team acknowledged the order. Michael slipped into a burned-out shop and put on his chromaflage cape. After a careful check to make sure that nothing more than a tiny slit across his eyes had been left exposed, he set off to Papa-Six, a derelict factory ten blocks from where Hartspring was quartered.

* * *

340

Tucked away out of sight behind a pile of scrapped machinery, Michael and the team watched the holovid feed from the holocams Kleber had set up.

Hartspring's unit was billeted in a school; like many of Cooperbridge's buildings, it was damaged, though not as badly as some. It still had most of its roof and walls. The yard in front was clear of debris, filled instead with marine all-terrain vehicles mounted with a mix of crew-served weapons: heavy machine guns, light antiarmor and air-defense missiles, and 120-millimeter mobile mortar launchers along with microdrone, grenade, and infrared smoke launchers. As Michael watched, the crews were busily throwing chromaflage netting across all the ATVs.

"Looks like they've just gotten back," Shinoda said, shifting the holocam down into the infrared. "Yup, lot of heat coming off those vehicles."

Michael nodded, trying to stay positive and failing. "That's good, I guess," he said. "Means they should be around for a while."

"Probably, but we need to do this fast, sir. The cart's been kicked over. The Hammers will be coming after us."

"They will. What's this?" Michael added as a small convoy of truckbots pulled up, black jumpsuited figures spilling out of the back.

"DocSec," Shinoda said. "Wonder what they're doing here."

Mallory leaned forward to look at the screen. "I know what they are," she said. "You're looking at a DocSec search team."

"How do you know that?" Michael asked.

"I worked with them once … in another life. See those boxes?"

Michael nodded. The DocSec troopers were manhandling plasfiber crates out of the trucks and carrying them into the schoolyard.

"The large boxes are perimeter security equipment: laser trip wires and so on. The small ones will be full of searchbots. Let me see … Yes, looking at how many boxes they've got, they've got enough to seal off and search a couple of city blocks at a time."

Michael swore. Searchbots were like sniffer dogs, only smarter and with better noses, and they never tried to hump your leg. They hunted for traces of carbon dioxide in the air; no matter where you hid, they'd find you. The only way to dodge them was to wear one of the absorbent face masks the special forces teams used. Since he didn't have any masks at hand, the only other option was to stop breathing, and even then the bots would find him thanks to sensors capable of detecting warm bodies, body odor, and the smell of fear.

Michael swore some more. He did not like what he was seeing. He did not know what it meant, but his instincts told him it was not good. But what he did know, even if he could not explain why, was that it was time for him to go it alone. He could not—he would not—risk the lives of his team any longer.

Michael swung around. "Okay, guys," he said. "This is nonnegotiable, so don't argue with me, because if you do—" He reached into his belt and pulled out his laser pistol, a squat, ugly weapon good only for killing at very short range. "—I'll shoot each one of you in the damn foot and keep shooting until you do as I say. Understood?"

The shocked silence was total.

"I'll take that as a yes, then," he went on. "Sergeant Shinoda, the team's yours. If you leave now, there's half a chance you'll get out of the city before the DocSec search teams get rolling. Go and go now. And yes, that is an order."

Shinoda stared back at Michael for a moment. Then she nodded. "Yes, sir," she said. She turned to the team. "Okay, everyone. We'll head down Velici to Juliet-Two. Chromaflage capes on until we get there and move slowly; there'll be surveillance drones over us for sure. From Juliet-Two down Armada until we hit the Kumasi road, then head south. Don't forget your countersurveillance drills. If we get separated, the initial rally point is Quebec-Four. If that's been compromised, then head for Mike-Nine. Questions? None? Good. Kleber, go check that our egress is clear. The rest of you wait for me by the old generator room. Go!" she snapped when nobody moved.

"I'm staying, sarge," Delabi said, her face a hard, stubborn scowl.

"No, you're not, trooper. You heard the colonel; you're going even if I have to shoot you myself."

Delabi gave a reluctant nod and got to her feet. She looked at Michael. "DocSec killed both my grandparents and my brother," she said, "so I want you to kill the motherfucker for me."

"I will," Michael replied. *I'm not sure how, though,* he thought. *Not anymore.*

"Good luck, sir," Kleber said, and with that the troopers turned and left.

"I don't like this, sir," Shinoda said.

"Nor do I do, sergeant, but I might have a chance on my own. You'd best go."

Shinoda put her hand on Michael's shoulder. "Just make sure you come back, okay? I don't want to have to explain to Anna what happened."

Her words ripped at Michael's soul. He cursed his one-eyed pursuit of Hartspring. All logic said he should be leaving with Shinoda and the rest. He'd have done better riding shotgun on Anna, and he knew it, just as he knew he'd never rest until Hartspring and Polk were dead. "I'll be okay," he said, his voice soft. "I'm a survivor."

"That you are, sir. Good luck."

"Thanks. Get the team back safely."

"I will."

With that, Shinoda left, leaving Michael feeling more alone than ever. He shook his head. Shinoda hadn't asked what his plan was. Why would she? She knew full well he didn't have one unless hoping to evade the DocSec search teams long enough to kill Hartspring was a plan. Who was he kidding? That was just make it up as you go along.

Something will turn up, he thought as he turned his attention back to the holoscreen. *It always has.*

The Hammers had been busy. The truckbots had parked. The boxes with the tiny searchbots had been opened. The ground was cluttered with small turtlelike shapes, the shells studded with small antennas, stubby sniffer probes, and infrared and acoustic sensors. And for every ten turtles, there was a command bot with comm lasers and antennas on its back to control its flock and provide a datalink to the search commander's drones orbiting overhead.

As he looked at the scene, something bothered him the way the fact that ENCOMM always knew where Hartspring and Team Victor were did. It was him they were after; that much was obvious. But he could have been anywhere in Cooperbridge. So why were the search teams setting up their bots at Team Victor's headquarters when they had a whole city to search? It didn't seem a very efficient way to do business. Michael could only assume that Hartspring was the man in charge of the search, and that was what he wanted.

The more he thought about it, the more his confidence returned. All he had to do was be careful, take his time, and stay clear of the DocSec search teams as they ground their way block by block across Cooperbridge. As long as he did that, he would be safe. And his time would come. Cooperbridge might not have been in the front line, but it was too juicy a target for the NRA to leave alone. They'd attacked it already, and they would go on attacking it. And that was when he would get his chance. He would slip through the chaos and confusion, kill Hartspring, and be gone before the last NRA lander had unloaded its bombs.

An hour later, there was a flurry of activity. Twenty or so of the DocSec troopers dropped what they were doing and grabbed the boxes containing perimeter security equipment. The troopers followed the boxes into the back of the trucks. The truckbots roared off. The minute they'd gone, a DocSec officer—a major from his rank badges and probably the man in charge, Michael reckoned—sprinted across the yard and disappeared inside the school.

Now, what is this all about? Michael wondered.

Ten minutes later, the DocSec major reappeared, waving his senior NCOs over into what was clearly a briefing. The major did a lot of talking, even drawing a mud map in the dust of the yard. Finally heads nodded, and the group dispersed, moving now with clear purpose, the men galvanized into action with much shouting and waving of arms.

The school's front door opened, and there he was. Michael's heart kicked hard when he saw the familiar figure of Colonel Hartspring, dressed like the rest of the DocSec troopers in black fatigues under a combat vest and carrying a stubby machine pistol. He strode out into the yard followed by what Michael assumed were the marines of Team Victor. They made their way to their ATVs and climbed in, Hartspring getting into an APC.

That's his command vehicle, Michael thought, looking at its array of aerials and datacomm lasers. Fusion plants came online.

After a short pause, the vehicles set off, some turning right to head west along N'debele and the rest turning left to go east. A moment later, the search teams followed on foot. Again, half went left and half went right.

Now Michael really was confused. If their plan was to start searching the city, they'd have all gone off together and they'd have gone in truckbots. No, they had something more specific in mind, and it was close. They—

It hit Michael like a brick between the eyes.

You are a fucking idiot, he raged at himself. *They're not searching all of Cooperbridge. They don't need to; Hartspring knows where I am.*

Michael's heart turned to ice. Somebody's chromaflage discipline must have slipped long enough for a DocSec surveillance holocam to pick up the mistake as the team—*or me,* thought Michael—made its way to Papa-Six. That was the only explanation.

Good thing I ordered Shinoda and the rest to go when I did, he consoled himself. *My conscience is bad enough without adding them to the list of people I've gotten killed.*

Now Michael could see Hartspring's plan as if it had been drawn on the ground in front of him. It was obvious. Backed up by Team Victor's firepower, DocSec would throw a cordon of laser trip wires around the area, one even a flea couldn't get through. When the perimeter was secure—*it already is*, he realized—Hartspring would send in the search teams to flush him out. And they would. It was only a matter of time.

Michael's time had all but run out. He had to find a way out of the trap Hartspring had laid for him. The man had played him for a fool, and what a fool he was.

Of course ENCOMM always knew where Team Victor was. Hartspring had made sure of that. And he'd changed his strategy. Kidnapping Anna might have been his original plan, but that would have been all but impossible in the chaos of combat. So instead of going after Anna—or Michael, come to that—he had sat back and waited for Michael to come to him. Which he had just done.

Michael cursed his stupidity, his pride, his arrogance.

He took a deep breath. Beating himself up was only wasting time. He had to get out. But how? A careful look around the ruined warehouse provided no options. It was built on a ceramcrete slab, and so there was no way into any sewers or drains that might run below it. The building's simple plasfiber-covered frame and handful of offices offered nowhere to hide, and even if they had, the searchbots would sniff him out. Make a run for it? No, that wouldn't work. He had delayed too long. He'd never get past DocSec's trip wires.

With fear now threatening to turn to panic, Michael cast about in a desperate search for a way out. But no matter how hard he looked, there was none. As if he were looking for divine intervention, his head went back. That was when he spotted the control cabin on the massive gantry crane spanning the warehouse. *Wait*, he thought with mounting excitement. *My breath is warm, and warm air rises, which means the searchbots won't be able to detect the carbon dioxide I exhale. It'll mix with the sun-heated air under the ceiling and escape through the holes in the roof.*

"Yes!" he hissed, exultant now that he had a real chance to escape Hartspring's trap. He should be safe. Searchbots couldn't climb ladders as far as he knew. Better still, their infrared sensors would not see him. The metal cabin would be so hot that any heat his body added would go unnoticed.

If the Hammers wanted to find him, they'd have to climb the ladder, and even then they had to spot him under his chromaflage cape. But Michael hoped they wouldn't even bother to look for him in a place so exposed, so obvious.

He did not wait. Jumping to his feet, he ran hard for the ladder, pulling himself up rung by rung, wincing as flame-seared hands took his weight; then he moved along the access catwalk and into the cabin, its interior hot in the sun-baked air.

Forcing the safety gate half shut, Michael went to the very back of the cabin and slumped to the floor, all but his boots and head tucked away out of sight behind a large junction box. Pulling his cape over his body, he did the only thing he could do: wait.

* * *

Michael awoke with a start, for a moment confused by the unfamiliar surroundings. Then it all flooded back; he cursed his lack of discipline. This was not the time to be snoring his head off; searchbots had all the senses except touch, and so they would hear him if he did.

His heart thudded in his chest when he heard a skittering, scratching sound: the sound of dry leaves being blown gently along, the sound of a searchbot legs as they made their way across the ceramcrete floor of the warehouse. And not just one set of legs; there were lots, and for all its gentleness, it was a truly frightening sound: the sound of mindless machines hunting for him.

There was a heavier sound now: the noise of boots. "Dubcek, Carmichael, take that end," a voice boomed, rattling and echoing around the warehouse, "Mishra, Kowalski, the other."

Don't look up, Michael prayed, heart pounding and mouth ash-dry with fear. *Please do not look up.*

The boots crashed their way up and down. "Nothing, sarge," one of the men said.

"Okay, outside. Mishra?"

"Nothing here. The bots say the place is clean."

"Fine."

Michael had been holding his breath so long that his chest burned in protest; exhaling in a long, slow silent hiss, he let a tiny flame of hope spring to life.

It did not last, snuffed out by a few simple words. "What about up there?" the corporal said.

"Kraa's blood," a voice protested. "Nobody's going to hide up there."

"Get your fat ass up that ladder, Kowalski, and make sure that's the case."

"Oh, come on, corp. What's the point?"

"The point, Marine Kowalski, is that I will kick you from here to sunset if you don't. Now move!"

"Yes, corp."

"What the fuck are you doing, Kowalski? Take the damn probe with you."

"Do I have to?" the voice whined. "Those things are heavy."

"Kowalski!" the corporal roared; his voice was incandescent with rage.

"Okay, okay. I'll take it."

Michael looked around, frantic now. His chromaflage cape might fool Kowalski; nothing would fool the probe. At best he had thirty seconds left before the marine found him, and then his life was over.

Defeat swamped him. He slumped back. Thirty seconds or thirty years; it made no difference. This was the end, and there wasn't a damn thing he could do about it except raise his pistol and wait, peering at the door to the control cabin through the tiniest of gaps in his cape.

He counted down the seconds as booted feet clumped along the catwalk. The man stopped. "Like I said, Corporal Shit-for-Brains," he muttered when he looked in, "there's not a damn thing up here."

For one glorious moment, Michael thought the man would leave it at that. But it was not to be.

With a grunt, Kowalski lifted the probe—a bulky box, its front studded with sensor wands—and balanced it on the safety gate. Buttons were punched; a soft hum told Michael that the machine had started to work.

Michael let the cape slip away from his face. It took Kowalski a few seconds to notice; by then Michael had his pistol pointing right at the man's face. He put his finger to his lips. "Shhhhh," he hissed.

The man stiffened. He blinked and stared back but said nothing. But only for a few seconds. "Corporal!" the man shouted, starting to back away.

Michael shot Kowalski between the eyes. The crack of the laser pulse sounded horribly loud. Dropping the pistol, Michael scrambled to his feet. He lunged out even as the body started ever so slowly to fall away from him. Hampered by the gate, Michael was not fast enough. His hands flailed the air, but now Kowalski was toppling to one side, his head and chest already over the guardrail, the rest threatening to follow. With one last desperate effort, Michael locked one hand into the man's assault vest, the other grabbing the probe an instant before Kowalski's hands let it slip.

"What's up now, Kowalski?" the corporal shouted.

"Having trouble with this damn probe, corp," Michael said, wincing at his piss-poor attempt to copy the man's voice. He pulled Kowalski back and let the body slump forward over the safety gate. "I'll be a while."

Michael might have been unhappy with his impersonation, but the corporal wasn't. "Just get a move on, you fat fuck," he yelled.

"Yes, corp."

The boots walked away; Michael urged him on. He let a minute drag past. Gun in hand, he ran along the catwalk, half climbing, half sliding down the ladder until his feet crashed into the ground. He turned and headed for the door, then stopped.

Killing Kowalski had changed nothing. He was still trapped with nowhere to run, nowhere to hide.

Corporal Whatever-His-Name would be waiting outside, wondering what the hell had happened to Kowalski. He would come back, Michael would shoot him too, and then all hell would break loose as the rest of Team Victor came crashing in and shot the shit out of him.

The corporal did come back. "Kowalski, you useless toe rag, what the—"

Michael shot him, the racket of the assault rifle shockingly loud, then dived for cover. "Come on, you fucking Hammer bastards," he shouted. "You want me, you come and get me."

The silence was complete. It dragged on. Michael wondered what was going on. Where were they?

He got his answer soon enough. A series of flat cracks preceded the arrival of more microgrenades than Michael could count. The small black shapes arced through the warehouse door and landed on the ceramcrete floor, bouncing for a few meters before bursting into boiling clouds of smoke.

Oh, shit, he thought as the clouds rolled across the floor toward him. *They're gassing me. It's over. Survival; that's all that matters now.* He ripped off the chain holding the gold sunburst Vaas's troopers had taken from Hartspring and tossed it away. Then his lungs caught fire, and the lights went out.

Pain hammered at Michael's skull, his mouth and throat burned, and his chest was a searing ball of flame. When he tried opening his eyes, he wished he hadn't. It just made things worse.

A pair of hands dragged him upright; the pain redoubled. "Come on, you little bastard. I know you're awake. Throw some water on him, sergeant."

The water hit Michael full in the face. A hand followed, a stinging slap hard across his cheek. He cringed back, hands coming up to keep his unseen attacker away.

"Open your Kraa-damned eyes, Helfort, or I'll make you wish you had."

Michael did, squinting through agony-filled eyes at a face he had hoped to see only on a dead man, a face dominated by eyes so pale that only a hint of amber remained, the eyes of a killer.

"Fuck you, Hartspring," Michael whispered, "you asshole."

Hartspring's fist lashed out, stopping only millimeters from Michael's face. For an instant, it hung there, utterly still. Then it pulled back. "You are lucky, Helfort, that Chief Councillor Polk has ordered me to deliver you to McNair without a single scratch on that pretty face of yours."

"Good for Mister Polk, you piece of Hammer sh—"

This time Hartspring's fist did not stop. It smashed into Michael's stomach with tremendous force, hitting just below the ribs to blast the air out of his lungs. The enormous power of the blow lifted him bodily into the air to drop with a sickening crash on the floor.

Thin, bloodless lips pressed tight in a sneer of disdain, Hartspring leaned over Michael as he lay on his back with his mouth working to drag air back into tortured lungs. "Unfortunately for you, Helfort," he said, "Chief Councillor Polk said nothing about not hurting you." He straightened up. "Let's get you cleaned up, and then I'll tell you what happens next. I'll come back in an hour, and when I do, I suggest you cooperate. If you don't, I will hurt you, and I will go on hurting you until you do."

"Screw you," Michael whispered to Hartspring's back.

"A public trial?" Michael said.

Hartspring nodded. "That's what I said. A public trial in front of the full bench of the Supreme Tribunal for the Preservation of the Faith."

"Why bother? Everyone will know it's a farce."

"We both know that," Hartspring said, "though I'd prefer, let me see … yes, I'd prefer to call it a piece of political theater. You're a celebrity, you see, a bit of hero to many, so we can't just shoot you out of hand. We need to be seen to be doing things in the right way."

"What a crock."

"It certainly is a crock, but what do I care? There will be a trial, you will be found guilty, and you will be sentenced to death, only this time your friends won't be there to help you escape justice. Oh, no; when the Hammer of Kraa sentences someone to death, they die." Hartspring paused. "The only difference with you," he continued, "is that you won't be shot. No, that'd be too quick. No, we'll make sure you die the slowest, the most painful death a man can suffer …"

Michael shivered, the fear all-consuming.

"… because after all you have done to us, it's the least we can do to you. Now, enough talk. We leave for McNair in an hour."

"Where am I being taken?" Michael asked the man sitting opposite him as they waited for the armored personnel carrier to take him to McNair. As much as he could like any Hammer, he liked Corporal Haditha. He was one of the few marines to treat him with any consideration, not that he deserved any. He had shot one of Team Victor right between the eyes, after all.

Haditha took a while to answer. "The Gruj," he said at last. "Where else?"

Of course, thought Michael, his pulse accelerating as a frisson of fear shivered its way up his spine. Where else? He had spent long enough with the NRA and the

Revivalists to know all there was to know about the Councillor Carlos C. Grujic Building. There were precious few born on the Hammer worlds who did not know some poor unfortunate who had been through the place—there had been tens of millions of them over the years—and every last one of them feared and hated it.

The Gruj's reputation as the very heart of the Hammer's all-pervading system of state terror was well deserved.

Michael had talked to an NRA trooper who'd been through the place, one of the very few to survive the experience. Her story had been one of pure horror, and Michael was not looking forward to sharing the experience.

Below what looked like an office block no different from any other lay a cold world, a world silent apart from the subdued hiss of an air-conditioning system set to maintain a temperature not far above freezing, a world that never slept, a world created for the endless stream of black trucks that shuttled DocSec's prisoners into the Gruj.

Hounded mercilessly from the arrival dock down bleak corridors, the new arrivals were fed through the heavily armored security post, then down to the first of four levels of unpainted, bare-floored plascrete rooms and into the massive in-processing center on Level A. There the bewildered and terrified sweepings of three worlds were stripped naked, searched with callous indifference, doused in icy water, and microchipped before being bundled, dripping wet and shaking with cold, into orange coveralls and plasfiber boots, their identities torn away along with their clothes and dignity, their identity a number stenciled front and back.

From Level A, prisoners would be herded down to the holding cells on Levels B and C by silent but always brutal guards who were never slow to use their plasteel batons. There they would stay, sometimes for minutes, sometimes for days, sometimes for weeks. But in the end, they all ended up being dragged to Level D for interrogation in rooms harshly lit by banks of halogen overheads that threw a pitiless white light from which there was no escape. The rooms were bleak and functional, fitted only with chairs and a simple metal table bolted to a plascrete floor pierced by a small drain to make it easier for blood to be hosed away.

The process was so assured, a guilty finding so certain, that the lucky few released without charge—and they were very few—were often violently sick on the pavement outside the Gruj as they waited for someone to pick them up. DocSec troopers called them boomers, because they always came back. The troopers had never been good losers, and every boomer was a challenge to their infallibility. And DocSec's view of things was simple in the extreme: Everyone who ended up in the Gruj was guilty of something even if DocSec hadn't yet worked out what that thing was.

For the overwhelming majority, the next stop on their journey through the bowels of the Gruj was preordained. In the interests of efficiency, the Gruj had its own investigating tribunal tucked away in a corner of Level A, the last stop but one for most prisoners and the only area underground that was even close to being comfortably warm.

Staffed twenty-four hours a day, seven days a week, the tribunal was an organization intensely proud of its ability to listen to the evidence presented by the DocSec prosecuting officer and hear the accused's response—if the tribunal could be bothered, though it rarely was—before bringing down the required verdict of guilty and recommending the sentence. The efficiency experts had decreed that the process should take five minutes if everyone did his job properly, and to nobody's surprise, almost every case was dealt with in less. The record, proudly held for more than ten years by Investigating Tribune Corey MacMasters, was fifty-seven seconds from the moment the state prosecutor opened the proceedings to the handing down of the sentence.

Because of DocSec's unshakable belief in guilt by association, it was rare for a case not to involve at least two hapless Hammer citizens. The record, once again held by the energetic MacMasters, was the trial of the entire crew of the Verity-Class heavy cruiser *Jossarian*, more than a thousand of them, their only crime having been to serve with a handful of crew members who complained too loudly about the conduct of Marshall Fench, *Jossarian*'s protector of doctrine and a man so irredeemably corrupt that even DocSec had been forced to bring him to account, but only once the misguided spacers had been consigned to the Hammer penal system after a trial in front of a tribunal temporarily set up in one of the Gruj's huge underground garages.

MacMasters had finished the entire process in less than three minutes.

The final stop for the guilty was outprocessing, and then their journey through the Gruj's little slice of hell would end where it started, back at the loading dock. There DocSec guards would ram the guilty into the back of black trucks, some for McNair State Prison and an appointment with the DocSec firing squad, some for the living death of the Hell system's mass driver mines, most for the hard labor camps scattered the length and breadth of the three settled planets of the Hammer Worlds.

Michael shivered again. Hartspring had told him he was to be treated like any other DocSec prisoner. It was his misfortune to know in cold, clinical detail what that meant.

The door banged open, and a marine stuck his head in. "The APC is here, corp," he said.

"Get the escort lined up," Haditha said. "On your feet, Helfort. Let's go."

Michael's journey down into the hell they called the Gruj had started.

Wednesday, October 20, 2404, UD
Level B holding cell, the Gruj, McNair,
Commitment

The cold had seeped deep into his body. He was chilled right down the bone. For hours his body had been racked by uncontrollable shivering. *Hypothermia*, Michael thought. *If this goes on much longer, I'm going to die.*

Michael sat with his head back, eyes looking up at the single recessed light in the ceiling, leaning against the ceramcrete wall, at the point where he did not have the energy to care anymore. After days of relentless interrogation and physical abuse, his reserves of courage, of resilience, of self-belief, had run dry. He had nothing left to absorb the appalling shocks that life dished out. He was empty. He did not care. He had nothing left to care about. He was just a number in orange DocSec coveralls waiting to die.

He laughed softly, a laugh that mocked his obsessive determination to hunt down and kill Hartspring.

The cell door banged opened, swinging back into the wall with a crash. Michael did not even look up, unable to summon the slightest interest in the man standing in the opening.

"On your feet, 775," the DocSec trooper said.

With an effort, Michael dragged himself upright.

"Outside!"

Michael stumbled after the man and into a bleak, harshly lit ceramcrete corridor. It reeked of chlorine. The

Hammers used tons of the stuff to scour the blood and shit out of the cells. Two troopers waited for him. They took him by the upper arms and set off. Michael forced the men to take his weight. His feet dragged, one last tiny act of defiance.

If it bothered the troopers, they didn't let it show. After a bewildering succession of turns and two elevator rides, Michael was manhandled into a small room and thrown into a chair; his arms and legs were secured to small rings. Job done, the troopers left, the door slamming behind them. Michael looked around, confused. He wondered what this place was. Unlike the interrogation rooms he'd been in over the last few days, this one was warm, softly lit, its floor not bare ceramcrete but carpeted. And the table was timber, not scuffed and scarred metal like all the rest.

He was left on his own for a long time. The minutes dragged past, but Michael was content to sit there to thaw out. The warmth soaked the chill out of his bones until his head fell back and he drifted into sleep.

A smack to the back of the head jerked him awake. "What the fuck?" Michael mumbled.

It was Hartspring. "Wake up, you sack of shit," he said, his riding crop stabbing at Michael's chest.

"What do you want now?" Michael muttered.

"You have a visitor, Helfort. And I'm warning you: Be polite, or by Kraa I'll make you wish you were dead. Understood?"

Michael glared at Hartspring. His silence earned him a savage slash across the back from the man's riding crop. "One day," Michael hissed, "I'll make you eat that fucking thing."

Hartspring sniffed. "I don't think so," he said with a disdainful sneer.

The door opened. Michael sat up; he could not help himself. "I'll be damned," he whispered as he saw who it was.

"So, Colonel Hartspring," Jeremiah Polk said as he walked in, "this is the young man who has given me so much trouble."

"Yes, sir."

Michael stared up into Polk's face. It was a hard face, lined and drawn, the eyes hard too, a deep brown, almost black. They glittered in the harsh light.

Polk nodded. "Not very impressive," he said. "He's much smaller than I expected. So, Helfort, I hope the colonel's treating you well."

Anger flared. "This is the Gruj," Michael snapped, "so that's got to be the stupidest thing I've ever—"

Hartspring's hand shot out. It locked itself around Michael's throat and choked him into silence. "I won't tell you again, boy," he snarled. "Mind your manners."

"It's all right," Polk said with an expansive wave. "Let him babble on. It won't change anything."

"Yes, sir," Hartspring said, letting go of Michael's throat.

"I am disappointed, though," Polk went on, talking over Michael's choking fight to get air down his bruised windpipe.

"You are, Chief Councillor?"

"Yes. I was rather hoping you would have caught that woman of his as well. What was her name?"

"Anna Cheung Helfort, sir."

"Yes, her. I would have enjoyed seeing the pair of them die together. So romantic—"

"You slimy son of a bitch!" Michael shouted. He hurled himself forward, arms flailing in a fruitless attempt to get free of their restraints. "I'll fucking kill you."

Polk laughed. "I don't think so." He turned to Hartspring. "Your prosecutor is taking his time," he said.

"We need to take the time to get this right, sir. The trial is scheduled to start a week from tomorrow."

"Humph!" Polk snorted. "It's all taking too long, but I'll defer to you on this one. Who's the investigating tribune?"

"Kostakidis, sir, Marek Kostakidis."

Polk frowned. "I don't know him. He's solid?"

"As a rock, sir. He was one of the tribunes who dealt with the MARFOR 8 mutineers."

"Kostakidis … Ah, yes, I remember him now. Seemed very efficient."

"He is, sir. But more important, he's very precise. There'll be no mistakes."

"Good. We have—"

"Hey!" Michael said. "I'm still here, assholes."

This time Hartspring did not hold back. The riding crop was raised high before slicing down, a vicious slash that laid Michael's cheek open, blood pouring down hot into his orange coverall.

"Now look what you've done, Colonel," Polk said. His voice displayed no emotion whatsoever. "You seem to have spoiled that pretty face of his."

"My apologies, Chief Councillor," Hartspring said. He wiped the blood from the crop and stepped back. "It won't happen again."

"Really? That's a shame. I rather enjoyed watching you do that." Polk put his face close to Michael's. "You do know," he said, "that I've told the colonel that he can do what he likes with you once the trial's over? Yes, I think you do." He turned back to Hartspring, wagging a finger in mock rebuke. "But you must not let him die, Colonel Hartspring … well, not until I say you can."

"Oh, don't worry, sir. He'll wish he was dead, but we'll make sure he hangs on. I've instructed my best interrogator to keep Helfort alive for three weeks at least."

"I like the sound of that. And the film crew?"

"Briefed and ready to go. I think you'll enjoy my daily reports."

"Oh, I will."

Michael had had enough. "So how's the war going, Polk?" he said. "Not well last time I checked. The NRA won't give you the three weeks Colonel Asswipe here—"

Another savage slash from the riding crop cut Michael short, but this time he expected it, twisting his head down and to one side to take the blow on his head. The pain was excruciating; the crop opened a cut deep into his scalp that send blood pouring down his neck. But it was worth it, Michael thought, staring from pain-filled eyes up into Polk's face, worth it to see the fear on the chief councillor's face.

"Well, well, well," Michael said, forcing a smile through the pain, "so it's not going well, then. Maybe you're the one who'll be looking at a firing squad—"

Michael was still focused on Polk when Hartspring's fist slammed into the side of his face, the blow so powerful that he blacked out for a second.

"I don't care about how the little bastard looks, not anymore," Polk said to Hartspring. "I want you to hurt him. Make him scream, Colonel. Just don't kill him. I want him in court next week, unmarked and on his feet."

Hartspring smiled. "Yes, sir," he said. "It'll be my pleasure."

Twelve hours later, Hartspring followed two DocSec troopers as they dragged the bloodied wreck that was Michael Helfort into the Gruj's sick bay. They dumped him on the floor.

"You!" Hartspring barked at the duty medic, snapping the man out of a half doze and onto his feet. "This man is a Class A prisoner. I want him fixed up now, and if he needs to go to the hospital, then organize it. Just let me know before you move him so I can organize security."

"Yes, sir."

"And you two," he said to the two troopers. "You do not let Helfort out of your sight. Understood?'

"Yes, sir," the pair chorused.

"Good. I want an update in an hour."

Wednesday, October 27, 2404, UD
High-security ward, McNair Memorial Hospital,
Commitment

Michael was bored rigid.

Even the prospect of appearing in front of Investigating Tribune Marek Kostakidis was not enough to get him excited. In fact, he was looking forward to it in a strange way. It would be a change from the tedium of being locked in a secure cell inside a secure ward with nothing to do and nobody to talk to. It also would give him a chance to say his bit, even though he knew full well he would not be given more than a minute or two, if that, to say anything.

The trial would be a farce. That much was not in doubt. The attorney appointed by the tribunal to defend him had handed him the brief of evidence only the day before. The meeting that followed had been a complete crock, and the attorney not much better. Over and over, he had refused to respond when Michael had pointed out inconsistencies in the evidence, saying only that the brief had been prepared by DocSec, was accurate, and could not be questioned.

Michael had never met a man so spineless. A jellyfish would have been more useful.

He pushed himself upright and swung his feet out of the bed before standing up, doing his best to ignore the protests from his abused body. Thanks to the best medical care the Hammers had to offer—as good as anything the Federated Worlds could provide—he was well on the way to recovery, his system still loaded with nanobots busy repairing the damage Hartspring's interrogators had inflicted over the course of those terrible hours of unremitting punishment.

Michael stood swaying until the light-headedness had passed. He slipped on his plasfiber half boots before forcing his body into its regular routine of pacing out the few meters his cell afforded him, stopping every few circuits to do squats and push-ups. It was a huge effort, but he forced himself to move, relieved to feel his muscles loosening in response to the exercise, the pain that had wracked his frame the first few days now reduced to a mass of dull aches.

An hour later, his body had made it clear that enough was enough. Five more minutes, he told himself, and then he would stop. For the umpteenth time, he reached the wall and turned, but as he did, the floor shivered, a fleeting tremor that was gone almost before he realized what was happening. An instant later, the air filled with a heavy rumble that rolled on and on. Puzzled, Michael stopped, his head swinging from side to side as he tried to work out what the noise was and where it was coming from. It was an impossible task with the heavy plasglass windows and the thick ceramcrete walls robbing the sound of all life. There was a short pause; then the noise returned, louder, and this time it did not stop, building into an irregular thudding that shook Michael's cell.

His mind raced. Only one thing made that noise: high explosive and tons of it. It had been almost two weeks since Hartspring's men had captured him; could the NRA have broken through the Hammer's defensive line along the Oxus River since then? They must have; why would the NRA be using its precious air assets over McNair if they hadn't?

Without any warning, the door banged open. "Stand back!" the DocSec sergeant in charge of Michael's security detail barked. Lojenga was the man's name. Like every other DocSec trooper Michael had ever met, he was a brutal psychopath who was way too fond of using his baton and stun pistol.

Michael did as he was told, and Hartspring appeared. The colonel looked down his nose at Michael for a good minute. He made Michael feel like he was a piece of dog shit on the sole of one of his mirror-polished boots. Finally he nodded. "He'll do," he said, turning to Lojenga. "Talk to—"

"Wait, Colonel," Michael said. "I'll do for what?"

Hartspring's lips thinned to bloodless slashes. "Did I speak to you?" he hissed.

"I don't give a shit whether you did or not," Michael snapped. He stepped back as Lojenga unholstered his stun pistol. "What will I do for?"

Hartspring waved Lojenga away. "Your trial starts tomorrow," he said.

"No way. The doctor said I couldn't be moved for at least another three days."

"The doctor?" Hartspring smiled. "You think I care what the doctor says? Now shut your damned mouth or I'll let the sergeant's stun pistol finish this conversation." He turned to Lojenga. "Have him ready to move out in ten minutes."

"Yes, sir."

Wrists flexicuffed to leg restraints, Michael watched Hartspring's second armored personnel carrier reverse up to the hospital's prisoner transfer dock. He wasn't bored anymore; the opposite, in fact. His heart pounded as he contemplated his return to the Gruj and the start of his trial the next day.

It was the beginning of the end. He knew that. After all the humiliation and embarrassment he had heaped on Chief Councillor Polk and the Hammers, they would finish him this time. Their determination was obvious; an APC blocking the access ramp to the transfer dock was just the start. Outside, in the harsh glare of massed floodlights, waited four all-terrain vehicles, cannon- and missile-armed, their crews dressed in full combat gear and carrying assault rifles. Beyond them were two more

APCs. Decoys, Michael supposed, and probably packed with yet more marines.

It would take an entire NRA battalion to get him free of the Hammers.

Hartspring was taking nothing for granted. His briefing over, he was walking the line of vehicles to have a final word with each of the commanders. Michael could understand the man's obsessive attention to detail. If Hartspring let Michael get away, Chief Councillor Polk would tear his heart out with his bare hands.

Hartspring took a final look around; he nodded and walked back where Michael waited. "Mount up," he shouted, waving a hand. "Sergeant Lojenga! What the hell are you waiting for? Get that bloody man into my APC!"

"Sir!"

Lojenga pushed Michael down the ramp to the waiting vehicle. Too hard. Unable to move his feet fast enough, Michael stumbled a few halting steps before gravity took over, dragging him down in an awkward, twisting fall that his flexicuffed hands could not break. His body crashed into the ceramcrete dock, tumbled down the ramp, and came to a stop at Hartspring's feet, newly healed injuries screaming in protest.

"You bastards," Michael hissed through clenched teeth.

Hartspring ignored him. He pulled out his pistol and stepped over Michael. In a single fluid movement, he ran up the ramp, put the pistol to Lojenga's head, and pulled the trigger. The shot echoed around the transfer dock, a flat crack that faded into the silence.

The DocSec sergeant stood for a while, eyes wide open in shocked surprise. With a sigh, he crumpled to the ground at Hartspring's feet. "You always were a useless turd, Sergeant Lojenga," Hartspring said. He spit on the black-jumpsuited body and stood back. "You! Rajith, Craxi!" His finger stabbed out at two DocSec troopers. "Get that bloody man on his feet and into the APC. Move!"

The two men sprinted down the ramp. They dragged Michael to his feet and bundled him into the APC, and none too carefully. They ignored Michael's protests and followed him in. It was hot; the air smelled of hydraulic fluid, burned gun oil, and spent ammunition and was filled with the muted chatter of radio circuits. The interior was cluttered with weapons racks, storage boxes, comm equipment, and workstations. The marine operators looked like they'd much rather be somewhere else; the glances they threw at the two troopers were loaded with contempt.

The men pushed him into a crash seat and strapped him in, securing his arms and legs to small rings on the bulkhead and the floor, the restraints pulled so cruelly tight that he could barely move. "Thanks so much, you pair of DocSec dipshits," Michael muttered.

One of the troopers put his face close to Michael's. "Enjoy the ride, you Fed cocksucker. Where you're goi—"

With all the force he could muster, Michael smashed his forehead into the bridge of the man's nose. The blow hit with a terrible crunching thud that sent the man howling back across the cramped compartment with his hands to his face and into one the marines, who pushed him to the deck with a curse. The man sat whimpering, blood spurting scarlet from between his fingers.

"Big mistake," Michael said, smiling though the pain.

The smile did not last. The second trooper whipped his stun pistol out and jammed it into Michael's stomach. The charge jolted Michael's body rigid, his entire nervous system screaming in protest.

"What the Kraa is going on?" It was Hartspring. Even through pain-slitted eyes Michael could see he was seriously pissed.

"The prisoner attacked Trooper Rajith, sir," the DocSec trooper said. "I have the situation under control."

"You'd better, Corporal Craxi. Rajith, get your useless hide out of here. I'll deal with you later."

Hartspring ignored Michael. He made his way up the compartment and slipped on a headset and boom mike. He climbed into the commander's position behind the driver, a center-mounted crash seat flanked by two large holovid displays; fingers flew across a small control console.

Finally Hartspring nodded, obviously satisfied that everything was as it should be. "Tango Niner, this is Box Cutter," he said. "Move out."

The APC lurched forward. Michael craned his head to look at Hartspring's displays. They were clearly readable in the subdued light. "You're not taking any chances, are you?" he said under his breath when he worked out what the clutter of icons meant. And Hartspring wasn't. His APC was accompanied by three more. Two ATVs led the convoy, two brought up the rear, and two more covered the flanks. Surveillance and attack drones orbited overhead.

It was an impressive amount of firepower to keep one man in plasticuffs and leg restraints in custody. Michael allowed himself a moment of satisfaction. Better all those assets and men were tied up escorting him across McNair than facing the NRA, he thought.

Satisfaction turned to jubilation when Hartspring opened out the range scale to reveal an ugly red line slashing down across the northeastern suburbs of the city.

Yes, yes, yes, Michael thought. *The NRA has broken the Hammers' defensive line between Yallan and Cooperbridge to cross the Oxus. Now it's only a matter of time before the Hammer of Kraa is history.*

His jubilation vanished. Behind the front line, red icons marked the positions of the attacking NRA units. And there was the only icon that mattered, the icon for a mechanized infantry battalion: a rectangle enclosing a cross, the symbols | | above, and the numbers 3/120 to the right. *That's Anna's battalion*, Michael thought, *and they are only 10 kilometers outside McNair.*

Knowing she was that close almost tore him apart. She might as well have been a million klicks away.

Michael forced himself to look away. His head went back, and his eyes closed in despair. He was slipping into sleep when, with no warning, the brakes slammed on, bringing the APC to a shuddering halt.

Something is up, Michael thought, *and I'll be it's something Hartspring hasn't planned for.*

The colonel's body language told the same story. He sat crowbar-straight in his seat, one hand locked into a grab handle and the other stabbing at the command display while he muttered orders into his boom mike. Whatever Hartspring was saying got the APC moving again, only this time it was really shifting. It swayed from side to side, its tires scrubbing as it was pushed hard into corners. And over the noise of the APC came the heavy concussive thud of bombs, the metallic racket of heavy machine guns, the heavy thump of cannon fire.

I'll be a son of a bitch, Michael thought. *Hartspring's convoy is being gone over by NRA ground-attack landers.* An image of a smart bomb coming down through the roof of the APC right into the man flashed across Michael's mind.

Without any warning, a single massive explosion picked up the APC and tossed it high into the air. The blast crushed Michael down into his seat and drove the back of his head hard into the headrest. For a moment, the APC hung weightless. Then it rolled onto its side and plunged back to earth, hitting in a sickening crunch that tossed men around the crew compartment like so many straw dolls.

The last thing Michael remembered was the butt of an assault rifle hurtling toward him before it punched into his forehead and sent him spinning down into darkness.

Michael ignored a blinding headache and opened his eyes. Groggy with pain, he looked around the APC. It was a shambles, a terrible sight in the feeble glow of emergency lights. The front of the crew compartment was jammed with bodies. They lay one atop another, piled in awkward disarray against the side of the APC in a tangle of arms and legs. The air was filled with moans of pain. Michael thought the two DocSec troopers and most of the marines were dead.

He realized how lucky he had been. Unlike the crew, he had been strapped in tightly when the APC was blasted skyward by what must have been a very close miss, his hands and feet restrained, his head and body cradled by the crash seat. Michael reckoned a glancing blow from a wayward rifle was a small price to pay for surviving the mayhem.

But surviving had left him with a small problem. The crash seat and restraints might have saved him, but he had to get out before help arrived. But how? He twisted his head around to look at Hartspring's body. Was the man alive? If he was, Michael wanted to be long gone before he woke up. Michael could see no way to get free. He swore long and hard under his breath, his frantic attempts to wrench his arms free only making bruised muscles protest in pain.

He swore some more when the side hatch opened. The sound of cannon fire and explosions flooded in. A head sporting a bloodstained field dressing appeared. "Anyone alive in here?" it shouted over the racket.

It was Corporal Haditha. "Just me, I think," Michael called up. "Rest are either dead or unconscious."

"Hold on." Haditha's feet replaced his head. The marine lowered himself. He looked around. "Kraa!" he hissed. "What a fucking mess."

"Can you get me out before this thing goes up?"

"It won't," Haditha said. He was already checking for survivors. "I've shut everything down." He paused, turning to Michael. "Besides, why would I help you? What I should do is blow your fucking head off, you piece of Fed crap."

Hope vanished, replaced not by fear but by anger. "You think this is what I want?" Michael shouted. "It's not. I just want you fucking Hammers to stop killing each other and to leave the rest of us alone." His head slumped back. "I don't care what you do," he muttered, closing his eyes. And he didn't. He had given all he could; he had nothing left.

Haditha worked his way over to Michael. "You think I'm just another stupid Hammer, don't you?"

"Piss off," Michael muttered. "If you don't kill me now, that son of a bitch Hartspring will, so what do I care?"

"Believe me, nothing would make me happier than to kill you."

"So do it."

Haditha sighed. "No," he said. "I won't. You can give me a hand to see who's alive, and then I don't give a shit what you do. This fucking war's over—" They both flinched as a second explosion punched the wrecked APC bodily to one side. "—and there's the proof. I never thought I'd see the day the NRA would be bombing the shit out of McNair. But today's the day, and it is. Now shut up and let me get you out of there."

It was the work of only seconds for Haditha to cut away the restraints. "That's it," the marine said. He threw off the safety harness that had kept Michael alive. "Now help me see who's still breathing. You can start with your friend, the colonel. I'll take the humans."

Michael wanted to kiss the man. Instead he grabbed a medical kit off the bulkhead. He pushed past Haditha to where Hartspring lay, moaning softly. For an instant, Michael's hands were around the man's throat, but sense prevailed, and he let his hands fall away.

Hartspring's eyes opened. He peered up at Michael. "Couldn't do it, then?" he croaked. "You Feds always were piss weak."

Michael put his mouth to Hartspring's ear. "Don't worry," he whispered, "it's only a postponement. I need you."

He was wasting his time. The man had slipped back into unconsciousness, so Michael turned his attention to the rest of the survivors, though not before relieving Hartspring of his pistol.

Fifteen minutes later, he and Haditha had done what they could. It wasn't much. Only one of the marines was conscious; the rest were either dead or so severely wounded that they would be if they did not get medical attention soon. Michael did not fancy their chances. By the sound of it, the NRA had launched a full-scale assault on McNair. The noise was incredible, the hull of the APC shaken repeatedly by near misses, its hull battered by a relentless shower of shrapnel and wayward gun and cannon fire.

"I think we've done all we can," he said to Haditha, "but these guys need help and fast."

"I know," the marine said, rubbing his face with a bloody hand. "I've radioed for the medics, but Kraa knows when they'll get here."

"What now?"

"Up to you." Haditha waved a hand at the hatch. "It's not too good out there, so I'm not going anywhere. This is the safest place to be right now."

"I can go?" Michael asked.

"If you want to. I don't give a shit."

"But I do," a voice said from the front of the APC.

Michael and Haditha swung around to find themselves looking down the barrel of an assault rifle held in the wavering hands of Colonel Hartspring. Michael cursed his own stupidity; he'd assumed that Hartspring was too badly wounded to pose a threat.

"Now, Corporal Haditha," Hartspring went on, his voice weak, "I will give you an order, and if you do not obey me, I will shoot you. Is that understood?"

"Yes, sir," Haditha replied.

"Find some flexicuffs and make sure that little shit can't go anywhere."

"Yes, sir."

"You don't have to do this, Corporal," Michael hissed.

"Shut up," Haditha snapped, rummaging through the DocSec troopers' jumpsuits. "Bear with me, Colonel," he said, moving away from Michael. "I need to get cable ties from the spares—"

Haditha moved so fast that it was all over before Michael even realized what was happening. As if by magic, a stun pistol appeared in his hand, and he shot Hartspring right in the chest. The shock dropped the colonel into a trembling, shaking heap, his face a rictus of pain before his head went back and he passed out. "Fucking piece of DocSec garbage," Haditha said. He scrambled forward to take the gun from Hartspring's hand. "I think you'd best go," he said to Michael.

"I will, but I'm taking Hartspring with me. I need him to get me a meeting with Chief Councillor Polk."

"Polk?" Haditha's eyes flared in surprise. "You're joking."

"No, I'm not. Now, help me get the dirtbag out of here."

"I hope he breaks his fucking neck," Haditha muttered as they manhandled Hartspring's limp and unresponsive body up to the hatch and pushed him out.

"He'll live," Michael said, grabbing a rifle and a pistol before scavenging everything else he might need and jamming it all into a pack. "People like that always do. Right, I'm off. I'll see you."

"I hope not. You're too dangerous to be around."

Michael grinned. "True. Look after yourself, Corporal Haditha."

Ignoring the inevitable complaints from his badly abused body, he climbed out of the hatch and dropped down to land beside Hartspring's unconscious form. He looked around. "Holy shit!" he whispered. He was in a scene from hell. The road was littered with the shattered remnants of Hartspring's convoy. The vehicles had been ripped apart; now their carcasses burned fiercely, sending thick clouds of acrid black smoke boiling skyward. Only one was still recognizable as an ATV. Its snout was buried under the rubble of a collapsed building. Its occupants, shocked and dazed, had taken what cover they could beside the wreck. A marine bent over one of the survivors, lurid green woundfoam on his hands as he struggled to deal with an ugly gore-spattered chest wound. Intent on his work, he ignored Michael.

Spurred on by a wayward bomb that ripped the street apart only a hundred meters away, Michael slung the rifle across his back. Stripping Hartspring of his personal comm, he took the man by the collar. With every last grain of energy he possessed, he dragged the colonel's dead weight away, then down a side street and into the dubious safety of a half-collapsed office block. The effort was almost too much. Dropping Hartspring, he collapsed. His lungs heaved, and his heart pounded; he could only lie there, oblivious to the battle raging outside.

"This won't do," Michael said out loud, forcing himself to sit up. "This won't do at all."

Ferreting around inside his pack, he found the medical kit. Inside was what he was looking for: a blister pack of autoject syringes marked in red with the words "CAUTION: EMERGENCY USE ONLY. MORE THAN 1 DOSE PER DAY MAY KILL."

"One dose per day? Well, screw that," Michael said. He broke three out. Taking one, he smacked it into his arm. In an instant, an unholy cocktail of ampakine-derived stimulants and painkillers flooded his system. A tsunami of energy and exhilaration flushed the fatigue and pain out of his body. He turned his attention to Hartspring. Working fast, he propped the man up against the wall, flexicuffed him, and ripped the sleeve of his black jumpsuit off. He drove first one and then a second autoject home.

For a moment Michael thought that he'd overdone it, that the drugs had killed Hartspring. The colonel lay motionless. Then, to Michael's relief, his eyes opened. He looked around in wild confusion before his body shuddered upright, quivering and shaking.

"What the hell did you just do to me?' Hartspring asked, his voice firming as the drugs took hold, eyes now alert but wary.

"I smacked two of these babies into you," Michael said, waving an empty autoject.

"Kraa! No wonder I feel so good."

"I'm pleased to hear it," Michael said. "Now it's time to talk about how you're going to help me."

"Hah!" Hartspring snorted his derision. "Me? Help you?" he said with a sneer. "Why would I do that?"

"How about this?" Michael raised the laser pistol and fired into Hartspring's shin, the sharp, metallic crack of the hair-thin laser pulse loud even over the noise of the battle raging outside. "Will that do for a reason?" he said.

Hartspring did not flinch. "You're wasting your time," he said. "I didn't even feel that."

Michael swore under his breath; he should have known Hartspring's drug-laden system would absorb the shot without complaint. "Okay, then. Let's try this." Michael shot Hartspring again, this time in the stomach, low down and to one side. "I don't suppose you felt that, either," he went on. "Now, I'm no doctor, but my guess is you'll be dead inside six hours if I don't get you to a hospital. And if not dead, then pretty close to it … and in agony as those drugs wear off."

Fear flickered in Hartspring's eyes. "What do you want?" he said.

"I want you to set up a meeting with Polk for me."

Hartspring stared at Michael in open disbelief. "Polk?" he said. He shook his head. "You're kidding. Those Kraa-damned heretics are tearing McNair apart, and you want me to set up a meeting with Polk? Dream on, sonny boy. I can't do that."

Michael shot Hartspring in the stomach again. Hartspring looked down in disbelief at the tiny smoking hole punched through his black jumpsuit.

"How're your guts going?" Michael said. "Not too good, I'd say. I think I'll try for the liver next time. You'd better hope I don't hit one of those big blood vessels, because you won't have six hours left if I do. Hell, you might not even have one. Now, will you help me or not?"

Desperation joined fear in Hartspring's eyes. "It's not possible," he said.

"That's crap. Polk wants me real bad, remember?"

"Not anymore. Please believe me. The man's paranoid about security. He won't let you get anywhere near him, and even if he did, what would be the point?"

A tendril of doubt slipped into his mind. *Let it go*, it whispered. *Polk's not worth it*. Michael stomped down hard on the slender thread. This was not the time for second thoughts, he told himself. A promise was a promise, and if he didn't kill Polk, the man would get away. Besides, Polk would want to see him; he too was obsessed by thoughts of revenge, and that was the lever Hartspring would use.

"This is what we're going to do," Michael said. He tossed Hartspring's personal comm over. "Call the man.

Tell him that you're bringing me in. Let's start with that, and we'll see how it goes. Come on, Colonel. Time's running out, and don't try anything stupid or the next shot will be through your throat."

"Okay, okay," Hartspring said. He fiddled with the comm, then put it to his ear. *Primitive*, Michael thought. There was a long pause. "Polk's not answering. Nobody from his office is answering. He's gone."

"Fuck, fuck, fuck!" Michael shouted. "So where is the bastard?"

"No idea. Probably off-planet by now if he's got any sense."

"Get back on your comm and find out where he is or I'll leave you here to rot. Do it! Now!"

"How am I going to do that? It's chaos out there."

What was left of Michael's self-control vanished. Without a second's consideration, he shot Hartspring in the gut a third time. "I don't care. Just do it," he said. He ignored the man's whimpering protests.

"Polk was last seen in his office around midday," Hartspring said ten minutes later. "After that, nobody's seen or heard from him. I'm sorry; that's the best I can do. Get me to a hospital, now! For Kraa's sake."

"You're lying. He's there, isn't he?"

"Maybe, but I don't think so," Hartspring bleated. His face was twisted with pain. "The NRA attacked the Supreme Council complex this morning; the place is a ruin, and the Hammer of Kraa is finished. Why would he still be there?"

385

This is not good, Michael thought, angry and frustrated. *What the hell do I do now?*

The sudden appearance in the road of a Doctrinal Security colonel pointing a rifle at a disheveled man brought the mobibot to a screeching halt. A window opened. A man poked his head out. "What the hell are you doing?" he demanded. "Get out of my ... oh ... ah, sorry," the man stammered when he realized who he was looking at. "How can I help?"

"Get out!" Hartspring said. "I'm commandeering this vehicle."

The man could not get out of the mobibot fast enough; he did so without a word of protest.

As they set off, Michael took his assault rifle back from Hartspring and replaced the empty magazine with a full one. "Now, Colonel," he said, "you sit there and enjoy the ride. We'll be at the complex soon."

Hijacking the mobibot had been too much for Hartspring. His face was now a death mask of pasty, sweat-slicked white. "You promised," he whispered. "You promised to take me to the hospital."

"Yes, I did promise," Michael replied, "and I will, though let me see now—" He frowned, a finger tapping his lips. "—I don't think I ever promised to get you there alive. No, I'm pretty sure I didn't."

"You bastard," Hartspring mumbled. His voice was so soft that Michael had to strain to hear him.

"Yeah, yeah." Michael shook his head. "Anyway, after all you've put me and Anna through, did you really think I'd let you live? You're a damn fool if you did. But let's look at the upside," he continued. "Chief Councillor Polk ordered you to bring me in, and that's exactly what you're doing, though it's a pity the bastard won't be there to say hello. When he finds out, I think he'll give you a medal. Mind you, you'll be dead when he pins it on, but then, you can't have everything, can you?"

But Hartspring had stopped listening. His head fell back. With a soft choking rattle, his lungs emptied for the last time.

Hartspring was dead.

Still wide open, his eyes looked back at Michael in silent reproach. Michael leaned over, closed them, and sat back. His mind was filled with a confused jumble of emotions. Nothing made sense anymore. He had killed Hartspring, so why didn't he feel ... whatever he should have felt? Fulfillment? Satisfaction? Pleasure? He felt none of those things. He just felt flat and empty.

All he wanted was for it to be over, to go home, to be with Anna, to live a normal life.

But it was not over, not while Polk still lived. The nightmare would end only when the man was dead. Michael took a deep breath and forced himself to think straight.

In the chaos raining down on McNair—as if to make the point, the mobibot shook as a flight of NRA ground-attack landers swept overhead, the air torn apart by the

howling screech of rockets as they pounded some unseen target—finding Polk had to be close to impossible.
Unless Hartspring had been lying, of course. But if Polk
was in the complex, how would he ever find a way past
his security detail to kill the man?

And even if he managed to kill Polk, that still left the
small problem of getting back out alive.

You're making this up as you go along, Michael told
himself. *You have no fucking plan and no fucking idea.* He
would have to take things one step at a time, he decided.
Much as he hated winging it, what choice did he have?

But I will find Polk, he promised himself, *and then I
will kill him, and if I can't do that without getting myself
killed, I should—I will walk away.*

There was too much to live for not to.

The mobibot swept around a long, sweeping bend.
Ahead the road climbed up to the Supreme Council
complex. It braked hard and stopped.

"Shiiiit," Michael hissed. He was looking at what
once must have been an imposing collection of buildings: classical in style, massive, designed to overawe the
people of the Hammer Worlds, each one a monument to
the brutality of Hammer power. Most had been reduced
to blast-shattered shells that were sending thin skeins of
smoke drifting into the sky. He'd thought the NRA would
leave the place alone, and for good reason. This place
was the single most heavily defended site on all of the
Hammer Worlds. That might well have been true, but it

hadn't stopped ENCOMM from sending in the landers to give the place one hell of a pasting.

Except for one wing, the Supreme Council building, the heart of the Hammer of Kraa, remained standing. *I hope you're in there, Polk,* Michael thought, *because I've come a long way to see you.*

The mobibot could go no farther. The blockhouses flanking the entrance through the outermost ring of razor wire had been blown apart, scattering ceramcrete rubble across the roadway as it threaded its way through an elaborate chicane of dragon's teeth, massive pyramids of ceramcrete big enough to stop an Aqaba main battle tank. And it was not just rubble, Michael saw. There were bodies everywhere in the black uniforms and gold brassards of DocSec's elite 201st Assault Regiment, the unit responsible for protecting the Hammer's senior apparatchiks. For a moment Michael considered trying to clear a way through, but that idea died when he spotted a double row of meter-high metal bollards spanning the road. He'd have to lower them before the mobibot could get past, and because the controls probably were buried in one of the wrecked blockhouses, he did not fancy his chances.

Time to walk, Michael, he said to himself.

He opened the door of the bot and eased himself out, rifle swinging from side to side. He looked around. The only Hammers he could see were dead ones. Where was everybody? This checkpoint might have been trashed, but there had to be more DocSec troops around if Polk was still holed up inside the complex. He swore under his breath. Where was the 201st?

Hard as he searched, there was still no sign of anyone. Michael swore some more. Hartspring had been right. No 201st meant no Polk, and without Polk he was wasting his time.

What the hell, he said to himself after thinking things through. *I don't have anything better to do, so I might as well go have a look, and if Polk has already abandoned McNair, then I'll call it a day.*

Staying low, Michael scuttled over to the shattered remains of the nearest blockhouse and peered in. It was a charnel house. The sight and smell of what was left of the DocSec troopers caught inside made him retch. Forcing his body back under control, he dropped to his stomach and squirmed past the jagged remnants of the building until he could see up the roadway to the next checkpoint. It too had been trashed, and so had the one beyond it. With all the concentration he could muster, Michael scanned the area for any signs of life. But nothing moved amid the luxuriant flower-studded foliage, not even the leaves, the humid air still and thick with dust and smoke from the battle raging across the city.

The road up into the complex was horribly exposed. Michael hated the idea of using it, but he had no better option. He'd read the ENCOMM intelligence reports. Ten meters on either side of the road, where the greenery started, the ground was seeded with antipersonnel and antitank land mines backed up by laser autocannons positioned to provide interlocking fields of fire. And if that wasn't bad enough, the entire area was patrolled by groundbots—the NRA called them pigs—with optical sensors linked to pulsed lasers. Without the right IFF patches, Michael's chances of getting past them were nil. If the mines didn't get him, the pigs would.

So the road it was.

Michael took a few deep breaths to settle a sudden attack of nerves. A soft sobbing broke his concentration. He swung around. He cursed himself for not checking that the DocSec troopers littering the area were all dead.

Michael slithered back to where the wounded man lay. The trooper stared up at him. "Please ... drink," he whispered through blood-encrusted lips. He looked young and afraid; for a moment, Michael was able to forget that the man was Doctrinal Security.

Michael found a canteen and held it to the man's mouth. The trooper drank greedily, dragging at the water in great gulps. "Thanks," he said, letting his head fall back.

Michael leaned over him. "What's your name, son?" he asked.

"Rossi, Lance Corporal Rossi." The man's voice was as soft as falling dust.

"Where's the rest of the 201st, Corporal?"

"All gone. After the NRA smashed us ... couple of hours ago, not sure."

"What happened?"

"Everyone ran … They ran like rats; they—" Rossi broke off. A choking cough wracked his body, and fresh blood bubbled from his mouth. The scarlet froth was shocking against bloodless lips. "We didn't know what to do," Rossi went on when he had recovered. "They were afraid of the NRA … I'm afraid of the NRA. We were just leaving when those heretic bastards came back again. Their damn landers … blew us all to hell."

"So who's left? What about the chief councillor? Did he leave?"

"Don't know … I don't feel so …" Rossi's voice faded away. His eyes closed. He sighed, a long sigh that took him by the hand and led him quietly into death.

"You poor bastard," Michael murmured, getting to his feet, "even if you were a piece of DocSec shit." He stripped the body of its armor and microgrenades. He abandoned all caution and walked up the middle of the road. Fear turned his stomach over the whole way.

Michael arrived, unchallenged and, he hoped, unseen, at the innermost ring of razor-wire fencing that protected the most senior Hammers.

How, he asked himself as he scanned the debris-littered ground around the complex, *did it ever come to this?*

The men who had squatted like obscene toads at the blood-soaked peak of Hammer power had gone. There was not a living soul to be seen anywhere, just more bodies. He walked through the chicane, heading for the largest of the inner compound's buildings. A scarred brass plaque proclaimed it to be the offices of the Supreme

Council for the Preservation of the Faith. It had been badly damaged, one entire wing reduced to a smoking shell, the walls pocked with cannon fire and slashed by shrapnel, glassless windows gaping empty-eyed at the world.

Michael slipped past the security point and stopped in the main entrance. A pair of impressively large doors lay on the floor, ripped off their hinges. He stopped, stunned by the arrogance of the huge atrium. The floor was black granite with flecks of gold; it was littered with splinters of glass from the roof. The far wall, also of black granite, was dominated by a Hammer of Kraa sunburst that was a full 20 meters high. Recessed lights had been arranged to strike brilliant spears of light off the beaten gold surface. Two staircases led off to left and right. Amid shattered glass and granite was the evidence of panic-stricken flight: shoes, coats, personal comms, uniforms, papers, a security briefcase complete with chain, the chairs behind the elaborate reception desk pushed away and toppled onto their backs, the desk itself thrown back against a wall, bottles, broken cups and mugs, a pot that had toppled over, spilling a dusty lake of coffee across the floor.

The place was a shambles. The miasma of defeat hung thick in the air.

Michael stopped in the center of the atrium. He looked up and turned slowly on his heel. The hubris was breathtaking. He stood at the center of Chief Councillor Polk's megalomaniac universe. It was hard to believe.

Except Polk wasn't there anymore. Nobody was. The place was empty. Everyone had gone.

Anger erupted into incandescent fury. The assault rifle in Michael's hands exploded into life; he emptied the entire magazine in a sustained burst at the sunburst. Hypersonic rounds chewed a jagged path of destruction across its golden frame. Shards of metal and fragments of granite blasted outward to tumble and spin through the air.

"You are such a dumbass," Michael said, angry with himself for losing control. He dumped the empty magazine and slotted home a new one. If any of Polk's people were around, they'd be—

"Welcome, Lieutenant," a voice boomed. "I was just thinking about you."

Polk, Michael thought, spinning around, searching for the man. *It's Polk*. But there was nobody to be seen. "Is that you, Polk?" he shouted. "Where are you? Hartspring said you'd left."

"That fool! I'm in my office. Where else would the chief councillor be at a time like this? Take the stairs. You'll find me on the other side of the building."

"I'm on my way," Michael shouted, elated now. He had him. The blood roared in his ears. "And when I get to you, I'll blow your goddamned head off."

"Now, now," Polk chided. "Let's not be too hasty."

"Just watch me," Michael muttered, half convinced that he had slipped into a crazy parallel universe where enormously powerful men like Polk sat alone amid the ruins of empire even as retribution bore down on them.

It was insane. If the Hammer of Kraa was good at anything, it was producing fanatics, so where were they all? Surely Polk could have scraped up a few to protect him.

Michael started up the stairs, nerves jangling in anticipation. Reaching the top, he checked every door and every passageway with care to make certain he was not walking into an ambush. But still there was no sign of life.

There was no mistaking Polk's offices when he came to them. The embossed gold sign was hard to miss. Michael moved past the security desk and into a sprawling reception area studded with chairs and low tables. He walked on and into a second reception room. This one was smaller, more intimate, the lighting soft. He followed a short corridor with rooms off to both sides, some elaborately furnished and some set out as simple meeting rooms. The corridor led to a sprawling open-plan office. It was as stark and functional as the public rooms had been relaxed and comfortable. Michael headed for a door on the far side. He eased it open with the toe of his boot.

Instinct had Michael's rifle up before his brain had worked out that the man waiting inside posed no threat. "You!" Michael hissed between gritted teeth.

It was Polk.

He held his arms out wide, hands empty, a disarming smile on his face. He was smaller than Michael remembered, his lean, wiry body dressed in a pale gray one-piece jumpsuit and sporting a small Hammer sunburst in gold on his lapel.

"Oh, for Kraa's sake," Polk said, "put that gun down. Come into my office. Come on, Michael. It's over, so let's at least try to be civilized."

"On your face, Polk, with your arms out, and do it unless you want me to shoot you."

Polk sighed. "You'll find I'm clean," he said, dropping to the floor.

"We'll see."

Polk lay there in silence while Michael searched every last square centimeter of the man's body, ignoring Polk's muffled protests. "Okay," he said finally, "you can get up."

"I told you I was clean," Polk said, getting back to his feet and brushing himself down. "Come on; my office is through here. We can talk. I'd like that."

"Go through. I'll be right behind you, and if I think you're about to pull anything, I'll blow your brains out."

"Michael!" Polk protested. "Please relax."

An enormous plasglass window dominated the chief councillor's office. It looked out across luxuriant gardens below a dust-filled afternoon sky thick with towering columns of smoke. It was sparsely furnished: a desk empty of anything but a comm box, two armchairs flanking a coffee table, a pair of Hammer flags, a wall-mounted holovid screen, a small coffeebot in a recess. Nothing personal, Michael noted: no memorabilia, no paintings, no pictures. It was strange. It looked as if Polk rented the place by the hour.

"What's through there?" Michael said, pointing to a door in one of the walls.

"My private rooms, the VIP entrance, and the elevator. Up to the lander pad. Down to the garage, war room, and emergency shelters."

"Show me."

Again Polk sighed. "There's nobody out there. Everyone's gone. It's just you and me."

"Move!"

Polk was right. The place was empty.

"Okay," Michael said. He allowed himself to relax a fraction. There might be fifty Hammers holed up in a room he hadn't spotted, but there were limits to what he could do on his own. "Let's go sit down. No, not your desk—there." He pointed to one of the armchairs. "And keep your hands where I can see them."

"Fine, but first some coffee?"

"Yes, please," Michael said, struck by the sheer absurdity of it all. Coffee and small talk with a power-crazed lunatic. It was beyond absurd. "You know why I'm here, don't you?" he asked as Polk placed two steaming mugs on the table and sat down.

"Of course," Polk replied. "You want to kill me."

"I do, and I will. I wanted to look you in the face first."

"Well, we'll see." Polk paused, a thoughtful look on his face. "I had it all, you know," he went on, "the chief councillorship, my councillors where I wanted them, you Feds on the ropes." He stopped and shook his head. "You know," he said a moment later, "I've never met anyone quite as stupid as that Ferrero woman. Did she ever stop to think what she was doing, what she was risking?"

"I don't think she did."

"No, she didn't. We were only months away from getting our new antimatter plant. Nothing could have stopped the Hammer of Kraa. I was going to be humanspace's first emperor, you know. I got so close … and then you came along." Polk's face, which had been animated up to then, soured into a bitter scowl.

"You give me too much credit."

Polk shook his head. "No, I don't think so. You were the catalyst. Without you, the Feds and the NRA would have screwed around until it was too late. You made things happen. That's your genius." He stopped, a faraway look in his eyes. "I would have destroyed the Federated Worlds, you know. I'd already given the orders. The operation was scheduled for December. Did you know that?" Polk's eyes glittered. He had a half smile on his face; his tongue flickered across thin, bloodless lips. "The Hammer fleet would have reduced your planets to smoking wastelands."

For the first time, Michael saw the evil in the man. It was a terrifying sight. With sudden certainty, he knew he would not live to see Anna again. Polk's depraved soul would never allow it.

"I'd have enjoyed that," Polk went on. He shrugged as if the destruction of an entire system and the deaths of millions were matters of no great import. "I hate you Feds. I always have."

"You're mad."

Polk laughed. "Looks that way, doesn't it?" he said. "But I'm not. After we'd dealt with the Federated Worlds, how much of a fight do you think the rest of humanspace would have put up? I'll tell you: none. They'd be on their knees begging for mercy, which I, Emperor Jeremiah the First, would of course have been happy to grant."

"Emperor Jeremiah the First," Michael said; he shook his head. "You really are mad."

"I'm the madman?" Polk said. He waved a dismissive hand. "I don't think so. I'm not a Fed renegade sitting alone in the office of the Chief Councillor of the Hammer of Kraa Worlds. Oh, no; you're the one's who is mad. And for Kraa's sake, stop pointing that rifle at me. Put it away! It's no good to you."

"I don't think so."

Polk's eyes scanned the room. "Let me see … Yes, there are twelve lasers pointed at you right now, and they will kill you the instant your finger tightens on the trigger."

"I don't believe you."

"You should. My laser system is very good. It was a present from the Pascanicians. It'd take a battalion of marines to get past it."

"Your lasers didn't stop me from getting to you."

"You idiot! That's because I let you walk in. You are no threat to me. From the moment you walked up to the building, your life has been in my hands. Now I decide whether you live or die."

Michael's stomach knotted, his every instinct saying that Polk was telling the truth. "Okay, so you have lasers on me," he said, tapping the butt of his rifle, "but I can still blow your damn head off before they get me."

Polk shrugged. "I doubt it. The system has motion sensors, and it monitors heart rate, blood pressure, brain activity, pupil dilation, skin conductivity. And if you do fire at me, the lasers will destroy the bullet before it even gets close to me. I've seen them kill men who are better and faster than you'll ever be. Trust me, Michael; it's a very good system, and that's because it's all controlled by an AI."

"Now I know you're lying. AIs are proscribed by the Word of Kraa."

"They are, but I'm chief councillor." Polk shrugged. "If I want an AI, I'll have an AI, and the religious primitives out there can go screw themselves," he added, angry now, his forefinger stabbing out at Michael. Polk took a deep breath before continuing. "And the AI is very, very smart; I can see why you Feds are so fond of them. It knows when you are about to shoot me long before you do."

"Bullshit!"

"You should also know that I only have to say a special code phrase and the lasers will kill you.' Polk glanced at Michael, who stared back, stony-faced. "You still don't believe me, do you?"

"No."

Polk sighed. "There's no trust anymore. Fine, have it your way. Watch this. Red Canal," he said, and a microsecond later a laser pulse snapped from a recess in the ceiling and punched a small smoking hole in the carpet. Polk sat back, looking smug. "There you go," he said. "That was a test pulse. The real thing is much more impressive, as you'd find out if you tried anything stupid."

Michael nodded his defeat. He'd heard about these systems. They could be beaten, but that took months of training and a neuronics-linked needle gun. "Fine, I believe you now," he said.

"Good, but we can't just sit here swapping small talk. Come on; what's your plan? You do have a plan, don't you?"

Now, that is a very good question, Michael thought. *What is my plan?* "I will kill you," he decided after a moment's consideration, "and if you kill me, that's the price I have to pay."

Frustrated, Polk threw up his hands. "Haven't you been listening? You *cannot* kill me. No matter how hard you try, the lasers won't let you. Anyway, you don't want to die, and we both know it. You're young, you have a good woman waiting for you, and I must say your Anna is such a lov—"

"You mention her again," Michael shouted, "and I'll blow your fucking head off. You hear me?"

"For Kraa's sake, relax," Polk said, putting a hand out as if to fend Michael off.

"I'll relax when you're dead, you asshole," Michael barked. "You think I've forgotten what you and that scumbag Hartspring had planned for her?"

"Michael, please. That's all in the past."

"Not for me, it isn't, as Hartspring just found out."

Polk's eyebrows lifted. "You killed him?"

"I did."

"Ah, I was wondering why he hadn't shown up. Look, Michael, much as I'm enjoying your company—and I am—time is against us, so we need to move along."

"What's that mean?"

"I have a proposal for you."

"I'm not interested," Michael muttered, frustrated, consumed by impotent rage. He knew he sounded like a spoiled child.

"You should be, because it's the only way you'll escape from here alive. You are a fool: a fool for coming here, a fool for thinking you could kill me, and a fool for even imagining you can just walk away. You've let emotion tell you what to do. Unless you start using your brain, you'll end up dead, and why would you want that?"

Michael knew Polk was right. He had let emotion take over, and he did not want to die. It was galling, but he would have to hear Polk's proposal.

"What do you want, Polk?"

"To leave, both of us."

"You could have left with all the rest of your loyal subjects."

"That's what everyone thinks I did, but me taking to the streets of McNair?" Polk shook his head. "Way too risky," he went on. "The mob wants my blood, and they if they didn't get me, the NRA would, so I stayed put. You see, with everything that's going on out there, this is the safest place for me to be. Hiding in plain view it's called. The NRA will think I went with my chief of staff and the rest of my people. This is the last place they'll come looking."

"So what's the deal?" Michael said.

"An orbital shuttle is coming to pick me up … let me see … yes, in less than ten minutes. Thanks to friends of mine inside ENCOMM's air tasking group and an obscene amount of money, I plan to be onboard a Kallian fast courier when it breaks orbit less than an hour from now. You see, Michael, I never expected it to come to this, but I always knew it might. So I made plans just in case. Oh, yes, I intend to have a very long and very comfortable retirement."

"Why do you need me? Sounds like you have all the bases covered."

"For heaven's sake," Polk said with an irritated frown. "Are you always this slow? Why do you think you're still alive?"

"What, I'm a hostage now?"

"Of course you are. The NRA will never shoot down a shuttle that has you onboard."

Michael shook his head. "You are delusional, Polk," he said. "Have a look out the window. It's a bloodbath out there. No shuttle will get within ten klicks of here."

"An NRA shuttle will, a shuttle under orders to check that Kallian courier to make sure I'm not onboard. Those orders have come from ENCOMM, Michael. Why would anybody question them?"

"It won't work, Polk, not when the shuttle has to drop in here to pick you up. Bit of a giveaway, don't you think?"

"That's why I'm so pleased to see you, Michael," Polk said. A huge grin of self-satisfaction animated his face, a grin Michael wanted badly to wipe away with the butt of his rifle. "Now, instead of putting down to deal with battle damage, it'll respond to a comm from you, a comm to say you've been wounded—nothing too serious, of course—and need to be casevaced. And you, Michael, are the best insurance I could ask for."

Michael could only stare. Polk had him by the balls. All he could do was hope that fate would give him the chance he needed to kill Polk without being killed in the process. "Fine," he said eventually. "If I agree to go with you, then you'll let me go?" Even to his ears, he sounded pitifully weak, but what choice did he have? He needed time for something to turn up, and if he had to beg to get it, he would.

"Once I'm onboard that Kallian courier, yes. You have my word on it."

"Your word? That's fine, then. What are we waiting for?"

"Don't be sarcastic. The crew will be coming with me; the shuttle's AI will fly you back. All of this is finished—" Polk waved a hand around the office. "—so what do I care? What you did, it's history now and I'm over it. Now we need to go. Either come with me or I'll give the word and the lasers will kill you. Last chance. Coming or not?"

"I'm coming."

Polk got to his feet and made for the door to his private rooms, Michael close behind. "We'll take the elevator to the roof," Polk said over his shoulder. "Once the shuttle appears, we need to be quick or it will leave without us. And in case you're tempted, don't try anything. There are lasers everywhere, even covering the pad. Those Pascanicians are very thorough. It's the only thing I like about them."

"I just want to get this over with," Michael replied.

The elevator opened into a small reception room. Polk checked a wall-mounted holovid screen showing the rooftop landing pad. "Good," he said, tapping a small data window superimposed on the image. "Our shuttle has received the message about you and is inbound."

The holocam tracked the shuttle in. Its nose reared up for landing. Belly-mounted thrusters blasted jets of incandescent gas into the pad. It slowed into a hover and started to drop to ground.

"Let's go," Polk said the instant the machine settled onto its undercarriage. He pushed through armored doors and walked briskly across the pad to where the shuttle waited, its ramp down. Michael struggled to keep up; belatedly he worked out why. The cocktail of stimulants he had injected into his body was wearing off. By the time he reached the ramp, it took a huge effort just to keep moving. His body was beginning to collapse with frightening speed. He staggered up the ramp and into the shuttle. A crewman—the only one Michael could see in the cargo bay—waved him into a seat, his pistol trained on Michael's chest, as it had been from the moment he had appeared at the foot of the ramp.

"I'll have the gun," the man said. Pistol in one hand, he reached forward to take Michael's rifle. But, as he did, the pilot fed power to the thrusters for liftoff and the artgrav twitched, forcing the crew member off balance for an instant.

Michael had his opportunity, and he took it. Purely on instinct, he pushed himself out of his seat and whipped his rifle up, driving the butt into the crewman's stomach with sickening force. The impact doubled the man over, and he half fell, half stumbled back. It gave Michael enough room to bring his rifle to bear, and he shot the man full in the chest, the noise of the gun shockingly loud even over the roar of the shuttle's main engines.

Shock had frozen Polk into immobility. Before the crewman even reached the deck, Michael was bringing his rifle up. Polk saw death coming for him. He threw his body to one side as Michael fired. The burst plucked at Polk's sleeve and smashed into the bulkhead, spalling metal and plastic into the air. Michael tried to get the gun to follow Polk around, but he was too slow.

Polk ducked under the rifle barrel and launched himself into a desperate leap that threw Michael onto his back, the rifle ripped out of his hands as he cannoned into the deck.

Now Polk was on top of Michael. One hand was around Michael's throat; the other arced down in a glitter of quicksilver. Michael only had time to bring his left arm up to deflect the attack but not fast enough to stop the knife from slicing through his DocSec-issue coverall. In a searing blaze of pain that shocked Michael into a frantic, scrabbling fight to win the knife, it opened a gash across the corded muscle between neck and shoulder.

With an awful clarity, Michael knew that this was a fight he could never win. His adrenaline-fueled energy was fast running out, and Polk was attacking with a manic ferocity that was truly terrifying, his left hand battering punches into Michael's face while the knife in his right slashed and cut and stabbed past Michael's flailing hands, a desperate struggle that left both men drenched in Michael's blood.

Michael rolled the dice for the last time.

Calling on the last of his reserves, he arched his back, a violent movement that brought his right leg up hard and gave him the space he needed to twist his upper body away from Polk's fist. He lunged for the knife with both hands, forcing it down, the sudden move throwing Polk off and onto his back. Polk fought to regain the initiative, but Michael's right fist was free now. A punch exploded upward into Polk's jaw. The blow hit home with a sickening crunch of broken bone that drove Polk backward, screaming in agony.

Kicking to get clear of him, Michael broke free. He scrabbled across the deck to grab his rifle. He leveled the gun at Polk. "It's over," he shouted.

Polk wasn't finished. His right arm whipped across his body. The knife was a blur that moved so fast that Michael had no time to react. It buried itself in Michael's right shoulder. Overwhelmed by pain and shock, Michael staggered back across the cargo bay. He hit the bulkhead and collapsed into a seat, the gun still in his hand across his lap. He glanced in disbelief at the knife lodged in his shoulder.

Polk struggled back to his feet. Terrified, Michael watched the man come toward him across the deck, a bloody-jawed horror with death in his eyes. Polk scrabbled into a pocket and pulled out a pistol. "Yes, Michael," he mumbled; scarlet froth dribbled from his mouth as he raised the gun, his hand shaking. "It is over, but it's not—"

Michael needed to move the gun only a fraction. He fired. The shot hit Polk below the heart. Polk staggered backward. The second shot hit him in the center of his chest, and he slumped to the deck, arms out wide and legs twisted beneath his body. But his eyes stayed locked on Michael's.

Michael stared back. "Where are your Pascanicians and their lasers now?" he mocked. "I know we had a deal, but I decided not to honor it. You should have killed me when you had the chance."

"You'll … never make it … Helfort," Polk said, the effort it took to force the words out twisting his face into a grotesque mask. "The pilot will know … so you're … dead too."

"I'll make it," Michael said. He fired again and again into Polk's body. "Unlike you, Chief Councillor Polk."

Michael looked down on the bloodstained wreck of what once had been the most feared man in humanspace. It was done, and now all Michael wanted to do was lie down and sleep, but he knew he could not. Polk had been right. The pilot would have watched the fight on one of the cargo bay holocams; now Michael had to make sure not to let him finish what Polk had started.

Where he found the energy, Michael would never know, but he bullied an unwilling body to lean forward as he worked the straps off his shoulders, whimpering in agony when one caught on the haft of the knife that still stuck out of his shoulder. Free of the pack, he reached in and pulled out the packet of autojects. With a silent prayer that his badly abused body would cope, he injected a second shot into his arm.

The change was immediate. Stimulants and painkillers flooded his system. They scavenged the last reserves of energy from his abused body, and it jolted back to life. He sat there for a few seconds. He wondered what to do about the knife. A tentative attempt to ease it out of his shoulder gave him the answer: Do nothing. Despite the massive dose of chemicals he had just injected into his arm, the pain was all but unbearable. Working with one hand, he did the next best thing: He slathered his entire shoulder with woundfoam before packing a crude dressing around the knife.

Reenergized, he got to his feet to make sure Polk and the crewman were dead. They were. Michael looked around the cargo bay, dismayed to see a row of body bags laid out on the deck up forward. *Now I know where the rest of the crew gotten to*, he thought; he felt sick. He counted the bags and then did it again to be sure. He'd been lucky. Judging by the number of body bags, the shuttle had lifted off from McNair with only two crew members: the command pilot and the man Michael had killed just after he and Polk had boarded.

That was the good news.

The bad news was that the command pilot was tucked away safely behind the armored door to the flight deck. He'd need a thermic lance and an hour to get at him, whereas all the pilot had to do was—

Heart racing with sudden panic, Michael bolted to his feet and launched himself at the nearest emergency equipment stowage. He ripped the door open with his good hand and pulled out an emergency oxygen pack. He clipped it onto his belt, slipped the mask over his face, and switched on the gas.

And just in time, he realized when he checked the air pressure in the cargo bay. *You are one slimy little shit*, he thought when he saw the readout. The pilot had been depressurizing the compartment, but so slowly that Michael would never have noticed. Another few minutes and he would have been breathing air with too little oxygen to maintain consciousness. A few minutes after that he would have been dead.

He patched his neuronics through to the flight deck. "Nice try, shithead," he said when the command pilot's face appeared. "Now do us both a favor and turn this thing around and take me back."

"Are they dead?" the pilot asked.

"Yes, they're both dead. And so will you be if you don't abort."

The pilot shook his head. "No, I don't think so," he said with a self-satisfied smirk. "You're a spacer; you know perfectly well you can't get to me up here, so sit back and enjoy the ride."

That was not an option. Michael knew what the pilot would do: override the airlock controls to trap him in the cargo bay while he transferred to the courier ship via the flight deck's emergency hatch, but not before he had ordered the shuttle AI to head dirtside under full power.

Which is not going to happen, Michael told himself.

He would have to force the shuttle to turn back. That meant some creative destruction, and he understood shuttles well enough to know what to do. Whether he and the pilot would survive the experiment was another matter, but he was out of options. There was no way he would allow himself to sit back and wait for the end. If he had to die, he would do so looking death right in the face.

Michael emptied his pack and refilled it with his supply of microgrenades. He made his way aft to the ladder that accessed the hydraulically powered locks that clamped the shuttle's massive ramp closed. Pack around his neck, he climbed the ladder. It was an awkward, jerky process with a knife in his shoulder and a useless arm, but he made it finally. He locked his left leg around one rung to hold himself in position, removed the pack, and set to work.

Even one-handed, it was easy enough to arm the grenades and place them behind a junction box directly below the shuttle's port reaction-mass feed line, an exotic alloy pipe 15 centimeters in diameter pressurized to 3,000 atmospheres.

Michael had just finished when the command pilot called him. The man did not look happy. "What the hell are you up to, Helfort?" he demanded.

"I've asked you to turn back," Michael said, working his way down the ladder, "and you won't, so now I'll have to make you."

"And how will you do that?" The pilot's voice dripped skepticism.

"Never underestimate a desperate man," Michael said, his voice calm even though his heart was racing. "I've put microgrenades under the port feed line. If you don't turn back, I'll set them off."

The command pilot's face went dirty gray. "You wouldn't," he said.

"Oh, but I will," Michael said. "Unless you want me to trash your main engines and a whole lot of other stuff as well, I suggest you turn back right now."

"You're bluffing." The pilot had recovered his composure and some of his color. "There's no way you'd do it. You'd kill us both."

Michael swore some under his breath. He'd been so sure the pilot would turn back. "I might kill us both," he said, forcing himself to sound nonchalant, "but since I'm a dead man either way, what have I got to lose?"

"You are so full of shit, Helfort." The pilot sounded confident.

"I'll take that as no, shall I?" Michael asked. "Right, Captain Asswipe; watch and learn." Michael picked up his rifle and made his way to the very front of the cargo bay, stopping just short of the passenger galley. He clipped his safety line to a ringbolt, then brought the rifle up and rested it on a seat back, an awkward business thanks to his damaged shoulder. "Last chance," he called out.

"Fuck off!" the pilot snapped. "You won't do it."

"I think I will," Michael said. He took careful aim and put a single round into the junction box packed with microgrenades.

For one heart-stopping moment, Michael thought the grenades had failed to fire. Then they did. The blast filled the cargo bay with a sheet of intense white light and a cloud of ionized gas and smoke, the shuttle bucking under his feet as the shock front ripped through the airframe. "That should do it," he said, throwing himself behind the galley bulkhead.

Nothing happened. A few seconds later, a lot did and in a very short amount of time. A small explosion followed the first; then the shuttle shuddered as a massive blast ripped through the cargo bay.

There goes the reaction-mass feed line, Michael thought, cringing back while the cargo bay filled with pulverized driver mass, a malevolent black cloud that tore the cargo bay apart, the overpressure rupturing both of his eardrums in a blaze of agony even as flying debris ripped the flimsy gallery bulkhead apart and debris clawed at his body.

The shuttle lurched hard to one side into a slow tumbling roll as more explosions followed. Its overtaxed artgrav gave up the unequal fight. It shut down, and Commitment's gravity took over. Thanks to the shuttle's extreme nose-up attitude, the deck was now so steep that Michael could not stand up. His feet shot from under him. He dropped to the deck and into the shattered remnants of the galley. Around him, the whole shuttle shuddered, a hammering so violent that he thought complete structural failure had to be only seconds away.

Michael commed the command pilot. "Having fun now?" he asked through pain-gritted teeth, head spinning and nausea rising as his overloaded brain tried to work out which way was up, a problem thanks to his ruptured ears. He blinked the tears out of his eyes and wondered if he might not have overdone the microgrenades a touch. "I certainly am."

"You've killed us all," the man screeched. His face was white and beaded with sweat. Around him, the flight deck was raucous with the cacophonous racket of multiple alarms.

"That all depends on how good a pilot you are," Michael replied. "Now, it's only a guess, but I'd say you've lost the port main engine, the starboard main engine's tripped out, and all of your primary and backup hydraulics have gone as well. Am I right?"

"You maniac," the pilot snarled.

"I'll take that as a yes, shall I? Michael said. "I hope you've been practicing your dead stick reentries, because that's the only way you'll get us down alive. Just thank your lucky stars I pulled the pin before we reached orbit."

"I going to tear your fucking heart out," the pilot screamed.

"Since that means we'd have made it dirtside, I look forward to you trying. Now shut up, get us down, and let me know when we can bail out."

Michael cut the comm before the man could respond. He released his line and slid down the deck until he reached a crew seat. He dragged himself into it and sat down. Jury-rigging the safety harness to avoid the knife, he armed the seat's escape capsule and sat back to wait, doing his best to ignore the pain that consumed his entire body. There was nothing he could do now. His life was in the hands of the command pilot. Provided that his little stunt hadn't done more damage than he'd planned, the man had a reasonable chance of getting the shuttle down low and slowly enough that they could both bail out and survive.

A thought struck him. He commed the pilot. "Hey, asswipe," he said.

"What?" The man still looked terrified.

"Settle down. You can do this."

"You don't know what you've done, do you?"

"Tell me."

"As well as everything else, we've lost hydraulics, and that means I'll never control this thing long enough for us to slow down and bail out. There's a limit to what the reaction control system can do, you know. We're dead, Helfort."

Oh, shit, Michael thought. *This is not good.* "Patch me into the command AI."

"Why would—"

"Because you want to live, you idiot! Now do it."

"Okay, okay."

It took Michael only seconds to see the damage for himself. The command pilot had not been exaggerating. The shuttle was doomed. Without hydraulics, the wings would stay fully retracted, and no wings meant no control as the air thickened. The problem was that the pilot had to do two things at once: keep the shuttle stable and slow down. If he failed, the shuttle would disintegrate and they were both dead men.

"Damn, damn, damn," Michael swore under his breath. If only … An idea popped fully formed into his head. Michael put it to the AI, and ten seconds later he had his answer. It would be touch and go, but they might still have a chance.

"Captain," he said. "Can you bring the starboard main engine back online?"

"I can, though it's not in very good shape. I don't know how long it'll hold up."

"We won't need it for long. How's the reaction control system?"

"The RCS is nominal, unlike everything else."

"Okay; I think there's something we can do."

Hope brightened the man's eyes. "There is?"

Michael forwarded the AI's analysis. "Have a look at this," he said. "The AI thinks it'll work."

"Mmm," the pilot said. "Not sure if the RCS can keep us stable long enough, but I can use the main engine to vector the thrust, which will help. Anyway, it's worth a try."

Michael nodded. "Sure is," he said. "Hey, look. I'm sorry about the Captain Asswipe thing. What's your name?"

"Karroubi, Jakob Karroubi."

"Good luck, Jakob."

Michael sat back and patched his neuronics into the holocam behind Karroubi. It was if he were sitting on the pilot's shoulder. He looked at the same screens, the same status boards, the same everything. It was unnerving, and for a moment Michael felt for the man. With the crippled shuttle now plummeting earthward, he had a huge challenge on his hands.

Karroubi fired the reaction jets to spin the shuttle around. Now the stern faced the onrushing air. A fresh set of alarms bleated in protest at a maneuver that appeared in no manual Michael had ever read. "Stand by," the command pilot called. "This will be very rough."

No kidding, Michael thought as the pilot fired the starboard main engine and rammed the throttle to emergency power, provoking yet more alarms. With the artgrav off, the airframe kicked hard in protest, the seat underneath Michael bucking as the pilot fought to keep the shuttle stable.

"Throttle down, Jakob," Michael shouted. "Throttle down. Too much and you'll lose her."

"Roger," Karroubi said; a moment later the vibration wracking the shuttle's frame eased off a touch.

"Better," Michael said even though it was still worryingly bad. But there was some good news: Karroubi was a natural on the sidestick controller. With a confident hand, he kept control of the stern's tendency to slide away from the oncoming air, and the shuttle was decelerating hard, riding a pillar of flame down to earth.

"Looks good," Karroubi said, "so stand by. It won't be long before we can go."

"Just say the word," Michael replied. "I'm ready to—"

In one terrible instant, everything changed. Karroubi lost control. The stern whipped up and over with frightening speed, the airframe hammered by endless cracking bangs. "Shit!" Michael screamed as the status board told him the controls had been overwhelmed. Condemned, the shuttle tumbled to destruction; it was beyond anything Karroubi could do to reverse the situation.

"Sorry about that," Karroubi shouted, his body a blur as the shuddering thrashed him from side to side.

"Don't be," Michael replied through clenched teeth, marveling that the pilot still was fighting against impossible odds to regain control.

"Go when I say … best I can … do."

"Good luck, Jakob."

Time ran out. The shuttle began to come apart. Damaged clamps failed, and the stern ramp sagged open far enough to let the slipstream grab it. The air tore the massive piece of foamalloy off and whipped it away.

"Now!" screamed Karroubi.

The ejection system took over. It blasted Michael out into the night and into a violence that overwhelmed his senses.

This is wrong, he thought as darkness claimed him, *all wrong*.

Michael awoke.

Rain hammered at the plasfiber capsule, the noise audible even over the insistent ringing in blast-damaged ears. It was light, a murky gray day thanks to the thick clouds that scudded overhead. He had been unconscious for … He tried to make his mind to do the math, but it refused. Since it had been early evening when the shuttle had picked him and Polk up, it was a long time. Commitment's nights were prolonged affairs. He lay there for a long while, tired beyond belief. It was only with a huge effort that he summoned up the energy to get free of his safety harness and crawl out of the capsule, his shoulder and the rest of his body screeching in protest.

He tried to stand up. That was a mistake. He never made it past one knee before gravity reasserted itself and dragged him back down.

Guess I'm staying put, then, he said to himself. He pulled the survival pack out of its stowage and wrapped himself in a space blanket. He was almost asleep when a voice snapped him awake.

"Over here," the voice said. It was a man's voice, a Hammer voice. Michael's heart pounded. *Not now*, he thought. *Not after everything.*

Every instinct urged Michael to get away, but he knew he could not. He lay there and stared up into the rain. A face appeared over his. "Here," the man called out. He knelt down beside Michael. "You okay?"

"Don't think so," Michael whispered. "Who are you?"

"Corporal Singh, B Company, 2/284th, NRA."

"Where am I?" Michael asked, overwhelmed by relief.

"Just outside of McNair."

"McNair, that's goo—"

At which point Michael passed out.

Sunday, November 7, 2404, UD
McNair, Commitment

Arm in a sling and right shoulder buried beneath an impressive bandage, Michael sat atop a captured Aqaba main battle tank as it threaded its way through the milling throng, a mix of civilian and NRA, looks of dazed happiness and relief on every face. The tank slowed to a stop, and the commander stuck her head out of the hatch. "Central Station's 500 meters that way, Colonel," she said, pointing down a broad avenue. It was a sorry sight. Once blessed with a double row of imposing trees, most now reduced to shattered stumps, it was lined with bombed-out buildings and littered with the burned-out wreckage of Hammer fighting vehicles. "Sorry I can't get you any closer."

"That's okay. This will do fine."

"You look after yourself. We owe you big time."

Michael's face flushed with embarrassment "Not sure about that," he said. He'd lost count of the times he'd been thanked for sending Jeremiah Polk into oblivion.

"Well, I am," the woman said, a broad smile across her grease- and dust-smeared face, a face startlingly young, a face that radiated uninhibited happiness and faith in the future.

Michael looked at her; he felt a million years old. "Thanks for the lift," he said.

"Need a hand?"

"No, I'm okay," Michael replied. He eased himself down one-handed. It took a while. His body was still a long way from forgiving him for all it had been put through. He grabbed his pack and set off, trying to ignore the nervous twitching of his heart.

And there she was, sitting with her back against a wall, head back and eyes closed. "Anna!" Michael shouted as he forced his body into a reluctant trot. "Anna!"

Anna looked up, and then she was on her feet and running hard toward him, skidding to halt when she saw the sling. "Oh, Michael," she said; she pulled him into an awkward one-armed embrace. "What have you done now?"

"Flesh wound," he said; he buried his face in her shoulder. "It's nothing. I'm fine … I'm sorry. I was so stup—"

Anna pushed him back. "Stop!" she said. "It's over. Let's leave it at that, okay?"

"Over?" Michael looked around at the shattered buildings flanking the debris-littered plaza. "I know it looks that way, but it's not over, not yet. We still need to—"

"Michael!" Anna snapped. "Stop! It *is* over. Polk and most of his councillors are dead, every Doctrinal Security trooper still alive is being hunted down, the Hammer of Kraa is headed for the trash can, and General Vaas has sent a special ops team to destroy the Hendrik Island antimatter plant. The war's over, and the threat to humanspace is gone." Her voice softened to the barest of whispers. "You've done all you need to, so let it go. Please, let it go."

"I have to make sure, Anna," he said, eyes casting left and right. "I can't just walk away, not now."

Anna looked at him for a long time. Her green eyes dragged him back until nothing else existed but the two of them. "I've got something to tell you," she said at last.

"What?"

"I'm pregnant."

Michael heard the words, but they made no sense. He shook his head, confused. "Pregnant? What do you mean … Ah, you're pregnant!"

"Ten points, Einstein," Anna said with a smile.

"Oh," Michael said. He choked. Unable to speak, he pulled her back into an embrace that lasted five lifetimes.

"Hey, spacer boy," Anna murmured at last, "we have to go."

"No, we don't. I'm not moving. You're pregnant … I don't believe it."

"You should, and yes, it's yours in case you're wondering."

"Anna!" Michael hissed in protest.

"Sorry," she said; she kissed him full on the lips. "My idea of a bad joke."

"You're right. It's over. So what now?"

"I've got us a ride to McNair spaceport. We've got places on the *Morkosh Star*, and we'll be onboard when it breaks orbit tomorrow. I never want to see this asshole of a planet ever again."

"Whoa, slow down. The *Morkosh Star*. What's that all about?"

"All the Feds are shipping out over the next few weeks, but I've fixed it so we go tomorrow with the first batch."

"Why the rush? It'd be good to catch up with Admiral Jaruzelska. Vaas too."

Anna frowned. "I'm sorry,' she said, her eyes filled with anguish, "but Jaruzelska's dead."

Michael's head slumped. "Why her?" he said after a while. "After all she's done, after all she's risked, she deserved ..." He couldn't say any more, crushed by the brutal injustice of it all. "She was a brave woman," he said at last. "I'll miss her."

"We all will. But she died—"

Michael put his fingers to Anna's lips. "Not now, later. I just can't take any more, not right now. I'm sorry." He took a deep breath to flush the emptiness out of his soul. "What's the plan?" he asked.

"General Vaas says the Feds have done their bit and we should leave the Revivalists and NRA to finish the job. Having us around will only confuse things. The locals have enough to think about without worrying that we might be trying to take over."

"But I can't go anywhere near the Federated Worlds. FedPol … they'll arrest me. You know." Michael shivered. "I can't risk it."

"I know, but who said we were going home?"

Michael frowned. "Where else would we go?"

"The *Morkosh Star*'s first port of call is Scobie's. I've booked us on a ship to Jagnesh, and once we're there, we'll find the most exclusive resort the place has to offer and then take … oh, I don't know … a month to make that decision. Maybe two."

"I'd like that," Michael said. "We can get the family over as well. I have some serious apologizing to do, not just to my mom and dad but to yours too."

"You don't need to apologize for anything."

"We'll see, but there is one tiny problem. You said Jagnesh?"

"Yup. No extradition treaty with the Federated Worlds and great beaches."

"Isn't it the most expensive system in humanspace?"

"Not quite, but it's in the top hundred for sure. But so what? Who cares?"

"Money, Anna. We don't have any. I spent all mine chartering that freighter I trashed, and the last time I checked, an NRA colonel's pay is peanuts."

"All true, my love," Anna said with a smile, "which is why General Vaas asked me to give you this." She whipped out a card and waved it at him.

Michael stared at Anna in disbelief. "Vaas gave you a cash card?"

"He sure did: a million FedMarks, to be precise. Reimbursement for expenses incurred, he said. He'll be in touch when things settle down. Now, our lift won't wait forever. Are you coming or not?"

"Try and stop me," Michael said, the urge to leave all the pain and suffering behind almost overpowering.

They picked up their packs and walked across the plaza in front of the station to where a massive truckbot waited, its Hammer markings obscured by crude slashes of black paint.

Five minutes later, the bot set off. Michael was utterly content to lie with Anna beside him and stare up at the sky.

Not once did he look back.

PLAN VIEW OF HUMANSPACE (TO GALACTIC NORTH)

Rogue Planets (1,493 LY)

East Sylvanian Reef

Sylvanian Federation

Sumijo's Worlds

Lost Worlds

Morrissen Group

Al-Quereshi

Abdoollah Merritts Reef

West Sylvanian Reef

Confederated Stars

Damnation's Gate

Serenity

Sertanius Reef

Ashadzeth

Karolev's World

Burana Coalition

Abdicheh Reef

Sorigbaya

Xenophon

Dewanrata-C

Sorigbaya

Zhuang's Ocean Reef

Kelly's Deep

Colburn Reef

Matovik Reef

Wu

Piquet-D

Federated Worlds

Praderhorn Reef

Old Earth Alliance

Xrang Reef

Vijver Reef

Kazbukc Cluster

Zhuang See

Zhuang-B

al-Harrasid

Jaggredo

Branski's World

New Kaalyerik

Caerton-G

Perano

Payson-N

Gok-3

Nadrion

Jaxnola

Wenighalizz

al-Stirri

Sutta-Nipata

Scobie's World

Bosanta

Brosan Reef

Szent-Gyorgyi

West Kent Reef

New Anatolia

Hammer of Kraa

New Noravood

Sechani-V

Xetnook-IB

Noppine

Merritt's Stars

Kostoya's Worlds

East Noran Reef

Obvery

Devastation Reef

Javitz Union

Siveschni

West Noran Reef

N Nutis Systems

Frontier Worlds

Far Planets (373 LY)

Holderrausn (125 LY)

Weocomna

Pascanici League

Gongbit-B

Delfin Confederation

Alemszerh

Marskoff Consortium Planets

Rejapsalos Reef

Kumanti

0   50   100
Light Years

About the Author

Photograph © Andrew Sharp Paul

Graham Sharp Paul was born in Sri Lanka. He has an honors degree in archaeology and anthropology from Cambridge University and an MBA from Macquarie University. He joined the Royal Navy in 1972; he qualified as a minewarfare and clearance diving officer in 1977 and reached the rank of lieutenant commander before transferring to the Royal Australian Navy in 1983. Graham left the RAN in 1987. After working on a range of business development and corporate finance projects, he retired in 2003. He lives in Sydney with his wife, Vicki, has three sons and two granddaughters.

71400500R00246

Made in the USA
San Bernardino, CA
15 March 2018